Kamand Shabani was born and raised in Kermanshah, Iran. She started learning English when she was only four years old and she's fluent in both English and Persian, aka her mother language.

Although she mostly speaks Persian, she never gives up on English and evolves her knowledge daily.

A good music, and a fine cappuccino are the only supplies she requires to write. And when she isn't found writing, she's probably daydreaming about her books' characters or other fantasies.

I owe myself a special thank, for NEVER losing faith in me.

**Kamand Shabani**

# 15.53.52.44

AUSTIN MACAULEY PUBLISHERS™

LONDON * CAMBRIDGE * NEW YORK * SHARJAH

A CIP catalogue record for this title is available from the British Library.

ISBN 9781035805112 (Paperback)
ISBN 9781035805129 (ePub e-book)

www.austinmacauley.com

First Published 2023
Austin Macauley Publishers Ltd®
1 Canada Square
Canary Wharf
London
E14 5AA

# Table of Contents

# Chapter One
# A Not Pleasant Start

**February 13th, Moores' Family House, 18:34 P.M.**

He was exhausted and confused and his ears were beeping. Not everyone is used to bury their best friend, attend their funeral and pretend like everything is alright and under control just in case of not being asked, 'Are you alright?' Oliver Johnson was only dreaming of himself, being just a four-year-old boy who could sit on the ground, cover his ears with hands and close his eyes just to be able to hear the voice inside telling him that everything is temporary, all the monsters he fears them; but death…Not temporary, forever and always.

"Hey Ollie," said the curly boy, "How are you dealing with—"

Oliver interrupted, "With Bradly's death? I'll be fine, Ezra."

Ezra Moore was the nine years younger brother of Bradly, the guy whose funeral caused Oliver's and everyone else's presence at that house. Ezra knew Oliver since he was born and Oliver was the best friend of Bradly ever since they entered the kindergarten. Oliver has been always treated him better than Bradly did so as a consequence, Ezra always liked Oliver better than Brad. But that didn't change the fact that Ezra was mournful either.

Dakota—the youngest sister of Oliver—came to them and said, "It's time for the speech. Ezra should talk and Ollie, Mr Moore said you can talk if you feel like doing it."

Ezra and Dakota left. Oliver was furious; well, who would be relax after seeing the stabbed body of their best friend?

"What in heavens have you thought, Robert?" Oliver thought, "A speech? Man, I just cried my eyes out!"

He felt breathless. Living room could be taken no more so he left the place to the back yard. He wiped away the snow off the stony bench and sat on it. He crossed his arms and looked up to the snowing red sky. God was sending pearls off the heaven.

It was hard for him to make up his mind in that specific situation; the detective of Bradly's murder case, Mr Richard Henry, who has been dealing with heart decease for five years and finally had decided to retire, asked Oliver to do his job for case. Crime psychologist. Or as some would know, forensic psychologist. Oliver…did not accept immediately and ended their conversation by saying: "I'll think about it, Richard."

The ringing of his phone notification pulled him out of his chamber of thoughts. He had seven messages from Richard, seven initial and incomplete information of seven people who found the lifeless body of Bradly Moore at the guy's home. Seven suspects.

Anya Barton, Sebastian Bell, Olga Durov, Theodore Rivera, Marika Lensher, Pietro Schwarter, Morgan Geller.

These were the names of seven people who were at Bradly's house when the police arrived and arrested them all; among Oliver…

**Flashback: February 9th 23:39 P.M.**

All could be seen was the red and blue lights of the police cars. Oliver remained silent in case of get over the blood bath he just witnessed. He noticed a young brunet girl who was crying out loud and two officers trying to get her in the car. He stood up took a look around him; beside the brunet girl, six more people could be seen that Oliver saw them on Bradly's body like twenty minutes ago.

"Oliver!" Arthur Black said, "What happened here? When did you arrive? Do you know these people?" Arthur was asking question in hope of getting an answer to help Oliver. He was Oliver's brother-in-law and also a sergeant at London's police department.

Arthur madly yelled at him, "Talk to me!"

Oliver shouted out: "Tell you what? I don't even know what is happening! I saw Brad's body! He is *murdered*!"

Arthur spent few seconds looking into Oliver's eyes; asked confusedly: "And what were *you* doing here?" Arthur closed his eyes and whispered: "I've been told that you were here when police arrived…And you weren't the person who called the police, Sebastian Bell was."

"Listen…Its…It's complicated. I got a message from Brad. He said it was an emergency. I arrived, the door was open, I rushed in and saw five or six people on Brad's stabbed body, I wanted to call 999 but a guy said that they already did."

Arthur put his hand on Oliver's back and pushed him slowly. "But you're currently counted as a suspect. Bill Oliver Johnson, you're under arrest by the accusation of the murder of Bradly Anton Moore. You have the right to remain silent."

## February 10th, 00:31, London's Police Department

Oliver sadly looked at Mr Robert Moore, Bradly's father. Mr Moore, as far as Oliver could remember, was an introvert, almost ice-cold man that Oliver and Brad used to think that he never cries; But the night of February 10th, was the first time Oliver saw him cry.

The station's hallway was quiet and the only sound that was breaking the silence, was Mr Moore's crying. Arthur came out of the interrogation room with one of the suspects who Oliver believed was "Morgan Geller;" Oliver was next. Before Oliver got to stand up, detective Henry came out of the room, went to Mr Moore and started a conversation with him:

"Mr Moore, sending you my deepest condolences for the loss of your son."

"Please…tell me what happened to my son?" Robert begged while crying and shivering.

"I'm afraid I can't tell you enough since we don't know either. All I can say is that he had been attacked. There is evidence of self-defence in the living room but the body was found in the hallway…stabbed." Richard informed.

"Do you have any suspects?" Robert asked sorrowful.

"Yes, we have Oliver plus seven other people."

"*Oliver*?" Robert asked out loud to make sure he heard what he heard.

"I…I'm not suspicious to him personally. He was the last one who arrived at Brad's house and he was here with me all evening."

"Then why is he here?" Robert whined.

"We can't let him go without his witness…Have you told your wife about…" Richard left his sentence unfinished because Robert interrupted: "The death of our son? You tell me detective; how am I supposed to tell her? Grab the phone, dial her number and say that we only have one son left for the rest of our lives?"

Oliver felt a hand on his wrist; he looked up and saw his brother-in-law or his saviour angel, better to say. Arthur took him to the interrogating room and, helped him sitting on a chair and sat on the chair in front of him.

"So?"

"So what?" Oliver whispered.

"Tell me everything. When did you arrive? Do you know any of those people? And most important of all, why would you go to Brad's house that late of the night? That timing is so not you." Arthur asked all the necessary questions and remained for an answer.

Before Oliver said anything, Arthur said: "Listen, Henry interrogated every single one of the people who were at the crime scene. All of them received a message from Brad like you did."

"I've already told you everything!" Oliver said, "What are you expecting to hear?"

"I'm your damn brother-in-law, I married your sister three years ago! Why would anyone waste their time by listening to what I say about my brother-in-law's confession in front of the house that he just saw a corpse in? Who would believe it, Ollie? Even a child can figure out that is totally illogical!" Arthur lectured.

"Breathe!" Oliver said, "Fine, I'm gonna explain everything all over again."

## February 13th, 19:01

"Ollie?" Oliver heard from the living room. It was Olivia, Oliver's younger sister, Dakota's older sister and Arthur's wife. She continued: "Would you like to come and…"

Oliver interrupted: "No, Liv. I don't want to come inside and tell all those people how I feel about the death of my best friend…so you go in there and tell them that Oliver is just as dead as Bradly!"

Olivia shamefully smiled: "I just wanted to ask if you want to come inside and eat? You haven't eaten anything in three days."

Oliver crossed his arms and said: "We don't call it 'you-haven't-eat-anything-in-three-days.' It's anorexia nervosa." He added: "Plus, I had some of Mum's soup this noon. I haven't got any hunger signals from my stomach."

"Do you mind if I sit?" Olivia sat on the other side of the bench next to his old, dear brother, "How are you feeling?"

"Fine. I'm fine," Oliver said quickly.

"Don't lie to me. I'm your little sister, you're my big brother," Olivia said caring and kind.

"Special thanks to you, I didn't know how are you my sister!" Oliver joked.

"You idiot!" Olivia laughed, "That's not what I meant! I mean that I know you better than yourself and I know that currently, you are not fine."

"You are totally right." Oliver sighed, "I'm dealing with multiple feelings inside my mind. It's…like I have dissociative identity disorder and these different faces keep taking place."

He took a deep breath and said: "I think I'll apply for Brad's case but there's one thing blocking my way."

"What is it, Ollie?" Olivia asked.

"Questions I've never asked me before. Like, what if I fail finding out who the murderer was and let Moores and me and…Brad down? This is just not any case that I can go to the victim's family, tell them that their beloved's case is out of my abilities."

Oliver felt like crying, "I mean, what if I am that bloody murderer, I'm looking for but I somehow don't remember the memory of getting a man killed?"

"Nonsense, nonsense, nonsense! Ollie, you are one of the best people I know. Despite all the madness in the world, you are one in seven billion I know that is still sane and honest not just to himself but to everyone."

"Thanks…It was sweet to hear. One more thing I'm thinking of is that there are seven suspects. I've never worked on seven people with seven different personalities and beliefs at once. It's too much work for a normal situation. I've just faced a massive loss and I'm clearly vulnerable."

"All correct but Ollie, this is Henry's one last case before he retires. And you know that he can't get along with other psychologists," said Olivia, "You know, like Daisy! You knew Daisy, didn't you? Do you remember how awful Henry treated her? He would never do such thing to you."

"How do you know about Daisy? Did Arthur tell you?" Oliver asked.

Olivia confirmed with head and said: "I felt so bad when he told me about it."

"*Three years* has passed and you two still got subjects to discuss?"

"Weird, isn't it? We eat breakfast together every day, sometimes lunch and usually dinner and you do the same routine the next day and the days after!" Olivia said with a divine smile.

"And still, people keep asking me why don't I get married? I'm inefficient in making small talks!" Oliver joked.

"That is not what I'm talking about. What I mean is that you must be the crime psychologist of Brad's case. Mr and Mrs Moore want you to do it; Brad wants you to do it." She stood up, "I'm gonna go bring you some coffee milk. Think about what I said, take your time and don't make any decisions until midnight, okay?"

## February 15th, 9:58 A.M.

Oliver walked into the police department and looked for Arthur or Richard immediately. "Mr Johnson?" The young officer who was standing next to Oliver said, "Follow me, sir."

Oliver followed him to the office of detective Richard Henry; the officer left them without saying or doing anything more else. Oliver sat on the chair in front of detective Henry's desk. Detective begun: "You know that I'm being retired, right?"

"A flawless sentence to start a conversation, nice. Yes detective, I'm aware," said Oliver.

"You thought it's normal that everyone here is so higher than the clouds?" Richard placed his hand under his chin.

"They should be, you are leaving!" Oliver smiled.

"Wow. Surprisingly blunt. I'm glad you're back in the game!" Richard smiled.

"Thank you, sir. I'm still recovering."

"Could you eat after all?"

"Not much but I did. Mum made me mac and cheese. I had some of that."

"Good. Are you back to your place?"

"I did. Mum finally unleashed me," Oliver laughed.

"It's good to see you back here Oliver. We could really use your help. Let's get to work, shall we?" Richard said.

"Okay. Why did Arthur say that I should be here half an hour earlier?"

"Not a half, but one! The meeting starts at 11 o'clock. They all know."

"All but Oliver. I would've been here 10 minutes earlier, anyway...*One hour*?" Oliver said miserable.

"What is it, princess? Did I hurt your sleep time? Are you gonna have a bad day? Do you want my head off my body?" Richard cruelly joked.

"Detective! Can please we move straight to the point? Are there any other information I should know?"

"Your question requires *your* information first. What do you know about them?"

"Seven suspects, four women three men, Bradly Moore got to know them in the past year, they have all received the same emergency message from Brad as I did. There's an Australian, a Scottish, a Norse, a German, an English, a Swiss, a Russian and here you see an American." Oliver informed everything he had on the suspects.

"Why are you so interested in being a suspect? You are no longer a suspect to the court and prosecutor."

Richard frowned. "Yeah, so?"

"So, what is this all about?"

"It is about the fact that somebody stabbed my best friend, my brother to death! 32 traumas of stabbing...only on his chest! 2 traumas on his arm and one trauma on his thigh! So, excuse me if I can't be as cold blooded as you," Oliver said with a nervous smile.

"Easy, boy, calm down. We're in a crucial situation while a murderer is out there and God knows how many more people he might send to Lord if we don't stop him. We're all at the same page here; titled 'finding a murderer'. We're here to work together not to be mad at one another. I eliminated all the accusations against you because I was sure that Oliver Johnson is the psychologist that we need for this case," Richard said seriously.

"Nice speech. You mentioned a 'HE'. Did you find any DNA?" Oliver said.

"Not really but the coroner thinks that due to Brad's anatomy, the attacker was a man because it seems like Brad didn't or couldn't defend himself. They are not certain; I spoke to them; they need to do some more tests."

"With a...corpse?"

Detective looked desperately: "You really had to talk?"

***

## 10:29 A.M.

Eight people, including Oliver were sitting in a cement room covered with white colour. "Good morning, everybody." Oliver began, "My name is Oliver Johnson, crime psychologist of the case of Bradly Moore's murder."

A black girl said: "Nice to meet you, Mr Johnson. I am Morgan Geller. May I ask, how is this process going? I informed the police with everything I knew and I believe the others in this room did as well."

Oliver said: "I know, Ms Geller. We all did. But the forces believe that we must have eight meetings together. Not a routine and certain time is considered and all meetings' time will be emailed to you maximum seven days before."

Everyone had different reactions; indifference, surprised, confused.

Oliver: "Any questions?"

The blond-haired boy asked: "Excuse me Mr Johnson…"

Oliver interrupted: "Oliver, please."

The boy continued: "Oliver; I saw you in Brad's house the other night. If it is any of my concern, am I allowed to ask if you are a suspect for the murder or not?"

"Of course; you have the right to know. I wasn't a suspect from the beginning. I met detective Henry, the detective who's currently working on the case at the evening of February ninth and we spent the rest hours working at this very station. Detective and three other officers witnessed that they saw me the whole evening and neighbours witnessed that I got in that house the last. Now let's communicate, shall we? Tell us a short bio."

The blond girl started: "I'll start. Hello, I'm Olga Durov, Russian and 28. I was born in Saratov. I have five sisters; three older and two younger. I was married to an English man for three years, that's how I got to this country."

Oliver replied: "Thank you, Olga. It's nice to have you here. So, who's next?"

An albino man started to talk with a hidden German accent: "Hello everybody; my name is Pietro Schwarter and I am 28. I'm a musician. I was born in Erfurt. I have a younger sister."

An English boy introduced himself: "Greetings. I am Sebastian Bell. I'll be 34 this year. I was born in Oxford and unlike Olga and Pietro, I don't have any siblings because my parents got divorce when I was only two and I grew up with my mother."

"I'm sorry about your parents' divorce, Sebastian," said Oliver, "May I ask, how is your relationship with your father ever since?"

"We're fine. He got married again but I see him every week. We're fine and I'm okay with his wife, we don't have any problems. She has a son from his previous marriage, Baron. He's older than me."

Oliver: "Thank you Sebastian."

## Bus Stop, 14:03 P.M.

Oliver was sitting aimless in the bus stop, thinking about the suspects' lives.

Anya Barton who insisted to be called by her mother's last name, LaVey, was an Australian law scholar in London. She was living in London with her aunt since her family, including her brothers 'Lukas' and 'Thomas', was living in Sydney. She was 21.

Theodore Rivera, twenty-three, was born in Geneva, Switzerland. He was the son of a Swiss writer named Aneska Olsen. He had a seventeen-year-old brother named 'Hendrik' who was about to immigrate to London and move in with his brother.

Marika Lensher was a Norse nurse, 34, Married to Edwin Tømas who was also Norse and library owner. Marika was the only child because her mother left her sweet little daughter alone. Her mother was gone. Marika was raised without her mother but her father never allowed Marika to feel lonely. He was a dentist and that's exactly why Marika chose to be a nurse.

Oliver's phone rang. He took the phone out of his pocket and looked at Arthur's name on the screen. He answered: "Speak of the devil! I was just thinking about you!"

"Were you? How lucky am I?" Arthur asked.

"Since you married my sister and I appreciated you every single day for putting some space between me and that psychopath for almost four years!" Oliver joked.

"Yeah…thank to you for calling my wife a psychopath, man." Arthur said indifferently.

"Seriously, sometimes I think that I owe you, you know? Like I should pay you; I never thought someone would risk his life and marry Olivia!" Oliver said gratefully.

17

"You remember my wedding day? When we got pizza together?" Arthur asked after a moment of silence.

"Not really."

"You said, living with Olivia is like living with a civilised person. But that thought belongs to a waste basket."

"Oh, I do remember now! I did also say that you are too innocent to live with Liv but you don't have the right to get a divorce!" "Why did you call?"

Oliver laughed: "I remember. Why did you call?"

"To tell you to speed up the process. I know it might be a lot to do in a day but go talk to the suspects in person…today."

"Today?" Oliver asked, "Do you and Richard realize that I just got back to work despite my vulnerability?"

"Yes, Oliver. We do. But it is your job. It doesn't take excuses such as being unwell to be left undone." He added, "Plus, you only have a month to come up with an answer. Don't waste time."

"Fine," Oliver said angrily but before he hung up the phone, Arthur said: "By the way, Olivia asked me to invite you to dinner tonight; Dakota will be there too,"

"No promises," Oliver said in low voice.

***

## 14:40 P.M. University Of London

The class was quiet and the only sound that could be heard was the professor talking about the disappearance of D.B Cooper in 1971.

"And yet, after forty seven years, there is no evidence to prove that Mr Cooper died after jumping off the plane or remained alive; we don't know anything about his fate or the money he stole. The case remains open and for our next session, I want you to…"

Professor's speech was cut after the principal opened the door, "Mr Denzel, if you agree, there's a gentleman outside waiting to see one of your scholars, Anya Barton," said the principal.

The professor said: "What's his name? I allow only if my scholar knows him."

"He said he is Oliver Johnson," the principal said and Anya replied: "Yes sir, I know him. Professor, may I be excused?"

In a minute, Anya left the class ignoring her friend asking, "Who is Oliver Johnson?" Repeatedly.

Anya went to the yard and looked for Oliver. "Anya!" Oliver said and she paid attention, "Hi. Sorry for interrupting your class…"

Anya interrupted: "No, no worries. It was getting boring. I know about D.B Cooper."

"You know, once I had the assignment to get to know his motivation of hijacking."

"You studied here?" Anya asked.

"I used to, which is why the principle allowed me to speak to you now. I was a good student."

"What a cool man! I thought he is that kind of person who is loved by nobody but his dog!"

"I mean, you weren't wrong but…any way, I came here to talk to you. About you, your life."

"I believe that I have told you everything this morning." Anya raised an eyebrow.

"I want to know everything like I've known you for a long time."

"Wait…shouldn't we discuss these stuff in a session among the others?" She asked.

"I have plans for what I am doing. This doesn't relate to the case. Let's call it a friendly exchange of personal information. What do you say?"

"Exchange?" Anya asked, "Like, I tell you about my life and you'll tell me about yours?"

"No. It's a one-way deal. You talk, I listen." Oliver smiled.

"That's not fair. Why should you know me so well and remain unaware of everything about you?" Anya said seriously.

Oliver rolled his eyeballs: "Fine. I believe in afterlife despite my religion. You're a Catholic and you probably believe in the same subject."

"You know my religion and yet, you came all the way here to know about my personal life?"

"Exactly. Let's start with…What is this whole LaVey thing?"

"LaVey is mother's last name. My father is Barnabas Barton so technically, I am also a Barton but thought LaVey is more unique than Barton so I asked everyone I know to call me Anya LaVey."

"Interesting. Continue."

"Continue what?"

"Everything. I want to know everything."

She breathed out and said: "I, Anya Manuela Barton aka Anya LaVey was born on August 20th, 1997, Mater hospital at 10:03 a.m. My father is an insurance employee and my mother is a portraitist. I have two older brothers, Thomas Christopher and Lukas William who aren't fans of abbreviating their names to Tommy and Luke. These two brothers are so overly fond of their baby sister as much as allowing themselves to interfere in her decisions; that poor little thing! Tommy married a shuffle dance teacher named Rachel who is seven years older than him and before my dad got the chance to oppose, he said that we have no right to tell him what to do because he is old enough to make his own decisions. My pet was a cobra snake named 'Cutie' but she got drawn in the ocean. When I was seventeen, I wanted to see the world out of Australia so my parents agreed to send me to USA but those two goats imposed their old-fashioned ideology that US is so far and I'm better to go to UK and live with my aunt Ada and his husband Jackson."

She added: "I did it. Jackson died last year while he was hiking so I got to be alone with Aunt Ada. Ada's mourning didn't take so long and she said that no one will ever be able to fill Jackson's shoes but you know…they were about to get a divorce but no court was needed, death separated them pretty easy and it cost me a black shirt, a pair of black jeans, a pair of black sneaker and a perfect ponytail. Meanwhile, I met Bradly Moore while I was searching about a case for a class of mine and he happened to be the doctor who did the autopsy. After I was done, we became friends and we would give each other a call or meet sometimes. We continued our lives like this until that night I got his message, I went by to see what is going on but I saw Olga, Marika and Sebastian on his body and I assume you know the rest," Anya said, inhaled and exhaled.

"Thank you, Anya. Your information was really complete," Oliver said and smiled.

"Aren't you gonna tell me something else?"

"My biography? Fine." He coughed to straighten his voice, "I was born on the fourth of July, 1986 in Pennsylvania. My family moved to London when I was only three months old. I am the big brother to my two sisters. I met Bradly in the kindergarten and we became best friends. I studied crime psychology in London's university and got hired in the police department, needless to say that

I have solved at least ten cases among the other detectives of the police department. Nothing else to know." He continued: "You see? By personal information, I meant short and concise info not a Wikipedia kind of biography!"

"In my defence, you didn't want to know me *better*, you said you want to know *everything* about me and I agreed and told you everything. Now if you excuse me, I have one more class to attend today," Anya said with laughter.

"Okay. Have a nice day, see you again. And…never sleep in Mr Denzel's class, he is a friendly man but he would never forgive the person who sleeps during his teaching! He sees you as his son-in-law if he sees you sleeping!" Oliver joked.

"What's with his son-in-law?"

"Nothing, he just hates the guy," Oliver shrugged.

"Noted. See you again!" Anya said and walked away from Oliver.

*** 

## Gym, 15:20 P.M.

Oliver entered the gym that he knew Morgan works there as a coach. He asked the secretary where can he find Morgan and they led Oliver to a salon that people were training. One of the coaches came to Oliver:

"Hello, are you here to enrol, sir?"

"Good afternoon. I'm afraid I've already enrolled somewhere else. I was hoping to see Morgan Geller," Oliver said and smiled politely.

The coach smiled: "I will send her to you in a minute." And he left.

Oliver stood where he was until Morgan came to him with a smile: "Hello Oliver! Didn't expect you here!"

"Hey…well I was hoping that maybe we could spend some time and I didn't really know if you're here," said Oliver, "I can return if you're busy."

Morgan laughed: "No issues! I was just warming up. I can postpone my exercise. You don't mind walking, do you?"

"Not at all. Let's go, shall we?"

"Sure," said Morgan, "Just give me a minute to take my bag."

"I'll be waiting outside," Oliver said and shook his head.

He went out and wait for Morgan and meanwhile, he texted Olivia: "I'm not so sure if I can make it to dinner. Don't wait more than nine."

Oliver waited two more minutes for Morgan until she came out of the gym and broke the silence: "So, you are a crime psychologist, Oliver. How long has it been?"

"I got hired eight years ago. I was twenty-five back then."

"Are you thirty-three? I assumed you would be younger."

"It's always sweet to hear people claim you to be younger than what you are," said Oliver, "I'll be thirty-three this year."

"I am twenty-seven. I'm too afraid of being thirty; how does it feel like?"

"Being thirty? Nothing! It is like you're on a carousel and when you get up there, you are like, 'is this what I got on the carousel for? Where is all of the excitement?' It's not that big of deal. Trust me."

"Liked your explanation." Morgan's smile disappeared, "But I don't see myself numb about being thirty."

"You will." Oliver shrugged and looked in front.

"Compared to the other suspects including me, you seem to be more hurt about Brad. May I ask why? Did you know him longer?" Morgan asked with careful choice of words.

"I did. Brad was my best and longest time friend," Oliver said with a sorrowful smile and intentionally said: "And I won't give up until I find who shut his eyes for good."

Morgan put his head down. Minutes passed in silence and neither of them knew where the destination will be. They just walked in London's streets until Oliver decided to say: "I decided to meet all of you in person. I want to know you better. Tell me everything about your life that I don't know."

"Like, personal information?" Morgan asked doubtful.

"Yes please."

"Well…My accent proclaims I'm Scottish. I was born in a not so wealthy family. I have a twin sister; we don't look alike at all. The two of us moved here four years ago. Karla is a purchasing manager. We're also engaged to a pair of twins as well! Brad and I met at the library in October. This is it. Do you want to hear something else?"

"No. Thank you Morgan. I wish the best for you and your fiancé." Oliver friendly smiled.

"Thank you so much," said Morgan, "What about you? Aren't you seeing somebody?"

"Me? No! I'm not the perfect marriage guy. My father once said that if I get married one day, the girl would be found in the mental hospital the next day!"

Morgan laughed: "You can't be that hard of a person to tolerate!"

"Oh, I am! You have no idea!" Oliver laughed.

***

## 15:57 P.M. Lorenté Coffee House

The young waiter opened the restroom's door and said: "Theodore! Where were you, boy?"

"And here I was, thinking that bathrooms are supposed to be private!"

Waiter laughed: "There is this guy named Oliver outside. Asking about you."

"I will be there in…a minute!" Theodore said hasty and the young waiter left.

Theodore looked at his reflection in the mirror; frowned and asked himself: "What is he doing here?" In a second, he shook his head and said: "Theo, you are talking to yourself, mazel tov!" He left the bathroom to the hall looked for Oliver and went to him.

"Mr Johnson," said Theodore, "Wha…What are you doing here?"

"Thank you for welcoming me pretty friendly and asking me what I would like to have!" Oliver said as a sarcasm and smiled.

"Oh…I apologise, my bad; what would you like to have?"

"I would say a cup of hot chocolate and since there are four other people are working here among you and the place is not that crowded, I might ask you to take an hour off so I can talk to you."

Theodore spent a moment in silence and asked: "Is there anything left from this morning?"

Oliver rejected with his head and said: "No. I've said everything I should've. This conversation is just necessary."

Theodore shook his head and left. Oliver took his phone and dialled Olga's number. The phone rang several times until Olga answered: "Hello?"

"Olga, hi. Can you speak?"

"Yes. I'm not busy. Go on please."

"I just called to see if you have plans for the rest of the day. We must talk in person. Today, necessarily."

Olga thought and answered: "I have no plans for the rest of the day. Give me a time and a location."

"Lorenté coffee house. One hour from now."

"Fine. See you in an hour."

"See you."

Oliver hangs up the phone. Theodore came to him with a cup of hot chocolate and as Oliver noticed, he had his apron taken off. Theodore put the hot chocolate in front of Oliver and sat on the chair next to him. Oliver unlocked his phone and read his information to Theodore:

"Theodore Stephen Rivera. Born on February 13th, 1996, in Geneva. Your father is a mechanic and your mother is a famous Swiss writer named 'Aneska Olsen'. You have a younger brother named 'Hendrik' who is seven years younger than you and due to his birthday and my perfect skills in math, he is seventeen by now. You are both trying to earn England's citizenship but troubles keep knocking your doors because Hendrik is underage."

Theodore looked miserable. He didn't feel quite comfortable about his personal life being read through a screen. He asked: "May I speak now?"

"You may."

"Let's begin with my homeland. Back in Switzerland, I wasn't actually living my life the way I supposed to live so as a conclusion, I migrated to here. Hendrik is going through the same problems that I've been through with my parents. We have parental issues that doesn't allow us to live with them. They are a little bit…barely at home. I mean, sure we're mad at them but they're our parents and we love them anyway. I talk to my mother every day and call my father every weekend, he is usually busy."

"Are you happy about your decision?"

"I'm fine, Oliver. I will probably get happier when I see Hendrik in London."

"You certainly will. You're a strong person, Theodore. Now, tell me about your childhood. How was it and tell me more about not living life the way you were supposed to."

"I barely remember Geneva for the first ten years of my life because we used to travel a lot. Because of all those travels I can speak German, French and Italian. Thirty-two days after my seventh birthday, Hendrik was born and you know…My father was usually at work and my mum was always writing a new novel upstairs and their job led them to hire a babysitter, an Italian babysitter for me and Hendrik; actually, she thought me more Italian than any trips did in those five years." Theodore smiled after remembering a lovely period of his life.

"Why did she stop babysitting you guys? Was it because of your age or something else?"

"She got married when I was ten and when I was twelve, she announced her pregnancy, moved back to Italy I think to Florence or Palermo. I visited her a couple times after that."

"What was her name?"

"Marina Esposito, then she got his husband's name, 'Russo'."

"What about your parents?"

"I remember my dad literally more than my mum, I used to see him more. Mum was usually in the guest room writing a novel or an idea of a novel and despite all these, we used to host a lot of guests and I played with their children. And honestly, if my dad had any free times, he would've spent most of it with us but Mum, I don't remember if she had ever done the same."

"We used to host a lot of guests too. I barely even remember their names. I would've forgot my cousins' names if we weren't related!" Oliver joked because he saw Theodore's unpleased face even though it was a lie of prudence.

Theodore laughed: "Why is that?"

"Not all of them were relatives. Most of them were my father's co-workers and partners. I used to see relatives mostly on holidays. Almost all of them live in America."

"You're American?"

Oliver drank a gulp of his hot chocolate and asked: "Doesn't my accent turns me in?"

"How long has it been? Living in London, I'm talking about."

"I was three-month-old. My sisters are younger, they were born here."

"What brought your family here?"

"My father. He is an architect and he had this tower to build and as he says, it changed all of our lives."

"How did you meet Bradly?"

"Bradly?" Now Oliver was uncomfortable to talk "Umm…We met at the first day of kindergarten when we were three."

"Wow, that is a literal lifetime. I had no idea."

Oliver smiled and kept himself busy with looking at the empty cup: "It was. Now it's just a finished story. A new spin off has been started."

After a moment, Theodore asked: "Oliver, can I ask your opinion on something?"

Oliver looked at Theodore. He said: "Okay, here's my opinion. This whole case sounds so planned to me and cliché. It just seems like a Hercules Poirot kind of thing. Eight people at a same place at a same time? And all of us were responsive to an emergency message? And some parts don't even make sense."

Oliver raised an eyebrow: "Like what?"

"Like…you being on an emergency list is compatible but the guy didn't even put his brother on the list, why should he put *me*? And of course, Brad didn't have enough time to send a message not to even one, but to eight people? I mean, who sent them? Brad or the killer?"

Oliver got quiet. Theodore wasn't wrong, her mother was a writer who had published at least three crime stories and by reading them, Theodore was familiar with the administrative system of the police department, who was Oliver fooling?

Theodor shook his hand in front of Oliver's eyes: "Hey Oliver!"

"Yes?"

"Don't worry. I won't talk to other suspects about it."

Oliver stared at him for few seconds and whispered: "You know too much; it freaks me out!"

"Johnson! I'm not a killer, I mean yes, I kind of am; I killed my goldfish because it didn't blink and I thought its eyes were burning and I tried to make a favour!"

"It was really kind of you! Now I am totally freaked out, I'm gonna sleep at some hotel from tonight!"

Theodore laughed: "You see, I'm no police but if there's somebody who knows my mother's books better than her, it's me! Mum always chooses the criminal with a 'TPQ'"

"What's that?"

"TPQ stands for 'The Potential Question'. My mum spends hours, days and sometimes weeks asking herself 'Who has the potential for doing this?' And then she designs mind-maps or just write about each one of them, the biographies."

"So, then she can follow each one of them as a clue! Like a string that the end of it is the answer! God, Theo, I must meet your mum! I have so many questions to ask!" Oliver said and laughed.

Theo looked at him scared and confused: "She is in Germany now...I believe should call and warn her to stay away from London!"

"I'm kidding! But I certainly have to meet her someday!" Oliver laughed and said.

"Oh, it's 16:42. My shift will be over in twenty minutes; can I get you anything else, Oliver?"

"No, thanks. I'm just waiting here for Olga. I must talk to her too."

"Well, good luck with that. I'm leaving and umm...when is the next meeting?"

"I haven't decided yet but thank you for your time."

"Any time."

They shook hands and Theodore left. Oliver called Sebastian to set a time for meeting and Sebastian said that he can only meet Oliver at 8 o'clock because he had so much work to do since he was a photographer who worked until 8 p.m. but he spent all morning at the police department. After Sebastian, Oliver made contact with Pietro and they agreed on 19:30 at Pietro's house.

\*\*\*

## Lorenté Coffee House, 16:59 P.M.

Olga walked in and looked for Oliver; she achieved to find Oliver behind the table next to the window. Oliver got extremely surprised seeing Olga wearing a pullover sweater and a thin cardigan.

After their greeting finished, Olga smiled: "I see you're amazed of my choice of dressing!"

"Yes, I am. Honestly, I'm dying to ask you 'How'?"

"How *what*? I'm Russian!"

"Yeah, but a Saratov kind of Russian! Saratov is not as cold as Moscow!"

"South-western Russia, it's still Russia and it is cold, I mean a cold that probably freezes *you*!"

"You won! But seriously, how isn't that weather cold for you?"

"Well," said Olga, "It's like a cool spring breeze."

"Got it…you see, I called you because I wanted to learn more about you."

"Why is that?"

"Listen, Bradly was my best friend and now he is murdered. It is my duty to find out everything about this murder because Brad was my best and oldest friend; I was his best man!"

"Best man? He was married?"

"Yes. I mean, not when he died. It was eight years ago."

"Back in 2011?"

"Yes. Elma and Brad married in June first, got divorce in October because Elma was a fashion designer and she was offered a job opportunity in Italy but the contract took her for a year so they had no choice but moving to Italy, Brad didn't agree so they had to split up and I can't believe I just told you everything about it!"

"It's alright. I knew him for almost two years but he had never mention anything about his marriage."

"He didn't like to talk about it much. Anyway, as I said, I asked you to come over because I wanted to know everything about *you*."

"You mean…from the time I was born in Saratov, my parents, my three older sisters and two younger, my marriage, my divorce and my friendship with Bradly and the way I came here to sit in front of you and tell you all these things?"

"That is exactly what I meant, so go ahead!"

Olga pointed to the waiter who was going to their table and whispered: "Coffee first!"

"Ladies first." Oliver leant back to the chair.

Olga ordered iced coffee with extra sugar and three ice cubes and Oliver was gonna ask, "*WHY* and *HOW*?" but he refused.

Olga started: "Let's begin. I was born on December first, 1990, in Saratov. My parents were both working for different units of military and as I remember, they left the six of us at home sometimes and it once led us to burning the kitchen when I was sixteen and I will explain that later. I met 'Gary Pine' when I was twenty-three, he was an oak wood merchant in Russia and England. Long story short, we got married after nine month and moved to London when I was twenty-four. We lived together for three years and ended up divorcing but we're still in touch. I met Bradly because of his younger brother, Ezra; their cousin Louis was my student and Ezra brought him to my class one time, that's how we became friends. I met Bradly later at a mall with Ezra, he introduced us to each other and Brad asked me to teach him some Russian."

"Thank you for being honest with me and I'm sorry for your divorce, it was certainly for the best. Now, would you like to tell me the story of you and your sisters burning the kitchen?"

"Yep. Oldest to youngest, it's Melody, Madeline, Melora, me, Zeena and Dinah. Our parents left us alone when I was sixteen which means that Melody was twenty-two, Madeline was nineteen, Melora was eighteen, Zeena was fifteen and Dinah was twelve. We were trying to make beef stroganoff but it went wrong, we all forgot to turn the oven off, we noticed that pretty late."

Oliver put his elbows on the table: "What did you do?"

"Well, Melora couldn't do anything, she is paralytic but the others tried to put out the fire with water."

"The others?"

"Yeah. I didn't do anything. If we were meant to die, we would be dead by now!"

"I appreciate your point of view!"

"It's some sort of life philosophy. I told you about it."

"Do you believe in destiny?"

"Just a little bit. I think of it as a book, a book that has every detail but you can edit some parts of it."

"Again, I appreciate your point of view."

"May I ask you something Ollie?"

"Sure."

"What is your point of view? About death?"

Oliver thought for a while: "I don't know. I used to believe in some idea but lately, I'm giving it more time. My beliefs have been altered and I've been doing anything to find my answers. I currently think of death as a brutal mother. Ones who cruelly take their kid away when the kid is playing with other kids. When their kid still wants to play."

Both of them spent minutes in silence. Both thinking about Oliver's way of thinking of death.

"Oliver, I know that we don't know each other so long," said Olga with dignity and sympathy, "But I think that you got this. I think you will find your answers and all your questions will no longer hurt you."

"Thank you so much, Olga. It was good to hear that," Oliver smiled, "Now if you excuse me, I should leave now; I should meet the rest of you guys."

"Who? The suspects? Why?"

"I need to know more about each one of you. I've already talked to Anya and Theodore."

"Good luck with that. Oh, Oliver?"

"Yeah?"

"Zeena and Dinah are arriving here tonight and they are gonna stay with me. If the eight of us are going to meet, I can't attend…until Wednesday."

"No matter. We've got an entire month for that."

***

### Greenwich Hospital 17:39 P.M.

Oliver stopped in front of the hospital, Marika's workplace. He called Marika on the phone and it took a bit for her to answer: "Oliver! Hi! To what do I owe the pleasure?"

"Hi," said Oliver, "Listen I, really need to come to the hospital right now."

"Why? Are you alright?" Marika asked concerned.

"No. I cut my arm."

Marika thought for a moment and suspiciously said: "You're too relax for someone whose arm is cut."

"Yeah. I need to talk to you, it's important as much as a cut arm!"

"Fine. My shift will end at six. Can you come to the hospital?"

"I'm coming in!"

"What?"

"You heard me! I will be waiting in the cafeteria."

"I will be there in ten minutes."

They hung up the phone. Oliver went to cafeteria and sat on a chair next to the counter and ordered a hot chocolate, the third high sugar meal of the day after cereal for breakfast and the hot chocolate he had early that day. Marika joint him after ten minutes as she said before. Marika sat in front of Oliver and ordered 'just as usual' and began the conversation: "What was super emergency that brought you here?"

"I wanted to talk to you about...*everything*."

"Do you want to know everything? Well at first, it was all darkness...some sort of endless nothingness. Then happened an explosion that manufactured the oceans and all creatures..."

Oliver interrupted: "Are you explaining me the big bang?"

"Didn't you want to know *everything*?" Marika smiled and raised an eyebrow.

"Not about the creation of the universe; about yourself. And speak of the creation, do you believe in evolution theory or Adam and Eve theory?"

"Evolution theory, is what I believe." She put her hand under her chin.

"So, you're one of us, good sign. I want to know about your life, your personal life from the beginning 'till now."

"Like, my past?"

"You're smart."

"I, Marika Scarlett Lensher was born in October thirty first, 1984 in Oslo. My father is a dentist and my mum was a physiologist and what they did for living motivated me to become a nurse. I don't remember my mum at all because she died soon after I was born, I grew up with my father and I don't have any siblings. I actually can't remember my past clearly but I do know that I used to study a lot. I was a nerd and a book worm. Six years ago, I married Edwin Tømas, he is a library owner just as he was in Oslo. We met at his library. We moved here three years ago in case of improving our careers. If you want to know about Brad, we met here in this hospital because he had his ankle broken, I nursed him at the night he was hospitalised. I was at my night shift which he called it 'The graveyard shift'! We spoke all night long that night, we met times after and became friends."

"First things first, I'm terribly sorry about your mother. Growing up with no mother is nothing I want to even imagine but I have no doubts that you can make an excellent mother someday...or if you already are!"

She smiled beautifully: "Thank you."

She took a look at the hot chocolate Oliver ordered and said with a smile: "I guess I owe Pietro ten dollars!"

"Why is that?"

"He thought that you are a hot chocolate person, I said you are a coffee person."

"You guys were gambling over me?"

"Maybe. It depends on how you see it!" Marika said, "Let's just call it a game."

Oliver looped his hand around his hot chocolate and said: "Yeah. Vegas is filled with game centres!"

Marika laughed.

Oliver said: "I'm neither a coffee or a hot chocolate person, I'm a milkshake person but now it's February and it's chilling!"

"Got it! None of us won the bet!"

"None of you guys did; actually, I'm about to meet Pietro in…fifteen minutes, I'll tell him about this whole thing and if you excuse me, I should go now."

"When will be the second appointment?"

"There will be no meeting until Wednesday. I will let you know."

***

## 19:31 Pietro's House

Oliver knocked at the door and it opened in less than ten seconds: "You're a minute late!" Pietro said and smiled, "Come on in."

"I beg your pardon, your majesty, I was occupied with meeting other people before you, should I kneel now?" Oliver joked and walked in.

Pietro said: "No, saints have asked me for your forgiveness…How are you, Oliver?"

"I'm good, hope you're the same."

"I am, do you want anything to eat or drink?"

Oliver smiled: "I see what you're doing! Marika told me about it! I'm not a hot chocolate person or a coffee person, I'm a milkshake person but now is February, no time for it!"

"So, tell me, what do you prefer instead?"

"Mocha, I suppose."

"Do you want any of us win or what?"

"Or what!"

"You know what? Forget about it! What do you eat or drink?"

"You've got peanuts?"

"It's on the top of my list!"

"So, I would like some peanuts and a glass of water."

Pietro went to kitchen to bring them some peanuts. Oliver sat on the sofa and looked around and appreciated Pietro's decoration in his mind. The major colours of the house were dark red and wheat. Pictures of musical notes could be seen on the wall which perfectly showed Pietro's job: Musician.

Oliver noticed a song lyrics, written with musical notation and a name above it, 'Moonlight' so Oliver assumed it is Moonlight by Beethoven. Pietro came out of the kitchen with two bowls of peanut and a glass of water for Oliver and sat on the sofa next to him and began the conversation:

"You said that there's something emergency you need to talk about, I'm all ears."

"Well, I was managing to meet you all in person this afternoon, I talked to everyone else but you and Sebastian. The fact is that I want to get to know you in person, I want to know about your personal life back in Germany and after migration and knowing Bradly."

"So, let's see. I was born in July seventh, 1990, you're invited to my birthday, by the way. My parents were both teachers and my dad is Albinos that's why Paula and I are both Albinos; Paula is my little sister, she is twenty years old by now. I moved here in 2013 and got addicted a year after but I wasn't that kind of addicted who slept on the street, I have obsession. Anyway, Dad understood that I've got addicted in…2015 and we haven't talk since then. I could quit drugs in last year, I met Brad when it was happening. We met by social media. I posted one of my videos that I was playing violin and he appreciated."

"Thank you or telling me about it. You know, for a German you have a nice American accent."

"Yeah, I hear that a lot. My father was an English teacher and a lot of accents could be heard. American caught my ears."

"What instruments do you play?"

"Violin, Cello and Piano."

"Wow! You're super talented!" Oliver said amazed.

"Thanks for your opinion"

Oliver pointed to the pattern on the wall: "Is that…"

"Moonlight by Beethoven? It is!"

"Can you play it?"

"Yes. It was the first track I completely played."

Oliver looked at his watch and stood up: "Nice communication. I better get going, I told you that I have to meet Sebastian too."

Pietro stood up: "I'll walk you to the door."

***

## 20:01 Eden's Photography Studio

"Smile a little bit more…There you go," Sebastian said to the infant boy who was sitting in front of Sebastian's camera and took his picture.

He continued to the little boy's father: "You may come and get the picture tomorrow at four o'clock."

"Thank you so much, should I pay for the picture now or tomorrow?"

"Tomorrow is fine."

Sebastian walked them to the exit door and came back to Oliver. Sebastian asked Oliver if he wants to share a chicken Pesto pasta. Oliver rejected despite his sense of starving because he couldn't risk his red pepper allergy.

"You know, I don't usually eat my dinner at work, tonight was an exception because I spent the morning with you," Sebastian said and sat on a table, holding a foil plate of pasta "No complains. It's alright."

"Sorry about that," said Oliver, "I'll try not to make any appointments in the morning."

"That would be better," said Sebastian, "So, can I eat while you're speaking?"

"Oh, I'm not the one to talk, you are."

"What should I talk about?" He raised an eyebrow.

"About your personal life, contains your childhood, adolescent, family and Bradly."

Sebastian thought and ate some pasta and said: "My dad is a drowned saver and my mum is a literature teacher. They got divorce when I was two years old and Mum took responsibility of my tutorship and we moved to Oxford, we…used to live in Birmingham before. I was always this energetic and playful kid who made jokes about everything at the class but all my grades were acceptable."

"Tell me more about your parents."

"Mum's name is Eden which I named the studio after her. The reason of their divorce was that they were about to welcome another baby after me but the baby didn't make it and somehow, it led Eden and Ethan to divorce. Dad got married again and his wife Celine has a son with her first husband, Baron. He's a nice guy, he has a wife and a new-born son named George. We're not that close but we can get along. Mum was engaged to an author for two years but didn't last."

"And about Bradly?"

"Brad brought a little girl here to take some pictures together. Things went wrong and I mistook his name with a client. I had to call him several times and we made friends."

"Who was that little girl?"

"I don't seem to remember her name, I'm afraid. But she was blond and her eyes were light blue."

"Have you ever met Brad's brother?"

"Ezra? I just saw a picture of him, first I thought it was Brad himself."

"Yeah, they're just the same!"

"How do you recognize them?"

"Recognize?"

"My bad, recognized."

"Ezra is more curly and shorter than Brad, like five centimetres."

"Oliver?" Sebastian asked, "How did the two of you meet? You and Brad?"

"We were friends for *twenty nine years*. We first met at the kindergarten when we were both three," Oliver said and looked at the floor.

"I didn't know…I can't even imagine how hard it was for you to see him like that," Sebastian said sympathetically.

***

"*What* did you say? How can you be so mean? I wasted *all my time* so you can *ditch* me? Oliver, you're *so* dead! Don't walk ten kilometres near me or I will shoot you with a machine gun! *Don't you dare* to call me again! I wish you burn in hell you *pathetic loser*! Do you think I'm yelling? *Do you think I'm yelling*? Guess what? I don't even care! I'm waiting for you to die! I will bury you with bare hands and dance on your grave! Oh, I just remembered, eight years ago you said that I'm losing too much weight, I should say that it's fine if you don't have belly fat until you have something up on your mind! Oh God, I wish you burn in hell! Don't forget to say hello to Grandpa Andrew!"

These were things that Olivia was snapping on the phone when Oliver said that he is too tired to have dinner at their house and Oliver, well since he was used to it, he didn't hang up the phone, just kept the phone away from his ear in case of preventing his ears from being deaf. Olivia's curses were always the same but Oliver heard something new this time: Grandpa Andrew.

Andrew Johnson was an exorcist. Not that kind of people who are looking for money or attention, he was a real one and the whole family knew it. Oliver and Olivia knew it more than anyone else because when they were kids and went on vacations to Andrew's house in America, they wouldn't return home without seeing a jar or sofa moving without being touched by something invisible! The worst part was when they were at Andrew's house for the last time when he said that he will die in twenty hours by a heart attack and it happened! Andrew died because of a heart attack without having any health issues! Dakota was born three weeks after the death of his grandfather and Olivia and Oliver were praying to God for Dakota, not to be their grandpa's afterlife form!

Oliver, however, didn't understand why did Olivia mentioned him. Andrew was a terrifying man who never cared his grandchildren might have a heart attack when he talked about ghosts or hunted houses; beside all these stuff, he was a good man, an amazing and caring dad and a wonderful grandfather. A lovely man.

"Hey Billy, are you listening to me?"

"What did you say, sis?"

"Don't you dare to call me sis, you're like Hela to Thor!"

"Actually…"

"Actually *what*? *Huh*? Actually *what*?" Olivia yelled.

"Nothing. Move on, sweetheart. I'm all ears."

"Oliver…get the hell away from my sight."

"I'm not! I'm standing on a street far from your home!"

"Dear Lord! Hang up!" Olivia said miserable.

"*You* hang up!"

"Why don't *you* hang up? *You* called me!"

Oliver hung up the phone which meant that he just had his death contract signed.

While listening to Olivia, Oliver was standing in front of the house of Moores' family.

## 20:54 P.M. Kitchen of the Moores' Family House

Elizabeth Hills-Moore put a plate of grilled chicken and mashed potato with two buttered toasts in front of Oliver, just as he always liked; he also liked something else, eating food all alone and in silence so Elizabeth left him alone in the kitchen.

After a few minutes and hearing footsteps from the left, Oliver looked up and saw Ezra coming into the kitchen.

"Get out," Oliver whispered.

"You're making me get out of my family's house kitchen? *Dictator*," Ezra said indifferent.

"You know I like to eat all alone, don't you?" Oliver took a tired look at Ezra.

Ezra stayed put.

"I don't see you getting out."

"Yeah…You see, there is something that I just found out about, like this morning. I wasn't sure if I can tell my parents first, I decided to tell you."

"What is it?"

Ezra sat on a chair next to Oliver: "I received a call, from an orphanage. Apparently, Brad gave them my phone number as a backup number or something."

Oliver stopped chewing: "Did orphanage call you to check on Bradly and give you the status of a little girl?"

"Yeah…How do you know about it?"

"Like I told you and your parents, I went to meet all the suspects in person. One of them who is a photographer said that Brad brought a little girl to his studio. What do you know more?"

"The girl is named Ava Florence Wintergreen. Bradly took the entire responsibility of her costs four years ago when she was two or three. Bradly was allowed to spend time with her three days a week, lately four days. Brad was so qualified they were even managing for Brad to adopt Ava." Ezra sighed, "They were wondering why Bradly didn't show up to see Ava for the past week. So, I told them why."

"My head will blow up in ten seconds," Oliver thought.

37

"Ad...adopt?" Oliver's mouth was dried, "Why didn't any on us knew about it? How come he didn't tell anyone?"

"I have *no* idea," Ezra said upset and stressful, "I noticed Bradly was changing the decoration of one of the guest rooms. I asked him and he just said that he wants to do something with the theme."

"*Dear God*. How come I was unaware of everything?" Oliver hided his eyes before his hand.

"It's not your fault. We should now think about Ava. Orphanage didn't even know that Bradly is gone. I told them that I will tell Ava what happened."

"Brilliant. It's really easy that her godfather's bother who looks like his twin, tell Ava everything!" Oliver yelled angrily, "Sorry...I just...don't think it's a good idea."

Ezra crossed his arms: "Then what do you suggest?"

"I guess I go see her and explain it step by step. It's for the best. She's just a kid."

Ezra took a deep breath: "What about my parents? Shall we tell them?"

"No! *Absolutely not!*" Oliver said hastily, "I must make sure of everything first. We must give them some time. Their current level of grief is crucial. They should get better and we'll explain to them together."

He then whispered: "Don't do anything without my permission. Let me know if you decided to do make any decisions."

# Chapter Two
# Help Me, Brother

**February 19th, Oliver Johnson's House, 11:22 A.M.**

It was the kind of day that Oliver wanted to stay home, watch some superhero movie, order some fried chicken with cheeseburger and answer no calls from work, family and friends. Besides, he hadn't slept last night AND thanks to that, he was feeling kind an angry and everything sounded intolerable.

Oliver was usually awake. It had nothing to do with sense of responsibility for his job or being an early morning bird, no, none of these options. Oliver was an insomniac since he was sixteen.

See, Insomnia is a sleep disorder in which you have trouble falling or staying sleep; Oliver has been dealing with this disorder for years; lack of sleeping made him anxious so Oliver was always anxious.

Most of the times, at least.

February nineteenth was the day of the second appointment with the suspects. Oliver asked all the seven suspects to go to the police department but since he couldn't sleep, he texted them to meet Oliver at his own home.

Oliver was waiting for them at home, planning to ask them the necessary questions, Oliver had his own way to interrogate!

It was the day that suspects were going to be asked about their life after Brad's death; and of course, seeing a body covered in blood.

Oliver's sadness might've not been more than Brad's family but it wasn't anything less.

Brad had this saying that he used its benefits throughout his thirty-two and a hundred and fifteen days of lifetime: "The feeling of losing somebody is like a hairstylist balding you. You dislike it at first, you hate it, you're upset at first but then you get along with it."

Bradly Anton Moore II was not a secretive man. But just after his death, it was revealed that he was a mysterious guy and that made his loved ones upset by the very truth, they would feel that they weren't that trustable they thought to know his secrets. At least this was what Oliver felt like.

He stopped staring at the wall when his phone rang. Looked at Richard Henry's name, Oliver looked away and tried not to scream.

Richard Henry *was* actually a horrible boss…not really a *horrible* boss, that's excess, he was a strict boss who never accepted any excuses for anything, everything he wanted to be done should've been done in one hour maximum or the person who was in charge was fired! Oliver was lucky about this habit. Fortunately for Richard's employees and co-workers, he was being retired but he agreed to be the detective of Bradly Moore's case as his last job.

Oliver eventually answered the phone and the first thing he heard was Richard shouting:

"What took you so long?"

"Hello, I'm fine, thank you for asking. How are *you*?" Oliver said sarcastically and smiled.

"Oliver," Richard said angrily, "I wish I could fire you."

"Lucky for me, I don't work for you, Richard."

"Why did you cancel the meeting?"

"About that, I didn't *cancel* it. I changed the location because I didn't sleep last night and I couldn't make it to the station so I told them to meet up at my place." Oliver explained rationally.

"Do you realise how dangerous is it to invite them to *your own* house, Johnson?" Richard miserably asked Oliver.

"Richard don't worry. I'll take care of everything," Oliver said and thought of a perfect lie: "And maybe I'll stay the night at Olivia's house. Happy?"

Richard took a deep breath: "You're the one to decide." And asked: "How come you didn't sleep last night?"

"My pills don't seem to have effects on me anymore," Oliver said sadly, "I'll see my doctor if I get the chance."

"Are you alright?"

"I weirdly am. Even though this is like a habit that you never get used to it."

"You are the golden key to all of our questions. It's important for you to be fine."

"That was nice to hear. I'll take care of it. Trust me," said Oliver, "We'll talk later."

They hung up the phone. Oliver began to seek his phone for the first meeting's video.

The day of the first meeting, after the suspects were introduced, Oliver asked each of them to tell him about their concepts of death.

He found the video and played it. Anya was the first one to speak, to keep the alphabetical arrangement.

She said: "*I believe in the afterlife. If you die a good person, you will return to the world as an alluring, delicate flower and someone will take good care of you. If you die guilty...and by guilty, I mean guilty of the sins that you never asked for their forgiveness. God would forgive if you just asked; I agree with this idea of Martin Luther. Where was I? uh-huh! If you die guilty, you may return as some weed that everyone wants it gone.*"

At that point, Oliver said: "Marika, your name's second letter is A. You go on, please."

Maria started to talk with her friendly and kind voice: "*Dead ones are alive if you don't stop remembering them. I grew up thinking the same.*"

Olga was next: "*I think that life is overflowed with pain and suffer and of course, it has good experiences but death is like a mitigation. That in which, everything you've been worried about, back in your living days just become meaningless.*"

Morgan talked: "*I mean...I have my religious thoughts but I think that dead people will come back to life again. If not, what is the whole point of living? I believe in afterlife.*"

Pietro said: "*I'm Jewish. I grew up learning and believing that when we die, our souls leave our bodies and keep living in Sheol.*"

Sebastian said his own idea: "*I just think that our lives come to an end when we die. And the only living things about us will be photographs. And memories. Nothing more.*"

Theodore was the last one to talk: "*I just...think that death is the end.*"

## 11:42 A.M. The Living Room of Oliver Johnson's House

Folded his arms, Oliver took a quick look to everyone and calmly asked: "Why isn't anyone answering?"

"Answer to…what question?" Theodore asked.

Anya said: "Oliver, you didn't ask anything."

"Didn't I?" Oliver asked, "Well…pardon me for lack of attention, I thought I asked. The question is that, how much Brad was close to any of you? I saw some of you got back or trying to get back to your old lives, I want you to tell me how you managed to do it and how Brad's death has affected you. You have a few minutes to think about it. Take your time."

Those few minutes were definitely one of the hardest moments Oliver had ever experienced. At that moment he thought: "A dead friend, a job that hurts you me somehow, an insomnia that doesn't go away, seven people in my living room that one of them is a murderer, damn headache and a memory of being in a burning building can teach me a good lesson. What lesson? God knows. I'm too tired to think about it now."

Oliver couldn't think more clearly than that. He couldn't tolerate nausea and headache anymore. He left his chair to the kitchen, took a sedative and came back to the living room after feeling better—Ignoring the nausea. As soon as Marika saw Oliver, she squinted her eyes and said: "Oliver, you seem to be ill."

Oliver sat on the chair and smiled: "It was just insomnia. I'm fine."

Pietro asked: "Are you *sure* that you don't need medical attention?"

"I wouldn't have been permitted to work if I wasn't fine…you guys tell me, why isn't anybody starting?" Oliver hastily tried to change the conversation.

Marika began: "May I? Well, I met Brad at the hospital. He broke his ankle and should've stayed at the hospital for a night. That night was my night shift. We spoke until six o'clock. He fell sleep and I switched my shift with another nurse…Brad's attitude was wonderful and somehow indescribable. He allowed me to go to his work and talk to him while he was autopsying, it was educational for my job. He once said that I don't know if he said it as a joke or not…but he said that he chose to be a coroner to see if dead bodies grab his hand when he worked after midnight! He was a really nice friend, he was excellent. We didn't get to spend more time together but I will always appreciate the time we were friends. I hope he felt the same about me." And she smiled with tears in her eyes and shake in her voice.

Oliver smiled: "Thank you for telling us about your feelings and Marika. I remember Brad always refused to make friends with doctors but he appreciated nurses."

"My turn," said Olga, "I'll say next. It all started with my ex-husband. After we got divorce, I started to work more and I met Brad as a consequence to that, I first met his little cousin, then his brother and eventually himself. He asked me to teach him Russian in case he could visit the country some time. Losing him is like the hot weather in Russia, it doesn't make sense."

Anya asked: "Am I allowed to ask that, did Brad help you accepting your divorce?"

Answered Olga: "Da. But as babushka used to say, *Nikogda ne vikhodi zamuzh za pervogo vstrechnogo parnya*; never marry the first guy you meet."

"Was your husband the first guy you met?" Morgan asked and answered Olga: "Of course not! I just quoted."

Sebastian said: "I beg your pardon, ladies. Olga, who is this babushka guy?"

"It is a word for grandma."

"Am I the only one whose grandparents are too old to speak?" Sebastian asked, "How old is she?"

"About ninety, maybe even more. Believe it or not, her life is a masterpiece. She can speak Russian, English, Italian, Spanish, German, French, Romanian and Persian. She had sixteen children, four of them weren't even born and three of them died because of old age, she is now an athlete and her record for weightlifting is eighty kilos," Olga said and smiled proudly.

Everyone was shocked and remained silent. Oliver broke the silence and asked: "Is your grandmother a terminator?"

Olga laughed and said: "She might be. She likes to wear black leather!"

Oliver smiled: "Thank you for sharing your feeling and introducing babushka. Who's next?"

Started Pietro: "It'll be me. I moved here and I got addicted a year after, I was addicted for four years, I was quitting when I met Brad. It was…hard for me to believe that he is gone. He was that sort of people who had plans for everything, every moment of their lives and I thought that he was going to live longer. I hope he is resting in heaven."

Oliver said: "Thank you Pietro, he certainly is. Next?"

Anya began: "I'm not so sure if I want to talk, it seems really creepy. I'm a lawyer; well, scholar but call me a lawyer. I met Brad while working on an old and solved case as a mid-term project. He volunteered to tell me about the found body and its autopsy. We met several times to work on my project, we got even friendlier when he came to my presentation of the project. I still can't get along with the fact that he is…gone. Even hard to say it. He was so young and it was too soon I think."

"I'm afraid to say that he thought he would reach forty, at least. You make memories during years and in a second, it all goes away. You should just take care of the memories you make; you better make good memories; because the more memories you make, the more you live in people's minds because one day forever, no one will ever remember who you were and what you've done," Oliver said calmly and sadly. Ignoring that one of those people in that room had blood on their hands. What he said, needed to be said.

Everyone kept the room quiet. Truth hurts, but Oliver was right. In that specific moment, Oliver could swear that everyone's face was showing their one common thought, 'what if *I* die?'

Morgan tried to change the mood: "You know, I thought he is a chatterbox, it turned out to be true! We talked about the books we read, we met at the library so we knew what to talk about. Honestly, I don't even know how to feel about his demise. I have no idea how to react. I just know one thing and that thing is that we shared great times."

"You found him a chatterbox? You haven't met his seven-year-old version, he would never shut up!" Oliver joked.

"Oh, well, he might've been talkative but he usually said useful things!"

Oliver tried not to laugh. None of his conversations with Brad were serious, *literally none*. Like Oliver remembered Brad's grandmother's funeral, they whispered 80s songs all along.

"Okay Morgan, thank you. Now we would appreciate a guy who talks."

"May I?" Theodore said, "I had a good friendship with him. He thought I'm a good brother. He came to the café I work several times and ordered apple juice but this one time that I brought him apple juice, as usual, he said that just because he had apple juice for the last seven times doesn't mean that he always wants it!"

Everyone laughed. Theodore continued: "Despite that one time, we were good friends. He used perfect perfumes, can't deny. I'm going to miss him and his perfumes!"

When Theodore finished, Sebastian finally decided how to choose his words: "We met in my photography studio and we got to know each other because of this talking guy's clumsiness. I printed the wrong picture for him. He sometimes told me what I'm doing wrong about my job. And Oliver, he mentioned you once."

"Did he?" Oliver raised both of his eyebrows.

"Yep. He said, 'I have a best friend named Bill Oliver who thinks is Oliver Bill. Extremely handsome, unbelievably insane.' Not sure about the second characteristic but the first one is so true!" he quoted and beamed.

Oliver smiled: "You see guys? If he was alive, I would've bought him a creamy cake and delivered it right into his face!"

Marika asked: "Sadism?"

"Absolutely not!" Oliver smiled, "The guy never admitted the fact that I'm more handsome than him!"

Everyone laughed. Oliver started a speech: "I believe that everyone talked. You see, Brad was sort of the friend who always tried to exhale positive energy. He might've not talked to any of us about the rest, I understand that this was a choice for him to keep his personal life really private, I can't see why but I respect it because all I remember from Brad are good memories that I decided to keep for good. What I heard from you was all good memories and blessing. There are usually five general steps of grieving; denial, anger, depression, bargaining and acceptance. I want all of you to go home and relax, maybe try to take a leave if possible. I want you to spend a day doing nothing. Forget about your diet, eat junk food, watch a movie and try to focus on these steps. I need you to skip all these steps just like road runner because when your mind accepts a fact, it can go along with other facts. It allows you to think more specific. Imagine a box full of paper balls, there are some extra balls that are on the top and keep falling, you're upset because you can't fit all the balls and more balls you were planning to fit. Instead of being upset, just take out some of the extra balls and try to fit in the useful balls."

## Oliver Johnson's House's Hallway, 13:09 P.M.

After an hour of miscellaneous talks, everyone was ready to go except for Anya, who asked Oliver to stay a little bit more to talk to him about something—she was so careful that no one else but Oliver understands what she asked for.

After everyone exited, Anya came back to the living room and sat on the sofa. Oliver joined him a few moments later with two cups of coffee and sat on the sofa in front of Anya.

He handed the coffee to Anya and asked: "So, what up?"

"Listen, Oliver…I no longer want to attend these meeting. I *can't*."

"I'm afraid to say that there is a judgment for it, directly from the court. You and I cannot make a decision about it," Oliver explained.

Anya quietly starred at the floor.

"Is anything or anyone bothering you?" Oliver asked.

"No, no. Everyone's treated me so well. You see, it's not about *you* or *anyone else*. It's about *me*. I can't stand the fact being in a same room with an *actual* murderer. Bradly Moore's death was reported to be a homicide by several knife traumas. Brad was at least fifteen centimetres taller than me, he couldn't prevent his death, and how am I able to guarantee my safety?" Anya said and started to cry. "Are you *sure* you want to be lawyer?" Oliver wanted to ask.

Oliver handed him the box of tissues and calmly and kindly said: "Hey, easy. Listen it would be a lie if I say that I totally understand your feeling. I've been doing this job for a long time and each time, the fear is reduced. I have to do this not just for my career but for Brad." He continued: "And it's procurable by only your cooperation."

"*It freaks me out!*"

"I'm not so happy with this circumstance either, Anya. All I can do is to obey the law."

Before Anya got the chance to talk, Oliver said: "You know what? I'm going to take you guys to the police department for the next times, I promise. Today was an exception. And if the killer tries to hurt you or anyone else, me and a whole group of police members will be there to rescue."

"Can you *possibly* realise that my mental health is prone to *burn*?" Anya frowned.

Oliver bent his head: "You have my word."

"I can easily scream right now." Anya leant back and wiped his tears.

Oliver said with a relatively high volume: "Damn it woman, get yourself together! You are going to be a lawyer, is this how you want to meet a serial killer?"

Anya looked at him angry: "Thank you for reminding me of that. I was *entirely* unaware of that."

Oliver rolled his eyeballs and said: "Anya, I'm being realistic. You may face an assassin ten times worse than Dennis Nilsen. Would you ask them to postpone their blood chain until you get ready?"

Anya frowned: "Stop humiliating me, Oliver. I'm in no normal condition, it's been only ten days since I saw a friend, covered his own blood and you are asking me to be in the same room the person who drowned the same friend in his own blood bath."

Oliver took a deep breath and despite how offended he felt after what Anya told her, he maintained a calm, rational voice: "You're *not* listening to me. I said that today was an *exception* and there won't be any meetings in such private place and for your own good, we'll see each other at the station for the next meeting. Alright?"

Anya's lower lip imperceptibly went forward. She drank her coffee and whispered: "Alright."

Oliver smiled and asked: "Are you better now?"

She confirmed with head and stood up: "I hope so. I don't tend to be a lawyer who's insomniac."

## Chingford Cemetery, 13:40 P.M.

Oliver sat next to the cold gravestone which's person buried under used to be his best friend someday. Because Oliver was starving and couldn't wait to get a hot sandwich, he bought a Greek yogurt, a bag of potato chips and a soda for lunch. Casual lunch for thirteen-year-old Oliver and Bradly.

"Hey buddy," said Oliver, "It's been a while since we last talked…like ten days."

He stared at the grave, like he was waiting for a responsive. The grave was unresponsive.

Oliver had a reputation of being introverted, doesn't like to talk about his feelings. He was never that kind of people with the marvellous ability to expressing feelings. He felt like a whirlpool was taking pulling him in itself but he is too paralysed by the water to ask for help or swim himself out of it.

"No words, huh? I guess…I should tell you about your funeral. Cheddar was good, Dakota and I had coffee with Ezra…Your relatives are so cold, no one even cried; just flakily wiped their hypothetical tears off their eyes with velvet napkins…and you know, there was this disgusting lie all across the air, your cousins were telling everyone how you called them right before you died to tell them how they meant to you. Why do we hear this at every funerals? Or that they had a dream about the dead person the night before where they were wearing a white dress, happily walking around an olive garden." He chuckled, "Don't get me wrong. I don't know what to say. I've never been through this…Although, I am furious at you. For *not* telling me about seven new people! I could understand if they were like four, maximum. But *seven*?!"

He stopped to look around. He took a deep breath and continued: "You knew that I'm excellent at my job. I can look at a person for a second and say whether they are potential to commit a crime or not…You never introduced me to these people. I don't know them like you did. I can blame you for it, I'm not doing okay and these people are complicated. Complicated because they were in touch with you and *we* were best friends…or I thought we were." Oliver stopped to breathe, "You brought me into something that I have never been taught for. No clues, no evidence, no murder weapons…nothing, I have *nothing*. How am I supposed to find an assassin with having *nothing*? I wish you were here to tell me how to get myself back together and figure this thing out."

Oliver leant to the cold grave and whispered: "Help me, Brother."

# Chapter Three
# I Promise You

Oliver rushed to the mentioned room where he was supposed to meet the seven suspects for the third time.

"Bill?" Detective Henry called, "Where were you?"

"Oliver." Oliver corrected Richard and asked: "Am I too late?"

"Yeah, just a little bit."

"My apologies. My parents will host Phillip tonight. I had to help them with stuff."

Richard thought for a second and asked: "Your uncle?"

"Yes."

"Alright. Go get your work done. Go on."

Oliver entered the room. After meet and greeting and making sure everyone's fine with three cops being in the room, Oliver officially began the meeting: "First things first, I apologize for being late. Second things second, I have to leave so soon. Today, we are not gonna talk." He shrugged off, "But unless you have anything to say. We can give that some time."

"Hold on. We're not gonna talk?" Sebastian asked confused.

"No," Oliver said, "You are about to use every piece of your imagination and hippocampus to write whatever you remember from the night of February ninth."

Olga asked: "The night that Brad…"

Oliver interrupted: "Yes Olga. I need you to write whatever you remember from that night because I want to analyse the night from each one of your sights. We're not doing it now or here; it'll probably take some time which means that you go home or…any other place to write. Our next meeting will be at the same time but I will announce you the place. Any questions?"

## The Orphanage, 13:01 P.M.

Oliver walked into the orphanage, where he was about to meet Ava Wintergreen. He slowly walked at the hall until he ran into a teenage girl and asked her where he can find Ms Jonah.

Being aware of Ms Jonah's current location, Oliver went to the principal's room. During his very short journey, he noticed that orphanage's teachers who were spending time with children at the hallway and the rooms actually were nice human beings or…at least this was what Oliver saw!

That was his first time in an orphanage. Before that, the only imagination of an orphanage was the one created by daddy long legs' book and movies. So, for every possible reasons, Oliver was feeling like a kid who was just told that there are more than twelve hours. He silently chuckled about his foolish imagination.

He knocked and opened the door to the room of the principal's office. The room's theme was generally brown, hazel and Aegean blue and by the hard effort of the tiny window, the room was being blessed by little root of the sunlight, enough for Oliver to see the face of Ms Jonah's face. She was black and looked about fifty and it didn't take Oliver more than a minute to understand that Ms Jonah was affected by OCD. You know, it's unnecessary to be a psychologist to understand the obsession, the lined-up pens on her desk and everything set so symmetrical were shouting it!

"Hello Ms Jonah. My name is Bill Johnson, we spoke on the phone yesterday." Oliver introduced himself and smiled.

"It's a pleasure to meet you, Mr Johnson. We spoke about the death of Bradly Moore and Ava Wintergreen, correct?"

Oliver sat on the chair and said: "That's true. But before we start any conversations, I should say that Mr Moore gave you the phone number of his younger brother, Ezra. I'm afraid that most of Ezra's behaviours and thoughts emanate from the cycle of grief. He was unable to make it here so he sent me."

"I see. So, Mr Johnson, please explain how you and Mr Moore were related?"

"We were really close friends for almost thirty years. Twenty-eight, actually."

"That is a lifetime. I'm so sorry for your loss. You see, we haven't told Ava about Mr Moore yet. We were hoping that a family member could tell her."

"I'll do my best. I'm sort of a psychologist."

"*Sort of?*" She indifferently raised an eyebrow.

Oliver didn't catch Ms Jonah's tone, he however said: "I'm a forensic psychologist."

"Good luck with your job but if you mentioned it for helping Ava, I don't think it's really gonna use it. She's faced a loss, not a bank robbery," she said humiliating.

Oliver got so mad but kept his smile and said: "At least five psychologists are working her. *Child* psychologists, to be specific and no one was able to announce a death to a six-year-old!"

Oliver felt free about what he said, no regrets. He would've died if he didn't say it. People must understand that being crime psychologist is as important, vital and dangerous as a detective.

Ms Jonah directed Oliver out of her room to the playground where Ava was playing.

During the way, Ms Jonah asked Oliver about what she was dying to ask: "Mr Johnson, am I allowed to ask the reason Mr Moore's death?"

"Yes ma'am…The reason of the death was announced to be the homicide by several knife traumas up to forty."

She put her hand on her heart and asked with her opened mouth of shock: "Oh, Jesus. Who would do such terrible crime?"

"I'm not allowed to share more information with you," Oliver said and bent his head.

"I understand…The door to the playground is right down the hallway. Ava is the one with blonde bangs, she is wearing blue today."

Oliver walked to the playground. Several girls of any ages were playing together or talking to each other. Since Oliver remembered knowing about orphanages, he never understood why does God take parents away from their children?

When Oliver was nine—and more of a believer—he used to ask everyone, he knew about it. By the age of eleven, his uncle explained that every good thing that happens in life, follows a little bit of a hard time with itself and patience is the key to get rid of them because all of them are divine tests but Oliver was growing up, spreading his mindset and as a conclusion, he wouldn't believe most of the things he heard.

Oliver had never reached a decisive answer or even an answer to convince him for a moment.

Why does God take parents away from children?

If a happy ending is waiting for them, then why countless amount of them doesn't get their happy ending?

Oliver could remember his grandpa Andrew crystal clear telling him the story of a man in the ocean.

A man is floating all alone in the ocean. A boat comes to help him, he answers: "No thank you. God will rescue me."

Comes the second boat for help. The man answers: "No thank you. God will help me."

The lonely man sinks and goes to heaven. He asks God why he didn't help him. The God answers: "I sent you two boats you *silly!*"

After a minute of looking around, Oliver found Ava and asked her to sit on a bench with him:

"Ava, right? My name is Bill, my family and friends call me Oliver, since you are a very dear person, you can call me Oliver."

"Do you know Bradly? I remember he told me about you, have we ever met?"

"No. We unfortunately haven't. What did Brad tell you about me?"

"He said that you're his best friend and I will probably like you because you are a nice person."

"Anything else?"

"That your name is Bill but you want everyone to call you Oliver!"

"It's getting contagious...But it's true."

"What did he tell you about me?" Ava said and a cute smile appeared on her face.

"He said that you're the sweetest, prettiest, *most* intelligent and kindest girl he *ever* met and he also thought that we'll become good friends." Oliver lied about the whole thing and smiled kindly.

"I think he was right!"

"So, Ava...now you know that I'm a friend of Bradly...And a friend of *you*, right?"

"I know."

"Due to that information, do you trust me?"

"What do you mean by that?"

"I mean, do you have this feeling of assurance and safety when I'm here with you? I want you to be honest with me. Tell me the truth."

Ava thought for a moment and said: "I do."

Oliver pointed to Ava's bottle of water and asked: "Is there any water in that?"

"Yes." Ava answered and grabbed the bottle to Oliver, "Do you want some?"

"No. I want *you* to drink some. Drinking water is the easiest way that helps us control our feelings."

"I can control my feelings." Ava cutely frowned.

"I have no doubts. Just in case."

Ava drank all the water in her bottle. Told Oliver to continue. If there was a priest, Oliver would've confessed that he couldn't think out of the box. He wished the time being frozen or get into Ava's mind to find out the best words to say. Nope, Bill Johnson wasn't Professor X or anything similar.

"What do you know about death?"

"It means to stop living and become dead."

"Oh, you know too much!…well, well, well…how would you confront the fact that someone is dead?"

"Who's dead?!" Ava raised both her eyebrows and asked.

"I'm just asking."

"Well, if as an imagination, I think that I'll cry and be upset for a while and then try not to think about it."

Oliver smiled proudly: "I appreciate this wisdom."

They both kept quiet for a minute. Oliver finally took the risk to tell the truth: "Hey…Umm…Do you want to see Brad?"

Ava smiled beautifully and confirmed with her head.

Oliver tried to smile, he failed. He looked like an idiot. He said with a shivering, low volume voice: "Ava. He's not as he used to be. He's different now. He's not like how you remember him."

"What? What's the matter? Is he alright?" Ava asked worried.

"Ava, there is no easy way to say this…I hate to be the one to announce this…Bradly is…gone."

Ava grudged and cried: "*What?*"

Oliver whispered: "It happened twelve days ago. I'm so sorry for not seeing you sooner."

Ava started to cry quietly and covered her face with hands. Oliver hugged him and he cried as well. He couldn't believe that he was crying after ten days, with the stepdaughter of the best friend who were supposed to tell their wives they are at work but they are actually watching rugby, whom were supposed to email each other after the birth of their children saying: "So what do I name this, dude?", whom were supposed to make their grandchildren sit and listen to their lies about hunting a bear with bare hands in Russia's rainforests.

All of a sudden, those plans were gone. Ten days earlier, they were all put in the white coffin and got buried in the hole that Oliver had dug for those dreams and plans.

"Oliver?" Ava asked with low volume, "Is he buried? Will you take me to the cemetery?"

"*Of course, I will,*" Oliver said while removing tears from his face "Go grab anything you need…We must buy a bouquet on the way."

***

### Chingford Cemetery, 14:49 P.M.

Oliver got out of the car, helped Ava to get off and they walked into the graveyard. It was drizzling and bitterly cold. Oliver asked Ava: "Aren't you cold?"

"No. My sweater is warm enough."

"Have you ever been to a cemetery?"

"Yeah. Two or three times. One time with Brad."

"Why did he take you to a cemetery?"

"We were talking about our comfort places. I asked him and he told me he gets so calm in a cemetery…Chingford, I think."

"I know. I thought it's weird but I respected his ideology anyway," Oliver lied. At that moment, he reprehended Brad for taking a kid to the cemetery.

Oliver was mad; just mad. Not exactly for no reason, he had tons of reasons to be mad but if there was only one thing this old boy was able to do pretty well, was to control his anger. Sure, there were times that he got mad enough to break the glass which he was holding. At that point, he had an energy provided by anger to shout out—but her mother always reminded him that cemeteries are holy and respectful places.

After seven minutes of walking, they reached the grave. You see, Bradly Moore's grave was not that poetic of the grave. There were no weeping willows next to it, the white gravestone didn't have designs of heavenly angels with harps on it.

It was just a temporary paradiso gravestone. The only engraved words were: *'Bradly Anton Moore II, 1986–2019, A Day of duty done and a day of rest begun.'*

That headstone was temporary. Ezra ordered it just until a black stone and golden writings was ready.

Ava put the bouquet on the grave and stared at it. Oliver felt sorry for her. A sweet young girl who was waiting for the one person to be her godparent, is staring at the godparent's grave.

By the short time that Oliver met Ava, he understood that Ava is mentally strong. She was a wise, smart and strong girl. Oliver knew that Ava will be alright but he decided to be there for him and ask the orphanage to meet her more. He also thought about asking the principle to let him know if Ava got new godparents, Oliver wanted to be aware of the process and the possible family.

"How did this happen?" Ava asked.

"It was a car accident. Concussion." Oliver lied again "He was driving real fast and someone collided him carelessly."

"Did he suffer?"

"You know, there was this seminar I attended eight years ago. The host was saying that death happens sooner than falling asleep. You go to an ever rafter sleep and at that moment, you remember everything and everyone you ever loved and then, you're just gone." Oliver explained, "So I don't think he suffered. I think he went on the journey with peace."

"Do you think he remembered me?"

Oliver kneeled on the ground next to her: "I think you were the first one he thought of."

"Is he in heaven know?"

Oliver smiled: "He was one wonderfully great of a person that he never needed anyone to pray for him at the funeral."

Ava put her head on Oliver's shoulder and cried in low volume: "I miss him so much."

Oliver put his head on Ava's and whispered: "I miss him too."

# Chapter Four
# Be Safe

**February 22, Oliver Johnson's House, 05:30 A.M.**

Oliver opened his eyes, checked the clock on his phone and leaved his bed happily after finding out that he was succeeded to sleep three and half an hour without waking up. He sat behind his desk and wrote whatever that was messing with his mind: "*I am literally freaked out. Freaked out and broken.*

*In the past 10 days I found out too much about my best friend that I never thought I would know. Like I never really knew him.*

*I asked these questions like a billion times:*

*Was I ever his best friend?*

*Did he ever, ever trust me?*

*If he trusted me, then what's with all the secrets?*

*Are there more secrets?*

*Did our friendship ever mean to him?*

*I don't know the answer to any of these questions. I just can overthink until headache stops me.*

*I can't sleep, I can't eat, I don't have the energy I used to have. I have NO idea about the killer.*

*Who the killer is?*

*I swear to the holy spirit of Jesus that if it wasn't for Moores' family, I wouldn't accept to work on the case. (I shouldn't ignore the fact that he kept so many secrets away from me, I feel so betrayed!)*

*I am starting to think that this job is killing me. Should I keep going on or let go? I need a sign from the universe.*"

After making his bed and taking a shower, Oliver called Dakota to wake her up for her university classes. This was not a usual thing for Oliver to do, Dakota was fond of sleeping and Oliver was worried if she missed a class—since he rarely missed a class back in college.

"Yeah, Ollie?" Dakota answered with no signs of sleep in her voice.

"Why are you awake?" Oliver asked as if he was interrogating.

"Is it a crime to be awake? Why are *you* awake?"

"I've slept enough."

"And I've watched movies enough!"

"Are you going to sleep *now*?"

"Maybe?"

"I won't tell Mum and Dad anything about their precious daughter being up all night only if you do something for me."

"You don't have to, darling. I will tell them that I was in a journey, seeking for wisdom and knowledge," Dakota said proudly.

"Like they're gonna believe!" He said, "This thing you're saying, I tested it *twelve years ago*!"

"Fine! What do you want?" Dakota asked greedily.

"I want you to come to Liv's house with me. Now."

"Now? Oh, Ollie, just because you couldn't sleep and I didn't sleep, doesn't mean that other people don't need sleep either!"

Oliver completely ignored her and said: "I'll be there in half an hour. Be ready."

And as Oliver said, he was in front of his parents' house in half an hour. Dakota joined him in two minutes. Oliver wasn't in the mood of going inside even though he could smell the fantastic omelette he knew was made by his father. Mr Edward Johnson.

In the car, Dakota played a country song. She knew that Oliver liked them because their mother went on shopping with Oliver once and when she returned, she was enthusiastically telling her that Oliver enjoys country as well.

What she didn't know, was that country wasn't Oliver's thing and he just said that for her mother's interest.

"Change the song, will you?" Oliver asked Dakota.

"Excuse me?"

"*Change...the...song.*"

"But it's country."

Oliver turned to her and smiled: "I know, change it."

Dakota, however, didn't really understand why but she changed the song and played a pop that she had no doubt that her brother enjoys.


## Olivia and Arthur Black's House, 08:19 A.M.

"Do you think that you can insult me, crumble my heart, question my effort and come to have lunch at my house?" Olivia said angrily. She would've yelled but she didn't mean to wake any neighbours.

"It's actually breakfast…"

Olivia interrupted him: "Don't correct me!"

"Okay," Oliver said and looked at the sky.

"Shut up!" Olivia whispered.

Arthur walked into the hallway and before he said anything, Olivia shouted: "Don't you support him, Black!"

"No, darling. I just came to ask if you want me to make some pancakes."

Olivia answered nicely: "Oh baby. Yes please and don't forget to put some chocolate between." She took a deep breath and continued: "And *you, Johnson*!"

She shouted: "What excuse do you possibly have?"

"May I talk now?"

"Spit it out." She frowned.

"It was about Brad's case. I was totally confused and I swear to the may-he-rest-in-peace soul of Grandpa Andrew that I was confused and freaked out. I felt like a ten-year-old who was watching 'The exorcist' for the first time! And…Umm…I thought that maybe I would come here and as an apology. See…I ordered two action figures for you and they'll arrive next week."

Olivia smiled like the blooming of a blossom and said: "No way!"

Oliver smiled satisfied and said: "There is a way. There is a way."

"Oh my God! Oh my God! Oh my GOD! Who's figures?"

"Reverse flash and green arrow."

"I had a green arrow," she continued loud enough that Arthur heard, "But Arthur broke it."

Arthur answered loudly: "It was an accident!"

"You don't say!" Olivia said, "Come on. Come in."

Oliver followed Olivia to the kitchen. What he said about action figures was true. He ordered them the night before as Olivia's birthday gift but as they were spoiled to her, Oliver was supposed to come up with a new gift. He relied to the frame of the kitchen.

Olivia sat behind the table and said: "Speaking of action figures, Ollie, I want a John Constantine figure."

Oliver answered: "I'm not buying you a Constantine figure."

"Why not?"

Oliver answered: "I already bought you two. You'll get none until June."

Olivia indifferently said: "Whatever." And purred some orange juice for herself.

Oliver sat behind the table and put two pancakes on his plate.

"What are you guys doing today?" Dakota asked and looked at everyone for their answers.

"I'll go to work now. I'll be back for lunch. I have paper works that can be done at home." Arthur answered Dakota and said to Olivia: "The dinner is tonight, right?"

Olivia shook her head and emphasized: "And Mum said that we can't miss it. *None of us*."

"I don't know…I have stuff to do." Oliver made excuses.

"Why? Could you sleep?" Dakota asked Oliver.

Oliver played with his pancake and said: "Three hours. I feel exhausted."

"Why don't you visit another doctor?" Olivia asked, "You've been Baldwin's patient since your insomnia begun."

"I don't know. Maybe I do," said Oliver, "I was getting better. I could sleep up to six hours until Brad died."

Dakota took his hand and said: "Ollie, we're worried about you."

Oliver smiled and warmly pressed her hand: "I'll be good again. Trust me, will you?"


## The Police Department, 10:31 A.M.

Arthur threw a five-hundred-paged book on Oliver's desk to get Oliver's attention since he had been calling him for the last two minutes.

Oliver frowned and asked: "Couldn't you just call me?"

Arthur rolled his eyeballs and said: "I've been calling you for two minutes."

"What's so important?"

Arthur was already tired and that was making him furious. He unconsciously asked: "Damn you Oliver. What's wrong with you?"

"Oh, I don't know. Maybe my best friend was murdered two weeks ago and I don't have any damn idea to find a killer?" Oliver angrily shouted out.

"No, it's not about that. You're being bipolar. You're alright for a moment and a second later, you're like this!" Arthur reproached "You knew that you weren't good enough to accept a case. Then why did you?"

"How can you say that?" Oliver yelled at him, "You have *no* rights to opine on my mental health situation when you don't know how much it hurts and what does it mean!"

Arthur finally realised that he had passed the red lines. He said calmly: "You're right. I don't know. But Bill, you were the best man at my wedding. You're my best friend and you always will be. Look, I'm aware that I'm not *your* best friend and I definitely am not the most trustable person you know but please, for God's sake, talk to someone about it."

Oliver walked out of the office and he heard Arthur said: "Richard asked to see you in his office."

He went to Richard's office, knocked and opened the door. Henry stood up and said without setting up: "Did you know that our dear Swiss friend, Rivera, lied to you about himself? Did you know about his mental disorders?"

Oliver stopped for few seconds to understand what Henry just said.

"Excuse me?"

"Theodore Stephen Rivera, I'm talking about. He lied to you."

Oliver sat on a chair and asked: "About what?"

"About his own life. Are you even listening?"

"I am. I just don't see your point. What did he lie about?"

Detective Henry gave Oliver a Folder and left the room saying: "I'm fed up, unable to handle it one more time. Read this."

Oliver took a look at the denim folder with his eyes full of tiredness, closed his eyes and whispered: "What have I done to be punished like this?"

Oliver opened the file. It was a calling detail history of Theodore's cell phone. There weren't so many names on the list; Hendrik was the most recurred name.

That paper didn't seem very useful so Oliver moved on to the second paper. It was a call history from 2017. Two German word could be seen 'Mutter' and

'Vater'. Oliver had an idea about the meanings but he called Dakota—Just in case!

Dakota answered immediately: "Yup?"

"Hey. Real quick, what's the meaning of these words? M-U-T-T-E-R and V-A-T-E-R."

"Wait, do you want the meanings?"

"That's why I called you!"

"Well, ummm, they are Mother and Father in German."

"Okay got it! Thank you for your cooperation! We'll catch up later! Love you, goodbye!" Oliver said quickly and happily.

"Hold on! Why did you need…"

Oliver hung up the phone and looked at the first and second history again. There were signs of mother or a father on the first paper which was the newest history call. Those papers could change so many things. Theodore hasn't talked to his parents for almost two years!

He rushed to Arthur's office to ask him for something. If Oliver could prove that Theodore hasn't met or contacted his parents in two years, he could make sure that Theodore was lying about one thing at least. Since Theodore told Oliver that he calls her mother every day and talks to his father every weekend, it couldn't be that hard to prove.

Oliver opened the office door excitedly and yelled recklessly: "He was lying!"

Arthur turned to him and asked: "Who was lying?"

Oliver threw the file on the desk and said: "Theodore Rivera."

Arthur opened and studied the file and it took him a minute to ask: "He hasn't spoken to his parents in two years?"

"Exactly" said Oliver, "He told me that he talks to them every day and weekend."

Arthur said: "Hold on just a minute." And he left his office.

Oliver leant on the table with his hand. He thought: "Why would you lie, Theo?…and if you lied about such a small subject, what else did you lie about?"

Of course, Mr and Mrs Moore had all rights to be aware of the process of the case but Oliver didn't think it was the right time; he needed to make sure that his word won't turn into false accusations. The only thing that could get Oliver rid of his insane excitement was talking to his mother.

He texted his mother, Katherine Smoke-Johnson: "Hi Mum. How are you? I have some news. Call me when you had time. Take care, love you."

"I must go check the crime scene." Oliver thought, "I'll tell Richard about it."

Oliver rushed outside and finally found detective Henry outside the building. Detective was talking on his phone. Oliver said gasping: "Detective…Hang up…it's…important!"

Seeing Oliver so thrilled, detective hung up the phone and asked: "What is it? What's going on? What do you want?"

"I…want to check the crime scene. Do I have your permission?"

"The investigation team has already given you everything, didn't they?"

Oliver shook his head and said: "They did. But I want to see Brad's house myself."

"Listen, I've been trying to consider your circumstances. Are you *sure* that you can go back to the crime scene again?"

"I'm fine, detective. I can handle it."

"Okay. I should be with you. We'll do it this afternoon; do you have time?"

"I do. Don't worry. I don't have plans."

"Be ready at two thirty." Detective said and went inside.

Oliver went back inside after a minute whispering to himself: "What did you do? *What did you do? Why would you do that?*"

You see, there was a little secret about Oliver that not many people knew; he could sometimes be affected by his own excitement so badly. This was one of those times. He got affected, he asked to check the crime scene himself.

He said that he is fine but Brad's house was the last place on earth he wanted to visit—even his aunt Donna's horrifying basement seemed more delightful to be at!

Oliver was picturing himself in that endless basement—which made him tingle every time—when his phone rang, it was his mother.

"Hi Mum."

"Hello, son. How are you?" Katherine said with her warm and motherly voice.

"I'm fine. How are you? How's Dad?"

"I couldn't be any better, I'm talking to my baby boy! Your dad has fallen asleep in front of the TV." Katherine said and laughed.

Oliver laughed and asked: "Baby boy, huh? Did you get my message?"

"That's why I called. Is everything alright, honey?"

"Actually, yes. Everything is good. I called to announce a progress."

"Oh, thank God! Tell me about it."

"You see…one of the suspects has lied about their backstory. I'm working on that. And I have decided to visit Brad's house after all."

"Oh, Ollie. Are you sure that you're ready for that?"

"Yeah, Mum. I mean…I should've done it any days now. His parents might ask me to go pack his stuff sometime."

"Oliver, we are not just mother and son; we're friends. I'm your friend. I'm a friend and a mother to three amazing children. One of those children has lost his best friend a couple weeks ago. He is so complicated and vulnerable at the moment but he never shows it on his face. He doesn't talk to anyone about any of his feelings. I need to know if he is alright. I have the right to know. Don't I?" Katherine said sympathetically.

Oliver didn't say a word. His mother was right. But Oliver was still really obstinate. Katherine continued: "Are you alright, Ollie? Will you be alright?"

"I'll talk to you later. Goodbye, Mum." Oliver ended their conversation with no answers.

She sighed and said: "Goodbye honey."

Oliver hung up the phone and walked to Arthur's office. Katherine was right. Oliver was very vulnerable but he never really wanted to show it. That's what he had learnt. At that very moment, he was more vulnerable than ever but he needed to get himself together. He needed to be the person that everyone expected him to be. Bill Oliver Johnson needed to refer to his intelligence not to his feelings.

What Oliver thought about the whole situation resembled a total insanity and chaos.

He was unable to take the ownership of his life or think out of the box.

Deciding to travel the world in 85 days but prolonging it to 85 years.

He needed to take the control of his life all over again. He needed to be delusional by the idea that none of these things ever happened to him.

Oliver walked in Arthur's empty office and opened his desk's drawer to find the box of cigarette.

He lighted up a cigarette and tried to smoke it as fast as he could. Oliver had no doubt that cigarettes are awful and harmful but…anyway. Let's ignore the fact that everyone smokes at least a cigarette at college. Everyone *even*

*Oliver*. Arthur wasn't a chain-smoker, not even a smoker but sometimes, his work itself magically lit a cigarette for him; Arthur hated it.

Arthur surprised him by walking into the office without knocking.

"No...No. No. No," said Arthur. "This is unacceptable."

"Oh. Hi bro," Oliver said innocently.

"Why are you smoking?" Arthur said, "It's disgusting!"

"I'm not smoking. I'm doing simulation and experimentation in case of improving human's science and knowledge about making cigarettes!"

"I'm worried about you. You're saving the destiny of the world all by yourself. Thor and Superman will kneel before you." Arthur humiliated.

"That's the plan! So, I was thinking that I can go to Theodore's workplace and talk to him now."

"Yeah? What will you ask?"

"I'm an expert on the matter. It's not like I meet him and reveal what I know. I know what I should do."

"Ollie, I believe in your wisdom but please, for God's sake, don't hurt yourself. We still need you around."

"Sweet." Oliver bent his head, "Now let's go get some coffee and interrogation."

***

## Café Lorenté, 12:01 A.M.

Oliver and Arthur sat behind a table and waited for a servant. A waitress went to them and asked: "Hello and welcome, gentleman. What can I get you?"

"I want to speak to Theodore Rivera. He knows me," said Oliver, "And a cup of black tea with honey to go, please."

And then he kept smiling weirdly that Arthur noticed it was freaking her out. Arthur said: "I would like a cup of chocolate coffee, please."

When the waitress shook her head and left, Arthur asked: "Why are you having a crazy eye, exactly?"

"I'm having a...what?" Oliver asked like he didn't hear Arthur. 'Crazy eye' wasn't some casual word for him to hear, like 'paper'.

"Crazy eye. Brad and I discovered it twelve years ago." Arthur explained, "It happens when your eyes are wide and you smile in a shaming and tingling way."

"I...don't have crazy eyes. You guys just made that up!" Oliver denied. Like he had never noticed that before.

"We made it up due to our knowledge of your super complicated personality. We know you, Ollie." Arthur joked.

"Where is this conversation going?" Oliver asked to change the subject.

"It helped the passage of time. I wanted to say that Oliver, no matter what happened, *you shouldn't lose control.*" Arthur emphasised.

Oliver breathed out: "Oh God, Arthur. I'm not a kid. I can..."

"Welcome, gentlemen." Theodore interrupted Oliver and put their drinks on the table, "Mr Johnson and...we weren't introduced."

"I'm Sergeant Black. Sit down, please." Arthur answered Theodore.

"Mr Johnson, you asked to see me. Is there a problem?" Theodore sat on a chair and asked Oliver.

"No, Theodore. I just found some inaccurate details about our conversation before and now I'm here to clarify," Oliver said and leant back to his chair.

Arthur said: "I'll leave you two alone."

"No, sergeant," said Oliver, "We'll talk outside."

He continued to Theodore: "Let's go, shall we?"

Theodore walked out first. Arthur caught Oliver's forearm and whispered to him: "Do not get in a fight with him."

Oliver whispered back: "I'm not a brawler!"

He left the café, Saw Theodore on the sidewalk and said: "I'll get straight to the point. I found out some evidence based on the fact that you were lying to me about your relationship with your parents. You haven't called them in two years."

"I...didn't exactly lie. I just didn't tell you the truth."

"But you *hid* the truth. And why is lie if it's not hiding the truth?" Oliver asked Theodore and sat next to him.

"Fair enough. I'm sorry."

Oliver took a deep breath and said: "Theodore, being sorry is not enough. I'm now so unsure about other stuff."

"What are other stuff?"

"Other stuff that you might've lied about. I'm talking about trust."

"Can I explain it?"

"Yes please. Go one."

"My parental issues started when I was a kid. We were hosting some of our relatives and one of them beat me; I can't remember why. I explained what happened to my parents but all they did was trying to convince me that what happened to me was a joke and no serious. I was too young to understand the difference between a joke and a serious situation but I can say this for certain, it wasn't a joke. I've been suffering from PTSD since then. Whenever I see people physically fighting, or when I watch an action movie, I panic." Theodore explained, "My reason for not telling you about my parents was not trying to hide something from you or the police, I just didn't want to feel like an orphan or a desperate person that his parents doesn't care about. I didn't mean to hide it."

They both kept quiet for a while. Oliver hadn't thought about it that way. There was now a good reason existing that discharged Theodore.

PTSD. A person that would panic by seeing people grapple, didn't really seem like a murderer.

"Are you convinced?" Theodore asked, "I didn't do it on purpose, *I swear*."

"What's always important is trust," said Oliver, "My best friend was murdered by one of you seven people I gather with. I gamble my own life on sitting with the killer, talking to the killer and being optimist that I won't get killed either."

"What do you mean?"

"I'm sorry Theodore. I truly am. I'm sorry for being unable to trust you. This situation, this sort of case is all new for me. Everyone's the killer and no one is...I'm...sorry I should go." Oliver felt a bit nauseous.

"And by the way" Said Oliver, "Our next gathering will be tomorrow at this café."

Oliver went back to the café to call Arthur. Arthur brought their drinks and got into Oliver's car. After some minutes, Arthur asked: "What happened?"

"Where are you going?" Oliver asked and unlike what Arthur thought, he looked calm. He didn't know that Oliver was too nauseas to talk.

"I'm going back to grab some stuff from my office." Arthur said, "What happened with Theodor, Ollie?"

"I'm now so sure that I can't trust these people anyway."

"Why would you think that you *could* trust them?"

"Please let me finish. Trusting them was my only biggest mistake. I managed to believe them anyway, whether they were reasonable or not. I was trying to look at the case with their sight and view."

"*But*?"

"But I was wrong! It was an unintelligent idea."

"So, what are you going to do about it?"

"I must ask each one of them 'Who do you think is the killer?' I think, *I think* it leads me to a clue."

"What can I say? Let me tell you my theories. Number one is that what if hypothetically, there isn't a killer? What if it was a group homicide?" Arthur said. "Think about it Oliver. There is a law scholar, a former addict, A photographer with AIW syndrome, A guy who his mother writes crime novels and most importantly, a Russian!"

"Alright. First of all, that would be racism! Second, AIW syndrome is not that good of an evidence to confirm a crime." Oliver shook his head "That's all about migraine."

"Oliver why don't you want to believe?" Arthur asked. "I remember having a case like this about three years ago. My squad's members were all a bunch of insane people by the end of the case."

"What was it?"

"There was a crowded party that the host was suffocated in the bathtub upstairs by the end of the night. The time of death was also estimated to be at midnight. There were still twelve people at the party by midnight. None of the suspects said anything useful while interrogations."

"So, who was the killer?"

"Five of them! They did a lot for a murder. We couldn't understand these things if other guests didn't testify." Arthur said, "Those five people, each one of them did some random thing to keep others away from upstairs."

"What was the murder motivation?"

"Murderer who was named Carter Duster had a daughter named Lilian and the victim who was Gunner Bronson was her Godfather. Seven years ago, when Lilian was three, his parents take a trip to oxford and Lilian was left with his Goddaughter. Duster's trip took longer than they expected so Bronson took Lilian to a road trip to oxford. Apparently, Bronson fell asleep while driving and his car was drowned in a river. Bronson succeed swimming out of the car but Lilian suffocated in the water. Dusters later knew Bronson as the reason of

Lilian's death and after four years, they took revenge for their daughter. Suffocated Bronson in his bathtub."

"That's…a sad story."

"Yes, it is," said Arthur. "I was trying to make a point. You should see if Bradly hurt any of them to make a murder motivation."

"Brad was a real nice person, I don't think he'd…"

Arthur interrupted: "I know he was a good person but it doesn't change the fact that he never hurt anybody. You don't know! Damn it Oliver he was secretly friend with seven people that you never heard of! How do you know if one of the suspects wasn't mad at him because something Brad did and decided to kill him? Some decisions happen at one second and get done before you even get the chance to think about what you're doing! When will you understand this?"

"I understand it, I completely do. You see, all these things happening only means that Brad didn't trust me in the way I trusted him. I wasn't even trustable for him to tell me that he is seeing seven other people."

Arthur shook his head around and asked: "Jesus, Oliver. Why would you think that?"

"Why not? I'm solving the case of a person who didn't trust me!"

"You're being unreasonable. You've helped in cases that you and the victim never met each other! This is the case of your life's best friend and you are the only person that I can trust his wisdom to solve it."

"Arthur, all my life I thought that Brad is the friend I'm going to get old with but I can't. I thought he is the friend who I would spend my retirement with, I can't do that either. What's left for me? A corpse that is six feet under? A cold grave that I will visit every weekend? What's left?" Oliver yelled.

Arthur glanced at Oliver and whispered: "You're so broken, aren't you?"

"I am. And I can't do anything. I feel so betrayed!"

"Do you need a hug?"

"Sure, I do!"

Arthur hugged Oliver and Oliver thought he had to ask for it before!

"You know that I'm always there for you for anything, right?"

"Thank you, Archie."

"You're welcome." Arthur whispered, "And don't ever call me Archie again, okay?"

They stopped hugging, got out of the car and entered the police department. A young cop came to them and said: "Sergeant Black, a lady is on the phone. She wants to talk to you."

He reduced his volume and said: "I think it's your mother-in-law."

"Alright. I'll take care of it," said Arthur. "Mr Johnson, would you mind waiting at my office?"

Oliver didn't say a thing and went to Arthur's office. Passing by detective Henry's office, Oliver remembered that he was supposed to check Brad's house for evidence.

Oliver took his phone out of his pocket to add a reminder when he saw eight missed calls from his mother. No wonder why Katherine called Arthur. Oliver walked into Arthur's office and sat on the leather chair behind the desk. Tired and sleepy, Oliver used the magical technique, writing down.

He found a piece of paper and pen; wrote down:

*I should…*
*Send email to the suspects for tomorrow's gathering.*
*Visit Bradly Moore's house this afternoon.*
*Invite Phillip for a meal.*
*Go to Moore's house and talk to Ezra.*
*GET SOME SLEEP.*

He carefully checked the list twice to make sure he wasn't missing anything. Arthur came to his office and asked: "Why don't you answer your mum's calls?"

"Why? What's up?"

"She wanted to remind you of the dinner tonight, reminding you that you're not given a choice and you have to be there."

Oliver rolled the chair and said: "I have plans."

Arthur stopped the chair and said: "No you don't…Oliver, two weeks ago, she called me at four in the morning to come check if you have committed a suicide!"

"Did you come over?"

"I come to work at eight every day. What makes you think I would spare my sleep?"

"Okay so you didn't come over to check on me; what did you do?"

Arthur put all the papers on the desk on one side and said: "I assured her that you won't do such an ugly thing."

"But what if I did it?"

"How do you find this conversation engaging?"

"Okay fine. We'll move on."

"You'll come to your parent's home for dinner tonight."

"You have my word, sir."

"Don't call me sir."

Oliver smiled and said: "Sir, yes sir." And added one more item to the list:

*Dinner at Mum and Dad's house tonight*

## Bradly Moore's House, 15:08 P.M.

Oliver and detective Henry arrived at the place. Oliver wasn't so sure if he still wanted to go back to that house again. Detective Henry said: "Listen boy, I'm going inside. I don't blame you if you can't come in. I understand that it's hard for you. I'll be waiting inside. If you can't come in, don't doubt; just leave."

"Thank you, detective. I'll be fine," Oliver said, "I'll join you in a minute."

Detective shook his head and left the car. Oliver looked at the house and the remembrance of his first memory at the house, made him smile.

## Flashback: 29 May 2010, 16:00 P.M.

Bradly and Oliver walked into the empty house. Oliver grumbled: "Bradly, this is the ninth and last house we're visiting."

"Last one?" Bradly sadly asked while looking around.

"I'm starving. Do you expect me to join you on this crazy journey?"

"Uh-huh."

Oliver angrily yelled at him: "Just get the house! What do you want, a Buckingham palace?"

"Explicitly," Brad said in cold blood, "We still have two more houses to visit."

Tiredness overcame Oliver and he sat on the floor.

Brad glanced at him and asked: "What, are you tired?"

Oliver glared and said: "No, I'm testing the seat."

Bradly optimistically shook his head and said: "While you test the seat, I'll go check upstairs."

Bradly went to see upstairs, Oliver stayed put and looked around him. It was a real pretty house; it had two living rooms connected by a slide door. There was a kitchen behind Oliver right next to the hallway. Oliver could see a small door that he assumed was a closet. A library was at his left side and at the right side, were the metal-wooden stairs.

Bradly walked down to the living room after ten minutes. He seemed excited.

"Dude!" Bradly excitedly said, "I love this house!"

"Great! You'll rent it?"

"Of course not!" Brad cheered, "I'm *buying* it!"


## 22 February 2019, End of the Flashback

Oliver took a deep breath to prepare to see inside the house.

Detective knocked at the car's window. Oliver said: "I'm coming." And got off the car.

He could barely stand all the memories that were surrounding him. They didn't seem to come to an end. Oliver felt weak in his knees, his legs were shivering.

Detective opened the door for him. Not a second longer after entering the house, Oliver felt breathless. He couldn't help recalling the night of the murder. He could remember everything about that night perfectly. Oliver could not dismiss Brad's crimson blood all over the hallway memory off his mind. He had seen plenty of crime scenes and dead bodies throughout his work-life and no doubt that those hurt them either but that specific memory of his friend didn't seem to be disremembered even for a single minute.

"Come on, Oliver! Get yourself together!" Oliver thought, "You're better than this."

"I found him right there," Oliver said while pointing at the corner of the hallway, near the living room door.

"Indeed. Due to our evidence, Brad took the killer to the living room. Brad later understands that the killer wasn't there for a pleasing reason. The killer stabs and Brad who apparently was holding a mug, hits the killer in the head with that mug." Richard explained.

"Wait, mug? Didn't they find any DNA on or in it?" asked Oliver.

"No. The only DNA they found was Brad's, milk and hot cocoa. The killer had been planning this crap for a long time," Richard said, "They knew how to not leave a mark."

"So, it's a first-degree murder."

Richard seemed surprised. He said: "Well, yeah. Black and I were talking about it two days ago. We thought you heard about it."

"No, I didn't. It's okay. I know now. That matters," said Oliver, "What about the security cameras?"

"There isn't one in this neighbourhood. This area is safe and crime-free."

"Crime-free *as hell*!" Oliver humiliated "So, what's next?"

"I had Myers analysing the suspects' body types."

"And?"

"Brad was at least fifteen kilos above our female suspects. Just consider Geller. She is a fitness trainer who does a lot of weight training. Female suspects are unlikable to be killers."

"Got it. What about male suspects?"

"Rivera and Schwarter are both ectomorphs. Bell occurs Bradly the most. Bell is an endomorph like Brad was."

Oliver wanted to share an idea when Richard said: "Before you say anything; when you said that Lensher told you that she met Brad at her workplace, the hospital when he broke his ankle, I called the hospital about it. Twelve days before he died, he called the hospital because of a non-union in his ankle. His ankle had been hurting him for a long time but Brad was too busy to see a doctor."

"When was his appointment?"

"February 10th."

"And he never made it…Right. What else?"

"The killer stabs Brad at the living room. Brad tries to defend himself with his mug. He holds his scar and runs to the hallway but he can't carry on with the trauma so he stops at the door frame. He touches the frame with his hand covered in blood, as you can see." Richard pointed at some red fingerprints at the frame and continued, "Then the killer kicks Brad in the knee from behind. Knee of the same leg that the ankle was broken, the left leg. Brad's fibula bone breaks, he falls down. Now from this point, we believe that Brad wanted to defend again by his hand and the killer steps on his hand and breaks Brad's metacarpus and…you know the rest."

"How long did it take to happen?"

"We've estimated ten to fifteen minutes. Considering the time that our witness said she saw someone with Brad until the help message was sent."

"But Sebastian arrived about eleven o'clock. How did you estimate?" Oliver asked confused.

"The time was estimated since ten twenty-five, when Brad was last seen alive until ten forty when his message was sent to you and the suspects. That makes fifteen minutes, son."

Oliver kept quiet until he started the scene analysis: "This homicide was planned. It's impossible to think it wasn't. No fingerprints, no DNA, no other witnesses. What are the chances?"

"Killer must've been very familiar with the neighbourhood. He or she knew about the cameras which don't exist, maybe even the crowd hours unless you can give me some good reason that how did no one was out of their houses at that specific hour!"

Oliver took a deep breath: "Detective, I think we're done here. Can we go now?"

"Yes, indeed. Let's go, shall we?"


## Moores' Family House, 18:59 P.M.

Mrs Moore happily invited Oliver to come inside. Oliver accepted her invitation; he wouldn't say no to a cup of coffee.

"Where's Robert?" Oliver asked.

Elizabeth blinked: "I beg your pardon darling?"

"I asked, where is Robert?"

"He went to see a friend of him."

"Where is Ezra? I didn't see him."

Mrs Elizabeth's smile suddenly disappeared and replaced with a blue face. She said sadly: "Oh dear; Ezra locked up himself in his room. He...just can't go on with what happened to Bradly. He still can't believe it."

Mrs Elizabeth started crying quietly. Oliver was shocked. He didn't see that coming. Ezra wasn't so logical enough to accept a death in a short time, even his brother's. His cold attitude was how Oliver knew Ezra. In fact, Ezra was a realistic person and he was proud of it. But it might've taken so long to get over with, even for Ezra.

Oliver wasn't so sure what word's he was looking for. He asked: "Mrs Elizabeth, why didn't you tell me sooner? How long has it been?"

"S…since yesterday morning…We wanted to tell you but we thought that he'll be fine."

"*Why* would you think that? He is now *unstable*. He is *not* trustable."

"I know, I know. I'm…I'm sorry. I'm so sorry." Elizabeth covered her face using her hands.

"There's no need to apologize," Oliver said to calm her, "I will talk to Ezra. Don't worry."

Mrs Elizabhet couldn't talk since she was crying so she shook her head as a 'yes' and she moved her lips to form, 'thank you'.

Oliver brought her a glass of water and sat next to her. "It's not proper to say that you're not supposed to be sad or move on. You lost a very close one. Someone you cared for. It's all so normal that you're unable to be happy or even normal for a while, you might think that your lost beloved deserved to be as same as happy as you are. It leads you to feel sorry and feel like you've made a mistake or it's a sin to be happy. What you should learn is that if Brad was still here, he never wanted to see you like this. He didn't want you to be so sad and broken."

She whispered: "He didn't?"

"No. Never in a million years. He wanted you to be happy. You're allowed to be sad but you must respect what Brad wanted. Considering what a lost person wanted is as important as everything they write in their will."

"I can't accept that Brad isn't here anymore. I can't even cook. Remember how badly he loved mac and cheese?"

"Why can't you?"

"What if…I mean…how do you know if he wasn't hungry? What if he died hungry?"

Mrs Moore started to cry again. Oliver had no idea what to do but lying to her: "Hey Elizabeth, don't cry. He didn't die hungry."

"He didn't?"

"No. Brad never gave up eating! He actually texted me that morning; he wanted to cook fries and steak for dinner."

"Did he cook?"

"I suppose yes. I…was at his house early this evening. His dishes were still on his table."

"How could you get in there? Tell me!" Elizabeth asked phenomenally, "I want to go there too!"

"Calm down, Elizabeth, calm down. Detective took me there for more investigation. I couldn't stand there longer than an hour."

"Do they know anything? About the killer or a murder weapon?"

"Coroners are still doing their investigations. They will give me an answer by the weekend."

"Oliver…Please…I beg you…Find whoever killed my son…Bring them to justice…You *shouldn't* let go of this case. You *can't*!"

"I won't let go, Elizabeth. I won't give up until I find the killer."

Elizabeth was a little bit calm. She had no idea how desperate Oliver was. Oliver was nearly giving up working on the case. He was destroying his own soul.

In case of talking to Ezra all alone, Oliver asked Mrs Moore to go to the supermarket and buy Ezra some junk food. Fortunately, supermarket was away from their home so Oliver could take as much as time he needed.

Oliver went upstairs and stood in front of Ezra's room…

\*\*\*

## 32 Minutes Later

Oliver punched the door and shouted: "Open the door or I'll break it!"

"Get away, Oliver. I don't want to see you." Oliver heard Ezra's enigma through the door.

"I am not so patient right now. I'm so messed up that I can even kill," Oliver indirectly threated.

"Like you killed Bradly?" Ezra slowly whispered but it was loud enough that Oliver heard and I can assure you, there is nothing scarier than angry Oliver.

He put a step back and kicked the door and opened the door. He entered the room, grabbed Ezra's collar and pushed him to the wall. He got closer to Ezra and whispered angrily: "*What…nonsense…did you…say?*"

Ezra didn't answer.

Oliver yelled at him: "Repeat again!"

Ezra pushed Oliver and yelled back: "Get off me! You know what I think? I think this whole thing is suspicious! You haven't cried for Brad more than once! I think whether you are the murderer or you are a *coward*!"

Oliver could allow patience to hinder him no more. He slapped Ezra that he nearly fell on the floor.

Oliver left the room without any delay. He soon left the house. Even though his car was in front of the house, he would rather to walk. He was breathing greedily. For the first time in his life, he wasn't regret hurting someone. Oliver couldn't think crystal clear, kept asking only one question: "What made him think that?"

Oliver finally stopped at a spot. He took a deep breath, tried to ignore his heartbeat, beating like a woodpecker in his chest and hurting him.

He sat on the edge of the sidewalk and put his hands around his head.

What Oliver's feeling at that moment was hard to explain. He felt like he is carrying the heaviest scales on his waist and due to that, his spine was pressing on his lungs are banning him from breathing.

He felt like the loneliest man alive. What he badly needed at that time was a trustable beloved to tell him: "It'll be alright, Ollie. Everything will be alright. You're not alone in this."

About the trustable beloved, inaccessible. Brad was off the universe and Oliver's family were all treating him sympathetic in a dramatic manner.

He had a second choice; getting his car and drive home safely to get a shower and be ready to see his parents for dinner.

Oliver was thinking about his second option when he heard a notification on his phone. It was a message from Mr Robert: "Where are you boy?"

Oliver texted back: "I'm out. Going home."

Mr Moore texted: "Send me your location. I'll bring you your car."

Oliver wasn't in the mood of texting so he called Mr Moore: "Hello Oliver."

"Hi. You don't need to bring me my car. I want to walk to organize my…thoughts."

"What thoughts? Job thoughts or little-fight-you-just-had thoughts?" Mr Robert didn't sound angry or anxious or even surprised and upset, he was totally fine and cool but in spite of that, Oliver didn't say a word.

Mr Robert Moore continued: "Listen. I'm *not* mad at you. Ezra told me what he said to you and I'm terribly sorry about that. He made a big mistake.

It's just that Ezra is really messed up after…you know. He has changed. I barely see him. He doesn't eat and he has a difficult sleep challenge, he wakes up having nightmares. Oliver he just lost his big brother and he is only twenty-five. Everything is happening to him so unexpectedly and I need *you* to be there for him because you are an *amazing* big brother; to your own sisters or to Ezra, you're an amazing and more than that…you're a good person, a fine human being. Would you do this for me?"

Oliver thought for a moment and said: "I'll consider that Robert. We'll catch up later."

He hung up the phone and put it back into his pocket. He felt really tired and sleepy that he could even sleep on the sidewalk! At that very moment, his thought was sleeping and nothing more.

Oliver thought about what Robert Moore said. He was right. As long as Oliver could remember, he treated Ezra way better than Brad ever did. Oliver wasn't so sure what he meant to Ezra but he was certain that they were not enemies. Oliver was really affected by what was happening. He didn't know what he was doing. He needed to pull things together and meditate. He should've reacted better. Oliver was better than that. He stood up and walk to his parent's house.

## Johnsons' House, 20:00 P.M.

Oliver knocked at the door and after a few seconds, Dakota opened the door:

"Hey big guy!" Said Dakota "Come in."

Oliver shook his head and walked in. Dakota held his hand and slowly asked: "Did you get what I wanted?"

Oliver turned to her and asked: "What did you want?"

"Didn't you get my message?"

"No. What message?"

"I wanted to get me some carrot muffins."

"Oh baby. I'm too tired to go get them now!"

"Why?" Dakota asked, "Ollie, *please*?"

Oliver continued his path in and said: "No."

Dakota breathed out with rage: "Doesn't matter. Walk in."

Oliver went in and looked for his uncle and father. He asked: "Where are Arthur and Liv?"

"They're on the way. Must arrive any seconds now."

Oliver walked into the kitchen to see his mother. Katherine was taking care of pots on the oven. He could smell a soup, maybe chicken or tomato soup. "Hello Mum!" said Oliver, "How are you darling?"

Katherine smiled after seeing her son. She hugged him and said happily: "Hi baby. My head is in the sky now! How are you?"

"Like a thousand bucks!" Oliver said, "Although I brought…nothing!"

"That doesn't matter son."

Dakota sat on a chair and asked: "So how was your day?"

"Like zero bucks!" Oliver laughed.

"Why? You okay?" Dakota asked.

"I'm not bad," Oliver said, "I still have a task for today. I'm seeing the suspects tomorrow and I have emails to send them."

"And?" Dakota asked like she was waiting for more information.

"And what?" Oliver bent his head to a side.

"What else? This is how your *whole* day passed?"

Oliver smiled and said calmly: "No. Not really. I went to two places."

"Spit it out! *Where*? *Why*? *With whom*? *How*?" Dakota asked quickly.

He smiled: "Hold on! Breathe! I'll tell you."

Oliver brought a glass of orange juice out of the fridge and sat on a chair. He continued: "I went to Brad's house with detective Henry. We went to see if we can help the investigation team and find anything more. I went to Mr Moores' house next." Oliver explained and inhaled his orange juice.

"Are you alright Ollie?" Dakota asked.

"I'm not bad…We did a great job back there. We didn't get anything new but we had a remarkable effort!" Oliver said with an optimistic smile.

"Son, are you sure it's fine? Did detective *make you* go there?" Katherine asked with her motherly anxiety.

"No, he didn't. I asked him to go there. He came along to make sure I'll get myself together," said Oliver.

"You said that you went to Mr Moores' house. What happened? How were they?" Dakota asked.

"I went to their house. Robert wasn't home. Only Elizabeth and Ezra. Ezra had himself locked up in this room. I talked to Elizabeth to go out so I could talk to Ezra. Things went wrong, he insulted, we got into a fight, I slapped him, came out of their home, I was too angry to bring my car, I walked and now I'm here with you beautiful ladies! Now if you excuse me, I think Dad is calling me. See you at dinner. Love you, goodbye!" Oliver explained generally and gave them his 'crazy eyes'.

"Wait a second. You got into a fight with Ezra?!" Katherine asked while trying not to be angry.

"Yes. I suppose yes," said Oliver.

"Bill, he just lost his big brother. What were you thinking?" Dakota asked angrily.

"First of all, I know what just happened. That man was my best and oldest. I was thinking that I'm being insulted," said Oliver.

"How could he possibly insult you, Oliver?" Katherine asked and slightly hit him on the shoulder.

"He said that he thinks *I killed* his brother. Mum, he thinks that I killed my best friend. How would you react to such an opinion, I'm willing to know?" Oliver frowned.

"Why would he think that? You got to the crime scene the last," said Dakota.

"That's what I'm keep asking myself. Detective Henry and a captain witnessed that I was with them at the police department when the murder happened." Oliver explained.

"This must've made you so angry Ollie, didn't it?" Dakota asked.

"Yes, it did. I'm so pissed off now. I didn't want to come here angry but I couldn't stand my house either, I'm sorry," Oliver said with regret.

"Angelina Jackson. Are you still in touch with her?" Katherine asked her eldest.

"Yes and no. I visited her on Christmas holidays." Oliver answered.

"Why don't you ask her for a little help? She could at least help you with your own feelings." Katherine advised.

"I think I'll give her a call. Maybe tomorrow. It depends on the meeting. I might have to spend my entire day at the station," said Oliver.

"Ollie, you *should* be fine. No one can work when they're not good," said Dakota.

"Okay D. I promise," said Oliver, "So what's for dinner?"

Katherine smiled and said: "Chicken soup and Jambalaya. Chocolate ice cream with slices of strawberry and banana for dessert."

Oliver smiled back and said: "Too perfect to be true! I'll go see Dad and Phill."

Oliver left the kitchen to the back yard. Edward was showing the garden to Phillip. As long as Oliver could remember, Edward had only a few certain things to do in a day. If he wasn't designing a building, he was taking care of the garden; if he wasn't doing that, he was reading a book or listening to a 50s to 80s music, if he wasn't doing them either, he was watching TV and if he wasn't watching TV, he was speaking with Katherine or he was outside of the house.

This time he was at home, taking care of his garden and of course, showing it to his youngest brother. Oliver headed to join them.

"Look at these delicate Orchids! Katherine likes it more than other flowers." Edward said excitedly.

"It is beautiful…Remember how Dad used to keep me away from his garden?" Phillip said with his permanent smile.

"Yeah? Don't you know why?" Edward asked him with sarcasm.

"So what? I liked the Jasmine's! They were delicious!" Phillip defended himself.

"Hello gentlemen!" Oliver interrupted their small talk.

"Hey boy! Look at you!" Phillip said, hugged Oliver and whispered near his ear, "Save me or I'll become a fern!"

"Hi son. You're late!" Edward said and hugged his son.

"You didn't give me a time to come. Plus, I had work to do."

"Right. What's up? How's the process?" Edward asked.

"It's normal. I have a meeting with the suspects tomorrow. I'm willing to get an answer. I was at the station with Arthur this morning. I asked detective Henry to take me to Bradly's house for our own investigation. I went to Mr Moore's house to say hello and now I'm here." Oliver explained.

"Are you alright? Didn't you feel bad going back to his house?" Phillip asked his nephew.

"I'm good. It was okay. Don't worry about me." Oliver said to calm them.

"So, what about the investigation? Did you figure anything out?" Edward asked.

"No. Nothing new. A new investigation team were there two days ago. They will give me their results by the weekend. We hope that their research will be useful." Oliver explained and while explaining, he felt sleepy.

"Do you have anything about the killer? Like a piece of cloth or a fingerprint?" Phillip asked Oliver.

"No, we don't. What you're saying is not that common. Most of the victims doesn't even get the chance to defeat the killer," Oliver said. He really liked to tell Phillip that he should reduce his obsession of watching crime movies!

"Answer my questions, Ollie. What was the murder weapon? Was it Bradly's? Where did you find the murder weapon? Why did you and seven other people were there? Do the suspects have witnesses that they weren't at the crime scene when the murder happened?" Phillip asked and waited for answers.

"He was killed by a knife and it is gone with the killer. Brad sent an emergency message to me and seven suspects to see him at his place, he was friends with all those seven people. Yes, they have a witness; detective confirmed their witnesses himself." Oliver answered all Phillip's questions.

"Let's go inside. Oliver, you don't have to work when your job hurts you. If your job hurts you, or make you think about other job, then it's not a good job. It's what my father told me." Edward said while going inside.

"Thanks Dad. But I'm cool with my job. I'm still not thinking of another job!" Oliver said while going to the stairs "I'm going up. I have work to do. Call me when the dinner's ready."

Oliver went upstairs. He opened the first door; entered the door, closed the door and laid on the bed. He took his phone out of his pocket. He turned on the night lamp because the place was too dark and the phone's screen was bothering his eyes. He composed the email: "*Hello and goodnight.*

*The fourth psychological meeting with Oliver Johnson will be tomorrow, February 23rd at 8 o'clock in the morning at Café Lorenté.*
*Please be on time. Thank you.*"

Oliver turned his phone off and dropped it off the bed right after sending the email. Before he even realized, he fell sleep.

## One Hour Later

"...I mean, why do some idiots have children to make things better with their lives with their partners? I arrested this kid this evening who was selling drugs. He said that his parents were experiencing a crappy time so they decided

81

to have a kid but then, his mother divorced and he has been a drug dealer ever since. If I could just say one thing to these stupid people, it would be a marriage psychologist address!"

Oliver didn't open his eyes but he was sure that it was Arthur, talking greedy on his phone or to someone else in the room.

He then heard Phillip saying with despair: "I hate such people. They're gross and their action is barbarian."

"Hi." Oliver sat on the bed and said with a thick voice, "What are you doing here?"

Arthur explained: "Olivia sent me to wake you up. Richard said that you didn't take enough sleep so I didn't wake you. I just called Phillip to come here and talk."

"What time is it?" Oliver opened his eyes. He could see that they are sitting on the ground, holding cushions.

"It's half past nine. I'm starving. I will eat you two if we don't go down!" Phillip said threatening.

Both Oliver and Arthur knew that Phillip wasn't joking. In fact, Oliver knew this habit since he was a little boy and Arthur... Well, he understood it in a little bit more complicated process.

About three and a half years ago when he was just engaged to Olivia, he took a trip to Philadelphia with her family to know the rest of Katherine and Edward's family who lived there. One of those days, a seventeen-year-old cousin named Karla convinced everyone that she can cook a Spanish food so delicious that they won't forget, same thing happened. Karla burned the food which supposed to be 'Spanish Tortilla' but Karla was succeeded to create carbon!

Long story short, Arthur understood that food is sacred to Phillip.

Oliver left the bed and made the bed after. He took a better look around. He noticed a big Prussian blue suitcase on the ground. The room he slept in was Phillip's room.

Oliver went downstairs, Arthur followed him but Phillip stayed a bit longer at the room. Olivia was watching TV. Oliver stood behind her, caressed her hair and commixed it. He asked: "How's my baby sister?"

"Hello Ollie." She said in cold blood, "You do this one more time and your baby sister will bury you alive!"

"You're violent. Cool!" Oliver said with a big smile on his face.

He saw Dakota coming out of the kitchen. He went to Dakota, hugged her and said: "You're the cutest sister *ever*!"

Dakota—Who was certainly confused—asked: "You okay?"

"Couldn't be better!" Oliver said happily.

Olivia asked suspiciously: "Why are you being weird?"

"I'm just being the great brother I always am!" Oliver said innocently.

"Ollie, what's the matter? Are you okay?" Dakota asked Oliver compassionately.

Oliver's smile disappeared and he sat on the couch.

"I knew this day will come. I knew that one of us will die sooner than the other one. It could be me instead of him. Eventually, the living one would have to follow his life," Oliver said sobbing, "I just didn't see a murder coming! I expected the day that he dies I just didn't see a homicide! This is what bothering me...*I can't take it*."

Oliver left the living room to the kitchen. He grabbed a glass and filled it with water. He leant to the alabaster counter and drank the water. He needed to clarify his thoughts to himself. He wished he was at his home sitting on the couch in front of the television waiting for his brain to get tired and sleepy.

He couldn't leave his parents and everyone else there. It would be rude. So, he just did what was polite; went out of the kitchen, had dinner with his family and spent time with them and by the end of the night, Arthur and Olivia drove him home.

***

## February 23rd, Café Lorenté, 7:43 A.M.

Theodore walked in and looked for a familiar face except for his co-workers.

He saw a blonde girl raised hand to have his attention from the end of the I. Theodore could barely see who she was. Wendy, his friend who was working in the morning shift that day, went to Theodore and asked: "Do you know those girls?"

"Is there another girl next to her?" Theodore asked confused, "Yes. Yes, I do. Thank you, Wendy!"

Theodore went to table number 10. The ten-seat-table with only two users.

"Morning! How are you?" Olga said to Theodore happily.

"Hi." Theodore said while sitting on a chair "How are you ladies?"

"Didn't you see Olga raised her hand?" Anya asked.

"I saw the hand! I didn't see Olga and, in my defence, she did a new haircut, I didn't recognize her!" Theodore said.

"Khoroshiy! I wasn't sure if these feathered bangs look good on me!"

"Did I…say that they look good on you?" Theodore asked Olga.

"*Do you dare* to say anything opposite?" Olga asked him with a cold smile.

Theodore didn't say a thing a finished their conversation with a smile.

Anya asked Theodore: "Do you need an optometrist?"

"I think I need to see one now!" Theodore said, "Hey, have you noticed that Oliver is a little bit…obsessed about this case?"

"Yes. I don't know Oliver so much but I think he isn't doing well. He's like, messed up," Anya said sympathetically.

"Okay guys," said Olga, "Remember what Sebastian said? Bradly Told Sebastian that his best friend's name is 'Bill Oliver' but he likes to call himself 'Oliver Bill'…I don't know if he met each one of you alone to know you better but he met me and told me that Bradly was his best friend and now it's his duty to find out who killed him. I think it explains why he is a little bit messed up."

"*A little bit*?!" Anya said, "The guy is killing himself! You know if I were the killer, I would've turned myself in right after I saw Oliver like this…I can't stand seeing someone so unwell."

"Speaking of the killer, who do you think the killer is?" Theodore asked and leant his elbows to the table.

Before they got the chance to say their opinion, Sebastian and Morgan came to them: "Hello everybody. What a *great* day! Isn't it?" Morgan said like she just won a billion euros.

"Can you believe her? She is *so energetic*. It's not even 8!" Sebastian said sleepy and sat on the chair next to Anya.

Anya smiled and said: "Girl, you're unbelievable! Take a seat."

Morgan sat on a chair next to Theodore and everybody starred at Olga who was sitting on the host seat.

For a few moments, no one said anything. Maybe they were so sleepy at that time of the day and maybe they didn't trust each other, assuming each other as murderers and avoiding to say a word that may've cost their lives.

Morgan said to break the silence fast: "So…I searched Pietro's name this morning. I listened to some of his tracks. He is talented! His music is delightful."

"I know, right?" Anya said, "I played one of his tracks for my aunt. He plays violin so satisfactory that she cried!"

"I guess we've all noticed that he is albinos and he has that two-eye colour syndrome. A complete masterpiece! I don't remember the syndrome's name!" Olga said as a complement.

"Is he?" Theodore said surprisingly, "What colours?"

"I think they were green and brown," said Anya.

"No. I noticed. They are hazel and grey." Sebastian corrected Anya.

"Wow!" Pietro said while getting close to the table, "I didn't know I'm so popular!"

He sat on the chair next to Sebastian and said: "Hi guys. How are you? I saw Oliver outside. He was getting out of his car…Olga, I like your hair. It suits you!"

Olga smiled beautifully.

Anya asked Pietro: "What instruments do you play?"

"Violin, cello and piano."

"Isn't it hard to play with both hands? How are you so focused?" Sebastian asked Pietro.

"It was when I started to learn. I had to meditate three hours a day. Now I don't need to meditate that much and, I can type on keyboard with both hands!"

"Pietro, I have a niece who would like to learn piano. I think she is pretty talented. She has a soul of an artist. She watches 'The exorcist' twice a day," Olga said to Pietro and waited for an answer.

"How old is your niece?"

"I think she is seven or eight. She's in Moscow."

Oliver interrupted their conversation by saying "Hello, good morning, everybody. Olga, love your new haircut. Can I take your seat? I want everyone to see me."

Theodore whispered: "Am I the only one who didn't notice her hair?"

"Thank you," Oliver said when Olga left the chair for Oliver and sat in front of Pietro "Marika called me, she'll be a little late. Did you write about the crime scene?"

Everyone gave their papers to Oliver. Everyone wrote everything down but Marika who talked to Oliver on the phone and told him that due to her time limitation, she will send an email.

"Thank you all. Today is the day of our fourth meeting, as I counted" said Oliver, "Today; I want you to empty your mind. I want you to dive into your thoughts. I want you to think out of the box. I should make a point first, I've noticed that you guys are friendly together which is good. Ignoring your friendship, I want all of you to tell me who do you suspect for this murder, without actually telling me."

"It got complicated. What should we do?" Pietro asked.

"I want you to send me a text. Text me that who do you suspect? I repeat, *don't* allow your opinion to affect your judgment about each other." Oliver explained, "You can start now. Take your time to think, text me when you're ready."

***

### Oliver Johnson's Car, 09:15 A.M.

Oliver was so surprised. He was so shocked by the meeting's results that he pulled the car over. He didn't expect this result!

Theodore, Marika and Pietro voted for Sabastian. Sebastian had 3 votes.

Sebastian voted for Theodore. Theodore had 1 vote.

Anya voted for Morgan. Morgan had 1 vote.

Morgan voted for Olga. Olga had 1 vote.

Olga voted for Pietro. Pietro had 1 vote.

Marika and Anya had no votes.

What really surprised Oliver was that Sebastian seemed to be a pretty nice guy; well of course, killers can treat people nice but sometimes you meet a person, you think yourself: "Can this person commit a murder? *Hell no!*"

Sebastian was one of those people.

Oliver thought about everything he remembered of the very first time he met Sebastian. February 9th…

When Oliver walked in Brad's house which an ambulance and a police car was parked in front of it. He was the last one who got there. Anya was scared and crying out loud. Olga crying in silence, she was too shocked to believe what was happening. Morgan was sitting down at a corner, holding her knees.

Marika was talking to a nurse, telling them that Bradly wasn't breathing ever since she saw him drowned in his own blood. Theodore was trying to keep himself away from crying even though he wasn't successful at all. Pietro and Sebastian were telling a cop about their information and Sebastian was hasted.

Oliver walked into this circumstance. He walked into his best friend's house and saw his best friend stabbed, laying in the hallway, drowned in his own blood, not breathing, cold, corpse…

Oliver couldn't forget that how he pushed the two nurses who were sitting next to Brad. Oliver put his hand under Brad's head, tried to wake him up by slapping his face slowly. He then opened Brad's eyelid; when that didn't work either, he started to cry. Weeping and calling Brad's name. Pietro, Sebastian and an officer hardly pulled him away from the body.

Before Oliver even understood, he was crying. He took deep breaths to calm himself. His efforts were useless, he cried again. This time harder.

He was crying when someone knocked at the car's window. Oliver pulled the window down and saw a fat old man.

Old man kindly asked: "Good morning young man. I was walking by and saw you crying in your car. Is everything alright? Can I help you with anything?"

"Hi sir. No, I wasn't, I mean…yes! I was crying because…" Oliver said everything that came into his mind.

"Because he has diarrhoea. No need to worry, he'll be alright!" Oliver and the old man looked behind Oliver to see who said that. It couldn't be anyone else but Oliver's brother-in-law, Arthur Michael Black.

Arthur came closer and shook hands with the old man and said: "I'm Arthur. This is my brother-in-law. Like I said there's no need to worry. It's just traveller's diarrhoea!"

Old man smiled: "Oh son. It's alright. I used to serve the royal navy, I used to have traveller's diarrhoea all the time! You'll get better soon."

Oliver took a "You're so dead" look to Arthur and said to the old man: "Thank you sir. Thank you for your attention."

The old man left Oliver and Arthur.

"Well, well," Oliver said threatening "Arthur Black…how are you, sergeant?"

"I'm feeling so alive! How are you?"

"How would you like to die? In a lava incinerator or in an incinerator full of lava?"

"In a lava that is filled with incinerators!" Arthur kept on joking with Oliver's word play.

"How did you even find me? We didn't talk today."

"Oh, I don't know. I'm a sergeant with a squad that happened to have a hacker. What do you think?" Arthur said and slightly bent his head.

Oliver surprised and his eyes were wide: "You *hacked* my phone?"

"It gets done so much easier when the hacker is Julia's former husband!"

"How many times have you done this before?"

"Hey, I done it for a good reason! I've done two times in the past year because I was worried about you. You didn't answer your phone, no one knew where you are! I had no other choice!" Arthur defended himself "can you blame me for that?"

"We have stuff to take care of. Get in the car. We should talk about the meeting."

Arthur got into the car. Oliver told everything about the meeting and the results to Arthur while he was driving.

"So, what do you think?" Arthur asked Oliver.

"Well, I…have to consider everything. Sebastian suffers from a syndrome named 'Alice in wonderland'. It hallucinates him. He sees things around him smaller or bigger than they really are."

"Ollie it's…not enough to consider him as the assassin," said Arthur. "AIW syndrome is caused by migraine."

"That's what I'm saying! He hypothetically grabs a knife and accidentally stabs Brad. Why would he repeat it thirty-one more times in his chest?" Oliver said, "it just…doesn't make any sense."

"Maybe it doesn't have to do anything with his syndrome. And maybe he isn't the killer we're looking for."

"I agree," said Oliver, "But I won't give up. I should at least check on him. I'll do it tomorrow afternoon. I should take a break for today."

### Oliver Johnson's House, 13:08 P.M.

Oliver bit the last piece of ham and cheese sandwich. He put the dishes in the sink and went upstairs to lay on his bed and maybe watch a movie.

Oliver felt sleepy right after he laid on his bed. His phone rang just before he fell asleep.

"Don't be Arthur. Don't be Arthur. Don't be Arthur." Oliver wished and answered the phone, "Hello?"

"Oliver." Arthur said on the phone. "I'm at work. Something happened. You should know."

"Did you get the killer?" Oliver asked tiredly. In fact, he didn't even understand what Arthur said for a minute.

"Detective Henry is so mad. He's tired of waiting. He wants to solve the case sooner. He wants to search everything, every single thing about the suspects. He wants everything's records. Bank accounts, phones, educational backgrounds, psychological records, crime records and even their family records!"

"Wait a minute. *What*? He can't do that!" Oliver wasn't sleepy anymore. He was enraged.

"Why can't he? He is the captain. Technically, he is our boss!" Arthur said greedily.

"When is this going to happen?"

"I bought you some time. I sent him home. He yelled at all of us and broke a couple of glasses!"

Oliver didn't say anything. Arthur said: "Ollie. He thinks that Anya Barton isn't that innocent. In his opinion, her youth is affecting our judgment. He thinks Anya is the killer and we shouldn't make any certain decisions about her. She is in danger. She might be locked up for a crime she didn't commit."

"Did you tell him about Sebastian?"

"I did. He said that your way was stupid. He has two strategies about our case. It was a group homicide or the most innocent suspect is the guilty."

"Someone must tell that old man that cases are different than '70s and '80s! Where are we? In the story of 'The murder on the orient express'?"

Arthur took a deep breath and asked: "What are you going to do about it?"

"I should go talk to Anya. She must do a second interrogation at the department."

"Fine. I'll be right here."

***

Oliver walked into the law college and looked for Anya Barton. It wasn't easy to find brown-haired law scholar in population of at least a hundred more brown-haired scholars. It was like finding a needle in a warehouse filled with haystack. It was hard and more importantly, it was futile and pointless!

Being a good, conscientious and punctual scholar benefits you with the euphoria of having your professors' trust. Lucky for him Oliver was still in touch with some of his former professors. Finding professors was a lot easier than finding a scholar.

Oliver asked to find Professor Denzel. He didn't have any classes, it meant that he is at his office. That was Oliver's next stop.

Oliver knocked on the door and opened it. Professor "Marvin Denzel" was sitting on his brown leather chair behind the desk, checking his scholars' tests. He looked up when he heard the door opened. He smiled when he saw Oliver, one of his favourite scholars. He stood up and said: "Bill! Hi! Long-time no see! Come in, take a seat!"

"Hello Mr Denzel. How are you?" Oliver sat on a chair and said with a smile.

"I'm good. Oh, I'm so sorry for your loss. I heard about your friend Bradly Moore. I knew him," Mr Denzel said sorrowful.

"Thank you, professor. He passed away two weeks ago. Murdered, honestly."

"Dear God. Are there any suspects?"

"He was murdered at his house. And yes, there are suspects, nearly ten."

"What a complicated case," said Mr Denzel, "Wait, is this case why Richard Henry is so pissed off? I ran into him yesterday and he was infuriated. He said that it was because of a case that he was working on as his last job."

"Yes, it is. We are doing everything we can. It's actually difficult. There are endless possibilities about it. They're like, really impossible."

"Oh please, even the word 'Impossible' says 'I'm possible'!" Mr Denzel smiled.

"Fair enough." Oliver shrugged with a smile.

"So, what's the occasion? Can I help you with anything?"

"I'm glad you asked. I'm looking for a scholar who is participating in your classes."

"What is their name?"

"Anya Barton. She is Australian."

Mr Denzel took a few seconds thinking and said: "I know her. She went home like—two hours ago."

"She went home?" Oliver asked again to make sure he understood clearly.

"Yes, she did. May I ask you that how do you know her?"

"We…" Oliver was managing not to say anything about the case "We were introduced by a common friend. We were supposed see each other here. I couldn't find her."

Oliver stood up and said: "Well, I…liked to stay here and talk more but I have a very important and boring thing to do. I'll come back later, maybe we even go out for a cup of coffee!"

Mr Denzel stood up to accompany Oliver. He said: "Sure. Why not? I'm so delighted for this small talk."

"Meeting you is always a pleasure, sir."

"Pleasure's mine. Goodbye and about the case, trust your wisdom."

Oliver shook his hand and left the office. He went through half of the hallway and stopped. Texted Arthur: "Barton isn't at the university. Send me her home address."

Oliver hoped that she can find Anya at her home or at least see her aunt to find out where else can he find Anya.

***

## Anya Barton's House, 15:29 P.M.

Oliver took another look at his phone to see if he followed the address correctly. He got off of his car and went to the door and knocked. Anya opened the door after a minute and asked: "Oliver?"

"I suppose I am. I've been called by this name as far as I can remember!" Oliver joked to hide his worry face.

"Very funny," Anya said confusingly, "What are you doing here?"

"Actually, there's a problem."

"What's wrong?"

"Some members of the investigation team have this theory that your youth and innocent has affected my judgment."

"I don't understand. What does that mean?"

"Means that you might be locked up for a crime that you didn't commit. I need you to go to the police department and ask to meet sergeant Black. Sergeant Arthur Black. You'll do a second interrogation with him. Tell him the same thing you wrote to me about the crime scene. Answer his questions exactly so he'll be able to help you. Go to the department today. The sooner the better."

"I might…go to jail?" Anya asked slowly.

"They can't put you in jail if I disagree. Do not underestimate me." Oliver assured.

"Can you promise me that? That I won't go to jail?"

"You have my word."

Oliver put a step back and as goodbye he said: "Be safe."

# Chapter Five
# They Might Know Things

Olivia walked into the living room and Arthur: "I'm leaving, Arthur. Will you join me?"

Arthur was writing a weekly report for the department on his laptop. He asked without taking a look at his wife: "Where are you going?"

"I told you. I'm going out to buy an anniversary gift for Mum and Dad with Dakota. Now, are you coming with me or not?"

"I'm sorry but I should finish writing this report in…" Arthur took a look at his watch and said, "fifty minutes."

"Okay. Don't you need the car?"

"No. We'll take Oliver's."

"Alright. I'll be back for lunch and if I didn't, you gentleman treat yourselves and order some food. Today's not the perfect day to face a blown-up house!" Olivia said while leaving the living room.

"Liv, that's rude. We're three adult men. We can cook for ourselves!" Oliver said while playing with his phone on the sofa in front of Arthur.

"You don't say! *Adult men*?" Olivia said sarcastically "Don't you remember the last time you and Arthur cooked at my kitchen? You had to contact the fire station!"

Olivia reminded everyone of a dark comedy memory and left the house saying out loud: "You might want to remember the night!"

Oliver and Arthur spent minutes in silence, staring at each other. What these two gentlemen did was unforgivable, unforgettable, unacceptable and irreparable!

Just because Liv didn't get mad at them and she was just grateful that they were both safe, doesn't mean she didn't regret not being there to prevent the event.

Phillip came out of the bathroom next to the living room. He asked: "What's for lunch?"

"Well, you men should figure out your own ways of survival in this brutal universe," Oliver said while going out of the living room, "I have to go see my therapist."

"Wait a minute, *you are* a psychologist and you are going to see one?" Phillip asked.

Oliver explained: "I'm a *forensic* psychologist. She's a *therapist*. These two are different like, a million years."

"Besides, Phill," sarcastically said, "What made you think that he *doesn't* need to see one? The fact that he's mentally stable?!"

"You're right, he must," said Phillip, "Good luck, kiddo!"

Oliver walked outside the house and thought: "*Kiddo*? man, our age difference isn't even a decade!"

\*\*\*

### Angelina Jackson's Psychotherapy Office, 11:58 A.M.

Oliver got in the room, smiled at the therapist and shook hands with her.

"Angelina Jackson" was Oliver's college professor and even though Oliver was graduated 9 years ago, they were still in touch.

"Hi Oliver," she smiled friendly, "Take a seat. How are you?"

Oliver sat on the leather chair in front of Angelina and started: "I'm not fine. Have you heard about my friend, Bradly Moore?"

"Yes, I have; and I'm sorry. I also heard that he was murdered. Is that true?"

"Yeah...And his family asked me to work on his case. I was upset so I agreed. But it's harder than I thought. There are seven suspects and it's not like movies that one of them say something and I accidentally find out who the killer is! It is way more complicated."

"That seems like a huge number," Angelina said, "There is so much pain, suffer and sadness inside you, Oliver. How do you cope with it?"

"I…I don't know. I used to think that if someday Brad dies, I would lock myself up in a room but I feel nothing! Literally nothing! I'm not locked up in a room, I'm simply outside."

Angelina placed her blonde hair behind her ears and asked: "Are you feeling paralysed about your loss?"

"No. I'm not okay but I'm acting that I am. It's like I have no control over my body! It's like I'm tearing apart and turning into pieces. Like when you're mad and tear a paper until the pieces are too small to even grab."

"Have you talked to anyone about it?"

"No. I can't explain my feelings. What I just told you wasn't even half of what I feel."

"Have you tried crying?"

"Yeah."

"The result?"

"Nothing. I can't. Seventy percent of my body is filled with water and yet, I can't cry a tear!" Oliver said greedily, "Oh, just once. I remembered the night it happened and I didn't even realize I was crying. And didn't even take long and not more than five tears!"

Angelina remained silent to think. She said: "When I was a little girl, I used to consider my grandparents as world's greatest lovers, because they were. They truly were. One day, granny left…she died…and my grandpa was left alone for the rest of his life. When my dad and uncles buried granny, he didn't cry. I could see an obvious sign of sadness and loneliness on his face. And I was wondering that how couldn't he cry? He lost the love of his life and he was just staring at the gravestone. Honestly, I really felt offended and insulted so I asked him about it. If I can remember clearly, I asked: 'Grandpa, I'm sorry your loss…our loss. I know what she meant to you.'

He didn't distract his eyes from the grave and answered: 'Thank you, Elina. You're kind and polite.'

I remember being so excited and proud and phenomenal after hearing that so I said with a big smile: 'I was wondering that why aren't you crying? Everyone is crying but you.'

He answered back: 'First of all, stop smiling, respect the dead! Second, I am trying to cry but I can't. This is a part of growing up. You get to know the meaning of the life, your own life and once you open your eyes and understand that the life you were trying so hard to survive it was nothing all along. Once your loved ones die, you should wish that they've lived the life the way they were willing to live; if they hadn't, that would be the time you should start crying for them.'

I was too young to understand what it means, when I grew older, I understood it. I understood the meaning of my life when my grandpa died."

"Did you find it?" Oliver asked while staring at is shoes.

Angelina smiled and confirmed with warmth: "Yes."

Oliver looked up to Angelina: "How do I know if Brad lived the life he wanted?"

"Dive into your memories with him. Think about whatever he said to you, even if it was only one percent close to his dreams."

Oliver closed his eyes and tried to recall. The first memory he recalled was four months before Bradly was married:

Bradly rushed into Oliver's house and said without breathing: "Dude, dude, dude!"

"What, what, what?"

"You should meet her! You should *definitely* meet her!"

"Meet who?" Oliver asked out loud.

"Elma! The girl I met today! She is so perfect!"

He didn't take time to breathe and continued: "I'm gonna marry her, I *swear* I will marry her!"

The next thing Oliver recalled was him and Brad at the age of eleven, eating hot dogs on a sidewalk.

"You know what, Ollie? I want to have a daughter."

"Get married and that would be possible," Oliver said indifference.

"I mean, even if I don't get married, I want to have a daughter. I can even adopt one!" Brad smiled and shrugged.

"It's September. 2 p.m. I believe that you're talking out of your mind because of the climate changes!"

"You never believe me! I'm serious. It feels fantastic to have someone to wait for you at home, it gets better when that person is your daughter! Look at you, you have Olivia and she is always waiting for you to go back home."

"Okay, Liv is not my daughter and she doesn't wait for me to go home when I eat her snacks. My question is that, are you in love with my sister?" Oliver undirected the main point.

"No. Liv is like my baby sister and I only used your relationship to prove a point, which I did!"

"Oliver?" Angelina called to have his attention, "Do you know what Brad thought of life? What was his prospect?"

Oliver thought for few moments and answered to his former professor: "Life…is more beautiful and delicate than a dandelion…This is what he thought of life."

"Answer my next question, Oliver. Did he achieve his goals? Did he get what he wanted?"

"I assume yes. He wanted to marry Elma, he did; even though they failed. He wanted to be a doctor, he became a coroner, not a galaxy different. He wanted to travel to Amsterdam, he did. He learnt French and Spanish and lately Russian as he wanted…He wanted to be a father and, yeah, checked."

"Excuse me, he had a child?"

"Oh, right, you didn't know. He adopted a girl named 'Ava Florence'. I met her a couple days ago and…I had no choice but telling her about Brad."

"How did she react?"

"She cried. She promised me she'll be fine. She's a strong girl as I evaluated" Oliver smiled, "I will check on her more in further days."

"You did the right thing. Don't forget to calm her. Her mental status might not be stable for a long time and cause her a long-term effect."

"I will. I promise. I was even thinking of asking the orphanage principle to let me know if another family or someone else asked to adopt Ava; I want to be aware of the process to make sure she'll get the caring family she deserves."

Angelina smiled and said: "You're a good man. You know that Oliver, right?"

"I think I do. Now I'm…just trying not to mess anything up. Just keep everything under control."

Angelina beautifully smiled and promised: "You're old enough to know how will your hard work will result."

Oliver smiled. He said: "Yesterday, I asked all the seven suspects about their own guess."

"What was their guess?"

"No one suspects Anya and Marika. I hate to use this sentence but I should; Anya is a kid. She's *just* a kid."

"Kid? How old is she?"

"She's only twenty."

"And Marika? What about her?"

"She seems pretty harmless. I know this much is true that doctors and nurses swore to save lives; not to destroy them." Oliver opined, "Besides, she's married, living a happy life with his husband. I don't think that she'd like to ruin her marriage like this."

"What about the others? There are seven people, there should be seven votes, right?"

"Right. Sebastian got three votes. Olga, Morgan, Pietro and Theodore have one. They all got one."

"Do you suspect Sebastian more than others?"

"I'm not so sure. He seems normal. I can't judge him and I can still see an obvious sadness in his eyes."

"Oliver, what was the most important thing that you learnt in your life?"

"Judge People by their personality...Do you know what I fear the most? Arthur, my brother-in-law, he is a sergeant and he assists detective in the case, he and his team works on the case; he has a theory. He thinks that it was a group homicide. In his opinion, everyone is guilty. He's looking for evidence to prove it."

"Did he have any improvements?"

"No. Maybe yes. I don't know. I didn't buy his theory so I didn't ask more."

"You should talk to him. Ask him politely about his investigations."

"I will. And you know what? I got into a fight with Bradly's younger brother, Ezra. He said that he thinks *I* killed his brother and I'm trying to suspect someone else; that's why I have no evidence or I'm a *coward*!" Oliver frowned and crossed his arms.

"Why would he think that way? Do you have any idea?"

"No. But what if hypothetically, Ezra killed his own brother? He wasn't home when that night. He said that he was with his friend and there is no evidence but that friend!"

"What are you going to do about it?"

Oliver took a deep breath and said: "I want to accuse him. I want to accuse Ezra."

"Oliver no! That's a terrible and selfish idea!" Angelina immediately disagreed, "You're not a ten-year-old boy! Just because someone dislikes you, you can't ruin their life and accuse them by such an unforgettable charge!"

"I don't want to put Ezra in jail! I just want a proof to prove that Ezra's proof is provable!" Oliver said fast, "I don't see any selfishness in it!"

"Can you repeat it again?"

"I want to prove that…" Oliver wanted to repeat but Angelina interrupted: "Okay I got it!" Angelina said and chuckled, "But Oliver, Ezra needs to be supported now. You can't let him feel lonely."

"Mr Robert asked me to be Ezra's big brother. I'm doing it. A brother has to check on his brother!"

"Answer my question; honestly. If Ezra never told you what he said, did you wanted to check if he's telling the truth or not?"

Oliver stared at Angelina and moved his lips: "No."

Angelina stood up and said with seriousness: "Don't choose regret as a result of action. Our time is over."

***

## London's Police Department, 16:15 P.M.

"No way!" Detective Henry yelled at him, "There is no bloody way!"

Before Oliver got the chance to speak, detective said: "Stop it, Johnson! Stop it now! You're giving me migraine!"

"*You're* giving me migraine too! Stop disagreeing, Richard. You can't deny!"

Richard Henry frowned and said: "Why can't I? I am your boss and I think you're being unreasonable."

Oliver said to calm Richard: "You're right, sir. I was crossing the lines. What I'm saying is that our job is to consider all the possibilities to get an answer."

"And you're suggesting that we further our investigations by accusing the victim's family members."

"No, detective. Not members; *member*. Victim's brother, Ezra Oscar Moore."

"Oliver" detective leant back to his chair and said, "I saw Ezra a couple days ago. He looks *terrible*. He is devastated. How can he possibly be a murderer?"

"Well, you can't judge people by the look on their faces. Do you remember that case from eight years ago? The one that you spent a year solving it?"

"Sure, I do. But Bill, this one is different. Consider the fact that Ezra lost his brother. You might be wrong. How do you think he will react?"

"But…what if I'm right? What if all those seven people are innocent? What if the killer is someone who's not on the list of suspects?"

Richard put his hand under his chin and tiredly asked: "What are you trying to say?"

"I'm saying that we don't know the gender of our murderer. It could be anyone!" Oliver said with a low volume "It also could be a neighbour. Remember what that young lady with a weak eyesight said during the local investigation? She said that she went out for a walk with her dog and she forgot her glasses."

"Keep talking." Detective whispered avidly.

A satisfied smile appeared on Oliver's face. He continued: "She told us that when she was passing by Brad's house, she saw someone in front of his door but she didn't say hello because she wasn't sure if it was Brad. Brad opens the door to the person in front of it when he sees his young neighbour with her dog and says hello…What we know so far is that Brad knew the killer and let them in. Or he didn't know and the killer made his way inside in."

"You said dog, didn't Brad have a dog?"

"Yeah, Margot. I don't think she can talk," Oliver said sarcastically and rolled his eyeballs.

Detective frowned: "I meant; dogs usually bark at strangers. Has anyone heard anything?"

"No. I'll check on the neighbours again. They should be more questioned."

"What are you going to do about Ezra?"

"I won't do anything. You're my boss. What can I do?"

"This is what we'll do. We won't accuse Ezra. We just ask him to come here and talk. We must know who his witness is."

## Oliver Johnson's Car, 18:29 P.M.

Oliver finished reading the last suspect's memories of the crime scene.

He learnt the order of each suspect's arriving to Brad's house; Sebastian, Olga, Morgan, Anya, Theodore, Marika, Pietro—and Oliver.

Oliver found Sebastian's information the most useful comparing to the rest of the suspects. The others just wrote repetitious details that Oliver already knew.

Sebastian had written:

*"I received Bradly's message about 15 minutes before I got to his house.*

*When I got there, I knocked at the door but I got no answers. That was when I heard Margot, Bradly's dog barking. She was barking so unusual and I could hear her hitting the door.*

*I told her to get away from the door because I want to break in.*

*I kicked and opened the door. So, I saw him.*

*I saw Brad on the ground. I saw him in a gallon of blood. I was too shocked to say or do anything. Margot was still barking.*

*After seconds, I understood that he was stabbed. I sat next to him and checked his pulse. He was dead and his body was cold.*

*I heard Olga coming in. She was freaked out but she controlled herself better than I did. She also checked Brad's pulse. I took my phone to call for the police or an ambulance. Within a short time, the others arrived.*

*I remember telling Olga one thing: 'I didn't do it. It wasn't me.'"*

Oliver finished reading it again. Detective was right. Margot would've probably reacted to the killer who killed the man who raised her.

Margot was at Moores' house. His next stop was at Oliver's house. Margot was going to sleep at Oliver's place for a while.

Oliver texted to detective Henry: "*Sir, I must go check on Sebastian Bell now. I should ask him about the murder night.*" And sent it.

He texted another message: "*I read every suspect's memories of the murder night. I found Sebastian's memory more useful than others. Olga got there after Sebastian. I should talk to her too but I need to see* Sebastian *first.*"

Waiting for answer could've take time. Oliver called Mrs Elizabeth Hills-Moore to see if he can pick up Margot.

Elizabeth answered the phone in two seconds but she hung up the phone by saying: "I'll call you back in a minute."

He put his phone on the front passenger seat and suddenly realised that he got into a fight with Ezra a couple days ago. It wasn't cool to call her and ask for anything. It wasn't cool.

Folding his hands and looking up, Oliver talked to God: "Dear God. Father of us all. I'm willing to ask you something as your nice creature. That other creature, Elizabeth Hills, she wants to call me in a moment. I don't have the courage to talk to her because I got into a fight with her son…well, it wasn't quite a fight. I just slapped him. Anyway! If you do me this favour and dissuade her from calling me, I'll be a really nice man. I'll visit the church every Sunday, I will take every stray dogs I see to an animal protection organisation. Just please, don't allow her to call…"

Oliver stopped talking when he heard his phone rang. The caller was Elizabeth Hills-Moore.

"God?" Oliver said sadly, "I thought we have a deal."

Oliver was compelled. He answered the phone: "Hello Mrs Moore! How are you?! I was just about to call you!"

"Hi Oliver. Didn't I say that I will call you back?"

"Yes, you did," thought Oliver, "Such a shame!"

He said: "Umm…I guess I didn't hear you!"

"I see. I'm sorry anyway. I was talking to a neighbour. Your call saved me! She was talking her tongue off!"

"I'm glad! How are you?"

"Oliver," said Elizabeth, "I know about your fight with Ezra. I'm not mad at you."

"You're not?"

"Of course not. I know what did he say to you and it was impolite and rude. He had no right to say that."

"I understand. I actually didn't take it so personal. I know that he is mournful. He just lost his brother and I don't blame him for crossing the lines of respect. This isn't him talking, it's his Unconsciousness talking for him." Oliver represented a sweet speech but in reality, he was thinking very judgmental and sinisterly.

"Thank you for understanding, my dear," said Elizabeth, "So, why did you call? How can I help you?"

"I called because I wanted to know if Margot is staying with you."

"Yes, she is. We're still waiting to find a proper and responsible person to support her."

"Good luck. How is she?"

"She is fine. She is so sad, I feel. We put a picture of Brad next to her, I think it makes her feel better. She doesn't know us much but we're doing our best to make her feel like home."

"That's admirable. Elizabeth, may I ask for something?"

"Is everything alright? Is there a problem?"

"No. Everything is good. We're still interrogating the suspects. I wanted to ask you if I can bring Margot to my house so you can take some rest and, I might ask Dakota to take care of Margot. She's a dog person."

"Sure, you can. But are you sure if you can handle the responsibility?"

"Yes. It's alright. I know how to treat dogs."

"Okay. When will you come to take her?"

"How about an hour from now?"

"I'll prepare her. See you."

"Bye."

***

### Eden's Photography Studio, 19:00 P.M.

"Mr Paulson, give me a beautiful smile!"

"There is nothing in my life to smile for!" The old, fat Mr Paulson said with sulkiness.

"Okay, I'll help you. Give me the face of receiving the annual salary!"

Mr Paulson with his lampshade moustache smiled like he heard a not-laughable joke and he's trying to smile and pretend that it was delightful!

"Sir" Said Sebastian "Mr Paulson, let's try something else. Give me the smile of the first time you saw your child."

"I'm not a father."

"I want to see the exact same smile of seeing your wife in a bride dress at the Alter."

"I'm divorced."

Sebastian smiled out of compulsion. He said: "You know what? The more I'm thinking, the more I find you handsome when you're serious! Stand put, sir!"

"Seems like you're busy!" Oliver walked to Sebastian and said, "Should I come back later or what?"

Sebastian looked at Oliver, smiled and said: "Or what. I'll be done soon enough. Go find yourself a chair."

Oliver shook his head as "Yes" and started walking in the studio. That place reminded Oliver of horror movies when the main character gets killed by the villain of the movie—who is always psycho killer or a ghost!—at a photography studio.

He found a tacky chair and sat on it. Multiple boxes could be seen. Sebastian's studio was messy. A lot of papers were fell down on the floor, too many plastic glasses of coffee were covering them. A big black notebook was next to the chair Oliver was sitting on. He grabbed and opened it. It was a list of Sebastian's clients.

"Hello, Oliver," said Sebastian, "Didn't expect it but apparently you're so interested in the list of clients!"

Oliver closed the notebook and smiled: "I'm not. How are you?"

Sebastian optimistically said: "Couldn't be any more tired! You?"

"So, who was that man?"

"Mr Paulson. Mr Paul Pascal Paulson. He's a new client. As you heard, childless and divorced...No sense of humour!" Sebastian said and laughed.

"It's weird that his middle name isn't Paul!"

"I saw a Paul Paulson coming when we first met. I was so offended when he said Pascal."

They laughed.

"So, to what do I owe the pleasure?" Sebastian asked.

"I just wanted to talk."

"Alright. I just need some coffee so badly," Sebastian said and looked at all of the coffee cups on the floor, "I just don't know which one is for today!"

Oliver pointed to a cup and said: "That one. It has water steam drops on its parapet."

Sebastian looked closely at the cup and said: "I think you're right. How did you notice that?"

"I'm sort of a detective, Sebastian. I notice every single thing."

"Yeah? Like what else?"

"Like you, moving from this building."

"That's impossible! I know it's messy in here but…" Sebastian said surprisingly and Oliver interrupted him: "Who are you fooling? I know you're moving! Don't deny!"

Sebastian smiled and said: "You got me! I'm leaving."

"Why? This place is okay."

"Yeah? You should see the renting expenses!"

"Financial issues, huh?"

"Yes. I found somewhere more affordable. I realised that we might be busy, until March, at least. So, I managed to move on April first."

"Great, thank you for the respect."

Sebastian sat on the floor next to Oliver's chair and asked: "What do you want to talk about?"

"Actually Sebastian, I'm here to talk about you."

"About me?" Sebastian asked with a tiny frown "What about me?"

"About yesterday's meeting, you got three votes. More than the others. See, I don't say it's normal but it isn't abnormal for them to think like this."

"Why it isn't?" Sebastian asked sadly, "Why do you have such an idea?"

"Because, Sebastian, you were the first one to arrive to the crime scene. That's why."

Sebastian didn't say anything.

"I know you're upset and you have every right to be," said Oliver, "I don't think you're the murderer that I'm willing to recognize. But I need reason to believe it. I need you to prove it to me."

"Oliver, I appreciate your patience and I respect you for your determination to work while you've just faced a loss," Sebastian said with melancholia, "But I can't respect you for thinking that none of us is as half upset as you are. Now, I'm not talking about the other six, I'm talking about only me. I didn't know Brad so long but that doesn't make heartless and it doesn't make the fact that I found his stabbed body any less hurtful."

Sebastian held his knees in his arms and whispered: "The next time that you wanted to judge everyone for not sharing their stories of losing best friends, you might want to do a reconsideration."

Oliver bent his neck. He wanted to hear more about what he heard. He whispered: "Sebastian?"

Sebastian glanced at him. He then looked at the floor and uncovered his most tragic story: "We were thirteen, Matt and I...We met on the first day of the second grade...from that early age, he had been dealing with a major depression. Since he was five...when we were thirteen, his parents called, they said that Matt was on the rooftop. I rushed to their house. I talked to him, tried to dissuade him, I failed...he jumped off and...he became the first dead body I saw. It was just...horrible."

Oliver didn't say a thing. He was frozen. *NEVER EVER* he could see that coming.

Sebastian turned to him and whispered: "I've seen two dead bodies. Smashed or torn." He continued: "I was just a boy."

Oliver took a deep breath and said: "Sebastian, I didn't know...I'm truly deeply sorry that you had to see such a thing as a child."

Sebastian shook his head and said: "Thank you."

He continued louder: "Hey, sorry I yelled."

Oliver shook his head and said: "Forget about that. That was my bad."

## Oliver Johnson's House, 20:45 P.M.

Oliver stopped the Car and suddenly remembered where he was supposed to be!

He called Mrs Moore to tell her what a dumb boy he was!

"Oliver?"

"Mrs Elizabeth! What are the odds? I just wanted to call you!" Oliver yelled cheerfully.

"Son, you just did!"

"Did I?"

"Yes. Where are you?"

"I...am...so close to your house!"

Mrs Moore took a deep breath and asked: "You forgot to come here, didn't you?"

"Umm...maybe?"

"Ezra and Rob went outside. I'm sleepy. You have twenty minutes to be here, Oliver."

"I'm on my way!"

Oliver knocked at the door. He looked at his watch. He'd made a new record! Fourteen minutes and thirty-five seconds!

Oliver was smiling at his watch so stupidly when Robert Moore opened the door.

"Crap!" Oliver thought while still smiling so stupidly "They're back!"

"Hello, Ollie," Robert said with a smile.

"Hi. I'm here to take Margot."

"Yes, Lizzie told me about it. Come on in."

Just as soon as Oliver walked in, Margot ran to him. Oliver sat on the floor and caressed the hair of the cream Samoyed: "Look who's here! Hey Mag! Look at me! I'm going to take to my place! We'll watch the X-men all night!"

Oliver was caressing Margot when Ezra came out of the kitchen and said: "Mum? Dad? Who was knocking at the door?" He saw Oliver, "Hello Bill."

Oliver looked at Ezra and said calmly: "Hi Ezra." He stood up and asked Mrs Moore: "Where are her stuff?"

"Come with me."

Oliver followed Elizabeth to another room. On the way, Elizabeth asked: "How are you?"

"I'm still grieving but I'm okay. Thank you."

"I meant you two."

"Me and...Ezra?"

"Technically."

"Well...we're cool. I think."

"That torment hello said the opposite."

"Elizabeth, we're fine. We don't have any problems. We're adults, we'll solve it."

"Doubt it," Elizabeth whispered. Oliver didn't care.

Elizabeth sat on the floor and removed the dog's stuff from a big brown suitcase: "This is her water dish. This one's for her food. These are her toys."

Oliver wasn't listening since he had taken care of Margot times before.

"So how are you?" Oliver asked, "Do you feel any better after the last time we spoke?"

Elizabeth turned around and looked Oliver in the eyes: "No. No I'm not. I'm worse."

"Why is that? What's wrong?"

Elizabeth frowned: "Are you really asking me what's wrong? How do you dare?"

"Elizabeth…"

Elizabeth interrupted Oliver: "Don't. Don't say a word. I haven't forgotten how I saw my son. Covered in blood and cold. Every time I close my eyes, I remember that my beautiful boy's eyes are closed for ever!"

Oliver didn't say anything. Elizabeth said with her sound shivering: "So excuse me if I can't move on so easily…Don't you want to talk?"

"You told me to shut up."

"I didn't say shut up and if I did, would it mean that you have to shut up?"

"That's my job, Mrs Elizabeth. You grumble, I listen. Quid pro quo; something instead of something else. You speak and satisfy your anger; I listen and get information. This is what I've been paid for the past decade."

Elizabeth leant to the wall. Oliver said: "Talk to me. Tell me about your nightmares. Your thoughts."

She closed her eyes: "I…keep thinking of Brad. I mean like, what would he think of me if he was here? Wouldn't he make fun of me if he saw me mourning for this long?"

Elizabeth sorrowfully explained, "You might remember that when he lived with us, he hated to see anyone mourning. He would've found it useless. He used to say that a dead wants to rest, not to be disturbed by the pathetic sound of us crying…"

Oliver completed her sentence: "Unless he is a rich and paranoid old man who wants his family to inherit nothing from his property!"

"Oliver I'm thinking of ending my life. I feel like this life means nothing to me anymore. Giving him birth was nothing easy. It took me nine months to make him a heart. I protected him for thirty-two years and in less than an hour, it was all gone. His heart was ripped and all those decades of protection was all gone. I lost my boy so bloody simple."

"Beth, you thinking of ending your own life is an irrational and emotional decision that happens out of fear and guilt. You had nothing to do with this murder. What could you possibly do? The coroner confirmed that his vital signs started to disappear just after the knife reached the heart. He got attacked on his upper body sooner than we know."

"I still shiver when I remember his body was filled with stitches. How he was laying in the coffin and we put lilies next to him, you and I."

"I remember once a girl gave him lilies. Brad took an amazed look at them and said 'Lilies? These are used at funerals. I love them!' I was shocked for a long time!" Oliver said and slowly laughed at that old memory.

Oliver said: "You know, I think of killing myself at least ten times a week."

"Why is that?"

"Because I can't sleep. It drives me crazy. I have these ideas of ending my life literally every day; but then I realize that it's not over yet. My life might end any minutes now but the world doesn't stop just because I decided to end me. Whenever I think of suicide, I think of all songs I haven't listened to, movies I haven't watched, foods I've never tries, people I haven't met yet, places I haven't been to and the memories I haven't made yet…Due to my experience, people commit suicide because they're mad at the universe and relate it to themselves somehow. It makes them feel inadequate."

"I feel inadequate. I think like my effort wasn't enough to save him."

"Which is a wrong feeling…Elizabeth, just think about it; what would've Brad thought if he was still with us?"

"That mourning is stupid."

"Yes. A dead wants nothing but respect. You should respect him, he never wanted to see you like this, so devastated."

"I'm glad that we have you by our side but I'm afraid I don't see your point."

"What I mean, is that Ezra lost his big brother like two weeks ago. Can you imagine how broken he will be if witness her mother's death?"

Elizabeth didn't let any words come out of her mouth. Oliver kept talking: "Do it for Ezra. He needs his family at this very point of his life. Robert asked me to be his brother but I can't. I'm not his family. Whatever I do, how much I be there for him, he eventually needs his real family. Don't let him lose more people he cares about…I remember my grandfather, Andrew. He lost his twin brother Andres when I was a child, he lost his dog a week after. He never said out loud but he needed us at that time."

"What did you do?"

"We stayed by him. We were patient until he was alright again."

"Did he talk about it later? About his loss?"

"No. I mean…not to his children. He used to tell his grandchildren stories at noon. I, Kai, Liv, Hailey and Ewan were the most curious kids there. We used to stay up until midnight for the horror stories. He then told us about Andres."

"I remember Andrew. What a nice man he was!"

"Indeed. But this isn't about him. It's all about you and your family. Think out of the box Lizzie, like you always have," Oliver said, "Can I take Margot now?"

"Sure. Thank you for talking to me. It means a lot."

"Any time," Oliver said with a smile and left the room to the living room. Margot was sitting right in the middle of the living room. Oliver went close and sat in front of her: "Maggie, my car is in front of this house. I'm going to take you to my place and you'll be there for a while."

He fastened Margot's collar around her neck. Robert and Ezra came out of the kitchen when Oliver stood up to say goodbye: "Alright, I took her stuff. I'll take care of her until we find a new house for her...It's what he would've want."

"Do you know anyone who can handle her?" Ezra asked.

"Currently no. For now, I'm considering Dakota or Olivia or even myself. I just take her to my house to see if she can come along with any of us," Oliver answered.

"Boy, you don't need to bother yourself; just tell us if you were uncomfortable. We'll just take her," Robert told Oliver.

"My thoughts exactly. Now come on, I'll walk you out," Ezra said to Oliver.

Oliver smiled and shook his head. Said to Margot: "Come on, girl."

Margot walked to Ezra and Robert snoring. She suddenly started to bark at them so angry and bothered. They put a step back. Oliver reclined and said: "Easy, Margot, easy! Calm down!"

Margot got a little calm but she was still snoring. For a second, Oliver noticed Margot's eyes. Filled with acrimony and enmity. The way of her look at Robert and Ezra made Oliver ponder a horrifying and pathetic question for the first time...


## Oliver Johnson's Car, 21:23 P.M.

Oliver greedily took another deep breath. His night turned into a disaster. He felt nauseas and his hands were shaking. He needed to talk to someone about what he had on mind. "I'm gonna die this weekend." He thought, "My time has come. This is the end."

He looked at Margot who was sitting so innocent on the front passenger's side and said: "You can't call or help if I pass out, can you?"

Margot didn't react. Oliver still felt bad. Perhaps, they could listen to a song. Oliver turned on the car's music player and played a song that didn't fit into the time at all!

*It's a beautiful morning,*

*I think I go outside for a while*

*And just smile*

*Just take in some fresh air, boy!*

Margot pushed a button and turned it off. What a polite way to disagree!

"Thank you cotton candy," Oliver said in cold blood, "No my night sucks even more!"

Margot barked once. Oliver domineered: "Hey, my car, my songs, my rules! Get along with it! We'll see each other around! Our lives are shorter than wasting them on changing my rules!"

Margot leant her head to her right side. "Who is this psycho?" Oliver thought Margot would think.

"We're both stuck with me, for now," Oliver said while shaking his head "Here we are."

They arrived to Oliver's house. Oliver noticed his father's grey car in front of his house. It wasn't his father, probably; Edward used to visit his children's house every ten blue moons in a while. It could be Phillip or Dakota.

Oliver stopped and parked the car. Opened the front door for Margot and got off the car. Phillip and Dakota were sitting on Oliver's house's front stairs waiting for him. Phillip stood up to welcome Oliver when he saw Margot: "Hi Ollie...What...is that?"

Oliver gave him a kind smile and said: "A smart, fluffy creature called 'Dog'! She's a Samoyed. You don't really have to know what she is, she can understand that you're a human, that's enough!"

Phillip frowned: "I know, you idiot! I meant, where did you get it?"

Dakota got close to them to participate in their engaging conversation: "That's Margot. Brad's dog. Ollie, what is she doing here?"

Oliver smiled ridiculously and answered Dakota: "Hello, dear sister! Thank you, I'm fine! How are *you*? Please stop asking why I'm so pale!"

Dakota bent her head. So, kind! Oliver answered: "It was hard for Moores to take care of her. I'll take care of her until we find her a new home."

"Why was it hard? They love dogs!" Dakota said.

"Elizabeth is too tired to take care of her and she barks to Ezra and Robert." Oliver explained.

Phillip wanted to say a thing but Oliver said faster: "I said, Margot the dog, *barks* at Ezra and Robert!"

"We heard you! What's your point?" Phillip asked.

"Consider it the way I do!" Oliver said like the times he was explaining some conspiracy theory.

"We'd be please if you just say it. It's not like Margot can go tell anybody!" Said Dakota humoured.

"When animals witness a crime, such as murder…they react wildly to the guilty!" Oliver said and waited for them to confirm.

"Oliver…*No!* Oliver no! *No, no, no, no! No!*" Phillip disagreed sooner than Oliver thought.

"I said *hypothetically!*" Oliver defended himself.

"No, you didn't!" Dakota said angrily.

"Fine! But it's still discussable!" Oliver said.

"Cut the crap, Oliver. We've known them for thirty years. You're falsely accusing Robert and Ezra!" Phillip said seriously.

"They just faced a loss. Their elder son. How do you think they would think if you stopped supporting them?" Dakota said, "You're their last flicker of hope. They expect you to find a killer and to put behind the bars not to accuse them!"

Oliver didn't say a thing. Angry Dakota didn't seem quite friendly. She continued: "Enough of this conversation. We're going inside now, like three adults. We pretend like this conversation never happened. Never."

She grabbed the keys from Oliver's hand and went inside.

Oliver and Phillip stared for seconds until Phillip grabbed Margot's stuff from the behind seat and told him to come inside with Margot.

Oliver walked inside with Margot and said: "Please, make yourself at home. You're always very welcome in here…My dearest, sweetest Dakota will give you some of your food and make me something to eat and consider the fact that I will faint in thirteen minutes!"

"You have so overestimated my powers, bro," Dakota said, "I can only feed her. Mind your own hunger!"

"I'll make us something to eat," Phillip said while closing the door.

"Thanks, you," Oliver looked at Phillip and shook his head.

Phillip went to the kitchen and after a minute, sound of drawers could be heard. Oliver left Margot with Dakota to feed her and took Margot's bed upstairs. Putting it in his own room seemed like the best idea. Truth be told, Oliver wasn't an expert about taking care of dogs, he had no idea what to do. Sure, Brad had left Margot with him once or twice for a few days but this time was entirely different. Brad was gone…FOREVER.

No one was there to take Margot this time.

"What am I supposed to do?" Oliver thought, "You just need to plan for it."

Oliver abruptly realized that he's talking to himself. He kindly thought: "You're still sane a quantum. Mazel tov."

He placed Margot's bed in front of his and called detective Henry. Detective answered his phone immediately: "Yes, Johnson?"

"Hello detective. Do you have a minute?"

"Of course. Go on."

"I went to Moore's house. Margot is here at my house."

"Bradly's dog?"

"Yes."

"So what? Does she want to say hello or something?" Richard joked.

Oliver smiled: "Your funny part of soul is a little bit scary for me. We spoke about her barking."

"I remember. Did she react to Ezra?"

"That's the utmost important point. She didn't just bark at Ezra. She also barked at Robert!"

Detective chose to remain silence. He obviously was asking himself questions. He asked after seconds: "What does that supposed to mean?"

"Listen, I…I don't know. I'm not sure. Did…did you ask Ezra to come to the police department?"

"Yes. I just did. Why? Do you want to accuse Robert, too?"

"Absolutely not. We'll interrogate Ezra tomorrow. See if he can tell us anything useful."

"Oliver, you're like my son. I find it necessary to warn you that this path that you're crossing over is dangerous. Dangerous and delicate. Watch your steps."

"Thank you, Richard. We'll meet tomorrow."

"Be there at seven."

The call ended.

***

### February 25th, 22:01 P.M.

Oliver was sitting on the sofa with Dakota who was holding Margot in her arms. Oliver couldn't believe that he actually got into argue with his little sister because he didn't want to watch 'Masha and the bear'; he failed anyway.

Phillip brought them sandwiches, he didn't neglect feeding Margot and put her dish on the floor. He sat on the sofa next to Oliver and nagged: "All delicious items can be found in your kitchen and yet, you haven't gained a pound. Its fact, you're absolutely in shape."

Oliver added: "I have six packs."

"No way." Phillip said, "I don't buy it."

"Just because you don't see them, doesn't mean they don't exist," Oliver said, "Hey, you two can go sleep in the guest rooms whenever you felt tired. I'm gonna do batman."

"Can't sleep, huh?" Phillip asked.

Oliver shortly answered: "You know it."

Dakota turned to Oliver and asked: "Do you have any nightmares?"

"All the time," said Oliver, "Stop asking. Eat your food."

Phillip and Dakota didn't say anything more. They understood Oliver wasn't in the mood to speak. Oliver was too tired to talk and what are the chances? Maybe he could sleep a little!

***

### An Hour and a Half Later...

Oliver was standing in the middle of Brad's house. The house was dark and empty. What was he doing at Brad's house at that time? He closed his eyes and then he realised that he can't hear anything. It was silent in there.

114

"Hello."

Oliver turned around to see who that familiar voice belonged to. It belonged to Bradly Moore.

Far from expectations, Oliver wasn't sad, angry, upset, mad, happy or thrilled. He was surprised of not being surprised to see a walking dead in front of him.

It was him. It was actually him. Bill Oliver Johnson was seeing Bradly Anton Moore once again. Healthy, pale as usual, smiling wistfully…*Alive.*

"What are doing here?" Oliver asked with a smile frown.

"I believe that the right form of your question is that how am I here? Well, I'm not here. I'm just a duplicate image of an old memory that your subconscious use to remind you of my identity, Ollie." Bradly explained.

"Are you…dead?"

"Yes and no. I am a part of a memory."

"I'm a living piece of memory. Like when you use a yellow pencil in a grey painting. They're not the same but they suit each other."

"You're the form of how my mind remembers you?"

"There you go! Man, you're the psychologist around, don't make me explain all this thing!"

Oliver put a step fore and said: "Brad, what happened? Let me help you."

Brad stood straight and said seriously: "You can't undo what's done."

"Don't talk to me like that. I want to know who did it? Who killed you?"

Brad continued with a mysterious seriousness: "Then what? Revenge me? Become a murderer?"

"I…I will get justice for you. Brad, you died for *nothing.*"

"What? What did you say?" Bradly asked and frowned scarily "How do you know if I died for nothing? How do you know I died innocent?"

Oliver was really confused. What was Brad's point?

"Because I *knew* you. You were a good person."

"I was no saint," Bradly said after putting a step back, "And you, Ollie? You stay out of it. Leave it or become the walking dead. Don't keep on doing what bothers you."

He continued: "And don't look behind."

Oliver didn't understand what Brad said until he felt a touch on his right arm. He turned his head to see who it is when he faced a faceless person. Oliver grabbed the person's neck and…

Oliver woke up, finding himself in his living room, grabbing Phillip's throat, trying to choke him. Phillip was totally aghast. A few seconds before, he wanted to wake Oliver but then within a moment, Oliver was trying to kill him.

Oliver realised what he was doing after understanding that it was all a creepy nightmare. He let go of Phillip and folded his legs. He was afraid. He wanted to kill a murderer not his dearest uncle.

"Damn it, Oliver." Phillip touched his throat and said with no signs of anger in his voice, "What happened? Are you alright?"

"I…I don't…I didn't…Where…are we?" Oliver asked stuttering.

Phillip grabbed Oliver face and said: "Hey, look at me. Try to breathe. You were having a nightmare."

"I…didn't want…to…"

"Kill me? I know. I know." Phillip said with kindness, "Now come on, let's get you to your room."

Phillip helped Oliver stand up and took him to his room. Oliver laid on his bed after Phillip left and said: "I'll be right back." He then sat straight on his bed. He grabbed his head and put his hand through his light brown hair and ran his hand through it cruelly and greedily. He couldn't clearly analyse the situation. But he knew for one thing, his hair was growing back and that was absolutely gorgeous.

His beard but was growing. It was the rightest time to shave it.

Comparing to his nightmares before, that one seemed to real to be nightmare.

Was his nightmare a sign?

Oliver didn't really believe in dream interpretation. He had no plans on stopping doing what he was doing just because a dead told him to.

Where were they, Dakota and Margot?

If Phillip was at Oliver's house, Dakota must've been there as well. Dakota had never felt safe to be outside the house alone after ten.

Phillip came back to Oliver's room, holding a mug. He sat on the bed next to Oliver and gave him the mug: "Drink this."

"What is it?"

"Warm milk and honey. Helps you go back to sleep."

"I'm far beyond traditional hacks," Oliver said tiredly, "Just give me my medicines."

"Where are they?"

"On my desk."

Phillip brought Oliver his medicine, one pill and two tablets and Oliver took them with the warm milk. He couldn't talk. He didn't know how to justify, honestly. Phillip also kept quiet because he knew Oliver so well that he knew speaking had nothing to contribute to Oliver.

"You're wasting your time," Oliver said after a minute.

"I know."

"Then go off to bed!" Oliver said ruthless.

Phillip bent his head and said: "About before, I'm not mad. I don't want to sound reprehensible either. I cherish you and all I want to do is helping you. I hope you understand that I can contribute nothing if you don't speak."

Oliver leant to the bed's headboard slat and whispered: "I'm alright."

Phillip sat on the bed next to Oliver and said: "Ollie, don't lie to me…Look, I was five when my parents told me that Ruth was expecting a baby and four months after, Robbie was crying in our living room. Then Kai and Hailey and Joe and then came you. You entered my life and you saved me, countless times. When I was injured, when I was sad, when I lost my dad. It is my duty to take care of you not just because I'm your uncle but because we're more than that, Oliver. We're brothers. I never felt like I have a brotherhood with Edward, Simon, Hugh, or even Steve but you and I, we were brothers since the beginning. You can't lie to your brother."

Oliver didn't say anything.

Phillip continued: "There's a visible, deniable difference between you and all the people I know. You always heal, no matter what. You don't wait for someone else to pick up your broken pieces off the ground because you do it sooner than anyone does. In this situation even, I know you'll be back on your feet again. Soon or late."

He took a sad, deep breath, stood up and whispered: "Good night, Ollie."

"I'm sorry," Oliver said shamefully "I truly am."

"Don't be. You're a human being. You have a legitimate right to be dumb. You're *not* perfect. No one is."

He walked outside the room saying: "Just try to sleep, okay?"

Oliver covered himself under his blanket and closed his eyes, wishing for a nightmare-free sleep.

## 5:25 A.M.

Oliver did his best but he couldn't get back to sleep. It was too annoying and boring. Not being able to control your bedtime, having a sick brain that wakes you up by its own discretion and you, being so compelled to do something about it was awful. Oliver understood that years ago.

He got out of the bed and looked around to find his phone. It was probably in the living room. "Will it seem so mean if I wake them up now?"

Oliver thought, "Or they will just think that I wanted to make sure that they're alive?"

He went to see which room Dakota was sleeping at. He found her sleeping in the room adjoining to Oliver's. He slightly got close to her and whispered: "D, hey, Dakota."

She didn't response. He asked again: "Are you awake?"

Dakota started talking angrily in a low volume: "I'm awake. What do you want? What time is it?"

"Oh, hi baby. I thought you're dead!" Oliver said with a stupid smile.

"Ollie, why in *heavens* would you think that? What time is it?"

"No reason. Just for fun. I don't know, my phone is not with me but I think it's like five or six."

"Oliver! Just get out!"

"Fine! You don't deserve my anxiety! I'm going to work. Tell Phillip when you wake up."

Oliver's next stop was the living room, where he found his phone on the sofa. He grabbed it and texted Arthur: "*Are you awake?*"

He received an answer just in seconds: "*Yeah man. Morning.*"

"*Why are you awake?*"

"*I was asleep the whole afternoon and evening yesterday.*"

"*I'm going to the department. I'll pick you up. We'll be back to my place for lunch. Leave the car for Olivia.*"

"*Okay. I'll be ready in ten minutes.*"

"How did everything happen?" Oliver thought for a moment, "How did we became brothers-in-law?"

**Flashback: 13 December 2016, 16:12 P.M.**

Olivia was sitting on a white chair in front of a huge mirror, watching a movie with Dakota when the hairstylist was straightening her hair and her mother was crying cathartic. Meanwhile, Oliver walked into the bride's room with the Margarita pizza that Olivia ordered. He knocked at the door and walked in; seeing his mother crying just before her older daughter's wedding wasn't the exact same thing, he expected a mother would do!

"Is she still crying?" Oliver asked with no certain feelings.

"You see. You hear," Olivia said in cold blood, "Although, I think she was faking those last tears."

Eighteen-year-old Dakota humoured: "Of course she was. We're all so happy that you're leaving that I don't even have the ability to describe it with words!"

"*Silence!*" Kathrine said to Dakota violently "How can you be happy about your sister leaving us?"

"Easy. Like when Ollie left our house! Life gets much easier when your siblings aren't around!" Dakota explained.

"She has a point, Mum. Life really got easier when I left. At least I could eat a whole pizza all by myself and no one was trying to wake me up on a Saturday morning with a vacuum cleaner!" Oliver defended Dakota.

Katherine said seriously: "This sort of attitude is rude, discourteous, inappropriate and unacceptable! You three should have a conversation with your father!" And she left the room.

Oliver gave Olivia the pizza and leant to the wall. What he was trying to figure out was the answer to the question 'Why do men get so emotional when they see their sisters getting married?'

Sure, their marriage was about to change some stuff but they were still siblings. Nothing was going to change about that. Was it?

Oliver wasn't acting emotional. As long as Olivia was satisfied with her choice, so was Oliver.

"Do you really want to get married?" Olive asked somewhere out of nowhere.

"Huh?" Olivia looked at Oliver and asked.

"Nothing. Forget about it."

"Do I *really* want to get married? Nah, I'm good." Olivia joked.

"What?" Oliver asked surprisingly.

"Don't get me wrong. I mean…Imagine that you get in some argue with someone, you block their number, you remove all of their social network accounts on your phone and they just open the door and come in and ask for food!" Olivia said, "It's *insane*. Marriage is like wonderland! I mean—how could Mum and dad keep on with this whole marriage thing?"

Oliver laughed and said: "They found it so interesting that they had me the year after!"

Dakota said: "And they didn't see that their children were mistakes until I arrived." She asked: "How long has this been going on?"

"It'll be thirty-one years this March." Olivia answered, "It doesn't sound terrifying until a year from now when people start asking us when we are going to have kids! Aren't I right you…hairstylist?"

"My name is Anika" the hairstylist said confused, "Olivia, I've been doing your makeup and hair for almost two hours. How can you not know my name?"

Olivia said: "Anika, I…don't think you told me your name."

"Well; fair enough. Now, don't move your head." And she went back straightening Olivia's hair again.

"How's Arthur anyway?" Olivia asked with her mouth full of pizza.

"He's nervous. Like panicking!" Oliver said with a big smile on his face "He is afraid he can't stand your belle and sincerity!"

## 27 Minutes Ago

"Baa, baa, black sheep

Have you any wool?

Yes, sir, yes, sir

Three bags full." Arthur was singing while tying his tie.

"One for the master

And one for the dame

One for the little boy

Who lives down the lane." Oliver continued the song.

"Two 10-year-olds that one of which is getting married and the other one is his best man!" Edward said while walking in the room.

"Mustn't you be nervous?" Edward asked Arthur.

"No. I'm fine. Thanks for the fret." Arthur answered and went back to tying his tie.

"I meant; you *must be*. It's Olivia you're marrying. She's precious. She is like…Cleopatra!" Edward said.

"Yeah. Dad? Cleopatra isn't the best example to describe my sister's specialty," Oliver said to make him a point.

"Why? What is it?" Edward looked at two of them waiting for answers.

"She married not one but two of his brothers. That's why." Arthur answered Edward in cold blood, not even offended.

"I'm not a historian. I'm the bride's father. And Black, if you ever, *ever* hurt my daughter emotionally or physically, I'll cost your family a funeral and a spread investigation in the Pacific Ocean. Watch your actions." Edward warned and left the room.

Arthur smiled: "I like your old man. He's discreet."

Oliver put his forearm on his eyes and said: "He is, for his daughters only." He continued: "But for real, why aren't you nervous?"

Arthur observed his hair closely in the mirror and asked: "When was the last time you saw me nervous, Ollie?"

"Never?"

Arthur turned back to him and said: "Exactly. When you're a cent percent sure about something and you accomplish it, you've got nothing to be nervous about."

Oliver presented a speech: "Arthur, for almost twelve years, I've had you as a friend by my side. In three hours, we'll no longer stay friends because we'll become family. So as a family member of mine, as my causal brother, I need you to protect Olivia with who you are and what you are. Arthur, I did my best not to be the reason of her concern and I did it successfully. Olivia loves you mystically. You're the one for her. Take care of her while I can't because she is everything I have."

Arthur smiled: "Wow, Oliver. It was, beautiful and…it just means a lot to me that you're trusting me with your everything and seeing me as your family…I want you to know that I couldn't do it without you. You're my brother, Oliver. Forever. You'll never see her blue face. None of us will."

"That's all I needed to know," Oliver said with a beautiful smile on his face. He stood up, "Welcome to the family, Arthur...Are you ready to get married?"

Arthur went to the door and opened it: "Not without taking some hot chocolate but hell yeah!"

They went out of the room and started walking towards the hallway. Oliver said: "You know...I have something to say. Something that you should know."

"Is it good or bad?"

Oliver shrugged: "Equal."

"Go on."

"Liv...Might act a little bit weird sometimes. Mostly when she's frustrated."

"And that weirdness is good or bad?"

"Equal!" Oliver said, "The best description is living with a civilized person. Imagine it, did you?"

"Uh-huh."

"Now throw that imagination into a wastebasket!"

Arthur stopped: "What does that supposed to mean?"

"Look! I've said a lot! Believe me, it's not that bad! You'll get used to it!" Oliver warned "Just don't make her that angry."

Arthur looked at him like a father looking at his son while watching his son taking a fish out of its aquarium to breathe and asked: "Oliver? You *do* realize that half an hour before a wedding ceremony is *not* the best time to tell a man how weird his wife can be, don't you?"

"I would've felt bad if I didn't tell you, okay? Now that you know, you have no legitimate right to divorce my sister unless you want to be dead!"

"Your timing is magnificent, Bill...Shouldn't you go out to get Liv's pizza for her?"

"Crap!" Oliver suddenly realized that he had a pizza to deliver.

Oliver rushed out to get the pizza he ordered an hour ago...


**A little while later at the bride's room...**

"Is he? I thought he is the one to be calm!" Dakota said.

"Ollie? What did you tell him?" Olivia asked Oliver with her suspicious tone.

"I said everything he needed to know. I'm your brother. It's my duty to make him understand some stuff," Oliver indiscreetly said.

"Can't disagree with that but please…don't scare the crap out of him! I'm not interested to look for a sneaked-out groom!" Olivia frowned.

"Don't worry. He is literally illuminated that he can't leave you!" Oliver said with a giant smile.

"Why do you think I was named Dakota?" Dakota asked somewhere out of nowhere.

"Dearest sister, you're now old enough to know the truth," said Olivia, "You weren't always meant to be Dakota. You were supposed to be Philadelphia."

"But Mum changed her mind at the very last moment. She believed that it would sound weird if we call you Philly." Oliver kept on with Olivia's humour.

"That was when we suggested names such as Texas, Florida, Alaska, Virginia, Pennsylvania, Montana, Indiana, Georgia, Arizona, Minnesota, Louisiana, Nebraska, Delaware and Vermont," Olivia explained.

"But Mum came up with 'Dakota'. That's when Dad asked, 'North or south?' Mum got really mad!" Oliver said with his eyes wide open.

"Are you guys alright? Do you need medical attention?" Dakota asked her two older siblings.

"She doesn't believe us Ollie. She's avoiding to accept the truth," Olivia said sadly to Oliver.

"I see. It's sad. I look at this young girl and all I can think of is that 'She didn't believe when we revealed that she was adopted and now she avoids believing the truth about her name!'" Oliver said unfortunate.


## End of the Flashback

Oliver smiled. The day of Olivia's wedding was a busy but great day. Oliver was glad that Arthur is the man who's marrying his sister. He knew Arthur for a long time, long enough to know that Arthur is the one and only for Liv.

Oliver made himself a cup of coffee and changed his clothes. He was ready to go. It was an unusual time for Arthur and Oliver to go to the police department. Night shift officers would've been pretty confused!

Streets were empty and if not, a person or two could be seen. Oliver tried to drive slowly to wake no one. The greatest thanks to his insomnia, he was crazy about sleeping. Who doesn't like to sleep? So as a result, he hated to bother anyone's sleep. Not even his nemesis! And as the old generation said: "Prefer what you prefer for people as well."

Oliver arrived at Arthur and Liv's house after fifteen minutes. Arthur was walking in the front yard with his arms behind him. He went to Oliver's car right after seeing it. After sitting in the car, Arthur exhaled and asked: "Ten minutes, huh?"

Oliver smiled and started to drive.

Arthur grumbled: "What took you so long? Even an arctic deer can't stand this amount of frost."

"And you, my friend just proved that you are more than a deer. Congrats," Oliver said in cold blood. He did it on purpose. It's mostly annoying when someone says something funny in cold blood.

"My brother-in-law is an orang-utan. Honour's mine."

Oliver changed the subject: "Colton is so damn lucky to have Mary-Kate. That woman is divine."

Arthur leant his head to the window and closed his eyes: "Colton is Married to Annie. Katie's still single."

"Anyway. How's Benny?"

"Don't call my brother by his nickname like you guys are best friends."

"How do you know if we aren't? I know Benedict, Benedict knows me." Oliver justified "There's always a secret between the people you know that it's decided not to be told to you!"

"Keep driving or I'll throw myself off the car!"

Oliver smiled. He had won a morning argue.

The police department was also deserted. Officers were setting a couple teens free. Oliver looked at the teens and said to Arthur: "We've never done what this generation does, have we?"

"Nope." Arthur answered, "They mustn't be banned too much but someone should bring them to their senses."

As soon as they walked into the building and old cop who Oliver believed his name was "Murphy" welcomed them: "Sergeant Black! Good morning! It's too early sir, may I ask what you are doing here?"

"Detective Murphy, hi. Yes, you may. I had some reports to complete and Mr Johnson asked to see the coroner for a case. I'll try to set them a date." Arthur answered, "What are *you* doing here? I thought you'll be a week off."

Detective Murphy smiled sadly: "Marriage issues."

"I hope you can work them out. See you." Arthur said and went to his office. Oliver followed him.

"I don't want to see the coroner," Oliver said, "I don't need to."

"Yes, you do. I want you to." Arthur disagreed, "This Coroner was Bradly's former co-worker. He checked Brad's body after the murder. I've met him few times before the funeral. You can talk to him for more information. Plus, Richard won't have the time to."

"And how do you know if he will inform me more?"

"He will not inform *you*. He will inform *us*. We'll go together."

"Arthur, did my mum ask you to do this? Did she ask you to be my nanny?"

Arthur frowned: "Nanny, Oliver? I'll put it on the process of the healing of your pains. Don't be so ingrate. We want to help you. Get out of your safe area and get some help."

Oliver was so ashamed at that moment. Arthur was right. He had every right to say what he said.

Oliver's greatest weakness was not getting help from anyone. He hated to get help. He used to do what he knew he can get done by himself but about what he couldn't do, he desired to figure out a way to do it.

Getting over the death of a person that close wasn't exactly what Oliver knew how to deal with it. Of course, Oliver was a crime psychologist and he usually had to comfort a family who was facing the murder of a loved one. But when it came to himself, Oliver didn't know how to feel, how to react, how to get over it or what to do to feel alright again.

Like all his knowledge was underground with Brad.

"The potter drinks water with a broken jar of water;" the point of this anecdote is that people do a better effort for people than themselves. This can describe Oliver.

Oliver went out to the coffee house in front side of the street to buy a cup of coffee for Arthur.

He went to Arthur's office, where Arthur was writing things down. Oliver put the cup on Arthur's desk and said: "There you go."

Arthur didn't look at Oliver. He kept staring at the computer. He asked seriously: "What for?"

"What do you mean?"

"Why did you buy me coffee?"

"Because I wanted to apology and confess that you were right. I insulted."

"Oliver" Arthur turned his chair and looked at Oliver, "The greatest apology would be asking for help...But coffee's fine. Thank you."

"This isn't coffee. It's white chocolate." Arthur said after drinking a gulp. He looked at the cup and continued: "Yes, it is and it's for...Bryan whose name was written with an 'I'."

"Is it?" Oliver asked, "I wonder how would do they write your name!"

"They write it the way I pronounce it. 'Uther'. You're written 'Uliver' I think."

"I think they do...Who is Brad's co-worker?"

"A thirty-two-year-old coroner named 'Ennis Arnálds'. His father is an Icelander and her mother is British. He wrote a complete report for Brad's case. The one you studied. I think a conversation might be useful. We'll see him this afternoon and you're sleeping at our house tonight."

"Ummm...I'm, not staying at your house. I brought Margot to my house until we find someone to take care of her."

"You're not given a choice. You have sleep issues; you choke people when you wake up. Olivia and I think you should stay with us for a few days so we can take care of you."

"Cut it out, man. I said no."

"Who are you, batman?" Arthur said back, "You can't handle everything by yourself. You're not an omnipotent!"

"Arthur, I don't need help! Especially with my insomnia!"

"Oliver! We went through this conversation twenty minutes ago! Let go of it!"

"Listen to me!" Oliver yelled, "Do it just a minute for the sake of God!"

He continued: "Yes, I do need help to get rid of this awful feeling...to get rid of this mourn but just this! You're not in charge of putting me to sleep! Let me take care of that!"

"Dude, you're becoming a maniac! Don't let your job take all of your thoughts and time and life for itself. Give yourself a break."

"I'm good. I don't need to get rest. I'm just doing my job."

"I perceive that. But you don't have to take it so hard. We can't always finish out job the way we should. That's why so many cases remain unsolved. I, Oliver...us...you and I have two cases that we failed solving them. A teenage girl's killer got bedridden in a mental hospital. Remember that? Brandon Grison didn't get his execution while we knew he deserved it!"

Arthur calmly continued: "Not everyone can be saved Ollie. Not everyone get justice. I don't like it; I hate it but I can't refuse accepting it."

"Excuse me but I don't really understand what you're saying. What you're trying to say is that...I'm not able to get justice for my best friend?" Oliver asked surprised.

"No, Oliver. What I'm willing to say, is that you can't take responsible for everything that happens in the universe. You can't blame yourself for the extinction of dinosaurs, global warming, Pluto getting out of solar system or the death of Elvis Presley. Convince yourself that you don't have to tolerate everything. Take responsibility for anything that gets done. I'm trying to prepare you for the worst. I'm trying to teach you that there are two scenarios as a result of what we do; whether it all goes wrong or it goes right. There's no situation between these two."

Arthur took a deep breath and continued: "Ollie, we're all seeing you are doing your best, your best to find out who the killer is and you have our utmost respect for your efforts. I know you think you owe this to Brad because you weren't there for him to save him but you shouldn't think that way. This thought is poisonous. What could you possibly do? See, Sebastian got there first but Brad was almost dead at that time. There was nothing anyone could do. Would you please, for the love of God, stop being stupid?"

"Can you accompany me to the cemetery this afternoon?" Oliver asked innocently after a few seconds of Arthur's perfect speech.

"Sure. No doubt. When?"

"Three. Three is fine. Then we'll go talk to Arnálds."

"And...you'll come to my house, won't you?" Arthur asked while hoping to get a 'Yes'.

"And then I'll come to your house. Yes. I just..."

"I'll make sure your parents take care of Margot."

"Thank you...I appreciate it. Isn't detective Henry here yet?"

Arthur checked his watch and answered: "He'll be here in twenty minutes."

Oliver leant his hand to Arthur's desk and asked: "I need a piece of advice. What should I do about Ezra and Robert?"

"You mean…what should you tell them about accusing Ezra? Oh well—you don't really have to say that it was your idea. You don't have to say anything about it at all, not until they ask."

"But what if they do?"

"We've been through this before. This doesn't count as an accusation. We'll be asking him questions. That's it."

All of a sudden, Oliver nervously said: "This whole thing, it was terrible idea. I'm calling them now to say that there was mistake."

Arthur frowned at him and whispered threatening: "You woke me up at five to accompany you here. And now what? You're just giving up?"

"You said that you were asleep the whole day!"

"I did because I was off today. I wasn't supposed to be here today."

Oliver got away from the table and flounced in the room: "Alright, this is it. I'm sick of this attitude. I hate it when everyone acts like I'm some sort of psychopath who shouldn't be left alone for a second because he might hurt himself. The death of my best friend isn't something casual and normal in my life but that doesn't mean I have no control over it."

Arthur tried to say a sentence: "Listen Ol…"

Oliver snapped: "No, *you* listen! How the hell do any of you expect me to heal when you don't even give me the time to? I'm not a child!"

Arthur was paralysed for almost a minute. He tried not to get mad or yell. He said with the calmest voice he could. He wasn't exactly successful anyway: "Since you're alright, Ollie, tell me why haven't taken your sedatives in a week? Why Phillip called me to say that your medicine box was full? Why did you wake up chocking him? Huh? Why did Dakota tell me that you talk while sleeping? Why did Marika Lensher told me that you were acting like an addicted at your house?"

Oliver had no answers for him. Arthur continued: "You know, I've been thinking a lot lately. Maybe I shouldn't have gathered your sisters and parents to talk to them about you. Maybe I shouldn't have told them to take it easy on you, to give you some time to figure out what's going on around you and to get back on your feet. I shouldn't have asked Phillip to leave his job and come here to cheer you up because he is your favourite uncle…I shouldn't have asked anyone for anything. I must've allowed everyone to interfere. To bother you with their disgusting conversations about life's going on and you shouldn't waste your time on mourning…I did it anyway and you know why? Because I didn't want to walk into your house and see a body with cut veins. I didn't want you to freak out and do something irreparable."

Arthur said and walked out of his office. Oliver was alone in the office.

He gave it some time and noticed three things that he'd never noticed before: Arthur being so mad at anyone; Oliver being so regret and ashamed of judging with lack of information; Arthur doing a serious intervention about someone or something irrelevant to his job.

Oliver sat on the desk and stared at the floor. He thought about what Arthur said over and over again. He focused on every word Arthur said. How was he so blind?

How come he never noticed any of that? The family that Oliver was raised in, was a family that preferred solving its problems by interventions and family discussions; Oliver's best and oldest friend was dead, murdered, his life was gone; and Oliver's family decided to do nothing? Decided to leave Oliver with himself and his feelings? They've decided to give Oliver space and never made an advisory speeches?

Of course, it was for Arthur. Arthur wasn't just Oliver's friend and brother-in-law at this whole time. Arthur was his dearest saviour.

He must've apologized.

Oliver left the office to the hall. He couldn't find Arthur there. He couldn't find him in the kitchen, the second floor or the restroom.

He was returning to the office disappointedly when he thought of one more place, the interrogation room. He went to the interrogation room and looked inside of it through the one-way mirror. Arthur was interrogating a teenage boy.

Oliver could hear them.

Arthur bent to the table and said: "Listen, Hartley. I'm not that kind of a person. Tell me who gave you those drugs and I might be able to rescue you from—let's say, two years of prison."

The boy who was named 'Hartley' arranged his black tapered undercut hair and said: "What do I call you?"

"Sergeant Black."

"Sergeant Black, sir. I don't know who gave the drugs to me. I didn't see his face. He just came to me and gave me the package."

"I know that part. You said it three times. Skip to the important part," Arthur said bored.

"There was an address on the package. I delivered it. The address belonged to a lady. She called the police and that's how I got here and you're scaring the crap out of me!"

Arthur leant back to the chair and said: "So this is what happened. You woke up at 5 a.m. and decided to go out for a walk, so normal. Then a person came and gave you that package; somewhere out of nowhere. You didn't follow to see who that person is and your honour told you to deliver the package?"

"Yes sir. This is exactly what happened."

Arthur covered his face with his hands and said: "Hartley, Hartley. I face at least two teenagers every day who tell me the same story as you're now,"

He put his hand under his chin and continued: "how do you expect me to believe that?"

Oliver opened the room's door and said: "Sergeant Black, can I see you outside?"

Arthur looked at Hartley and said: "Boy, I'll be back in ten minutes. I would welcome your honest answer, not some dumb story you learnt from some movie."

Arthur said and came outside. Oliver asked: "Who is he? What did he do?"

"Who? Hartley? A women called like thirty minutes ago. He said that this boy brought a package to her door. The package was carefully covered in tape and papers."

"What was it?"

"A hundred milligrams of diazepam. I interrogated her. She has no idea about the drugs with her address on them. We checked her financial records, there is no evidence of buying illegal drugs. She's now in the lab. I told Larry to do some tests and now if you excuse me, I have more questions to ask Hartley."

"Okay, just please, don't scare the boy because you're mad at me."

"I'm not mad at you."

"Oh, yes you are."

"I'm disappointed, not mad." Arthur said, "Richard must arrive any seconds now. Go wait in front of the station."

And he went back into the room again.

At that point, Oliver wanted nothing more than screaming so loud. What was the matter with everyone?

"Maybe The problem is me," Oliver said out loud.

***

## 42 Minutes Later...

Robert Moore was waiting in the hall while Oliver, Arthur and detective Henry were interrogating Ezra.

With the clock running, Robert was losing his patience. He had no idea why he was there. He had no idea why Ezra was being interrogated. Back in high school, Ezra was a bit of a troublemaker kid. He had the golden ticket of visiting the headmaster's office two to four times a week!

No one even thought that Ezra will become an Aerospace engineer with the Stanford University certificate!

From the very first day that Ezra started his education in California, Robert and Elizabeth Moore expected him to call and say: 'I just broke a nose!'

It never happened.

He educated so damn well and graduated proudly.

This time was different. This time wasn't about two kids fighting. This was the time that Bradly Moore was dead and no one had the answer to the question: 'Who killed Bradly Moore?'

Even a three-year-old could realise that the police wanted to interrogate Ezra because they thought that he killed his own brother. Pathetic! Pathetic, dumb and irrational!

Why would anyone kill his own brother? And if someone killed his brother, why would he be so upset and broken about his death?

"Ezra didn't do it," Robert thought, "I know he didn't kill Brad."

As Robert was being worried, Ezra's interrogation was going on.

"Okay, Ezra. I know this situation might seem uncomfortable and confusing for you. Don't consider this conversation as an interrogation." Oliver started the conversation.

"Shouldn't I?" asked Ezra with a sarcastic volume.

"Ezra, this choice wasn't made by a single person. My investigating team needs more information to focus on a suspect or two. There are seven suspects and they're all somehow connected to the murder. Focusing on every single one of them takes too much time and we don't want the case to be cold." Arthur explained to Ezra, hoping that he wouldn't get anything wrong.

"I understand your point, Sergeant Black. But you know what I think? I think you and your team were given a standard time to work on the case. You just haven't solved it yet because you are not using the bests," Ezra opined.

"We *are* using the bests, I assure. But we can't rely on a source or two. It's not like searching a book's list to understand the chapters. It takes time and Bradly's case is our top priority," Arthur explained.

Ezra said: "Still, I don't think you're doing your best. You're all professionals, I understand. But the effort might not be enough." He said, "I don't know, maybe I'm not aware of anything."

Richard didn't allow them to argue more. He said seriously: "Enough. Both of you. Don't waste time. This isn't what Brad wanted. Ezra, you're going to answer every single question with no aberrations."

Arthur asked the first question: "Where were you and what were you doing between 22:24 to 22:50 p.m.?"

"I was at a friend's house that night. I arrived at his house at 8 p.m. and I left when my dad called me to come here. I think it was half past 11," Ezra answered like Richard wanted, without aberrations.

"Who is your friend? Can he witness that you were with him the whole time?" Oliver asked.

"His name is Sean Gwan. He's English-Korean. Yes, he can because we watched football together that night."

Richard asked: "Which teams were playing that night?"

"Liverpool and Arsenal."

"Do you know any of the suspects?" Arthur asked.

"Yes, I do. I do know some of them." Ezra answered Arthur's question.

"Which one of them? How do you know them?" Arthur asked again.

"I know…Olga, that Norwegian nurse…Oh and I know Pietro."

"Tell us about them," Oliver said to Ezra.

"Pietro is extremely talented. He's a musician, as you know. I accidentally understood about him. I was surfing Brad's social media accounts when I saw Pietro's account" Ezra explained, "The next thing I remember is that Brad called me on the phone and asked me not to panic. He said that he broke his ankle and he also told me that our parents shouldn't know about it. I went to the hospital to bring him back home. There was a nurse that took care of him overnight, it was her; I think her name was…Maria?"

"*Marika*," Oliver said to correct Ezra.

"Yes! Marika," Ezra said, "We met Olga at the same time; we met her when we went to pick up our young cousin, Louis, from his Russian class. We met her two more times together. One time, we were at the airport and the weather was stormy. We saw her and suggested to go the airport's café and wait for our travellers to arrive."

"When was the next time?" Oliver asked.

"Brad and I were walking and we ran into her."

"Why were you at Sean Gwan's house that night?" Richard Henry asked.

"We spend so much time together. As I told you, we were watching football when my dad called me." Ezra answered. He was getting a little bored.

"Tell us more about the suspects. Pietro and Marika. Didn't you spend more time with them?" Arthur asked Ezra.

Ezra spent the next few moment thinking and said: "Pietro and I met when Brad took me to some opera to watch Pietro's performance. I went out with Pietro a couple more times. We once had dinner together" said Ezra "I haven't seen Marika since the hospital…sorry, sorry. I saw her the night I came here. The night that Brad died. She as sitting in the hallway and Sergeant Black was covering her with a blanket. I stood in front of her at the other side of the hallway for a second. Our eyes caught each other. She was crying. I haven't seen her since that night."

"Is there anything else that we should know about Olga?" Arthur asked about Olga.

"No…I…I'm not sure…I don't think so," Ezra said with his voice shivering, trying so hard not to cry for his poor, dead brother.

"Ezra, tell me, did Brad ever mentioned *anything* that might help?" Arthur asked him.

"Like what?" Ezra asked Arthur.

"Like, did he say that he was having problems with each one of the suspects? Didn't he say anything weird? Something like a code that you didn't understand at that time?" Arthur explained to Ezra.

"Sergeant, I'm not sure if this is a code or similar; but two days before he died, we talked on the phone and he said…he said that he wasn't alright," Ezra said and started crying silently.

Detective Henry was a man with low emotions but Ezra crying about his dead big brother, broke his heart. Like I said, man with low emotions; he asked in cold blood: "Ezra, please focus."

Ezra wiped tears off his face and said: "You're right, detective. Let's continue, shall we?"

"Yes. Ezra tell us, what did Brad say after he said that he wasn't alright? What did you answer?" Oliver asked.

"I asked him 'what do you mean?' then he ditched me. He said, 'I have to go rip a dead's chest open.' I called him later that day but his assistant, Ennis picked up the phone and he told me that Bradly was working." Ezra recalled the memory.

"Didn't you ask him about what he said later?" Oliver asked louder than he expected.

"Yes, Mr Johnson. I did. We had dinner at our parents' house that night. I asked him about what he said and he ditched again. He said that he was fine. He didn't even say that it was a joke and two days after...I lost him. I lost Bradly." Ezra answered.

Arthur breathed deeply and crossed his arms: "What about your parents? Did Brad say anything abnormal to them?"

"I don't know, Sergeant Black." Ezra said, "My father made it very clear to me that we are not allowed to talk about Brad with my mum."

"What do you mean? Why doesn't Robert allow you to talk to Elizabeth about Brad?" Oliver asked with a tiny frown.

"He believes that people talk about Brad enough. It's a lot of pressure like a piano on her back. He told me that we should be her safe place after Bradly is...gone. He said that I should be the shoulder that Mum can be able to rely on and me talking about Bradly and renewing her memories of her dead son isn't helpful; at least not for now," Ezra answered sadly.

"Why Margot barks at you and Robert?" Richard asked Ezra. He was too bored to take emotions.

Ezra looked at Oliver like 'what the hell did you tell these people?' but he answered anyway: "It was like, the first week that we brought Margot to our house and I didn't allow her to sleep in my room; you know, she confused me with Bradly and then I forgot to feed her twice...I was in the worst situation ever. I was impatient and sleepy and dizzy and drunk all the time."

"What about Robert?" Detective Henry asked.

"Because my father is allergic to dogs and cats. Even when Bradly was alive, Dad didn't go visit him at his place or if he did, Bradly had to keep Margot in a room. Robert is some kind of a stranger to Margot. An outsider," Ezra answered.

"Okay," said Arthur. "thank you for your cooperation, Ezra. Gentleman, if there are no more questions on your mind, we're done."

"May I leave?" Ezra asked slowly in a low volume.

"You may. Detective Henry will escort you out." Arthur said to Ezra.

Richard stood up and walked Ezra out. Oliver and Arthur stayed in the room for a couple more minutes until Oliver stood up and Arthur grabbed his forearm and asked: "What the hell do you think?"

"Huh?"

"What the hell do you think? Tell me about all the crap that's on your mind."

"Arthur, you can at least give me time to think of this cumbersome conversation," Oliver said miserably.

"Ollie, can I do an intervention right now right here?"

"Yeah, go on Erik Erikson!" Oliver said ridiculously.

"You are wasting time. I hate to but I must say it, this case is complicated but you're not using your intelligence either! You're smarter than that and I know it. You only have nineteen more days to at least get to some point! You have less than three weeks. Use the days, don't lose them."

"Sure, I will" Said Oliver, "I'll have lunch with Ava today. I had to check her drawings but I kept postponing that. Then I'll see Olga to see if she can tell me something more. After a very long and exhausting day, you and I will finally buy some dinner and go back to your house and spend a calm night with my beautiful sister."

"Yeah, that we can't do."

"What we can't do?"

"Spend time with your divine sister. Olivia is going to a baby shower with your mum and Dakota."

"Are they? Who is the party for?"

"Some woman named 'Jessie;' I think."

"Uh-huh. So, we're on our own."

"Yes, we are. Just answer me. Why do you need Ava's drawing?"

"Because children's drawing can explain a lot about their mental situation."

"Do you know how to interpret a child's painting?"

"No. No, I don't. But a friend of mine can. Do you remember Jessica Brandon?"

"I don't seem to recall her."

"Sure, you don't. We had some mutual friends and classes back in college" Oliver explained, "She's a child psychologist. She will interpret Ava's drawing for me."

"Alright. Why do you want to talk to Olga? Why her?"

"Sebastian was the first one who arrived at the crime scene. Olga was the second one. I want to know what she saw. I should talk to her outside of the meetings so she won't feel uncomfortable."

"Okay, as you wish. Have you called her? Does she know you want to meet her?"

Oliver smiled and said: "She has no idea. I don't even have her number. Which is why you're going to find it for me now."

"My friend, you don't have her number and she doesn't know that you want to meet her in like, four hours?"

Oliver looked at her watch and said: "It is 9 o'clock. I'll go pick up Ava in two hours. I should call the orphanage. Would you call Phillip and Dakota? Tell them to make some lunch for themselves."

Arthur bent his head and asked: "Is anyone aware of your plans or is it just you and me?"

"It's just you and me. Olga will find out in a minute and I'll let Jessica know as soon as you find me her number."

"Haven't you been in touch with her for the past ten years?"

"Oh, I was. We see each other every year for some college reunion or something else and she also invited me to her wedding last year."

"Did you go?"

"Yep. It was the wedding that I had a flu for the next two weeks after."

"What a fortunate wedding!" Arthur said with a huge amount of fake joy "So, Mr Obama, your honour, when will you honour us with allocating some time to discuss the latest interrogation of Ezra Moore?"

Oliver coughed and became the serious casual Oliver. He said: "Now. We'll discuss it right now. I'm just waiting for Richard to return. I don't want to meet Robert. Not today."

"Approved," said Arthur. "Aren't we going out of this room?"

"No. Why?"

Arthur shrugged: "Nature's calling me."

Oliver glared at Arthur and whispered: "Go spend a penny."

***

### 7 Minutes Later...

Arthur knocked and opened the door of detective Henry's office. Oliver was sitting on a guest chair in front of detective Henry. Arthur closed the door and said: "Thank you for waiting, gentleman. I appreciate your patience."

Richard said: "It is okay, Arthur. We've all been through what you're dealing with."

Before Arthur said anything, Oliver smiled and said: "I told detective that you're having a tough haemorrhoid."

Arthur looked at Oliver and realized, this was a revenge for what Arthur said to that old man the other day on the street. Arthur said: "Thank you for your sympathy, detective."

"Go see a doctor as soon as we were done, alright?" Richard said with worry "Weren't you off for today?"

"Thanks for your worry, sir. Yes, I remembered that we were supposed to interrogate Ezra today. I'll leave after we finish talking about him."

"I'll be leaving too, sir," Oliver said to Richard.

"Where to?" Richard asked.

"To see Ava. Ava Wintergreen. That girl who was supposed to be Brad's goddaughter." Oliver explained.

"I remember her. It's alright, both of you can leave."

"Now let's move on to our business, shall we?" Arthur asked the two of them.

"So, what do you think? How much do you think was true, Ollie?" Richard asked Oliver.

"To be honest," Oliver coughed and continued "despite my own suspicion, I think he was telling the truth. He might be suffering from a mild Alexithymia. Every time I talk to Elizabeth about Brad, she's like she has a lot to discuss. A lot of feelings to express. Robert doesn't allow any discussions about Brad run in the house."

"Do you mean that Robert is somehow…making limits for Ezra and Elizabeth?" Arthur asked him.

"How are you so sure about that mental disorder you mentioned?" Richard asked, "It's an issue with feeling emotions, correct?"

"Yes. I'm pretty sure. Ezra isn't so emotional as much as I recall. He used to be like a piece of ice; he still *is*, actually. The truth is that he was five when I last saw him cry! He isn't emotional at all but when something personally changes him of make an effect in his bloody life." Oliver explained, "My point is that Ezra Oscar Moore isn't an emotional man; but the death of his older brother and his family falling apart somehow and separation has affected his unusual cold nature. He must talk to somebody about how he feels but that somebody isn't me."

"Thank you, Ollie," Richard said, "I agree with you. My experience has taught me that family members are the best people to talk to about a loss. Family has an interpersonal connection. Robert is weakening this connection. Neighbours, relatives and friends can never understand how you exactly feel but your family *does*. I've known Elizabeth and Robert for a long time now, I can swear that they adore you. You're like a son to them. You're like a son to Elizabeth. She talks to you because she believes you. She doesn't talk to her husband and son but she talks to you. The limit we're talking about wasn't applied on you."

"Richard has a point, Oliver. You can talk to them and you should," Arthur said to Oliver.

"I'll consider that. But don't ask me to talk to Ezra. I wasn't his favourite person lately. He sure dislikes me now."

"He is just a kid!" Arthur yelled at Oliver, "He is *just a kid*, Ollie. I don't care if he lived in a foreign country for four years. I don't consider his knowledge. He has been *a* secluded for his entire twenty-five years of living. He is twenty-five but do you think he actually lived for the past twenty years? He is mad at you but he won't stay mad. He will be alright. He just needs time to realise what's happening. You can't blame him for having several feelings at the moment and you know that!"

"I see your point, Arthur. I really do. But as I know, a countless number of people refuse to share their thoughts with a psychologist because they think they might forget their loved ones," Oliver said to Arthur. "I will talk to Ezra so soon. I can't just walk into their house and force them to talk to me. I should take baby steps. I talk to Robert at the first place. When Ezra sees his parents talking about Brad, he will take it easy on himself."

"I'll appreciate it, Oliver," Richard said to Oliver and continued to both of them "As you remember, Ezra mentioned that Robert is allergic to dogs and cats. I asked Robert about it when I walked Ezra out. That part was true, he *is* allergic."

Arthur informed: "He said that he was at his friend's house the night of the murder. His name is 'Sean Gwan'. I told Juniper to find the guy."

"Can Juniper show me the criminal records of our seven suspects?" Oliver asked Arthur.

Arthur answered: "Sure she can; but Ollie, we studied their records at the first place. Why do you need them?"

"I know we did. Taking another look won't make a harm, will it?" Oliver said and shrugged.

"I'll go tell her." Arthur said and exited the office.

Oliver asked Richard: "How do you know if I didn't kill Brad?"

"Cut the crap, boy! Four people witnessed that you were here when the murder was committed."

"But" Oliver said, "What if I bought their witness?"

"Oliver?"

"Yeah?"

Richard frowned tiredly: "*I'm* one of your witnesses!"

"Yes, you are," Oliver said and smiled.

"Have you told Ava that Brad is dead?"

"Yes. But I said that he was killed in a car accident. Murder is a lot for a kid to process. I took her to Brad's grave twice."

"What are your plans? Will you adopt her?"

"No. I'm in no place to father a child. But I will be there for her in every steps of her adoption by a family. I'll make sure she'll get the family she deserves."

"Oliver...I've already lost a child. You may not pay attention to what I'm saying. I want you to be patient and wait for this case to be solved. Then you might like to adopt Ava. Having a daughter is the best thing that can happened is anyone's life," Richard said with a little, sad smile.

Oliver knew how hard it was for Richard to talk about his daughter.

Richard was born at the Christmas night, 1953. He married 'Anastasia Halloumen' in 1978 when he was twenty-five. Their first child, 'Andrea' was born two years after but she died within four weeks after her birthday. Her death was reported to be the sudden infant death syndrome. Two years later, their twin sons were born; 'Grant' and 'Thomas'.

Three years after twins were born, Richard and Anastasia were parents to another son who they named 'Harrison' and called 'Harry'.

Harry was also a crime psychologist. He and Oliver were friends since college. Harry was just as tall as Oliver, so much funnier and Oliver had no doubt that Harry could cook superior!

Richard barely talked about Andrea. In fact, he never had. All Oliver knew about her, he learned in college when he and Harry met. Oliver said that he has two younger sisters and Harry said that his parents' first born was a daughter who didn't make it.

Years after, Oliver asked Arthur about her.

"Do you really think we will solve this case?" Oliver asked Richard.

"I won't be discouraged. You shouldn't be discouraged too." Richard answered, "This is as far as I can say."

"I don't get discouraged, Richard."

Richard smiled: "Good boy."

"How are your sons? I haven't talked to them since Christmas."

"They're working as usual. What a coincidence, we were talking about you last night…Grant is a tour leader, still. He has a flight to Rockhampton next week. Tommy and his wife are expecting a baby. Harry said that he has been trying to get in touch with you since the funeral."

"First…" Oliver said excitedly, "You're going to be a grandpa! Richard you're living my dad's dream! Congratulations!"

Richard laughed: "Thanks! Why am I living his dream?"

"He is willing to become a grandfather. He thinks nobody knows but he actually wants to name his first grandson after himself."

"Does he?" Richard asked, "Like…Edward Black-Johnson the second?"

"Maybe. Yes. I don't think he knows that it sounds more normal if the baby would be Jacob Black the second."

Richard joked about Arthur's father: "I think he decided to name a boy after himself pretty late. His son is three and a half decades old now!"

Oliver laughed: "I was about to become Edward Johnson junior."

"How did you turn out to be Bill Oliver?"

"It's a funny story, actually. My mum believed that she's carried me for nine months so she can choose my name. Her favourite fictional character is Oliver Twist. Bill Gates was a millionaire. They thought about naming me Oliver Bill but Dad said that Oliver Twist was a pauper and Gates is the millionaire so I was named Bill Oliver Johnson!"

"That was a great story! I didn't see that coming, I admit!" Richard said with a smile.

"So, you said that Harry was trying to contact me since the funeral. I didn't see him at the funeral."

"Yes, he came. He was hoping to talk to you at the funeral but he said that you didn't seem to be in the mood of talking to anyone. He tried to call your landline but you didn't answer that either."

"I appreciate him. His effort means a lot to me but I rarely check my answering machine," Oliver said, "Is he in London? Maybe we can meet next week?"

"I'm afraid you can't. He's in Dublin now. He went there to work on a case."

"Too bad. I'll call him tonight."

"Thank you. Let's go outside; see if Juniper found Gwan."

Detective walked out first; Oliver baby-stepped outside the office to set an alarm on his phone for 08:00 p.m. He should've called Harry.

Oliver went to Juniper's desk. "Juniper Emily Linda" was a young red-haired girl who had the job with the computer at the police department, mostly at Arthur's investigation team; her honourable job was what people would like to call "Hacking."

Juniper was a cold blood, relax and indifference girl. As the matter of fact, nothing could surprise her even an alien attack! But still, she was a funny girl.

"Mr Johnson?" Arthur said while standing next to Juniper's desk, looking at something in her computer "Come here, please."

Oliver went to them. He shook his head and said: "Sergeant Black, Ms Linda."

"Mr Johnson, Ms Linda found Sean Gwan."

"Good. Where is he?" Oliver asked.

"He lives with his parents. Their house is an alley away from here. His mother, Martha Stein is an Obstetrician and his father is Choi Gwan; he is an Ophthalmologist." Juniper explained.

"What does he do for a living?" Arthur asked Juniper.

"He is a high school math teacher," Juniper answered.

"Sergeant?" Oliver called, "When will you interrogate him?"

"This afternoon. I'll take care of it personally." Arthur assured.

He continued: "Juniper, please give the phone number to Mr Johnson." And left them.

"How are you, Oliver?" Juniper asked without taking eyes off the computer.

"I'm fine. I'm just physically tired. Thank you for asking, how are *you*?"

"Couldn't be better. I'm getting some inspiration that I'm going to die this weekend." Juniper joked with her cold blood tone.

"I've known you for three years. You're saying that you're going to die this weekend every week. With a little bit of calculation...you've said this 150 times or more!"

"You are smart! I'm amazed!" Juniper said in the coldest way possible.

"Don't be too surprised, you would stroke!" Oliver humiliated "So, where is the number?"

Juniper tied her red hair ponytail and wrote two numbers on a small piece of paper. She handed the paper to Oliver and explained: "Jessica Brandon. First number is her phone number and the second one belongs to the clinic she's working at."

"Thank you, Juniper," Oliver said as gratitude, "Things get done faster when you're around."

"That was beautiful and made my day. I will give you the suspect's criminal records by noon," Juniper said with her cold blood attitude and a flicker of smile.

"Thank you. I won't be here by noon. Email them to me, okay?"

Juniper shook her head and Oliver went outside. He dialled Ms Jonah's number to see if he can take Ava out for lunch. As the phone was ringing, Oliver looked at the sky. It was drizzling, breezy and nimbostratus clods could be seen.

Oliver loved this sort of weather; So did Olivia.

Ever since she was a little girl, she would put on her yellow raincoat and black rain boots that had patterns of chamomiles on them and rush outside to play.

Unlike Olivia, Dakota hated rainy weather. Dakota was an extrovert, she liked to spend time at the yard while receiving sunshine. (P.S. Edward used to reproach Oliver and Olivia for being at home all the time!)

When the rain was pouring, Dakota would stay home, wear a cute pair of mid-calf socks, have a cup of peanut butter hot chocolate and read some story books; classic!

While Oliver was remembering a better part of his life, he also noticed that Ms Jonah rejected the call and in a second or two, a message from Ms Jonah appeared on Oliver's phone: "*I will call you back in ten minutes.*"

Oliver was still holding the phone next to his ear. You're making no mistakes if you think that Oliver didn't understand what happened for a moment.

Oliver went back inside to Arthur's office. When he opened the office's door, Arthur was talking on the phone: "I will, okay…Take care…Love you more, bye."

Arthur hung up the phone and asked Oliver: "What's with the blue?"

"Excuse me?"

"Your blue face. Why are you sad?"

"I was talking…or tried to talk to Ms Jonah. I wanted to ask her if I can take Ava to lunch. She didn't answer but she did text me that she will call me in ten minutes."

"Can I ask you something?"

Oliver sat on the chair in front of Arthur's desk and said: "Yes please."

"You told me before that Brad gave Ezra's number for an emergency. Has Ezra ever met Ava?"

"No. I don't think that they are ready to meet. Plus, what if by any chances, Ezra is the killer we're trying to catch and if he meets Ava, there is no guarantee that he wouldn't hurt her."

"Man, it's not 'Taken'."

"What?"

"Taken, the movie! It's not like we're going to have hostages!"

Oliver didn't say anything. Arthur continued: "Oliver, you know the process. We work on what evidence gives us, we have nothing to do with theories. I asked Ezra Moore to come here because I believe in your wisdom. Do you understand? Your wisdom. I knew that this theory might be totally erroneous but I decided to trust you, Oliver."

"Let me guess. You'll never do it again…unless we have evidence."

"I won't do it again. Please don't be sad about it and don't blame me. It's the protocol and we both know that."

"I get it. In fact, I was astonished when you agreed to accuse him. I didn't see that coming!"

"We had a little bit of evidence, actually."

"Margot?"

"Yes. She barked at Ezra for a reason. We needed to know why."

"Do you know now?" Oliver asked ridiculously.

"Ollie, spend a day having no thoughts on your job. Act like you are unemployed!" Arthur advised.

"I *can't*! I am *obsessed* with this job!"

"Then don't be!"

Oliver wanted to say something when he heard his phone ringing. He picked up the phone and answered.

"Hello Mr Johnson."

It was Ms Jonah. Oliver answered: "Hello Ms Johnson. How are you?"

"I'm good, thanks to God. How are you doing?"

"Me too; thanks to God. I just called you to see if I can take Ava to lunch today. May I?"

"Mr Johnson, I'm being concerned about your consecutive meetings with Ava. I'm afraid you can't see her today. You may see her next week." Ms Jonah said with certain and no sparks of doubt.

Oliver felt deeply insulted and offended. He was really infuriated but he tried not to be like Ms Jonah, offensive and insulting! He politely said: "Ma'am, with all due respect, I don't see any reasons indicative of not seeing her. Please don't talk to me like I'm breaking any laws or I'm not qualified enough to spend time with a kid. I work with the police and I do no harm to anyone. I don't have any sinister goals, as much as I'm aware unless you ponder trying to bring some joy into the life an orphan who just faced the loss of the man who was meant to be her parent is illegal."

Ms Jonah was even more infuriated than Oliver, but she couldn't deal with the truth. She corrected what she said a few seconds ago: "She'll be ready by twelve o'clock."

"Thank you. Please tell her to bring all her paintings too. I want to see them."

"I will. Have a nice day," Ms Jonah said with an uncovered enmity.

Oliver hung up the phone. "Dude!" Arthur said surprised, "What was that?"

"What was what?"

"You talked to Ms Jonah like that?"

Oliver smirked and said: "Yeah, she was. She said that I can't see Ava today. She thinks I'm a sick psychopath because I see Ava too much."

"I heard. Are you taking her?"

"Yes, I am." Oliver confirmed "Hey Arthur, I've got an idea. I've done a lot of thinking. I just wanted to hear your opinion."

Arthur leant back to his chair and said: "I'm all ears."

Oliver coughed and said: "So, I should start with a memory. When I was twenty, we spent the summer in US. You remember Joe, right? He had met Melissa back at that year's spring. He couldn't shut up about her. When he was talking about her, he mentioned that Melissa had prepared a list of everything she wanted to get done before she got married. I remember thinking that idea was weird but when came back to London and college, I had my mind changed. I made myself a list and I never spoke to anyone about it until now."

"Okay," Arthur said, "so what happened? Do you still have the list?"

"I do and I never edited my list again. I have seventeen check boxes on the list, I've done nine of them."

"Are trying to say what I'm thinking, Oliver?"

"I think I am. I want to have a kid. I want to adopt Ava."

Arthur nervously chuckled: "Are you for real? How much time did you spend thinking about this?"

"A lot. It's been a few days. What do you think?"

"I saw it coming but it didn't make it any less shocking." Arthur said, "Listen, it's not a good idea, it's not bad. We have to do more thinking. Make a pros and cons list; and we should talk this out in a better situation, alright?"

"Alright. You're—you're right. We'll talk this out tonight when we are calm and none of us are suffering from lack of sleep that was caused by an insomniac brother-in-law. We got to make a pros and cons list. Alright?"

"You got it Ollie."

"And we'll do it at our house."

"Yeah, about that…"

Arthur interrupted: "No, man. There's nothing about that. Or should I remind you what happened with Phillip?"

Oliver took a deep breath and said: "I hate you."

"You hate me or you hate the fact that I'm always, right?" Arthur asked proudly.

Oliver looked at him and said raged: "I will stay at your house; now will you stop?"

Arthur opened a book to read. He said: "If you're up for it, we can go see Ennis now. You'll make it to lunch on time."

Oliver stretched his hands and shrugged indifferently: "No complains if you drive."

***

### Autopsy Laboratories of Greenwich, 11:10 A.M.

Oliver and Arthur carefully walked into an autopsy room. The room was so unexpectedly neat and well-cleaned; it wasn't like some creepy movie, there were no signs of blood drops anywhere, everything was so clean like a mirror!

A very clean dissection table was placed in the middle of a room and behind it, a young blond guy was cleaning it obsessively. He looked up to Oliver and Arthur and smiled: "Hello gentlemen. How can I help you?"

His Nordic accent just revealed that he was an Icelander. He got closer to them and took of his scrub.

Arthur said: "Hello, I'm Sergeant Black, this is forensic psychologist Mr Johnson. Are you 'Ennis Arnálds'?"

He answered: "Yes, sir. I've been told that you will stop by. I suppose I met both of you at Bradly Moore's funeral. But we didn't talk."

"Do you mind if we ask you some questions about Bradly?" Arthur asked.

"Of course. Please come with me. We better talk outside and no one will be disturbed," Ennis said and pointed to the door.

Oliver smiled: "Sure. Lead the way."

And they walked outside to the hallway. As they were walking in the hall, Ennis began to talk: "I have to admit, Bradly's death was unexpected, like *literally*. I can't think of any reasons that someone would've killed him for."

"About that, Mr Arnálds, we want to know if he had an issue with anyone that you knew about?" Oliver asked Ennis.

Ennis opened the entering door of the labs and said: "Sure he did. I mean, he had some problems that I was aware of but I'm not sure if they're helpful."

"Everything might be helpful. Explain them, please," Arthur said and gently shook his head.

Ennis sat on a wooden bench, Oliver sat next to him and Arthur kept standing up.

Ennis explained: "Well, since July, Bradly and his brother Ezra talked several times on the phone and in person to talk about their mother."

"What about their mother?" Oliver instantly asked.

"As far as I know, their mother was being aggressive to Brad's dad and Ezra. Ezra was trying to convince Brad to leave their parents' house and get a house of his own."

"What did they do at last?"

"I don't know. Every time they talked about it, Brad would've been so angry that he hung up the phone or leaved the place they were talking at. I never asked him to talk about it."

"What else?" Oliver asked, "What other problem did he have?"

"He had a friend; I don't remember their name but they also had some problems. Apparently, Brad was interfering in their personal life and that made his friend upset."

"Can you be more specific? How did Brad interfere?" Arthur asked and put his hands in his pockets.

"You see, his family was living in another country or far from London. I once heard Brad was talking to him on the phone, trying to talk to him into go and visit his family but he refused," Ennis explained.

"When did this conversation happened?" Oliver asked Ennis.

"Early December, I think," Ennis answered doubtfully.

"Was his friend a man or a woman?" Arthur asked.

Ennis thought for a moment and said: "I don't know about that but I can say that he talked about his ex-wife, Elma for a couple days. He said that they were talking on social media for a while and he also thought that they had a

147

chance to get back together again…But then another day he seemed extremely sad and when I asked him why, he just said that Elma was married and they didn't have any chance again."

"Did he meet any of his friends or family members at work?" Arthur asked.

"Ummm, no, he did not—Oh I just recalled something!"

"What is it?" Oliver asked hopefully, wished for something more useful.

"Mr Johnson," said Ennis, "This is somehow about you. Do you want to hear it?"

"Yes. I'm sure I can take it."

"At the last days, he was talking about some new friendships he'd made. He thought that you would be bothered if you knew about them. And he was working on a resignation because he was considering moving to Wales by the year of twenty-twenty."

"Bloody hell," Oliver thought with a British accent.

Arthur deeply breathed. That would've been a great time to leave.

He put his hand inside the inner pocket of his long black double-breasted coat, brought a cad out and gave it to Ennis: "I'm afraid we must leave now. My number's written on this card. Please contact me if you seemed to recall more, Mr Arnálds."

Ennis smiled: "I sure will. Thank you."

Oliver did a quick farewell by shaking his head and got away from them with big steps. What really was making everything so upsetting and hard to take for Oliver, was the fact that he didn't know if he could share it with the Moore's. He had no clue whatever him, learning about Brad was old-fashioned to the guy's parents or it was just as fresh as it was to Oliver.

*** 

### The Orphanage, 12:03 P.M.

Ms Jonah walked to Oliver while she was taking Ava's hand as Ava herself was also holding a few papers on her other hand. Ava was wearing a yellow raincoat and brown boots. She couldn't stop smiling while walking to Oliver. Oliver sat on his knees and hugged Ava. He said: "Hey Ava! Nice to see you! We are going to have so much fun today, girl!"

"Yay!" Ava yelled joyfully.

Ms Jonah brutally ruined their happiness as if she had to: "*Not* so much, of course. Happiness must have certain red lines so it won't cause any troubles."

Oliver's smile lightly passed the process of fading away as Ms Jonah was talking. "How annoying is she!" Oliver thought with no regrets.

Oliver stood up, pointed his car and said to Ava: "You remember my car? Go stay next to it. I'll catch up in a minute."

As Ava walked to the car, Oliver asked: "Ms Jonah, Do you have a problem with me?"

"I certainly do, Mr Johnson."

"What an accident, I have problems with you either. My problem is with your paranoid attitude, to be specific."

"My attitude? Oh Mr Jonson, what about your disrespectful behaviour?"

"I was just telling the truth. And I don't regret it. Not even a word was against the truth."

Ms Jonah frowned and said: "Be back in an hour."

"Ms Jonah. Only the food takes one hour to get ready. I'll bring her in three hours."

"That would be too long and I do not allow it."

"I'll bring her back in three hours, maximum," Oliver said and went to the car. Ava waved her hand to Oliver. Oliver kindly smiled among judging Ms Jonah in his mind.

He opened the car's door for Ava, helped her sit and put on her seatbelt. After he sat in the car, he noticed that Ava seems gloomy and she was trying to hide it behind her smile.

Oliver asked: "So Ava, what would you want to have for lunch?"

"I don't mind. Just get us what you prefer," she said with a fake smile.

"My preference is what you want us to eat."

"I don't mind, really."

"Ava, is there something wrong?" Oliver turned to her and asked, "What are you not telling me?"

"It's Ms Jonah. He said that when I'm with you, I'm not allowed to make you spend a lot of money for me. She said that I should buy the cheapest things or I shouldn't buy anything at all," Ava sadly explained.

Oliver had another reason to hate Ms Jonah. He said to Ava: "You must know that I'm a little mad at Ms Jonah. I want to do something against her opinion. What do you want to eat?"

"But Ms Jonah…"

"What about her?" Oliver said quickly "I won't say anything if *you* don't."

Ava smiled and said: "It's been a long time since I wanted to try Salmon with fried rice."

"We're going to get some seafood!"

Oliver played a song and started to drive to the best seafood restaurant he knew. A few moments passed when Oliver's phone started to ring. Ava immediately grabbed Oliver's phone and spelled the caller's name: "O-L-I-V-I-A. Olivia!"

Oliver smiled: "Well done, Ava! Olivia is my sister."

"Are you twins?" Ava asked curious and handed the phone to Oliver.

Oliver said: "No, I'll explain." He answered the phone: "Yes?"

"Hey Ollie, what's up?"

"Hi Liv. How are you?"

"I'm good…Are you driving?"

"Uh-huh."

"Is Arthur with you?"

"No. He's at work. I'm taking Ava to lunch."

"Okay, I'll call his office. Say hello to Ava!"

"Thank you, dear."

"One more thing, one more thing! You're sleeping at our house tonight. Got it?" Olivia asked to make sure.

"I will. I talked to Arthur about it."

"Good. See you!"

"See you." Oliver ended the call and looked at Ava.

He said: "It was Olivia, she said hello. I have two sisters. Olivia and Dakota. Olivia is now twenty-seven, she is six years younger than me and she is a martial arts coach. She got married three years ago. Her husband is a policeman. Dakota is twenty-one. She is twelve years younger than me. She isn't married. She's a scholar."

"Do you have any brothers?"

"No, I don't."

"Haven't you ever wished for one?"

"No. Or maybe I have. I don't remember. But I do remember that I had a friend who was just like a brother to me; even better than that."

Ava paused for a second or two before she asked: "Bradly?"

Oliver glanced at her. He didn't see Bradly's memory coming right into their conversation. He confirmed with head and said: "Yeah. Bradly. He was my brother; my younger brother."

"I made him a birthday card last year. He said that he liked it."

"Did you know his birthday? Did he tell you about it?"

"Yes, he did. October seventeenth. Why did you call him your *younger* brother? When is *your* birthday?"

"July fourth." Oliver answered.

"That means…we're four months away from your birthday."

"Six months, actually."

"It's gonna take a lot of time! That's not bad, it gives me time to think of a beautiful card!"

"That would be my honour," Oliver said and smiled at Ava's cute and infantile world.

"I have another question."

"What is it?"

"Why didn't Brad like his birthday? I remember he seemed so sad on his birthday."

Oliver thought: "Does she even know what is divorce?…is she even ready to understand it?"

He answered: "Brad didn't like his birthday because he got divorce on his birthday eight years ago."

"What's a divorce?"

Oliver took three seconds to pick the right words and then he explained: "When a married couple realize that they can't live together anymore, sometimes because one of them doesn't want something that their partner wants or they can't share the same idea on a subject and these kinds of issues that can't be solved, they realize that it's the best to stop being married so they get a divorce." He explained, "Do you understand?"

"I think I did." Ava said, "I didn't know he was married. He never told me."

"I'm sure he had a very good reason for it, maybe he didn't mean to upset you."

"Maybe."

Five minutes or six passed in silence for Oliver and Ava, the car was still playing songs. Oliver took a quick look at Ava who was sadly looking through the window.

"Is everything alright?" Oliver asked, "Did I upset you?"

"It's not you. It's Brad I'm mad at."

"Why?"

"Why would he want to adopt me if he had a kid?"

"Kid? He didn't have any kids. What are you talking about?" Oliver raised an eyebrow.

"You said it. You said that he was married; that means he had kids."

"Oh, I see what's going on here. Ava, being married doesn't mean being parents."

"What?"

"Becoming parents is a choice, not an obligation. Some people get married and they decide to have kids but some couples choose not having any. Sure, Brad was married but that doesn't mean that he became a father."

Oliver's explanation sounded confusing to Ava. She asked: "That doesn't make sense. So why do your parents have three kids? Like so many other parents?"

"Because they chose to. I told you about my sister Olivia and her husband, right?"

Ava confirmed with head.

Oliver continued: "Well they are married too. They got married three years ago but for now, they have decided not to have kids. Do you understand what I'm trying to say?"

Ava beautifully smiled: "So he didn't have any kids?"

"No, he didn't. And he loved you so much that he wanted to be your father, he was ready for it."

"Was he?" Ava asked cranky, "Then why did he die?"

"Ava," Oliver called, "We talked about it. He died in a car accident. No one is able to postpone their death."

Ava frowned. Oliver guessed that she needed more reasons to convince her.

Oliver said: "Let me tell you a story about it, my teacher told me the story when I was five. The story happens in an unknown time but I know it's ancient. So, once upon a time a traveller reaches a city after a very long trip. As he walks into the city, people gently welcome him, telling the man that their king just died and according to the city's rule, the first person who walks in the city shall ascend the throne. The man, let's call him John Constantine, agrees immediately; who doesn't want to be king? Long story short, Constantine becomes the king. He does everything a good king would do, he builds schools, libraries, roads and such subjects to be called 'a good king'. He rules the city for ten years. Until one night when he was asleep, he hears whispers." He stopped to take a break.

Oliver resumed: "As he wakes up, he sees his guards around is bed. The king who is so terrified and confused, asks them: 'What's going on? What are you doing here?' A guard answers: 'Sir, your time has come. You're no longer our king and you have to come with us.' Constantine, however, doesn't lose his hope so soon. He says: 'Where will you take me?' Another guard answers: 'We are taking you to an island far from here. According to our rules, the king should be transported to that island every ten years and after that, the first person who comes to the city will be the governor and now it's your turn.' Constantine begs them: 'At least give me some time to pack a bag.' The guard says: 'Pardon us, we don't have time for that.' Man's requests were useless. Nothing stopped the guards from taking him to the island. The man lived on that island until he died."

Ava gave herself a few minutes to think and opined: "That was…a very strange story. It was sad."

"Indeed. Did you get the point?"

"I…don't think so?" Ava answered doubtful.

"Listen, we all have a specific time of lifetime like Constantine's time as the king. We don't know when will we die, man didn't know when he was going to be discharged. He wasn't even allowed to pack a bag for himself because he wasn't aware of the rule, neither do us. We don't know when will be our time to die because if we did, we would've been better people. We would've lived a better, more wholesome life. We wouldn't have refused or hesitated to do things that we wanted or buy things we wanted but didn't."

"We know that we will die, we just don't know when."

"Exactly, Ava, exactly."

"But it can be any seconds now. I mean we might die a minute from now. Why don't we live our lives in the way we want?"

"I don't have the answer to that. But I think that maybe…we're too afraid to live our life delightfully and we're too afraid of death at the same time."

"What's stopping us?"

Oliver shrugged and whispered: "Ourselves."

Their conversation came to an end when they arrived at the restaurant. Oliver got off the car first to help Ava out. As soon as they found a two-seat table and settled down, a woman came to them with a big gentle smile: "Hello and welcome aboard! What can I get you and your daughter, sir?"

"He isn't my father," Ava said real quick.

"I'm a close friend of his godfather."

"Yes, but he just died."

The waitress seemed a bit suspicious. Oliver said: "We know each other. I assure you."

"Alright…may I get your order?"

"Can I get some salmon with fried rice?" Ava ordered first.

"Salmon and fried rice, what would you order, sir?" the waitress said while writing the orders in her notebook.

"I also want salmon with fried rice, thank you."

"Alright, I'll make it a double. Do you prefer any drinks?"

"I would like to have a glass of water, what about you, Ava?"

"Ummm, orange soda!"

"Add an orange soda please," Oliver said with an artificial smile.

When the waitress shook her head and left, Oliver said: "Hey Ava."

"Yeah?"

"You know, you really don't have to explain that you were Brad's goddaughter and he is dead now."

"Why? She thought that you're my father. We should've told her the truth."

"Truth is valuable, I know. But people such as her are just trying to be nice. They mostly don't care if we are father and daughter or not."

"They don't?" Ava asked surprised, "Why don't they?"

"I guess they just aren't interested in people's family trees."

"You're right. I'm sorry."

"It's okay. Everything is fine."

Ava spent the next couple minutes looking around. That seafood restaurant was the only one Oliver knew that didn't look like a pirate ship and no one hung plastic fish models to the wall!

Those kinds of restaurants had Oliver thinking so many times, "Why would I want to see the live pic of what I'm eating?"

That place looked so normal and simply decorated for a seafood that some people would've thought that they could have chicken there!

But who cares? It's not like anyone wants to eat the decoration!

While Ava was looking around, Oliver texted Jessica Brandon: '*Hello. It's Oliver Johnson. Remember?*'

Oliver quickly received a message from her: '*Yes, I do! Hi! How are you?*'

'*I'm fine. Thank you for asking! Are you good?*'

'*I'm also good. BTW I'm so sorry for your loss. My thoughts and prayers are with you and I wish you all the best.*'

'*Thank you. Your concern means a lot to me.*' Oliver texted back.

He was kinda disgusted the '*Sorry for your loss*' messages. No one really meant any of those. But Jessica did. Oliver knew she did.

'*What can I do for you?*'

'*I need to see you. It's about my job and it relates to a kid.*'

'*Absolutely. Send me an address. Can we meet in three hours?*'

'*Of course. Thank you.*'

Oliver put his phone away after he sent Jessica the address of a coffee house near the police department.

"I have a question." Ava said to Oliver.

"Ask it."

"Brad once told me that he had a brother. What is his name?"

"Brad has a younger brother named 'Ezra Oscar'. Ezra is nine years younger than Brad."

"He has a weird name. I haven't heard it. What's the meaning?"

"Ezra is a Hebrew name. It means 'Helper' or 'Helpful'. Oscar is Irish, means 'The deer lover'."

"Can I see him sometime?"

"Why not?" Oliver answered, "But not so soon. He is not in a good condition. He is in grief at the time."

"Okay. Does he know about me?"

"Yeah, he does. Brad gave his phone number to Ms Jonah in case of an emergency. He wasn't so good so he asked me to see you first."

"How is he like?"

Oliver crossed his arms and said: "Well he is…as tall as me. He has dark brown hair; his hair is wavy unlike Brad. Brad was curly. And he has jade green eyes."

"Does he look like Brad?"

"Yes, actually," Oliver answered, "Facially yes. But you know, Brad looked like their mother. Ezra looks like their father, too."

"I should see him sometime. Whenever he gets better."

"Of course," Oliver said, "Hey did you bring your paintings?"

"Yeah, like you asked."

"Where are they?"

"I left them in the car. Do you want me to go get them?"

"No. it's not necessary. I just want to have them."

Oliver took a break to save time for thinking of subjects Ava might've enjoyed discussing. Taking care of a child might've been the hardest thing he had ever accomplished; because the souvenir of age difference is nothing but hardship.

You have zero ideas about other generation's interests, that's what making association so rough.

Ava saved Oliver from an absolute mind explosion by asking: "What do you do for living?"

"I'm a crime psychologist. A forensic psychologist."

"What does 'forensic' mean?"

"It's a word that relates your job to some methods about crime."

"How do you do your job?"

"When a criminal commits a crime, I spend as much time it takes to find out why did they do it."

"Is your job exciting?"

Oliver thought and answered: "Sometimes."

"What did Brad do for living?"

"He was a coroner. His job was to find out the cause of someone's death."

"Your jobs are connected to the police. Was it a coincidence?"

"Yes and no. When we were sixteen, we went to a library. The library was this enormous building which I think now is a residential building. So, the building was on fire later that evening while we were there. It was horrible. Fire fighters got there fast enough to put out the fire. When we got out of the building, we saw how happy and grateful were the survivors that we thought we should be helping people like that, saving their lives. We ended up as a forensic psychologist and a coroner." Oliver, unlike his will, recalled the one catastrophic memory that had been keeping him awake for almost seventeen years.

"Which one of you two's job is harder?"

"The easy job doesn't exist. They all come with a certain sort of difficultness but if you like your job, you'd probably pay less attention to those difficulties."

"Let me compare them…A coroner has a map of human's body because bodies but you don't have any maps or if they won't be enough since our mind-sets aren't similar. You both have to explore; coroners expect to face something familiar but you may face a new disorder! Your job is so much harder!"

Oliver was extremely amazed. Those words didn't seem like Ava's. She must've studied them on a book or heard it from somewhere else.

Just for his own information, Oliver asked: "That's brilliant! Where did you learn that from?"

"A few nights ago, I was unable to sleep so I went to see our psychologist and she said I could stay with her until I feel sleepy. I asked her about her job and what makes it difficult and she told me what I just said to you. I compared you with a coroner."

"What she said what she said so wisely but Ava, your job normally doesn't get easier if you don't enjoy it. Follow your dream job and pursue it. Okay?"


## Coffee House, 15:57 P.M.

Oliver was sitting in a café that he used to visit as a scholar. After he had lunch with Ava, he bought her an ice cream and they both took a walk before he brought Ava back to the orphanage.

Café was generally covered in Egyptian blue and tawny brown. Oliver was obsessed with this place's cappuccino and despite his passion for hot chocolate, he ordered a cappuccino when a waiter asked for his order.

Before Jessica arrived, Oliver took another look at Ava's drawings. He didn't really have any experience about analysing paintings but he knew that overusing colours have a meaning. Ava seemed to overuse some colours in her paintings. There was a couple paintings of Ava and Bradly; so happy, safe and sound.

Next painting was a weird red and black creature. Oliver didn't really understood what that creature was.

The other painting was a picture of a 3D building which Oliver understood that it was the orphanage; there were two small windows on the building and there were no signs of the sun in that painting, rain and clouds could be seen.

Ava's paintings were odd. Comparing to other children, Ava's paintings had at least one odd and unusual point in them. As Ava said to Oliver at lunch, she had drawn them after Oliver told her that Brad lost his life in a car accident; those paintings were able to represent an accurate explanation of Ava's mental situation.

Ava was an introvert like Oliver. That little girl knew how to hide her sadness and grief by putting on a happy face. Or maybe she just wanted to look good when Oliver was around; maybe that 5-year-old was so intelligent to feel that Oliver may not desire to talk about his dead friend.

Oliver could get some help from Jessica. Jessica could be Oliver's saviour angel at the moment.

Talking to a bereaved child wasn't a usual kind of task for Oliver. He usually talked to children to ask: "Where were you, what were you doing when the crime was committed?" Those children were later sent to a therapist. Jessica was a kid psychologist, for real. It was her job to talk, understand and advise children every single day; of course, she could guide Oliver with Ava.

Unlike Oliver's expectation, Jessica arrived soon. She sat on the chair behind the table next to Oliver after taking off her overcoat and cardigan.

Oliver looked at Jessica's thick orange sweater, smiled and said: "Typical Jessica. Still cold, aren't you?"

Jessica placed two pieces of her long straight brown hair behind her ears and said: "You have no idea!"

Oliver smiled and asked: "How are you, Jesse?"

"I'm good, I'm fine. I'm just sick of doing the laundry every weekend!" Jessica happily joked about her marital life.

Oliver laughed. It was good to see Jessica happy and energetic. He asked: "How's William?"

Jessica corrected him: "*Liam* and he's just fine. He's actually planning on inviting you over for dinner with mutual friends next month."

"That's very kind of him. I might have to reset my schedule."

Jessica suddenly recalled something. She took a small, wrapped box out of her purse and gave it to Oliver: "Here you are Ollie, I hope you like it!"

"Wow, Jesse. Thank you," Oliver said while slowly shaking the box near his ear to hear what's inside, "Umm…what's the occasion?"

"Christmas…But you know, it's for Hanukkah if you're a Jew now!"

Oliver finished ripping the paper and opened the box. It was a watch inside it that looked extremely familiar to Oliver.

"Ollie," Jessica called, "Do you remember that watch you lost at the senior year?"

Oliver looked at Jessica so amazed: "This is the same watch! I don't believe it! I thought they were out of production!"

Jessica clapped cheerfully: "It wasn't impossible! Even the word 'Impossible' is saying 'I'm possible'!"

"Oh my God" Oliver was still amazed "Jesse, you made my day! I didn't see this coming."

Jessica laughed: "I'm glad you liked it! Put it on, I'll go order something."

And she left the table to the counter.

Oliver took off his watch and replaced it with his new watch. He loved it! Oliver was obsessed with those cream straps, golden case and lug, brown case, golden Ionic Greek numbers and hands! Oliver would've never had enough of staring at that masterpiece.

Jessica came back to their table and Oliver said with a shameful smile: "You see, Jessica? Now I'm too embarrassed. I didn't get you anything."

Jessica generously smiled: "Don't think about it. I know how busy you've been." She continued: "So why did you want us to meet? Are you alright?"

"Yes. It's not about me," Oliver said while putting Ava's paintings in front of Jessica "I wanted to talk to you about these paintings."

Jessica looked at the paintings and said with a cute tone: "Aww, Oliver! You're such a great artist! I see your future almost as bright as Claude Monet!"

"You're kind and hilarious. But these are not mine. These belongs to a girl named Ava Wintergreen. Bradly Moore was planning to adopt her before he died."

"Oh," Jessica felt sad, "I wanted to talk to you about him, I just thought that you don't want to talk about it. I'm so deeply sorry about your loss, Oliver. I've never been there but I have no doubt that you're strong and you will pass this situation. I'm here for you."

"Thank you, Jessica. I appreciate your sympathy. Thank you," Oliver said with a grateful smile.

"How are you dealing with it?"

"I—am…handling it just right. I have some sleep issues and sure, I'm upset; but I'm getting along. I mean, just because Brad died, the world doesn't stop. I had a life before Brad, I just need to make plans for a new life without him."

"Don't rush into it. Take your time." Jessica said, "Tell me about Ava."

"Brad had decided to make a difference in his life. He always wanted to have a daughter. Ava was born in 2013. I don't know much about her parents. Ava knew Brad. And she loved him. Brad had promised her a new life. A new life that he was a part of it but as a living man. He even prepared a room for Ava at his house."

"Does she know about Brad?"

"Yeah, I told her. But I couldn't mention that he was murdered. It would've been too much for her. I said he died in a car accident."

"Does his family know about Ava?"

"Brad kept it a secret. Like, top secret. None of us knew about her before he died and we received a call from the orphanage. I haven't told them yet but I will so soon."

"Soon like—really soon?"

"No. Brad's parents aren't in a good situation to meet Ava. I'm trying to prepare them," Oliver said, "Imagine I go to their house with Ava! They're already carrying ten pianos on their backs."

"That's the best."

"Thanks," Oliver said, "So tell me. What do you see in these paintings? Analyse them."

Jessica took a few moments to process the first painting, the monster. She then looked Oliver in eyes and asked: "Would you tell me more about Ava's life and personality?"

"Does it…help the analysis?" Oliver asked confused. The confusion was because he didn't think that painting analysis might require personal information.

She moved her lips: "Yes."

"As far as I know, there are no clues of any of her real parents. About her life at the orphanage, she told me that she lives in a room with four other girls and Ava is the youngest. She also said that she's friends with them. They play together, share their meals and paint. They were so excited when Ava was about to move in with Brad but she promised them to convince Brad to take her back to the orphanage so they would be able to spend time."

"Those girls, do they treat Ava properly?"

"Apparently. She has never said anything unlikely."

Jessica turned the paper to Oliver and explained: "Look, this is a painting of a monster. The monster isn't generally the symbol of positive vibes. This monster is placed in the middle of the paper which means that Ava wishes to be seen more powerful. The monster has two horns that were drawn by black but they're filled with white which means that she's innocent inside."

"What about the colours? She has overused blue and red."

"Correct. Purple, red, blue and black are used in this painting. Purple represents wisdom and creativity. Red and blue show anger and depression, obviously. Black is used for mystery." Jessica explained.

"Monster can be what she's afraid of, can't it?"

"Maybe, but I assume that it's the way that she is trying to show her anxiety issues."

"She painted this after Brad died. Of course, she's angry and depressed, she doesn't even like Ms Jonah."

"Who is she?"

"She is the principal of the orphanage. She isn't pleasant at all."

"How is she like?"

"She's actually good. It's just that she has her strict rules that make her hard to take."

"I see. Let's move on to the second paper."

Before she started, Oliver said: "That is the orphanage."

Jessica shook her head as a yes and started observing the painting. She finished analysing way sooner that he did for the monster.

"So?" Oliver asked.

"Okay, we must skip the colours part straight to more important details. Take a look at the windows, only two."

"What does it mean?"

"Window is generally how you mean to communicate with people. Now what do you see through the windows?"

"Darkness."

"Exactly, she doesn't desire to communicate because she is too angry and depressed over the death of his godfather. Now the chimney. A chimney with no smokes. Do you what does a chimney stands for?"

"No, I don't."

"For the past centuries, mothers used to get foods ready on fire and chimneys would've sent the smokes out. When a mother wasn't there to cook, there were to smokes out of the chimney. Ava doesn't have a mother and she doesn't feel the dependence to anyone at the orphanage like a kid to their mother."

"What about the rain and the clouds?"

"Well, London hasn't been so rainy lately, mostly snowy. Rain is also depression and the proof are those grey clouds."

That was it. Oliver had another subject to overthink about. Typical.

He smiled: "Jessica, I'm so really thankful for your time and help. You did me a great favour today. I owe you one."

Jessica smiled back: "Don't mention it. I'm happy to help. Contact me if you needed any more help."

"Absolutely. Say hello to Liam." He said while standing up when Jessica was wearing her coat to leave.


## The Coffee House, 18:00 P.M.

Olga walked into the café and looked for Oliver. She found him sitting behind a table in the middle of the crowd.

She went to him: "Hello, Ollie!" She said to earn his attention.

Oliver looked up and smiled: "Hi Olga. Take a seat."

Olga sat on the chair in front of Oliver's and asked: "How is splitting the atom's nucleus going?"

"You're so funny, you know?" Oliver asked with utmost serious he could.

"I do know that," Olga said with a smile, "How are you?"

"Couldn't be better. How are you?"

Olga placed her hand under her chin. She asked: "You do realise that classic answers are not so acceptable if 'How are you?' was asked by a Russian, don't you?"

"I just learnt!" Oliver chuckled and said, "What do you rather to hear?"

"Something more than how do you feel right now. I want to know if your life is good, your recent plans and…anything that make me trust you to be my friend."

"Olga, we *are* friends."

"Doesn't change the tradition."

"You're insisting. I'm not alright; I'm just trying to be. I recently did a terrible thing which I don't tend to talk about it. I should be sorry and maybe ashamed of what I did but I'm not. Don't get me wrong, what I did was related to my job, I didn't do anything outside of the law! I'm done. How are *you*?" Oliver explained and asked Olga a question.

"Ignoring that I saw my friend's dead body which I still have nightmares about it, I'm fine or I'll be. Soon. My family called me. My second sister, Madeline, will be getting married in May. She asked me to be her maid of honour…and when we're done, I have something that I really want to talk to you about it."

"It'll probably take a while for all of us to be mentally healed. Congratulations to your sister, I hope she'll live a long healthy life. Don't worry, we will get to that as well. I'll now tell you why I asked you to come here," Oliver said, coughed and continued "First things first, I need you to know that I hate racism…There are hundreds of possibilities, Olga. My job and cooperation with the police induce me to analyse all those possibilities patiently and rigorously. There is a possibility that I personally don't like but I don't avoid giving it a shot; I'm not allowed to. That possibility tells me that you are the killer I'm willing to bring down to justice. I don't like it but I can't neglect making sure that it's deniable. This possibility that has a direct connection with your nationality. Some very racist people who I unfortunately work with, believe that you can be dangerous because you're Russian. I disagree. Their racial vision of Russians is what makes them feel superior, makes them feel valuable but it's wrong. It just makes them more stupid."

"I apologise Oliver. But I follow," Olga said curious. She indirectly asked for more information.

"Sebastian told me that he got to the crime scene first. You arrived after him. You were the second person there. He said that he didn't do it and it wasn't him. He never mentioned what was your answer. I want to know your answer."

Olga thought and said: "I told him that I knew it wasn't him. That was my answer."

"Now, tell me why you told him that you knew he wasn't the killer? What was your argumentation?"

Olga raised an eyebrow and said: "Well, I think his frightened attitude was too real to be faked. I think that guy's worst sin might be killing a bug!"

"John Wayne Gacy seemed innocent as well," Oliver leant to his chair and said calmly: "Ms Durov, why don't you tell me who did it? Who killed Bradly Moore?"

Olga was undoubtedly confused and felt insulted. A tiny, teeny frown appeared on her face and she asked with discretion: "Oliver, are you alright? How can I answer you when I don't even have an answer?"

"I meant the voting, the other day. Who did you vote for?"

Olga leant back to the chair and answered: "I voted for Pietro."

"Why did you?"

"I think that there is this voice inside me, telling me that Pietro is guilty. You know, the rest of the suspects...they have this particular innocence." Olga explained, "Don't get me wrong! Pietro isn't a bad person. He is actually a very affable and eloquent guy but—I don't know, Ollie. I really don't know. I feel that Pietro is the killer that you're looking for or...he knows who the killer is."

Oliver bent his head and closed his eyes a bit and whispered: "Do you think so?"

"Like you said, we must analyse all the possibilities. This is one of those. I don't like to accuse him but that guy is a world of mysteries."

Oliver didn't answer her. He was bemused. One of the hundred possibilities. What if Olga was right? And what if she was wrong? What if she was trying to put everything on someone else?

The number of possibilities weren't 'hundred'. Not anymore.

Thousands. Let's call them thousands.

It was like maze; every escape would've led him to another maze.

It was too much for him to take.

"It's *not fair*," he thought, "Struggling for the truth is *not fair*"

He looked up to Olga and said: "I have nothing else to discuss. Thank you for your time, Olga."

While he was talking, he saw Arthur walked into the café and because he saw Oliver was talking to Olga, he took a seat behind a table next to the door.

"Yes. I also think I'm done here," Olga said with signs of feeling insulted in her voice, stood up and took her purse "See you later, Oliver."

Arthur took a seat at Oliver's table just after Olga left the coffee house. He asked: "How did that go?"

Oliver took a serious look at Arthur's Nordic blue eyes and whispered: "She wanted to say something." Then asked: "Why don't you go back to your homeland sometime?"

"Where? Canberra?"

"Yes" Oliver asked, "I miss Pennsylvania sometimes even though I literally never lived there. How can you not miss Canberra?"

"Who said I don't?"

"You do?" Oliver said, "Then go back there and leave me alone."

"What's wrong, Ollie? Tell me about it."

Oliver said impatiently: "Just go get in the car. I'll be there. I'm waiting for the waiter. I want to buy pasta."

Oliver exhaustedly put his head on the table. Considering the fact that Arthur knew how hard it was for Oliver lately, he had to take Oliver home sooner.

Arthur raised his hand and a waiter went to them and said smiling: "Good evening, gentlemen. What can I get you?"

"Hi. I would have some Alfredo pasta for two, a medium cup of iced coffee and a large cup of hot chocolate. We'll take them."

"Right away, sir." And went to the counter.

Oliver brought his head up and whispered: "I ate you." He continued: "I told you to go get the car. Who are you to disobey?"

"Arthur Michael Black-Hall. Sergeant of London's police department. Thirty-three, Australian." Arthur represented a biography of himself in exactly three seconds.

"Sometimes I really, *really* hate you. I mean it."

Arthur shrugged indifferently: "I usually feel the same about you." He said with no feelings.

"Give me the car keys. I'm going home."

Oliver was extremely exhausted. At that very moment, his one and only preference would be taking some of his sleeping pills and get a good sleep.

Arthur asked: "Alright. But where do you mean by 'home'?"

"My own."

Arthur rolled his eyeballs and said: "Listen, Olivia made it crystal clear that you should stay at our house for a while and…"

Oliver interrupted him: "I am not staying anywhere other than my own house."

"Do not interrupt me," Arthur frowned, "I don't have the patience and ability to get engaged in a conversation about your mental health with your family again. I can't guarantee you anymore."

"Okay. You know what? Enough of my entire mental health problem. I'm fine and just because of the lack of desire to talk about my feeling, doesn't mean I'm not okay and anyone should interfere."

Although Oliver said what he said out loud and undoubtedly other people at the coffee house heard him, Arthur didn't react and that not-reacting, made Oliver feel embarrassed and frightened. All Arthur said was a four words sentence: "Get in the car." And handed Oliver the keys with a scary frown.

When Oliver walked on the street, the sky was pouring dogs and cats and by the time Oliver sat in the car, he was soaking wet.

He reviewed all the words that came out of his mind, transported to his mouth and said to Arthur. He could swear that all those creepy stuffs were side effects of tiredness. You know what they say, people can be described in three different types:

1. Those with side effects of hunger.
2. Those with side effects of tiredness.
3. Those with side effects of both hunger and tiredness.

So, there is this little fact which is that Oliver allows tiredness to defeat him; not once, not twice but so much more than that.

It was nothing prideful to Oliver.

He thought about Arthur. Arthur was always there for Oliver for the past fifteen years, whenever he was needed.

Arthur didn't deserve to be treated like he was being.

Oliver remembered a memory, all of a sudden.

It was the first day of work for Oliver. His first day of working among Arthur. That day, an underage boy was arrested for driving without license and for being high of cocaine. When his parents went to the station to set him free, they asked Arthur not to put those on the kids' profile with the excuse of 'All the teenagers do such things. Haven't you done such crimes back in your days?' and Oliver remembered Arthur's answer like day one. Arthur simply answered 'No, I had good and caring parents.'

Oliver had never heard a better answer. Ever.

Oliver felt like crying. He wasn't actually interested in sharing his feelings with anyone; even himself.

When he was younger, his genius hack was to pretend that nothing has ever happened. He would ignore the occurrence.

Growing up as a teenager having two younger sisters, an always-busy-taking-better-care-of-younger-children mother and a father who would spend most of his day at his office to design buildings, Oliver grew up as a shy and quiet boy.

Brad—May his soul rest in peace—was an extrovert person or as some people like to call "The cool friend;" not cooler. The cool friend. *The* cool friend. So as an extrovert and the cool friend, Brad was usually joyful, happy, head in the sky and cheerful. And when he wasn't, he was talking about it to Oliver. Of course, Oliver's feelings would always been considered too, but he was the one who didn't want his thoughts to leave his mind.

Long story short, Bill Oliver Johnson didn't want to share his feelings with his parents, his sisters, with his best friends but sometimes with a psychologist.

Now at that specific moment, he wanted to tell someone how he felt and what has got him crying but he was in doubt. He was crying rivers when Arthur opened the back door, put the dishes in the car and came to sit on the driver's seat.

Oliver wiped tears away off his face and grabbed his hot chocolate.

As soon as he saw Oliver's moist face, Arthur asked: "What's the matter, Oliver?"

"Nothing. I…it's nothing…I'm fine."

"Indeed, you are. Saying the man who is crying and hardly talking." Arthur said with a moderate level of apprehension "Why don't you just tell me? Or tell Liv or D or…your parents?"

"I don't do that. Entirely. I don't talk to anyone about this, at all."

"And why is that?"

"Because I don't know how!" Oliver yelled at Arthur. "Happy now?"

"What?" Arthur asked bewildered "What did you say?"

"What I said...was...that I don't know how to share feelings. It's always been tough," Oliver said calmly and turned his face to the window.

"Ollie?" Arthur called him after a few seconds.

"Hmm?"

"God forgive me for asking this but, are you sure that you're a psychologist?"

"I'm no psychologist."

"Your courtesy is one thing that I like about you."

Oliver instantly turned to him and yelled defensive: "God damn it, Arthur! A crime psychologist isn't a psychologist."

"It is, technically."

"Yeah? How is that? People voluntarily talk to therapists and psychologists. But me? People are brought to me and I should beg them to speak!"

"Oliver, I don't really care about your job complains. What I'm trying to say is that you're a psychologist; somehow at least. Basically, you should know that what has caused this issue."

"I know. I exactly know why," said Oliver with a significant sadness in his voice, "When I was growing up, Mum was filling her time with taking care of the little ones. My dad worked all the time. I didn't have anyone to talk to. I know you're thinking of Brad; he usually was the one who talked. I was the friend who listened."

Arthur didn't say anything. He understood that there are more things to be said and more things to be listened.

Oliver continued: "That was exactly why I got this job. Although I wanted to be a psychologist but you know...what I do brings more excitement to my life."

A certainly most beautiful smile appeared on Arthur's face. He said satisfied: "Look whose heart I found."

Oliver laughed and said: "Don't tell anyone, they won't take me serious anymore."

"You see, Ollie? This is what sharing feelings is," Arthur said and started to drive. He continued: "Do you know who you remind me of?"

Oliver drank a gulp of his hot chocolate and asked: "Who?"

"Will Graham," Arthur said with his eyes locked on the road, "You're both equally insane."

### 21 Minutes Later...

Arthur walked inside his and Olivia's house to turn the lights on while Oliver was getting their food off the car.

He went to the kitchen to get two plates for the pasta.

Oliver went into to the house, made his way right into the kitchen.

Arthur said: "Put the dish on the table. I must save some for Liv."

"You see, *this* is what I don't like about marriages. You should share your food with somebody else," Oliver said while removing the dishes out of their paper bags.

"You don't have to. It's a must." Arthur said with his head in a cabinet.

"That doesn't make it any less awkward."

"And no one's kneeling in front of you right now." Arthur said very straightforward.

"When's she coming back?" Oliver asked, pretended like he didn't hear Arthur.

"I don't know. I call her now." Arthur said. He brought his phone out of his pocket and called Olivia, "Hey dear, how are you?...How's the party?...Great, have fun...Oliver and I bought some food, shall we wait for you?...Okay babe, have fun...love you more."

Arthur ended the call and said to Oliver: "She's suffering there."

"How do you know that?"

"Let's start with the part that she was talking really enthused and she said that the party was amazing and she's having the time of her life."

Oliver laughed: "She's in a deep water!"

"But she'll have a lot to gossip about when she returns! Wait and observe!"

***

### About 2 Hours Later...

Olivia opened the door with her keys and removing high heels off his feet was the very first thing she did and she headed to the living room to find his brother and husband.

Oliver and Arthur had just finished their meal and were watching a Ted Bundy documentary without blinking.

"Hey guys." Olivia called but received no answers. She said with no feelings: "Oh dear God, I'm on fire, where are Bruce and Clark?" no answers again.

Olivia went standing right in front of the television.

Arthur said: "Hi love, how are you? Can you move? They're gonna show Ted's trial."

Olivia crossed her arms, raised an eyebrow and asked: "*Ted*? Who is he? My brother-in-law?"

Oliver bent forward and said: "Don't be sensitive and just move."

Olivia did move away; she sat next to Oliver and said: "He acted as his own lawyer at the second trial. He did a very great job, by the way; he was executed by the electric chair!"

"Yeah, we're not there yet." Arthur said without taking eyes off the television.

"Arthur?" Olivia turned to Arthur. "You've watched this documentary like eight times!"

You know it. Arthur didn't answer. So, Olivia gave up on them and maintained watching the rest of the documentary with them.

After half an hour, the documentary was finally over but all three of them were too tired and amazed to get up.

Oliver finally stood up and stretched his body: "I'm going upstairs. I should call Harry."

Olivia put her feet on Oliver's seat and put her hand under her chin: "Who's Harry?"

"Harrison Henry. Richard's youngest." Arthur answered her.

"Yeah. I saw him at the funeral," Olivia said.

"He was but I didn't see him. I'm gonna call him now, see you."

Oliver said and went upstairs to the guest room with his phone. He closed the door, turned on a night lap and sat on the bed. He called Harry and after a few moments, the call was made. In a second, Oliver saw Harry's face on his phone: "Hello, muffin!" Harry said happily.

Harry used the nickname 'Muffin' for Oliver ever since college because Oliver was addicted to blueberry muffins. He bought one of them every week back at the college.

"Hello Harry," Oliver said with a smile, "You have no idea how happy I am to see you."

"You too, Ollie. How's it going?"

"Not good…bad," Oliver said doubtful.

"I know, Oliver. I'm so truly sorry about your loss. My condolences. No words can explain how I feel and think about how you're doing since that night." Harry said sympathetically.

"Your father told me that you were at the funeral. Thank you for coming. Sorry we didn't catch up."

"It's okay Ollie. I get it. It wasn't a responsibility. You were upset and I didn't mean to bother you."

"Again, I'm thankful."

"Do you—want to talk about your feelings?"

Oliver thought for a few seconds and answered: "I saw Angelina Jackson, our former college professor, a few days ago. I think I lied to her…I'm failing at expressing how I feel. I am being bipolar maybe. I can be so mad at you right now and within a second, I can hug you." Oliver explained to Harry "I get mad easily and I don't even realise it. It makes me feel endlessly unstable."

"Ollie" Harry took a deep breath "I don't want any quick answers. Take your time and give me a convincing answer."

Oliver put the phone down. He laid on the bed and stared at the ceiling and went through every single memory he had made with Brad.

Every ice cream they had together.

Every place they'd been to.

Every mess they'd made together.

Every person they'd met together.

Every conversations and small talks they'd made.

Every laughter they had together.

Every time that they thought one another's idea was stupid.

Oliver could remember them all; well, crystal clear.

Oliver brought the phone up. Harry was still there. With his gorgeous and caring smile, he was still there. "Came up with a word?" Harry asked Oliver.

Oliver shortly answered: "Endless nothingness."

"Is that how you feel? Endless nothingness?" Harry asked Oliver.

"Throughout my life, my job has been my greatest accomplishment…And now it's turning into my greatest failure. I was so professional back then; I just needed to look someone in the eye and say if they're criminal. I can't do that now."

"Ollie, do you fear anything?"

"I'm afraid, Harry. I'm afraid that I might've killed my friend and I don't even know it," Oliver said with his voice shivering, trying not to cry.

"How do you think that's possible?"

"I don't know. I may have had drugs; I was drugged and I don't remember that time period of the night."

"When was the murder committed?"

"Between 10:30 to 10:50."

"And where were you at that time?"

"I was with your father. We were at work." Oliver answered, "Two officers and a detective approved."

"What is the matter then? My father witnessed that you were with him at that time."

"Yes! But I have a theory."

"What is the theory?"

"That I killed Brad somehow and I don't remember killing him. All of the people around me know that I've done it but they avoid saying anything. They keep quiet because they're afraid that I kill them too," Oliver said his theory and by all the thirty-three years of knowledge, Harry had never heard anything more insane...more dumb!

Harry took another deep breath, bent his head and patiently called: "Bill?"

"Yes?"

"I would've punched you in the face if I were there with you!"

"Why?"

"Because what you're saying is so unbelievably untrue! It has the potential to become a sci-fi book or movie!"

"That was...good to hear?"

"Oliver, I'm not like other people and other people aren't like me. I'm not going to tell you that everything will be alright. That might turn out to be a lie. I won't tell you that you will be alright, you might feel broken for the rest of your life. Don't expect me to tell you that time will heal your mental trauma; time isn't healing, time will just provide you a bit of itself to think. Time will provide itself for you to think and come up with a solution to heal you. Time provides you itself that leads to a situation, time won't change into scar tapes. You're all alone at this cycle. Others just open your eyes to an outlook that

172

you've been neglecting." Harry said and with every word, Oliver felt like those words were the exact thing he needed to hear.

"Keep talking," Oliver said curiously.

"Ollie, you are smart, sweet and caring. You are realistic and that is your key to success. The analytical part of you is invincible, the extent of your mind's thinking is limitless. Listen to me carefully; you are a human, Oliver. You are a human with a human body, a human amount of energy and a human need of breather. Give yourself a break or what you'd become after solving this case will be just a walking dead! A depressed man who isn't even forty." Harry warned and advised.

"How are you so sure that I can solve this case? How is everybody so sure about it?" Oliver asked the most important question that had been messing with his mind.

"Why not? Tell me, Oliver, why not? You have solved dozens of cases! No one can deny the truth. Someone says the sky is green, who believes? Everyone knows it is blue."

"*Eppur si mouve*," Oliver said in Italian.

"I beg your pardon?" Harry raised his left eyebrow.

"And yet it moves." Oliver translated.

"What do you mean?"

"It was the last thing that Galilei said after he was forced to claim that earth is still. 'And yet it moves.'"

"I know that. Why did you bring that up?"

"He was aware of earth's movements. He was forced to accept the ignorance of his regarding circumstances because no one thought that he was right."

"Is this a metaphor?"

"Yes, Sherlock. Analyse it."

"What you're saying is that you might not be as good as we think you are?" Harry asked in doubt.

"Yes."

"And what you're saying is that we're just blindly following our emotions that is appreciatively loving you?"

"Indeed."

"And what you said, Oliver, is that you are not god enough and none of us ever noticed that?"

"How brilliant! Yeah!" Oliver said cheerfully.

Harry was furious after all. He said infuriated: "Oliver! You are the best forensic psychologist that was ever born! Okay? Don't you dare to tell me that you're not enough while you are! Who is more obsessed with this job as much as you are? Nobody! Now you go get yourself a break and find a way to get this done! Understood?"

"What if I say no?" Oliver asked with a big smile. Just to mess with Harry.

"Oliver!" Harry yelled at Oliver.

Oliver laughed.

"Harry, how are you?" Oliver asked kindly.

"I'm good. Overthinking about you, but still fine. Why did you ask?" Harry said with an initial misery; but he was calm.

"Because we were talking about me since we said hello! It's rude to ignore you," Oliver said with a warm-hearted smile.

"I'm fine. I have this new case I'm working on; it's keeping me busy. Plus, I'm in love!" Harry said cheerful.

"That's fantastic! Who you love?" Oliver asked excited.

"Not who, what!"

"Huh?" Oliver asked confused.

Harry switched the camera and showed Oliver outside of his hotel room through the window: "Isn't this magnificent? Oh, I can stay here and watch this view for the rest of my living life and after!"

The view that Harry was talking about was the beautiful, splendid and extraordinary cloudy sky of Dublin. Harry was obsessed with that sort of weather, so was Oliver! No doubts that London was the best place for both of them to live!

Oliver said: "Thank you, Harry. Your advice was great. I'll certainly consider that."

"Bravo. I'm glad that I could help you, even a little bit. And don't you make me angry again!"

"Fine, man. I'll never do that again!" Oliver said, "For now!"

"End the call or I will come back to London now!"

\*\*\*

174

Olivia knocked at the door and opened it without waiting for permission. Oliver looked at her and said: "Just—What if I was naked?"

"Well, you should be so sorry and ashamed of yourself to discuss your nakedness with your own sister who is happened to be married."

"What the—you know what? Forget about it. What brought you here?"

"The fact that this is my house and I own the place," Olivia said, "I need you downstairs to redecorate." And she left.

Oliver didn't have anything to do for the rest of the night. Being physically active sounded like a good idea plus, Oliver hadn't exercised in a month.

He went downstairs and the first thing he did was going to the kitchen to get some juice but instead, he got Arthur sitting on the island cabinet. Oliver asked: "What are you doing here?"

Arthur answered: "I live in this place. Your questions should be asked by me. What are italic doing here?"

"Liv told me that she wanted to redecorate." Oliver answered and stared at Arthur. "And I never thought that you'll look so good on this cabinet!"

Arthur laughed and didn't say anything.

Meanwhile, Olivia who just finished mind mapping about the living room's redecorating, walked into the kitchen. She said happily: "Gentlemen, woman up! We are going to redecorate!"

Arthur gave her a beautiful, charming smile and said with honour and honesty: "Love, I'd love to help you but I'm too tired. Can we do it in the morning?"

Olivia grabbed her husband's face and said: "Come on, sweetie. Let's just do it now, you know that I don't do anything on a Saturday morning."

"I know." Arthur grabbed her forearms "But I was thinking of watching a movie with Oliver. You know, to see if he gets tired enough to sleep."

"And you think watching a movie makes him more tired than redecorating?" Olivia asked smiled and raised an eyebrow, "Okay, fine. I'll do it by myself. You two kids go have some fun. Take some snacks."

"Tell me if you needed any help, alright?" Arthur smiled out of satisfaction.

"Sure, honey," Olivia said to Arthur, kissed his right shoulder and whispered next to his ear: "You two are huge wastes of muscles!"

Arthur smiled at her. Got off the cabinet and went to the fridge that Oliver was standing next to and whispered: "Run! *Run!*"

Oliver wished to be a little more active to replace it with his workout-less month. He however went upstairs to the attic.

Unlike the attics of creepy thriller movies houses, Arthur and Olivia's attic was cosy, comfortable and well-decorated. Like that old saying: "A woman has made that house a home."

Olivia literally had made that attic *the* most beautiful room of the house. The wooden attic was covered in blue. A Teal three seats sofa and two singular benches with syrup cushions were put at the corner of the attic in front of a television.

A peanut and tawny carpet added extra beauty to the room but what was favourite to Oliver was several pots of Sansevieria all across the room.

As of the myths, no snacks should've been lived in that room and if it were any, the humankind would've been stuck in an infinite loop with no exits. Pretty cool, huh?

Oliver started searching the box of DVDs to pick a movie. He wasn't in the mood for horrors, fed up with crimes, sick of romances, no time for biographies, disgusted by sci-fi and watched a documentary an hour ago so as a conclusion, he picked a Jim Carrey comedy. Pure Perfection.

He was ready to put the CD in the device but he stopped when he saw Arthur.

Arthur's body, to be specific, no heads could be seen; he was holding a notebook and a pen, his laptop and a bunch of chips with two sodas and all of these items were almost covering Arthur's face.

Oliver grabbed the laptop and pen and notebook so Arthur could drop everything on the table.

Oliver asked: "Why did you bring your laptop? You've got work to do?"

"No," Arthur shortly answered, "I should send some emails. Notebook is for our pros and cons list. Remember?"

"But I thought we were gonna watch a movie."

"You know what? You're right. You've emotionally decided to adopt a little girl but watching a movie is so much more important than that." Arthur humiliated Oliver with a serious attitude.

Oliver rolled his eyeballs and said: "Let's just get it done."

Arthur sat on a bench and opened the notebook. He asked: "Does anybody knows? Except for me?"

"No," Oliver said, "I'll tell Liv after we finished the list. If it got accepted, I'll tell my parents and Moores."

"Fair enough." Arthur shook his head, "Okay, let's do this. We start with pros."

He wrote in his notebook:

*Pros:*

- *You won't die alone.*
- *You can share your joy with someone else.*
- *Your life will be filled with wonder.*
- *You'll have someone to teach them and learn from them.*
- *Someone is always there to make you laugh.*
- *You can see a little person becomes an adult.*
- *You may see your grandchildren before you die.*
- *Doing so many activities that you haven't done since you were a child.*
- *There is always someone to teach you how to work with technology.*
- *They would cause you heart attacks which helps reducing world's population.*

*Cons:*
- *Uncertain future for the kid.*
- *You may lose the opportunity of getting married.*
- *When they grow up, they might want to look for their real parents (if the kid is adopted).*
- *Having no extra time for personal activities such as hanging out with friends.*
- *Lending money to someone who will never pay you back.*
- *You get a roommate that you can't interview.*
- *They keep you up all night asking questions.*
- *They wake you up at 6 a.m. to get breakfast.*
- *You may get disappointed by their childish actions but you can't stay upset so long because they're your kid.*
- *You HAVE to share your meals with them.*

- *When you don't hear anything for more than 3 minutes, it means that they are making a mess.*

"Is that all?" Oliver asked while reading the list, "Can you think of anything else?"

Arthur took an exact look at the list and answered: "No. I don't think we missed anything."

"Right. How many cons and how many pros?"

"Nine pros and eleven cons."

Oliver didn't show it on his face but he didn't want to buy it. He grabbed the notebook and read it again. He asked after reading the ninth title on the cons list: "Why is 'have' written in capital letters?"

"That's a sign for emphasise. Sharing meals is no joke. That is the main reason why I don't have kids." Arthur explained, "When you're married, keeping meals is a must. When you have a kid, it becomes a should."

Oliver joked cold blood: "Yeah totally. So, these reasons doesn't seem logical to me. What if we analyse them in logical terms?"

Arthur bent his head and smiled: "There is nothing logical about having kids. Logic cannot defeat kids. They wouldn't have been kids if they knew what logic is!"

"I see what you mean. But I need real reasons," Oliver said and handed Arthur the notebook "Would you please ask Olivia tonight? My pills are affecting. I'm going to bed."

"I thought you weren't gonna take sedatives. You know, to evaluate your sleep at our house."

"I was but I really needed to sleep so…" Oliver said and shrugged.

"I get it." Arthur said and got off the couch "I'll talk to Olivia. Sleep well."

Oliver shook his head and headed to his room. By the time he entered the room, he fell sleep on the bed. He got unconscious, to be specific.

\*\*\*

### February 26th, Black's House, 8:45 A.M.

"Hey honey," Oliver said after walking into the kitchen with a smile.

"Morning, sweetie." Olivia answered back, "Take a seat. I made you some scrambled egg."

"You've got cherry tomatoes?"

"Yeah, they're in the fridge. Put the bowl on the table." She guided while going to the oven to put the eggs on the plate.

Oliver placed the tomatoes' bowl on the table and sat on a stool.

Olivia put a plate of Oliver's favourite egg in front of him: Scrambled egg with ham and parsley.

Oliver smiled and appreciated: "Thank you, dear."

"Anytime," said Olivia, "Hey, we must talk about Arthur."

"What about him?"

"You *do* know you've been his closest friend for the past seven years, right?"

"No, not really. Am I?"

"Yes, you are. He has other friends but he isn't close to any of them as he's with you," Olivia said with worry "He has been working a lot lately. He barely gets time to rest. Can you please talk to Richard about Arthur? Maybe Richard can reduce his involvement in the case of..."

"Wait, is it about Brad's case? Because we should talk about that too." Oliver stopped Olivia, "You know that I've always respected and cared for Arthur but I'd also believed that Brad was my best friend, correct?"

"Correct. That's true."

Oliver took a deep breath and said: "You can't talk about this to anyone...I recently have realized that Brad was my best friend, but I wasn't his. I mean, who keeps so many secrets from his best friend? Why did he even keep them in a closet? Wasn't I reliable enough to know about his friends? Or his daughter?"

Olivia froze for a moment: "Brad...had a daughter? With Elma?"

"Wha—no! No, they never had kids. The girl was supposed to be his goddaughter."

Olivia sat on the table and asked: "Who is she? Do I know her?"

"No, you don't. Her name is Ava Florence WinterGreen. She lives in an orphanage. I saw her a couple of times, I had lunch with her yesterday."

"Who else knows about her?"

"Arthur, Richard and Ezra. Brad had given Ezra's number to orphanage's principle in case of an emergency, that's how we found out about her. I asked them not to tell anyone else."

"Ezra hasn't told his parents yet?"

"Apparently not," Oliver said, "They would've talked to me about her but they haven't."

Olivia put her hands on her eyes and said: "Damn, Ollie, *damn*. Are we sure he wasn't cooperating with the SIS?"

"No ideas, although I wouldn't be surprised if he was!"

They both spent a moment in silence so that Olivia was able to think clearly about the entire situation and the information she received in the past minute.

She asked reprehensive: "Did you mean to tell anyone else about Ava? Like, *ever*?"

"Of course I did. I couldn't let you or Dakota know because you might've spilled the tea. We couldn't tell the Moores either. They currently aren't in a good situation to know so much."

Olivia raised an eyebrow and asked: "You promised them to find the killer, bro. Now you're worried if they find out about a little girl?"

Oliver defensively said: "I know that I broke the rules but, in my defence, I was being emotional!"

Olivia clapped and humiliatingly cheered: "Acceptable! Problem solved!"

Oliver frowned at her and quietly started eating his eggs.

Oliver obviously felt bad about that. Fortunately, or unfortunately, Oliver was a real emotional person. Emotional and judgmental. That didn't end well plenty of times.

When he promised Robert and Elizabeth, he certainly was emotional but the death of his best friend didn't cause it.

"Rob, Lizzie, I will find who killed Brad and bring them to justice; I promise." Those words came out of the mouth of a typical Oliver.

Unlike Oliver, Dakota and Olivia were logical. They would've knocked their hearts out if they dared to opine. Plus, the only use of their hearts was the blood transporter!

Oliver smiled at what he was thinking and Olivia looked at him weirdly. Perhaps she was thinking that her brother had gone insane, finally!

By the moment the door was knocked, Oliver stood up and said: "I'll get it."

Oliver got to the door and opened it. It was Arthur who apparently had been out of the house to some get milk, since he was holding a bottle.

"Morning, Arthur," said Oliver, "Why did you get up so early?"

Arthur walked into the house and as he was heading to the kitchen, he said: "It's the miracle of the weekend, Ollie. You can never get up late!" He then continued to Olivia, "Hi love. So, I woke up in the middle of the night, thought I'd drink some milk to go back to sleep but I found none. How come we ran out of milk?"

Olivia answered: "It came to the end of existence when I made you a jar of oatmeal last night. It's in the fridge."

Arthur smiled: "You're the *best*!" He said happily.

Oliver smiled as well. Nothing could've possibly cheer him up more than seeing his sister and her husband so happy and lovely.

Arthur took his oatmeal out of the fridge and put it on the table and when he was looking for a spoon, he asked: "How did you sleep, Oliver?"

Olivia suddenly said: "Oh, Ollie, I'm sorry I totally forgot to ask you about that."

Oliver said with the calm that was hiding his sadness: "It's not a big deal, Liv…I actually didn't sleep well…Technically didn't sleep at all."

"Why is that? What was the matter?" Arthur asked.

"Everything was fine with the room…There was nothing wrong with that. *I'm* the problem."

"How long did you sleep?" Olivia asked sympathetically.

Oliver thought and answered: "I slept…a forty five minutes, a forty minute duration and then an hour."

Arthur held his chin and said: "Two hours and fifteen minutes. That's not good, Oliver, that's not enough."

"I know it's not, but I can't help it." Oliver sadly shrugged.

"What are you gonna do about it?" Olivia asked sympathetically.

"Before you say anything, I suggest you spend one more night here. Maybe your brain hasn't got used to this place yet." Arthur suggested.

Oliver looked down and said slowly: "I was just fine before the ninth day of February. My mind has been disordered since then. Now I don't even know what I'm doing…It's all like a dream; when you're having a dream and, in that dream, you're doing something, you know everything such as the knowledge of why? But when you wake up, they're all gone and you know nothing. This is how I feel. I feel like I don't understand anything."

Olivia and Arthur spent moments in silence. They were seeing Oliver's path to devastation and yet, they could do nothing about it but listening and giving him time to fix it.

Olivia took Oliver's hand and said: "Ollie, you're not alone in this. We will help you with all we're able to. You'll pass this creepy time period and be fine so soon."

Oliver looked at Olivia and said: "Thank you, Liv. What you said meant a lot to me. And I'm so deeply thankful to have you guys by my side."

He immediately showed them a fake smile and said: "I'm going out for a walk. I'll be back for lunch."

Oliver went outside the house without taking any jackets. It didn't matter.

His black t-shirt, black and white plaid shirt and grey jean pants were warm enough.

He actually thought that Arthur had told Liv about Ava and Oliver's decision; apparently, he didn't and that led Oliver to keep the details to himself. He had all the time in the world. He touched his phone off his pants but didn't feel the phone. He didn't bring his phone.

"That's better," he thought, "No phone, no stress."

Oliver put his hands in his pockets and followed a path to the park. Besides his passion for America, Oliver would never want to leave England. He was in love with London. He was in love with the weather, the sky, the clouds that kept the sun in hide, the streets cobblestones and the smooth cold wind of the morning. Who wouldn't like these items?

As he was walking slowly, he closed his eyes for a moment and inhaled the fresh air.

For the first time in the past month, he felt like he was him; the one and only Oliver in his world. He felt like himself once more. He didn't want that delightful feeling to be gone so he sat on a bench beside the street and leant his head back to stare at the sky.

The sky was cloudy and beautiful and as always, it had rooms for birds to fly. How pretty.

Watching that divine view was so pleasing that Oliver felt sleepy and before he took a nap on a street bench, he decided to go back home.

"You know what?" He thought as soon as he got up, "Today is *my day*. It's weekend and I don't work on weekends!"

He haughtily went to the closest supermarket and did his best at buying ANY junk food he bumped into. He didn't withhold.

Despite the abundance of his shopping, Oliver placed them all in two bags and walked back to Blacks' house happily.

By the time he got to the house, the bags were showing him that they were heavy; but not as heavy as he couldn't take them. Oliver was nothing less than an athlete. Ringing the bell was no big deal.

It took a little while for Olivia to open the door. She opened the door and said: "Oh wow! Look who's been busy with shopping that he didn't answer any of my calls!"

Oliver handed her a bag and said: "I forgot my phone. It actually felt nice. I mean to destroy it!"

Olivia took the bag to the kitchen saying: "That is nice, honey. I'm glad you came to an understanding!"

Oliver laughed and went after her. He asked: "Where's Arthur? I bought him a cereal box."

"Thanks. He went to the gym. He'll be back for lunch. He said you could join him."

Oliver yawned with his mouth closed and said: "No I won't. Today is my day. I'll do nothing but taking extra calories with no bits of guilt." He added, "But you have my word, I will begin my exercise from Monday or Tuesday!"

"Why Tuesday?"

"I want to have the fifth meeting with the suspects on Monday. It might take a while; let's not promise anything for Monday."

"And…are they aware of your plans?" Olivia leant to the sink.

"No. But they will! Tell Arthur to send them emails for Monday, half past five in the afternoon."

"Fine. What do you want for lunch?"

He answered with no hesitate: "Chicken parmigiana. Australian recipe."

"You got it mate!" Olivia said with an Australian accent.

Oliver asked surprised: "How did you do that?"

She answered: "Did what?" She laughed, "I live with an Aussie! What do you think?"

Oliver glared: "Well be grateful for this gift, sis. If I had an Australian accent, I would've never shut up!"

And he left the kitchen to the bedroom, announcing: "I'm gonna go sleep. Do not disturb!"

***

He was confused.

He thought it through.

It had happened before.

Nothing was new about that night.

He looked around him.

Red and Blue lights of the police cars were lighting up the place.

Neighbours and pedestrians were staring that scene with their heads full of questions.

He jogged into Bradly's house but this time no officers stopped him saying: "You cannot enter, sir." so Oliver could reply: "I'm his friend. I know him."

He made his way into the house and entered the dark hallway.

No signs of a dead man's body or any other people inside the house.

The only murder accurate object was the blood on the dark brown parquet.

But it did not seem like its original form.

It appeared like someone was hauled towards the hallway.

The bloodline was continued to down the hallway.

Heavily breathing, he slowly followed the crimson line with eyes to the bottom.

The entire house was dark but he could see that someone was standing right where the bloodline was finished, facing the wall.

He put a baby step or two to the stranger.

Carefully walked so the stranger wouldn't notice him.

He took another quiet step but his loudness in breathing revealed him, unfortunately.

The stranger turned back, he sensed.

Less than a second later, the stranger was in front of him. Roaring insignificant.

Was the stranger even a human?

He felt a giant hand on his throat, chocking him.

That hand was disgustingly adhesive.

It made him think of three words: Monster, Sticky, Gross.

He took a not-so-clear look at the monster before he felt completely breathless.

The monster was faceless.

Black as the petroleum.

Sticky as the wax.

He tried to scream but he was too unable to even open his mouth.

He was helpless.

*All alone…*

## Black's House's Guest Room, 11:18 A.M.

Oliver woke up fearfully and sat on the bed. He was breathing real fast and heavy. He touched his throat, no one was grabbing it. No petroleum on his throat, only his cold sweat.

He looked around. He was alone in the guest room. He turned on his phone to check the clock. He succeeded sleeping for an hour; although he thought it would've been so much better if he just didn't sleep at all.

He laid back on the bed but soon, he removed the grey sheet off himself. He was too sweaty; he needed a shower.

Within an hour, when Oliver was showered and calm, he walked around the room to reformulate his mind. He knew exactly what to do. He had to call the sleep clinic. NO second thoughts. No hesitations.

He found the number of 'Balthazar Baldwin' to call. His sleep doctor. Balthazar didn't answer, his answering machine did: *"Hello, you have reached Balthazar Baldwin. I'm afraid I can't answer you right now. So…you know what to do!"*

And the phone beeped. Oliver left his message: *"Hello Balthazar. What's up? So…I called you to announce that something happened to me almost a month ago and I'm kinda sleepless ever since and if I sleep, nightmares don't leave me alone. So, I wanted to know if I can come to the clinic to evaluate my sleep. This is urgent so please answer when you heard this."*

Oliver went downstairs. He was starving. He entered the kitchen and saw Arthur and Olivia talking. Olivia turned to Oliver and asked with a low but horrifying volume: "What is Arthur talking about?"

Oliver simply answered: "You've got three days to think about it. I have something else to talk about." He leant his right shoulder to the door frame, "Guys I can't sleep. Last night I took my sedatives and I slept for only two and a half hours. I now slept for an hour. This isn't enough. Nothing works, even sleeping at your house. I left Balthazar a message. I need to go to the clinic."

Olivia crossed her arms and glared at him. Probably thinking of punching him so hard to break his jaw. She asked: "About your new decisions. Do you even allow yourself to ponder them?"

"Sure, I do," Oliver said, "Please, respect this decision. I'm not a kid who's afraid of medication. This is for the best and—about Ava? You guys have three days to think about it. I might go to the clinic this evening."

Arthur put his hand on Olivia's shoulder and said: "Liv, he's right. He isn't a kid. He's an adult man with the full ability of making decisions. If he thinks this might make him feel better, then why should we dissuade him?"

Oliver took advantage immediately: "See? Thanks, man."

Olivia breathed deeply and agreed, unlike her actual opinion: "Alright, fine. I'll be supportive. But I will not explain anything to Mum and Dad. You'll deal with them yourself."

Oliver smiled: "Fair enough."

"We'll talk about Ava later." Arthur said, "But for now, it's a bad idea in my mind."

"Three days you have to consider everything." Oliver whispered.


### February 28th, Baldwin's Sleep Clinic, 17:08 P.M.

After spending almost two days at Baldwin's sleep clinic, Oliver literally felt like an actual swank and he was spontaneously showing it off.

While he was bedridden; he had to chance to concentrate on himself and his thoughts. And he was finally ready to write them down. Oliver was a southpaw but because he had slept on his left side the night before, muscles were hurting so he had to write with the right hand. He started the note by drawing a twisted scrawl in the top left-hand corner and began to write the self-note with a terrible handwriting:

*This scrawl is the exact definition of I have been feeling recently. Indescribable. I'm trying to find only one meaningful item in the drawn lines. Why did Brad keep so many secrets away from me?*

*Was I a bad friend?*

*Did I do something to let him down?*

*What was his purpose of not telling me even about his friends? What if I don't get to solve the case and it remains unsolved for the next two decades?*

*The problem is that I'm incapable here. There is always a blonde American nurse who keeps drugging me with hypnotics and sedatives 24/7. Does she ever go home?*

*Just as soon as I'm ready to put a step ahead, I will get out of this damn clinic.*

*Today is the day of my fifth meeting with the suspects. Some of them have or had a mental disorder (dramatic!) and I want them to talk about the disorders today.*

*P.S. Marika has a daughter! How cute! I should ask for her name!*


The door was knocked. Oliver hided his note under the blanket and sarcastically said: "It's open! Always!"

Balthazar Baldwin opened the door and walked into the room. He smiled: "Don't be so sarcastic! It upsets Ms Kauri."

"Who is Ms Kauri?"

"Your nurse, of course. She's been nursing you for the past three days."

"That is Kauri? *The* Ms Kauri?" Oliver said sarcastic again.

Balthazar frowned and joked: "Stop it, alright?"

Oliver put his hands up and laughed: "Alright, deal. What is Kauri's last name?"

"Kauri is her surname. Constance Kauri. She's one of the best nurses here."

"I see. She's been working real hard this weekend. Isn't she coming today?"

Balthazar looked at Oliver so disappointed. He asked: "Oliver…she *just* left."

Oliver bent his head and smiled: "Did she?"

Balthazar shook his head and said: "Listen, I have to go." He continued, "And you do know that if it wasn't for the police investigation, I would've never allowed you to have people here?"

"I absolutely am aware," Oliver said, "I try to make it quick. They won't stay here for long."

"Please do. I should be going. I'll see you tomorrow."

Before Balthazar left the room, Oliver asked him: "When can I go home?"

"Tomorrow," said Balthazar, "Oh and one of them is here. Sebastian Bell; I will send him in."

Oliver grabbed the paper, climbed off the bed and wore his fluffy footwear, went to the closet and put the paper in his suitcase.

The room had no place to walk because Balthazar asked the nurses to put extra chairs in there for Oliver's meeting. Oliver sat on the bed anyway.

Not a long time after Balthazar was gone, Sebastian knocked and waked into the door. He saw Oliver and smiled: "Hello Oliver."

Oliver, who was slowly being affected by his drugs, sad ice cold: "Sebastian. Hi. Come in. Sit on one of these chairs."

Sebastian sat on the nearest chair to Oliver and said: "Before anything Oliver, it upsets me to see you like this. I hope you get your health back soon."

"Thank you, Sebastian. How are you? Did you move to your new studio?"

"I did, actually." Sebastian answered, "I was supposed to move on April first but I had nothing else to do, so."

"Congrats on that one."

"May I ask, how did this happen? Why are you here?"

"I had sleep issues, obviously," Oliver said and then he realised that he's being rude "I couldn't sleep. I came here to monitor my sleep…By the way, please forgive me if I'm being rude. It's the drugs' side effect."

"I see. It's alright. I understand that it is a tough time for you," Sebastian said, "Let's pass this, shall we? What is today's discussion about?"

"It's about Alice," Oliver said with dizziness, "In wonderland."

"Pardon me?"

"The syndrome. Alice in wonderland syndrome; which you got, right?"

"Is this meeting about me?"

"Not just about you. It's about the others, too. Some of you guys have or had mental disorders which we will talk about today." Oliver couldn't take it anymore. Sedatives were proving themselves to be so hard to defeat.

"What the hell were those sedatives?" Oliver thought.

"Sebastian?" Oliver called, "Go find Balthazar Baldwin. He's this tall and swarthy guy, he's wearing blue today."

Sebastian went outside to find Balthazar.

Oliver was just sleepy. Which meant that the new sedatives were effective; effective in the wrong time. Mazel tov!

## 24 Minutes Later...

Everyone was sitting on the chairs inside Oliver's clinical room, staring and waiting for him to begin—as he was concentrating on his cold coffee that Balthazar made him with reprehend.

Pietro seemed so confused and fed up that he asked: "Sorry, Oliver. This is a sleep clinic, right? Then why are you holding a coffee since like, ten minutes ago?"

Oliver looked up to him and answered with no feelings: "This is a sleep clinic and I'm so high on legal drugs. This'll help me avoid sleep." He coughed and said: "Move on to the subject."

Morgan miserably whispered: "Yes please."

Oliver glanced at her and decided to ignore what he heard: "Some of you have or used to have mental disorders, I tend to talk about them today. Any volunteers?"

"Oliver," Sebastian innocently complained "Is it necessary? Some of us don't really want to talk about our mental situation. It would be like exhuming buried memories."

Oliver took a sympathetic look in Sebastian's eyes: "I am aware and I'm sorry. But I'm afraid I'm not the one to be blamed. The murderer who gathered us together is the one to be blamed. Look around, see where I'm talking to you."

He turned his head to look at the others: "I swear I don't want anyone to see me like this. Even my parents. But I had no choice…Is it because of your harsh memories you don't mean to recall? Who doesn't have one of them? I mean, are they worse than seeing people burning alive, screaming while they know that it is the end and even being among them?"

Theodore bent his head and asked: "Oliver, what do you mean?"

"I'm talking about my adolescence, Theodore. I'm talking about what brought me here." Oliver answered Theodore.

"Do you want to talk about it?" Anya asked Oliver.

Oliver took a deep breath and began his story: "I was sixteen. Brad and I went to this library to study. I was too tired so I fell asleep. The next thing I remember is that I woke up hearing people screaming and Brad shaking my arm…I woke up and I saw flames burning up the entire library and you know; wooden shelves, wooden floor, wooden roof, wooden tables and chairs and books are made of woods, obviously. Everything was wooden. Everything was burning and people were struggling to leave the library but it was on the seventh floor and it seemed impossible to get out of it. I saw...*we* saw, Brad and I, we saw people burnt and screamed in the fire...the smell of a human burning is the most disgusting scent I've smelled. So, Brad took us to the window, there was this wide edge outside the window. We stood there until the firefighters arrived and brought us down. I don't quite remember what happened up there but I remember feeling terrified, holding on to Brad's arm too tight...and I could never sleep since that day." Oliver took a look at the others and continued: "That's it. That's my story. Who's next?"

Pietro raised his hand and said: "I'm not sure if it is counted as a disorder but I've been an addicted for the past four years, you know it. I moved to London in twenty thirteen and I got addicted to alcohol, ecstasy and amphetamine. Of course, addiction sucks but it didn't destroy my life...social life, I mean. So, I was addicted for four years. I met Brad last year and he encouraged me to quit. My father found out about my addiction a year later it started. And we haven't spoken since then. He thought that I'm a 'versagen' and 'enttäuschung'."

"Translation?" Olga asked.

Theodore answered: "Failure and disappointment."

"Yes, Theodore. Failure and disappointment. These were his words. We haven't talked since then," Pietro said, "But his day of birth is tomorrow and I want to call him to see if he has changed his mind."

"Thank you, Pietro for sharing," Oliver said with appreciation "Who's next?"

"Me, of course," Sebastian said, "My disorder is Alice in wonderland syndrome. AIWS, it's nothing rare. When I was a teenager, I went to my friend's house and something happened which I won't talk about it that because of it, I ran to the stairs and fell down. My head hit the wall and since then, I got migraines and AIWS. Sure, migraine *is* hereditary but AIWS isn't. I'm prone to a kind of the syndrome names Somatognoisa which makes me see myself bigger or smaller than what I really am. It has led me to anorexia nervosa plenty of times but I can handle it."

"Thank you for sharing it, Sebastian." Oliver appreciated, "This was it. Just the three of us. Any comments?"

Anya raised her hand: "Pietro, I'm so sorry about your addiction and yes, you must talk to your father. Sebastian, you experience the weirdest thing I have heard in my twenty-two years of lifetime. And Oliver? I won't lie. I don't understand your suffering but I'm sorry about it."

Marika crossed her arms and asked: "Is it just me or you guys do not get what's going on here either?"

Olga confirmed: "Neither did I. What was the point of this meeting, Oliver?"

Oliver sat straight on the bed, coughed to straighten his voice and explained: "These disorders are capable of deranging daily lives, almost every day. Being aware of their effecting methods is a coping tactic. This is not just about drugs or buildings or even syndromes; it's about the thread. History is learnt to understand what damages caused an overthrow. Human's physical and mental damages must be studied to cope with. You don't just jump off the cliff, you know the consequences. You understand what I'm trying to say?"

Theodore added: "Yeah, I think I do. When I was in high school, I didn't know what I wanted to do about a career. My father very wisely told me that a society needs vagrants as well or plenty of children would never decide to study. And about what you said, if there's a group with physical or mental disorders, there must be a group to study their disorders."

"You've got a very intelligent father," Pietro said as a compliment.

"Exactly," Oliver said, "Now, I don't know how Sebastian and Pietro feel about talking about it but when I talk about it, I feel like now that I have illuminated more people, it gets easier to take. This is what I meant."

## March 1st, Baldwin's Sleep Clinic, 09:12 A.M.

He placed his hands on the edge of the window and carefully pushed his body out with his eyes closed.

After taking a deep breath, he opened his eyes and stared at the ground. His room was on the second floor, five floors less than the original memory.

His eyes only showed coldness and expressionlessness but in his mind in his heart, there was a great flaming fire. An unstoppable chaos.

"Mr Johnson?" Oliver turned to the nurse who called him, "Do you want to go? Or you enjoyed our services that you decided to stay?"

Oliver got away from the window and smiled: "You're a good nurse, Eliot. Attitude, ten. Punctuality, ten." He lowered his voice and said: "Cigarettes, fifteen!"

Eliot was a smoker, Oliver accidentally found out about it and took three cigarettes as bribe to avoid spilling the tea to Balthazar; and also allowed Eliot to smoke by the window. Once a day. Oliver cared about his lungs!

Eliot slightly frowned: "We agreed on the fact that smoking has never happened in this room. Remember or are you still high?"

Oliver gave him a big smile. Eliot said: "Get dressed. Ms Johnson is waiting at the secretary."

"Ms Johnson?" Oliver asked because he thought that he was supposed to take a cab "What's her name?"

Eliot shrugged and left the room.

Oliver put on a black t-shirt and an orange hoodie with grey jeans. NICE outfit. He grabbed his suitcase out of the closet and walked the distance between the closet and the door in slow-motion. As he was walking so dramatically with a charming smile, a doctor who was walking in the hallway stood right in front of the door and stared at Oliver so weirdly. This is what makes everyone feel ashamed, including Oliver. His charming smile changed places with a shy smile, he said: "In my own defence, good sir, I was here for sleep analysis not psychiatry treatment!"

Doctor didn't care or react, just continued to walk and pretended like he never saw Oliver.

Oliver kept on his way like a mentally healthy human being and went downstairs to see which Ms Johnson was there to take him home.

When he walked down the stairs to the secretary, there was only one young lady there: Dakota Chance Johnson.

Dakota ran to Oliver and hugged him so hard that made him feel like his lungs were being tied.

"Ollie!" Dakota silently yelled, "I missed you teddy bear!"

Oliver hugged him back and said: "Nice to see you cotton candy. Where are the others?"

"Um, who are you asking about?"

"Mum? Dad? Liv? Arthur?"

"Oh yes. Liv and Arthur are at work. Mum and Dad are out of town with Phill. You and I will be on our own for lunch, cutie pie!"

"Fine. Do we have a taxi?"

Dakota looked at Oliver concerned: "Ollie, why are you being weird? I brought Mum's car."

"Correct. Do you have a license?"

Dakota pinched Oliver's arm and said: "No, you're the only licensee in the world."

They left the clinic. Before they went out, Oliver saw that the weather was cloudy through the glass door. He put on his sunglasses and went outside.

Oliver was kind-hearted and caring but he did not care what others would've thought of what he enjoyed personally.


## 10 Minutes Later...

Oliver and Dakota were stuck in a frustrating traffic. Oliver had a request that he was in doubt about bringing it up. He wasn't worried about Dakota's possible answers; he was anxious about how the result would've affected *him*.

He, however, took the risk and asked: "Dakota, can we stop somewhere before we get home?"

"Sure. Tell me where and I'll drive," Dakota said without looking at him.

"I want to go back to the building."

Dakota looked at Oliver like he misheard him: "Pardon me?"

"You heard me. Can you drive there?"

"Yeah, I can. But Ollie, are you certain? You just got better."

"Come on. It has been nineteen years. I'm better than that." Oliver optimistically insisted.

Dakota licked her lips and obeyed: "Ahoy, captain."

Truth be told, Oliver was stressed. He was unable to predict his reaction.

The seventh floor was rebuilt but Oliver's mental damage wasn't. Since January 11th, 2000, Oliver had never closed his eyes, estranged the thought that he might've been surrounded by chained flames. He could not estrange the thought that there might've been no saviours this time.

Traffic ended so soon. "What the hell did I do?" Oliver thought sadly, "I shouldn't have overestimated me."

As Dakota was driving to the building, Oliver was getting more nervous. He could feel the warmth of the blood, rushing in his veins. You know what they say, confront your fears or die fearfully.

Oliver was going over curse words in his head that he missed the path they covered to the library. He was still reviewing curse words in his head, until Dakota slightly slapped his face and said: "Get back to the real world, dude!"

Oliver turned to her: "What is it? Why aren't you driving?"

"Because we've arrived?" She nodded to the building in front of them.

"Oh" Oliver noticed "Okay, cool. Totally fine."

"You sure it's fine?"

"Yup. Yeah. Absolutely. You got it, sis!" he said and got out of the car.

Dakota followed him to the building. While she was following him, she asked: "You don't want to be here, do you?"

"Of course, I want to…I mean, I'm not a hundred percent certain but I think this is the time."

"What?" Dakota snapped, "You aren't even sure? Then what the hell?"

"Please, please, keep your manners, dear. What the hell is 'hell'?"

"Don't change the subject."

Oliver stopped, looked Dakota straight into her eyes and said: "I'll be thirty-three this year, not three. I am a strong, confident man who has no time for being stressed over a so-called issue that has occurred nearly two decades ago. I've got to face it."

"*So-called issue?* The death toll was over forty people, twenty-two people were hurt."

"Dakota, Dakota, I get that you're concerned but sometimes, we have no choice but to trust each other." He continued: "Like, I don't know. Like right now? I trusted you to give me a safe and sound ride. I could drive us home myself or even convince you to get taxi but what I did? I trusted you and now I need *you* to trust me."

Dakota didn't answer. Oliver kindly asked: "Do you understand?"

"I understand," Dakota said, "I trust you."

You can't fight the truth. Am I right?

Oliver smiled at his little sister and gave her a warm hug. They took the elevator to get to the seventh floor.

After a couple moments, the elevator's door was opened and the seventh floor appeared. Oliver and Dakota, both stepped to the seventh ceiling—which was rebuilt to a new library.

The first renewed item that caught Oliver's eyes was the ceiling that was equipped with multiple fire sprinklers. There were none back in 2000.

Oliver looked around. His panic attacks were coming to him. Hand sweats, pain in the chest and the sensation of not connecting to his body.

"Ollie," Dakota called slowly, "Look at this."

She pointed to a memorial section in a corner. They went to the section to take better looks. It was a memorial section of all the victims of that gloomy January. The wall next to the memorial was filled with black and white ribbons, teddy bears, bouquets and single flowers, chocolates and letter pockets. Oliver looked at the victims' pictures until he saw a familiar one. A sad smile took place on his face and said to Dakota: "Look at this, Caity Maroone."

Dakota looked at the picture of the young, beautiful brunette girls with a little note on her picture: "*Caitlin Anne Maroone was a smart and hopeful medical scholar. She was born on May 10th, 1979, and sadly died on January 11th, 2000, at the age of 20 after 82 percent of her body was burnt in the fire. She is no longer at our house but forever in our hearts.*"

Dakota said: "This is tragic. Did you know her?"

Oliver took a sad deep breath and said: "Yes. That day, she asked me and Brad if we could lend her a pencil and an eraser. She said that she wanted to be a doctor but, in her opinion, she could never see a burnt body or an injury caused by fire because she believed that getting hurt or burning alive is the worst was of dying." He sneered "She died an hour and a half later in what she feared of."

"Did you know that she was dead?"

"No, I didn't. Honestly, I thought about what happened to her once."

"When was it?"

"A few hours after I was rescued. I can't quite recall it but I remember that a doctor was checking me up for injuries. I remembered that she was dreaming of being a doctor and I wanted to ask about her but I fainted. And I never thought about her until now."

Dakota put arms around Oliver and whispered: "We'll leave whenever you say."

He closed his eyes and whispered back: "Let's leave."


## Johnson's Family House, 16:17 P.M.

Oliver laid on the ground and breathed repeatedly. After almost twenty days of not having any exercise, he forced himself to do an hour of cardio. During his workout, he heard Arthur and Olivia came to their house.

After he and Dakota visited the library, Oliver felt so much better, mentally and physically. They had a large chicken pizza together and Dakota had a cabbage salad that apparently, it didn't fit in her stomach, since she was throwing up in the bathroom.

Everything was surprisingly going well until Edward, Katherine and Phillip came back home early and Edward announced them that Moores invited them to dinner and they had to go.

Oliver had no plans and desires on going to an oppressive dinner party but he didn't disagree in case of not losing his energy for working out.

He stood up and left his room to the bathroom with shower, which they used to call 'bathroom number two'. 'Bathroom number one' was only a bathroom with toilet, the one that Dakota was throwing up in. He stopped by the bathroom number one to talk to Katherine. Before he started the conversation, Katherine frowned at him: "Why aren't *you* throwing up?"

"Sorry Mum. Is it good thing or a bad thing? I can't say."

"You both shared a pizza, didn't you? Why is she throwing up and you are not?"

"Well, your fallen angel ate cabbage salad. I didn't. Thanks for being so concerned about me, ma," Oliver said with no specific feelings.

"Whatever. Are you going to the shower?"

"Yeah."

"Make it quick for the supper. What do you want to wear to dinner?"

"I haven't decided yet. But I will, okay? Bye!" Oliver said fast and headed to the bathroom number two to take a shower. He did and it didn't take more than twenty minutes. The process of getting dressed, however, took more time than showering.

Oliver went downstairs to meet his lovely family. Men's voices could be heard from the living room and a warm, perfect smell of vanilla, revealed that Olivia was making a cake. Olivia was Oliver's first choice to meet.

He went to the kitchen and greeted: "Hey Liv."

Olivia looked at him and smiled: "Greetings, sibling of mine. How are you? How was the clinic?"

"It was helpful. I haven't tested my new sedatives outside the clinic yet, but I will tonight," Oliver said, "Did Dakota tell you that we went to library?"

Olivia sat behind the island cabinet and said: "She did. She mentioned that you took it very well. Tell me about it?"

"Not very well, but it was better than I expected. I panicked a little but then it was just easy to handle." Oliver sat on the island cabinet and expressed.

"That's good, I'm happy for you," Olivia said, "And about Ava,"

Oliver grabbed a tangerine and peeled it: "What about her?"

"Don't face this emotionally. Raising a kid is no joke. You see, even a plant needs too much attention and care and love. What if at some point you won't be able to provide it for Ava?"

Oliver gave half of the tangerine to Olivia and asked: "What do you suggest?"

"I think you have to be there for her until a nice family show up and ask for adoption. You have to make sure she gets what she worth. And then ask that family to spend time with Ava sometime. You get it?"

Oliver reviewed Olivia's suggestion. She had a point. He answered: "I think it's not a bad idea. I'll think about it."

Olivia smiled: "I'm glad you came to an understanding."

Oliver smiled, ate the last piece of tangerine and went to the living room. A soon as Phillip saw him, went to Oliver and beamed: "There he is!"

Oliver hugged him and smiled: "Hi Phill!"

Phillip looked at Edward and joked: "Ed, I really blame you for this! None of my nieces and nephews call me Uncle and *your* son started the chain!"

Oliver said: "Hi everyone." And sat on the couch next to Arthur.

Edward asked: "How do you feel? Aren't you affected by the food?"

"No Dad." Oliver hid his fed-up sense for the question behind a smile, "We shared a pizza and Dakota ate a bowl of cabbage salad. I think that's what making her ill."

Edward nodded and said: "The food system is being very unhealthy now days."

"Yeah, we should've been hunting our own food!" Phill whispered. Arthur heard it and by imagining it, he could only prevent laughter by chewing his lips.

"Did you say anything, Phill?" Edward asked Phillip.

"I...I was just umm...saying that I don't disagree with you. When I was a boy, foods used to be healthier," Phillip answered back.

"Not healthier, just healthy." Edward corrected.

Phillip looked behind Oliver and Arthur and said: "There she is!" And then stood up, grabbed the small blanket next to him and went to Dakota and Katherine who just entered the living room.

Oliver and Arthur looked behind them and when they saw Dakota walking in, they got up and made seat for her. Dakota sat on the couch, Phill carefully wrapped the blanket around her and fondled her arms and asked with sympathy: "Cherished, do you want me to get you anything?"

Dakota looked pale. She whined: "No. I can't eat anything."

Edward said: "Get her a glass of water, please."

Phillip shook his head and went to the kitchen. Edward was frowning; not because he was mad but because he was upset. His 'anger' for his kids was usually out of concern. They understood it during years Oliver understood it for three!

"Ed, will you massage her, please?" Katherine asked his husband.

Edward switched his seat and sat next to his youngest and started to massage her.

Arthur touched Oliver's shoulder, when Oliver turned to him, Arthur nodded the kitchen with his head and they both went to the kitchen.

When they entered the kitchen, Olivia and Phillip were talking and they turned their heads to Arthur and Oliver so scared.

Olivia went to them and closed the kitchen's room: "You scared us! We thought you were Mum!"

"Why?" Arthur asked, "What are you tending to hide from her?"

"I was telling Phill that I didn't want to go to Moores' dinner and he must tell Mum and Dad that we want to stay with Dakota."

"Okay, okay, okay!" Oliver interfered, "I have to stop you right there! What do you mean by *not* going?"

"I'm just measuring the circumstances. Dakota is ill and I should be with her," Olivia explained.

"So what? Phill is here with her." Oliver frowned unserious.

"If she's not going, I won't accompany you either." Arthur said and put his elbows on the cabinet. Oliver looked at him vituperatively and asked: "The…what?"

Olivia rolled his eyeballs and said: "Uh, Arthur don't start."

"Liv, I'm not a bachelor. It's not normal for me to attend a party without my lady." He added, "Plus, I'm not fond of Moores. Whenever I see them, especially now days, I have suicidal thought for at least three days!"

"Me either, bro, me either!" Oliver shook his head with disappointment, "But we must go and I swear I will not attend if none of you won't!"

Arthur put his hands up and said: "Fine! I give up but you owe me one, Oliver."

## Moores' Family House, 19:50 P.M.

Oliver grabbed the bathroom's knob and took three deep breaths. Faked a smile on his face and got out of the bathroom. Ezra was leaning to the front wall with his hands in his pockets, waiting for him. Oliver said: "You know, you don't really stand behind the bathroom door while people are...doing something personal."

Ezra raised an eyebrow: "Evacuating intestine and urinary are *personal*?"

"No. No it's not. In fact, it's quite public. We actually have a weekly family competition for it!" Oliver joked in cold blood.

Ezra laughed and said: "Oh, damn it man! Don't worry, I arrived when you were washing your hands."

"Thank you?" Oliver asked and walked towards the hall.

"Look, we must talk."

"Indeed. I wanted to talk to you too."

"Nice. You go first."

Oliver waited still: "Ummm...I was thinking that maybe it's time for us to wrap Brad's stuff. The investigation team is no longer working there."

"Hmmm" Ezra gave it a thought, "It's not a bad idea at all. I told Mum and Dad about it a few days ago but they said that they won't be able to do it at all and that I was too impudent to bring that up."

"Okay. How about tomorrow morning?"

"Fine by me. I'll be ready at nine." Ezra said, "Oh and the reason that you guys are invited is that as Dad requested, I spoke to Bradly's lawyer yesterday. We wanted to share it with you. We'll talk about it at dinner."

"That's fine. Oh! And what about Ava? It's getting so hard to keep her a secret."

"Tell them tonight. Don't worry about my parents, just tell them that I decided for both of us to keep her secret. I'll deal with them later myself."

Oliver shook his head and pointed to the dining room: "Shall we?"

Ezra shook his head and whispered: "You're the guest. Prior's yours."

Oliver glanced at him and opened the dining room's door. Robert looked at Oliver and Ezra walking in and yelled cheerful: "Uh! Here they come! Come here boys and take seats."

Oliver and Ezra took seats behind two sides of the table in front of each other. It didn't take long until Elizabeth and Katherine brought the food, two dishes of cottage pie and after settling them down on the table, they took places on the only two empty chairs.

Arthur smiled and said: "Thank you, Mrs Moore. You didn't have to do all these."

"Oh, please," Elizabeth said modestly, "I meant to prepare something better but I chose this because it…was Brad's favourite meal."

"We're really glad that you do what you're able of to keep your son's memory. It's remarkable," Edward said.

Robert knew that his wife would've started to mourn, so he anticipated to talk: "We appreciate that. And oh, Edward, you didn't say why your daughters aren't here. I believe I called you to invite your brother as well."

"Indeed," Edward shook his head. "Dakota had a bad lunch today, she was poisoned and Olivia stayed home with her for you know, emergency. Phillip also appreciated your invitation but he thought that it's a dinner for family."

"I'm sorry to hear that. I hope she gets better soon," Robert said and continued to eat his food.

Meanwhile, Oliver and Ezra constantly made eye contacts, waiting for one another to begin the top priority conversation.

After passing almost ten minutes, Oliver was running out of patience. He poured himself a glass of water, saying: "I think Ezra has something to tell us. Do you, Ezra?" And drank it without getting eyes off Ezra.

Eleven words were enough for everyone to pay attention to Ezra. Ezra looked at Oliver and whispered to him: "I'm eating."

Robert decided to start the conversation for his son and give him time to swallow his food: "The real reason that we wanted you here, was that we thought that Bradly might've had a will and his lawyer might be aware of which. So, we, Elizabeth and I, requested Ezra to talk to the lawyer and ask her about the will. We thought that we hear the result among you."

Ezra coughed. He had no choice but explaining: "This might not be the perfect time to talk about it but I spoke to Bradly's lawyer this morning. She said that ever since the judicial accusation, they hadn't met. Bradly had no written wills."

"There must be a mistake. What do you mean that *he doesn't have a will?*" Robert said while trying to keep his confusion down.

"Bradly and his lawyer knew each other for five years. Brad had never talked to her about a will. Even if there is a will, she isn't aware of." Ezra explained more to illuminate.

"Well, there must be something. Like—like a video tape or a recorded voice. Brad was an organised man. He must've had a plan for inheritance too." Edward opined.

"Dad," Oliver said with a low-key anger, "Please consider that he was thirty-two when he died. Things have changed from three decades ago. I was born when you were at my age! What am I doing now? Getting thrilled for watching SpongeBob!"

"What do you mean, Oliver?" Robert asked Oliver.

"My point is that our generation is experiencing a higher level of life expectancy. Why would we want to make a will when we hope to live longer that the previous generations? We are never ready to die."

"Listen, everyone, there's a lot of tension now. I shouldn't have brought it up at the dinner at all. I knew Bradly and I'm sure he had a reasonable excuse for all of this," Ezra said and tried to calm everyone.

"Pardon me for being so blunt, Ezra but I don't think that neither of us knew Brad as much as we thought we did," Oliver said to Ezra, "Who are you kidding? Don't shut your eyes on what's really happening. We've got *seven suspects*! Seven friends of Brad, Damn it! We didn't even know about Ava!"

AVA.

Those three letters name blurred out of Oliver's mouth.

Elizabeth who was quiet until that moment asked: "Who's Ava? Was my son seeing someone?"

Oliver and Ezra looked at each other terrified.

"Bloody hell." Ezra thought with his British accent.

"Mum, Dad," Ezra began to talk after a shockingly quiet silence, "Oliver had nothing to do with it. *I* told him not to talk about it."

Robert stood up and yelled with a so-called controlled anger: "Who's Ava?"

Arthur stood up as well and tried to take control of the atmosphere: "I want all of you to calm down and take a few breaths. There is a simple explanation for it."

"You knew about it?" Elizabeth asked confused, "Then how come we didn't know?"

"Let them talk, Elizabeth!" Robert snapped at his wife, "Talk, Oliver."

Oliver started to explain: "It started when we were claiming information to find a possible suspects. We needed to check on every place Brad had been and people he had met; his credit cards records and—you know, everything that could lead us to an answer. That was when Ezra received a call from and orphanage. They told him that Brad hadn't answered his phone for a while and got them worried. They also said that Ezra's number had been given to them in case of an emergency. So...Brad had been visiting that place for the past year and a half. He had been managing to adopt a girl named 'Ava Florence Wintergreen'. She is six...Do you remember the night I came here for dinner? The night you served me grilled chicken. That night Ezra told me about her and we decided to leave the matter in hiding until you two get better."

Ezra fulfilled: "At first, I thought that it was a mistake or a joke but Ms Jonah, the principle, she explained to me everything and that Bradly had given my number as a backup."

"I went to visit the orphanage the next day," Oliver explained with his eyes locked on the saltshaker, "I met Ava and I told her about Brad. It was hard for her to accept it and I'm still struggling with it. We, Ezra and I, didn't tell you about her because you were in the worst condition ever. We only did it for your own good and we thought that..."

"*Silent!*" Elizabeth sobbed and interrupted Oliver, "What else don't I know? What else are you hiding from me?"

"Lizzie, please!" Robert held Elizabeth's shoulder "Control yourself!" Elizabeth yelled again: "Don't tell me to control myself, Rob! My son is dead and—and..." Her tears didn't allow her to finish her sentence and took refuge in the kitchen.

After a couple moments, Oliver slowly said: "I go talk to her."

Katherine instantly disagreed furiously: "Sit down, boy! You're why she isn't here now. *I'll* go." Katherine said what she said very seriously and that scared Oliver.

By Katherine and Elizabeth's absence, Robert said: "You young men have a lot to explain. I'm talking to you too, Arthur."

"Perhaps we can keep on discussing the matter outdoor. Let's go to the back yard, shall we?" Edward suggested.

Oliver, Arthur and Ezra didn't disagree. How could they? They were the ones to set up the fire, without knowing how to put it out; Arthur was guilty less than the other two though. The three of them were referring to their hippocampus to find some legitimate answers for the possible questions.

It was lightly snowing and bitterly cold outside.

Robert wiped the insignificant snow off the bench and sat on it with Edward and Ezra. Arthur leant to the wall and Oliver sat on the ground and cuddled his knees. "Okay" Robert began, "I'm all ears. What's going on? I want to hear everything."

"I think we should start with your knowledge. What do you know so far, Robert?" Arthur asked.

"I know that my son was dead by more than thirty stab wounds and there are seven suspects; seven suspects that Brad knew them. And it was just revealed to me that he meant to adopt a little girl and he never even mentioned it to me." Robert informed "That's it. That's all I know. Tell me what I need to know."

Arthur scanned Oliver and Ezra imperceptible and thought: "You two idiots are better to save me soon," and explained: "Those suspects weren't just people that Brad knew. They were all friends of him and they didn't know about each other's existence. By the night of the murder, they all received a message from Brad to meet him at his house for an emergency."

Seeing Robert's apathetic face, Arthur decided to skip the part. He resumed his speech with his first-hand information: "I want to inform you with something that I found out at first blush…Oliver doesn't seem to know; detective should've let him know." At that point, everyone was curious, although Oliver seemed a bit displeased.

Arthur said: "Bradly and Elma had been in touch for the past almost three years. It was started when Brad returned home from the Italy trip."

Robert, despite what Arthur expected, welcomed that information. Edward asked: "How did you understand that?"

"I went through his emails, messages and phone calls records myself. Elma married an Italian guy named 'Santiago' two years ago and their twin daughters were born shortly after they got married. Elma had a miscarriage last autumn and Brad had been supporting him as a friend."

Edward asked: "Are there any chances that this Santiago guy was unpleased by their friendship and attempted to murder, Arthur?"

"No, I checked" Arthur answered, "he has never visited Britain."

Oliver turned to Arthur and asked: "Arthur, a word?"

Before Arthur got any chances to agree or disagree, Robert interrupted angrily: "No! No private conversations. Say what you want to say right here right now."

Seeing that there was no way to escape that bloody situation, Oliver who was so ready to yell at Arthur, took a deep breath and said: "Our protocol…the priority of sharing brand new information is with the investigation team. You had all day to tell me about it, why didn't you?"

"Like I said, *detective Henry* was supposed to tell you. I don't see why he neglected."

"But why didn't he?" Oliver asked again.

"I don't know," Arthur said, "But I can say that he's unsatisfied by your working progress. You better talk to him tomorrow."

"But his excuse is acceptable. He was bedridden, Arthur. Did you tell Richard about it?" Edward defended his son.

"Wait, you were bedridden? Why?" Ezra asked Oliver worried.

"No need to worry, I've been having sleep disorders for the past few days. I'm fine now." Oliver answered exhausted. He hated pity.

"What type is your disorder, exactly?" Robert asked kindly. So much different than his attitude few minutes ago.

"Insomnia and REM sleep behaviour disorder," Oliver answered Robert.

"Now that Robert is well informed, how about you two go apologize to Elizabeth for your misbehaviour?" Edward asked Oliver and Ezra.

"Yeah, you two better go and try not to mention Bradly; she's still not ready to talk about him," Robert reminded.

"And Oliver, tell your mother that it's late. We should get going," Edward asked his son.

Oliver shook his head as an agreement and stepped inside.

At such situation, you struggle to find the rightest words to say. You get genuinely concerned at such time, pulling ambiguous scenarios together to predict the confronting person's reaction.

Before Oliver went into the kitchen, he felt Ezra's hand on his shoulder. "What?" Oliver whispered.

"Let me talk first. Take it easy, Ollie," Ezra whispered back.

So, Ezra made his path to the kitchen first and falsely coughed to draw Elizabeth and Katherine's attention. Elizabeth was drinking a glass of pomegranate juice and Katherine was talking to her.

Ezra began: "Hi mum."

Elizabeth looked at him and opened her arms. Ezra went closer and hugged her. He said while hugging his mother: "We're here to apologise."

Oliver added: "Yes, Elizabeth. We're indescribably sorry. Your mental health's condition was our top priority. We just didn't mean to upset you any more than you already were."

"I know…I know," Elizabeth whispered and slowly separated from Ezra. She continued: "I'm not mad at any of you, but I judge you. It has been…twenty days since that ominous night and I know that you weren't able to share enough, because of your job or because you wanted to keep me and Robert safe. Since that night I have been, sad and angry and anxious and confused and you know what hurts me more? The fact that I knew you were hiding something from me and that I didn't have the power to understand what it was."

A tear fell of her green eye. She continued: "I'm so much tougher than I look. I saw them bury my dear boy's body and yet, I'm alive. I mean, what kind of a mother can see her child's dead body and still survive?…What hurts me is that I've been gloomy not just for the things I knew, but also for the things I didn't know and I still don't."

Oliver was looking at the floor all along. Elizabeth had every right to be complainant.

After a few seconds, Ezra said: "Mum, Oliver and Arthur also couldn't talk because of MPS. I'm also guilty for telling them to hold on because I would've told you everything at the rightest time. We've already told Dad everything. I'll tell you everything tonight. Okay?"

Elizabeth shook her head. Katherine whispered next to Oliver's ear: "I'll go out. We'll leave when you're ready." And she exited the kitchen.

"Elizabeth," Oliver called, "Will you *ever* forgive me for this?"

"There is nothing to be forgiven for, Oliver. And if there was, Bradly would've never wanted me to be mad at you."

Oliver cried silently: "I'm sorry."

\*\*\*

205

## March 2nd, Oliver Johnson's House, 7:00 A.M.

Oliver woke up and turned off the alarm, climbed off his bed and changed his clothes. When he was walking to the bathroom, even he was surprised by his unique amount of energy!

"Is it me? What was in the food last night?" He thought and laughed.

A fact be told, if you talk or make silly faces in the mirror, you are not alone. Oliver joins you.

Oliver is a funny ten-year-old boy in front of a mirror.

He was busy telling his reflection how attractive and pretty he was when he heard his phone ringing. He ran out of the bathroom and followed the ringtone to the bedroom and answered the phone right before it went off: "Hello?"

"Hi Ollie." It was Ezra.

"Ezr. Hi. Aren't you awake yet?"

"No. Unfortunately no. I'm now asleep," Ezra joked. Oliver laughed. Ezra asked: "Just called you to make sure you still want to go to Bradly's house."

"Yeah, yeah." Oliver assured, "Definitely. I'll be by your door at nine."

Oliver hung up and went to the kitchen to make breakfast. He was thinking of making a green smoothie for Dakota. It wasn't her thing but being sick is not a quantum about interests at all, agree?

He looked into his fridge, he had avocado, green apple, spinach and celery. He cut them very carefully and put them in the blender with a cup of milk and a spoon of honey and of course he didn't forget about ice. As the smoothie was getting ready, Oliver was jealous at his little sister for the first time; for having a charming and caring brother.

Oliver called Balthazar Baldwin to report that he slept well the night before. Baldwin's answering machine answered, typical. Oliver left his message: *"Good morning, Balthazar. I just wanted you to know that these new sedatives of mine are efficacious. I slept like a baby last night and, now I'm awake because I should see a friend. So...later, I think?"*

He took Dakota's smoothie and his car keys and then he was ready to go. His first stop was his parents' house. He texted Edward first to see if he was awake. It's so against the humanity to visit their homes at 8 in the morning, even if they are your parents. Luckily, Edward texted back in less than a minute. Oliver took the smoothie to the door and Edward opened the door: "Well, hello! I see someone has woken up early!"

"Morning, Dad. Is anyone else awake?"

"No, it's just me and Phill. Why are *you* awake?"

"Ezra and I are going to Brad's house. Maybe we could wrap some of his stuff."

"Good luck with that. How did you sleep?"

"Good, actually really good. I slept at midnight and I woke up an hour ago."

"I'm happy about it. Aren't you coming in?"

"No, sorry. I just stopped by to give you this," Oliver handed the smoothie to his father and said: "I made this for Dakota."

Edward smiled: "Thank you. She'll appreciate it."

Oliver shook his head and said: "Well, bon voyage!"

"Wait" Edward requested, he put a step front and hugged his son.

Oliver was surprised by his father's amount of love. "Wow!" He thought, "Am I dreaming?"

Edward separated from Oliver and smiled: "Join us for lunch, will you?"

"I don't know, Dad. I'll probably join if we finish soon. I'll text you."

"Okay. Take care, son."

Oliver shook his head and went to his car. Before he started to drive, he slightly—without Edward noticing—slapped his face to make sure that he wasn't dreaming. Edward wasn't a man of feelings; he would rarely express them. His sudden hug must've been a result of the night before.

Not that Edward was heartless, but he would always spend more love on his daughters. His love for Oliver was just enough.

Seeing Robert talking about his lost son, must've gotten Edward picturing the same scenario.

It didn't take much time for Oliver to drive to Moore's house and pick up Ezra; although Ezra said that Oliver was a minute and thirteen seconds late, Oliver believed that he was totally on time. By the time they arrived at Brad's neighbourhood, Oliver looked around through the windshield. Every neighbour who was sad about Brad's death was resuming life.

It's just how it works; when somebody dies, people who knew them would feel sorry or even grateful that death didn't stop by their house. At first, everyone talks about the dead's virtues and how they were amazing human beings, taking care of everyone and how their smiles used to bring the light to the room. But within a day or even less, they would be forgotten. Like they never existed.

Brad's neighbours were also people, correct? They went back to their daily lives too. Walking with their dogs, riding bicycles and even sitting at their front yards were their exclusives. None of them would understand what Bradly Anton Moore II's family and friends circle was becoming a nonagon. In fact, it was like no one else cared.

"You passed the house," Ezra said calmly all of a sudden.

"What?"

"The house," Ezra said, "you passed it man. Where is your mind?"

Oliver looked behind and said: "You're so right. I…was…looking for a parking spot. Yeah, a parking spot."

Ezra smiled ridiculously: "You don't say!" And he got off the car. Oliver actually went for what he said, a parking spot.

Although neighbours had gone back to their normal lives, they respected Brad's memory enough to leave his parking spot unoccupied.

When Oliver parked and left the car, he saw the front door's neighbour stared at him indignant. Oliver frowned back, of course.

The door was open and Oliver just pushed it. Ezra was standing in the middle of the hallway, right where it happened.

Ezra said: "You shouldn't have done this. You shouldn't have cleaned this place up."

Oliver said: "I didn't do anything. It must've been Richard. He didn't want you to see it. He did it out of compassion."

Ezra closed his eyes, breathed deeply and whispered: "Then He said, 'What have you done? The voice of your brother's blood is crying out to me from the ground…Genesis 4:10."

Oliver waited a few moments to get closer to Ezra and ask: "Why would you bring that up?"

Ezra turned to him and said: "I remembered a memory."

"What memory?"

"It was after Bradly was returned home from the hospital. It was January thirteenth, I think. I'm talking about that building's great fire," Ezra explained with his voice shivering, "So Bradly, he was returned home and Mum and Dad wanted to throw a party for his survival. I remember breaking my arm the day before it happened and within four days, I wasn't important anymore. Brad was alright, physically at least. But my arm was hurting at the very day but no one cared." He chuckled, "I remember sitting on the third stair, staring at the worried population around Brad and I—I was quietly crying because of my arm but no one even cared to ask if I was okay."

Oliver corrected him with sympathy: "I did. Remember?"

"Oh yes, you did. Unlike the others, you grabbed my unbroken arm and took me to the back yard. We played until Bradly showed up and the two of you left me alone. Bradly and I were never sensibly fond of each other but that disinterest...I know it would've never led to homicide."

"Ezr, I'm so sorry. I didn't..."

Ezra interrupted: "Don't...apologise. You're not the one to be blamed." He continued: "Robert and Elizabeth should be blamed."

"Why them?"

Ezra started to walk slowly with his hands in his pockets: "I'll tell you about it the moment you start to be Oliver and not a psychologist."

"I'm me. You just be you."

"I spent all my childhood hating my brother. I think it was legit to be. His attitude was so excellent as a son, as a friend, as a cousin and as everything he was good but being a brother. He ignored me all the time. Like I was never there. You were at least not as bad as him but never perfect. You ignored me less but he affected you like you were hypnotised. No one ever cared to know if *I* was okay, if *I* needed to talk to a therapist and not if I needed *anyone* in my life. And it's annoying that now, everyone cares."

Ezra explained while looking around with a sad smile, "Our parents never cared for my education. I remember when I told them that I was moving to Cali for the college. That was the only time when I can say they were proud...Rob and Liz care a lot now but it's not because of me. It's because they lost Bradly and all very unexpectedly, they realised that there is a second son here. I hate being their second preference."

Oliver hugged him and said: "Ezra you're not some second priority. You're my youngest brother."

Ezra cried with no sound: "Sorry, sorry. It's just...I had to do it. I couldn't take it anymore."

"It's okay. I'm glad that you said it at last."

"It has been really tough; you have no idea."

"I know, man," Oliver said sympathetically "I exactly know."

"You asked me why I chose that part of Bible; well, I chose it because since that day, I started hating Bradly and...and I wished him dead! I thought my life would've been so much better if he wasn't there. And now here I am! So drowned in agony!"

Oliver separated from him and sat on the floor: "You may laugh at this, but I used to think the same about my sisters. Dad was addicted this job as much as I remember and Mum spent more time on girls and I blamed sisters. But now, I can't imagine my life without them...I cried the night I moved into my house and I cried the night Olivia got married," Oliver said with chuckles, "Brad loved you. I mean, how couldn't he? He loved you and he would've been extremely unpleased if he saw you like this. Would he?"

"Honestly Ollie, I can't say. And I don't want to say."

## Oliver Johnson's Car, Somewhere near Johnsons' Family House, 10:30 A.M.

Oliver took a deep, angry breath and turned off the music. He was stuck in a traffic among uncountable number of cars. He and Ezra didn't really pack anything; they just indexed the biggest objects like Brad's tables and sofas and refrigerator. There was too much stuff to pack and they absolutely needed help so they left it for another time.

Oliver grabbed his phone to check his messages or Google some dumb question to pay less attention to the goddamn traffic. Among his messages, his eyes were caught by a voice message from Anya. He opened the voicemail and Anya's tired voice was played all over the car: "*Hi Oliver. It's Anya. There is something you need to know...I didn't think it was important and I wasn't sure. I thought it was all a coincidence but...I don't know. You have to know...So, the other day...I think it was two days ago, I think...I...didn't sleep ever since, I've lost the track of time...I believe it was two or three days ago that we met. When you were bedridden. I don't know when it was...These aren't important. Listen to me...that night, the night Bradly died, I was going to his house with a cab...ummm...When I was in the neighbourhood, I saw a man near Brad's house. He didn't seem fine...He...Looked drunk or confused. Walking around on the street like he didn't know where he was or...or why he was there. He was so confused...So because he was on the street, did I mention that he was walking on the street? Yeah, he was, ummm, walking on the street and the driver honked. The guy noticed and freed the path. I don't remember his face or his hair but I swear, Oliver, I swear he was wearing the same yellow hoodie that Pietro was wearing!...I say that I don't remember he was almost as tall as*

*Pietro and there was this giant Sol sign on his hoodie...Oliver you have to believe me, I'm so scared I can't even sleep!"*

Oliver definitely wanted to spend more time on it, to listen to the voice message more. But the cacophonous sound of horns dissuaded him and he started to drive to his parents' house to have lunch with them.

Olga suspected Pietro and Anya had seen him around the house like ten minutes before he arrived. That didn't seem meaningless to Oliver.

"They might know things," Oliver thought and frowned.

# Chapter Six
## It Wasn't Me. Was It You?

Edward and Katherine Johnson were sitting in the back yard with their so annoying neighbour, Bryce Davis; and of course, poor Oliver.

Bryce was at least twenty years older than Oliver but she always used to say that she is three years younger. She was British but she insisted on being American and she used to speak with a very naïve and awfully wrong American accent when she was around Johnsons.

It's notable that Bryce was black haired, one of those who dyed their hair blond and telling everyone that it's 'genetic'.

"And so, she apologised to me. That waiter won't do that to anyone ever again!" Bryce said proudly.

"Pardon me," Oliver who wasn't listening until that time asked, "I got distracted, the waiter won't do what?"

Bryce looked at Oliver and explained proudly: "I wanted my coffee with caffeine, that guy gave me decaf. So, I talked to his manager and he was reprimanded."

Oliver raised an eyebrow: "Over a *coffee*?"

"Oliver!" Bryce said disturbed, "How can you say that? Uh, never mind. You would've taken my side if you visited America half as much as I did!"

"No argues on that one. I spent my life in this country," Oliver said to finish the conversation.

"It's alright honey. No judgments here." Bryce said narcissistic.

Oliver stood up and smiled: "I'll go check on Dakota."

And he rescued himself from a miserable conversation leading by a pretentious inferior.

He went to the kitchen, where Phillip was working with his laptop.

"It must be really hard for you, isn't it?" Oliver asked sarcastically.

"What must be hard for me?" Phillip asked without taking eyes off the laptop screen.

liver continued sarcastically: "Staying here, sending your niece to battle with the enemy and not being sorry about it. It's so hard, Phill. Almost impossible." He sat on a chair.

"Bryce isn't an enemy, she's a worthless and unappealing human being who's wasting the other people's oxygen." Phillip answered in cold blood.

Oliver shrugged and picked up the potato chips' bag off the cabinet: "Can't disagree with that."

After a few moments, Phillip finished working with laptop and shut it down. He said: "Dakota is upstairs, getting ready. We want to go get some ice cream with Liv and Arthur. Do you want to join?"

"That sounds nice" Oliver said with a pleasant smile, "It's better than staying here with Bryce!"

"Go suit up and see which traffic has D stuck in."

Oliver went upstairs to get ready and find his sister.

Dakota's room's door was half open and Oliver just slightly pushed it: "Sis?"

"I'm coming!" Dakota snapped.

"Okay, take your time!" Oliver said frightened and passed to his own room.

He switched his informal outfit with something casual because he was thinking of going to the station and talk to Richard.

He was finishing buttoning when Dakota opened the door with rush; almost broke it.

"I could've been naked!" Oliver yelled.

"You don't talk about your nakedness so public." Dakota frowned, "Are we still feeding that demon with our souls?"

Oliver laughed at Dakota's comparison for minutes. He then answered: "Yes, unfortunately yes."

Dakota rolled his eyeballs and sighed: "Can I just, *not* see her?"

Oliver brushed his hair: "Not an option. She's here to see *you*."

"Who am I, Helen of Troy?"

"You are Dakota of Penna. Helen of Troy is who Bryce thinks she is!" Oliver joked.

Dakota breathed to recover her patience and suggested: "Here's the plan. We go downstairs and we leave the house so quietly like we were never here."

"Just greet her, Dakota. I tolerated her for an hour."

"And I couldn't be more proud," Dakota said proudly and grabbed Oliver's face "you deserve a championship belt, Brother. But our tolerations aren't at the same level."

"Agreed, agreed. But you'll have to deal with Dad yourself."

\*\*\*

## 30 Minutes Later...

"Finally, Neapolitan and cookie dough ice cream for our boy, Oliver," Olivia said and gave Oliver his ice cream and sat on the bench in front of the others.

"We should do this more often." Phillip suggested.

"We could; if you were settled here, man." Arthur reminded Phillip of his citizenship.

"I've got no plans on leaving Penna. I have a job, a dead dad and a living Mum there." Phillip said and drank a gulp of his caramel milkshake.

"Hey Arthur, is Richard at this office?" Oliver asked Arthur.

"He is. And he is so mad. No one even dared to greet him today." Arthur answered.

"Mad at me or something else?"

"I can't say. But don't talk to him today. You won't receive any good answers." Arthur warned Oliver.

They all continued eating and drinking their snacks speechless until Arthur's phone ringtone cut the process.

"Sergeant Black...Which one?...How?...Isn't detective Henry there?...I'll be there, I'll take care of it." Arthur hung up the phone and said: "Get up Oliver. Let's go."

"What happened?" Oliver asked with his frozen tongue.

"Pietro Schwarter is at the department. He's mad, *really mad*." Arthur shortly explained, "Come on, let's go."

Oliver left his unfinished ice cream cup on the bench and followed Arthur.

Police department wasn't far from the ice cream booth so they chose walking.

As they were walking the path to the destination, Oliver had a thousand thought and ideas about Pietro's appearance at the department.

Was he there to confess about being a murderer?

Did he know who the murderer was?

Did he have a lead?

Why was even mad?

And so many more question with hundreds of possible answers.

They arrived at the station sooner that Oliver expected. Or maybe he had lost the track of time.

As Oliver walked into the station, he found Pietro sitting on a chair, nervously shaking his leg.

He got close to him. What he meant to say was: "What the hell are you doing here you idiot? What the hell do you want?" But instead of being rude, he decided to be polite, kind and nice and so he asked calmly: "Good evening, Pietro. What brought you here?"

Pietro stood up and began complaining: "Your police force friends. They've been monitoring my house!"

Oliver didn't see that coming. He was confused and assumed that he misheard Pietro: "Excuse me?"

"Yeah. After the funeral, I kept seeing the same car with two men inside, watching me and my house."

"And," Oliver coughed "how are you sure that the men you saw were cops?"

"I saw two of them the night I was interrogated here. At first, I thought that I was wrong or paranoid. I thought maybe they wanted to break into my house so I stayed at a hotel for the past two nights and didn't leave there until this morning. When I came back home, they were still there and my house wasn't any different. It was just like I left it. I came here to see if my theory is correct."

"Did you talk to anyone?"

"I did. I talked to the case's detective. He said that I should be talking to *you*," Pietro said, "Oliver I *know* that my alcohol test was positive, but I don't deserve this. I *was* drunk but I wasn't *that drunk* to commit that huge of a crime."

Pietro was revealing information that Oliver wasn't aware of and apparently Richard was. Oliver, however maintained his confidence: "Okay, fine. Don't worry I'll be talking to detective Henry and see what's going on. Please stay here." And stepped away from Pietro to Richard's office.

Richard had some stuff to explain about. He had too much on his plate.

Oliver opened Richard's door office without knocking. He found Richard alone in his office, sitting behind his desk and doing paperwork.

Richard frowned: "What's wrong with you?"

Oliver took a step forward: "It's Pietro. I saw him in the hallway and he said that you've been keeping eyes on his house." He said, almost yelled furiously "Why do you mind sharing information with me? Why am I always *the last one* to be aware of everything? This is *my* case and I have every right to know."

Richard was enraged. He stood up and went to the door and closed it. Forced Oliver on the shoulder to put him on the chair and he took a seat in front of him.

He chastised: "This is not *your* case. Stop calling it yours. *I am* the detective and I decide what to share with you by my own discretion. You're only on this case because of your friendship with the victim. You weren't even my chosen psychologist at first."

Oliver frowned: "Then why did you ask me at the first place?"

"Because, Oliver, I knew that Moores would've asked you to help them and you would've accepted with no second thoughts…"

"No, I wouldn't." Oliver denied.

"Yes, you *would*. Your feeling overcome you most of the times. What makes you think you wouldn't?"

Oliver didn't answer.

Richard continued: "Pietro had taken alcohol that night. No tests were even needed, his breath could say. I couldn't tell you until I was sure. Besides, you weren't quite mentally stable. I decided not to involve you a lot."

"Excuse me?!"

"For God's sake, Oliver. You were bedridden in a hospital for three days."

"Your excuses still aren't acceptable."

"Schwarter is mad at the time. It is your mission now to go convince him to leave this place."

"Only if you accept not to watch his house again." Oliver insisted.

Richard frowned: "Why are you taking his side? He's a suspect, don't make me repeat that again."

"Will you, promise?" Oliver insisted again.

Richard rolled his eyeballs and said: "Fine. Now get out of here."

## 10 Minutes Later...

Oliver found Richard on a hallway after he sent Pietro home. "Detective Henry?" Oliver called and got closer to Richard, "I almost forgot that you wanted to see me. What is it?"

Richard explained: "It's about your working progress. It's not very satisfying. You've had five meetings with the suspects and yet, we have no leads."

"About leads, detective. Anya Barton told me that he saw a man at Bradly Moore's neighbourhood earlier at the night of the murder. She reported that the man was stumbling and he was wearing the same outfit that Pietro Schwarter wore on our fifth meeting."

Richard frowned. He was really mad at Oliver but still, he calmly asked: "You had a lead, *this important*. And yet you told me to *stop* monitoring his house?"

"Before you disclose your anger, that man could've been anyone else. I mean, Pietro isn't the only one with that shirt." Oliver hastily defended "And secondly, it was so inhumane to watch someone's house while the others are freely living lives."

"*Inhumane?*" Richard yelled, "You know what's inhumane? Killing an innocent man is inhumane! How the hell can you be so kind to a man who has possibly murdered your best friend?"

Oliver kept his calm attitude: "It's not about my kindness, it's about your discrimination! Don't pretend you haven't noticed it because you have!"

"*Discrimination*? *I discriminate*? Johnson, you have only two more weeks to light me up with a lead or I'll discharge you, not from this case but from your job! You hear me?"

## March 3rd, Greenwich Park, 08:58 A.M.

Oliver nervously shook his leg and checked on his watch again. It was his own fault; he was faulty for being too early.

Not even twenty-four hours after having a violent conversation with Richard and understanding that he only has two weeks to keep his job as a forensic psychologist, Oliver had planned seven private conversation with all seven suspects and he made it very clear to them that they couldn't tell anyone of the other suspects that they were having this conversation with Oliver.

Anya was the first suspect to meet. According to her own self, she had a very boring class that morning that she would rather to spend time with a man who suspected her.

They had to meet at nine but Oliver got there fifteen minutes earlier. Thankful for Balthazar's new medical treatment, Oliver could sleep like a baby. He no longer hated his phone alarm because he had slept perfectly before he heard it.

After a couple of minutes, Anya arrived and sat on the bench next to Oliver and said smiling: "Rise and shine, Oliver! Oh, first things first, thank you so much for helping me out for the class today. Aunt Ada was driving me crazy."

Despite her endeavour to wear a smile, she looked so exhausted. Oliver knew that insomnia was the cause. He answered: "You're welcome, Anya." He continued: "I called this meeting to talk about something really important."

"Which is?"

"You, Anya. I want to talk about you."

"I didn't see that coming," Anya said confused, "What about me? Do you want to know anything more?"

"I know…that you killed Bradly," Oliver said in peace, "Let's make the scenario, shall we? It is the night of February ninth, two thousand and nineteen. You go visit Brad, your head is filled with murder thoughts and methods but you've been planning this for a long time and you're equipped by your own knife. You arrive to the victim's house around half past ten, five minutes sooner or later. You two talk for ten minutes until you use the knife to stab Bradly in the leg and the chest, you rip his chest, his chest is filled with knife wounds and of course, it looks pathetic seeing all those bloody holes…I'm not sure if Brad does it or it is you but one of you two send me and the rest of the suspects including you, a message that Brad needs help. You exit the house and get far away from the house and wait for the other suspects. When you see that house is filled with some suspects, you enter and we you see Brad's body and act like this is the first time that you see him like this. No one will know that it was you. Easy peacy lemon squeezy."

Anya seemed stunned and defenceless. She stared at Oliver's eyes for a few moments until she could finally talk. She whispered, better to say: "Oliver? What was this?"

"Prove me that you're not the murderer I think you are. Prove me wrong. Right now," Oliver said determined with no doubts.

Anya thought for a short time and defended herself: "Oliver, I…tried, I struggled so hard and I did whatever it took to leave Australia, to come here and study because I was sick of my family…they didn't allow me to grow, to evolve. I have everything I want here. All I want now, is to just to prove my family that *I am a person* without them. Am I crazy to attempt the crime that would put me in jail for at least fourteen years?"

That conversation seemed over to Oliver. There was nothing else to talk about.

"I think this conversation is over. You may leave if you tend to," Oliver said with dignity.

Anya, for some reason she didn't know why, was visibly agitated at Oliver. She said inaudibly: "I think I go now." And she started to leave and she was walking, Oliver's voice stopped her: "Don't be mad at me. I would've never put you in the condition if it wasn't for the case."

A tear dropped off her left eye: "You're the one I blame; among the killer. You two are putting me through an inexorable mental damage," Anya said without turning back and then she walked away.

Oliver looked at the ground. For someone as affectionate, amiable and considerate as Oliver, it wasn't a piece of cake to see people with blue faces, let alone being the cause of blue faces. "Get yourself together, Oliver. It's the process. It's the job, it has to be done. Don't feel bad about it." Oliver thought.

After Anya was invisible, Oliver took his phone out of his jackets' pocket and wrote Anya's defence: "*Trying so hard to leave Australia to prove my family I can make it on my own.*" Now he had to wait for the others to arrive…

## Oliver Johnson's House, 12:04 P.M.

Oliver carefully put the lasagne's dish in the microwave and determined the baking time. He sat behind a table and breathed in an exhausted manner. He had seven engaging conversations with all seven suspects. It's all so true that they were seven different people with seven different manners and prospects but they all had a duplicate reaction: They found Oliver's scenario 'offensive'.

"Loki must've been exhausted all the time" Oliver placed his head on the table and thought, "Poor guy."

He turned on his phone and read the suspects' defences:

**Anya:** *I tried so hard to leave Australia to Prove my family I can make it on my own.*

**Sebastian:** *My parents separated when I was two because my mum had a miscarriage and my dad didn't act very supportive. That miscarriage got her thinking ever since and even though she doesn't talk about it, I know she couldn't forget about it. I perfectly know how does the death of a child affects a family and I would never make anyone feel the pain that my family did.*

**Morgan:** *I'm finally getting married after seeing twenty six springs. I'll be married to the man I love this summer and I highly doubt that Anthony would like the idea of marrying a murderer!*

**Marika:** *I'm not a murderer because I was the happiest person ever since Nilsa was born. I can't even imagine losing my child and if I can't, how can I allow myself to make another mother suffer from it?*

**Olga:** *Brad was a good friend of mine. He and Ezra shared happy moments with me. Returning their favour like that wouldn't be monstrous you think?*

**Theodore:** *My brother is trying to join me here. You know that, right? I don't think that neither of us would gratify a dead brother. How could Brad's brother do?*

It didn't end there. Pietro's answer's still left, which Oliver read it over and over and over again with different fonts. Still couldn't figure it out.

**Pietro** had answered: *Oliver, I'm so thankful for what you did for me yesterday at the police station but…I don't think that I'm the murderer or the other suspects. Honestly, I have this little feeling that it was you, or at least you had a small part in it. I did not kill Bradly Anton Moore. I couldn't be any more certain…it wasn't me, was it you?*

Oliver anxiously smiled and whispered: "You Adolfs."
Was Pietro the killer who messed up the lives of at least three people?
Was he at Brad's house before everyone arrived?

If he was the killer…

Was he so smart to leave no DNAs or leads?

Was he that discreet to set a perfect timeline, a perfect scenario to pretend being the seventh person who arrives?

What if all of these were just accidents?

What if the real killer was sabotaging for Pietro?

Pietro was drunk that night, was it volitional or the killer knew him and got him drunk?

Pietro was not a deferential person but he didn't deserve to be treated so cruel.

There was no standard evidence indicative of Pietro being the killer and you can't press charges against someone just because a young woman is scared and a woman finds him shady.

Oliver looked up to the microwave. There was still time left and he was starving, who thinks about job when they're starving?

He got up and went to the living room and laid on the couch in front of the television. He stared to the TV's black screen for a while but got eyes off it pretty soon. Since he was a boy, he had the phobia of seeing someone other than himself in that black mirror.

"I'm bored as hell," he thought, "I hate my life."

He turned to the other side and remembered something: "I have a landline on the other side of the couch!" He thought with a British accent.

He sat on the couch and picked up the phone from the table behind the couch to check his answering machine which was only one message. He played and the voice of the last person he thought it could be, changed places with silence. Oliver's dead friend, Bradly Anton Moore II. Bradly's voice was cheerful, like it always was…but the fear was obviously audible: *"Hey Ollie! How you doing man? I know you never check your answering machine…but anyway! So, recently, I've been seeing some friends, new friends and I swear I was gonna tell you about it but some of them are just jerks and this is not the point…I've been having some issues with one of them, some opacities came up, I talked too much, said things I shouldn't have and I'm so incapable solving them and he is a little…Dear heavens! A lot! He is irresolution; a lot! He is not the guy you can fairly discuss a problem let alone the fact that he's mad at me right now. He's got this sort of anger that leads him to maybe…just maybe commit some crimes, he has done some of these crimes! The point is, he is so mad at me and I don't feel safe enough, I feel like he is gonna do something to me, I don't know! maybe kill me!...He WILL kill me...I know that...If anything ever happened to me, check my mattress...You will find who he did it...Do not hesitate...Oh, Ezra's here. We are going to get supper at Aunt Marina's place, farewell! I love you bro, be safe."*

The message was over.

Oliver was staring at the wall for the next minutes, dismayed.

He couldn't decide which one was getting him thinking.

Hearing the *actual* voice of a dead friend again, or the dead friend informing him with a lead, a man that Bradly was having problems with? A *man*.

"It's a *he*." Oliver whispered. He yelled: "The killer is a man!"

Oliver dialled Arthur's phone so fast that he didn't even check the number. Luckily, it was Arthur and he answered right away: "Yes?"

"It's a *he*!" Oliver shouted.

After spending four seconds quiet, Arthur asked: "Oliver, what drug are you high on?"

"I didn't take any, Arthur," Oliver said angrily, "The killer we're looking for is a man! Hear me!"

"Wait, what?" Arthur asked confused, "How do you know that?"

"I'll explain to you on the way! We should go to Brad's house! *Right now!*" Oliver said excited.

"Okay, be ready in five." Arthur said, "And calm down for God's sake!"

Oliver hung up and changed his clothes instantly. He was thinking of not letting Ezra know but remembering the chaos of two nights ago, dissuaded him so a text was sent to Ezra about meeting up in Brad's place immediately.

Oliver left the house when he heard Arthur's car's horn. He grabbed his keys off the cabinet and that was when the microwave beeped. Oliver looked at the lasagne through the microwave glass. There was no time to eat it. What a shame.

When he sat in Arthur's car, Arthur said: "Hi. Explain."

Oliver began to talk after all: "Hello. I barely check my answering machine, you know that. I was bored today so I checked it and there was this left message from Brad. It belongs to...a month ago or two. He said that he was making some friends recently and he was having some problems with one of them. Brad mentioned that the guy is irresolution that Brad can't talk to him and fix the problem. He said that the guy might kill him."

Arthur frowned: "Didn't he mention what the problem was?"

"Apparently, Brad said things that he wasn't supposed to. I think he might've interfered in something that was none of his business." Oliver opined.

"Like a family problem?"

"Exactly. A family problem."

Arthur drove the car and breathed angrily: "Which one of the suspects have family issues?"

"Sebastian is alright with his family. He sees his father every week and his mother is very supportive. Theodore has parental issues but not very much serious. Pietro, on the other hand, was addicted between twenty fourteen and twenty eighteen. His father found out about his addiction and these two haven't spoken since then." Oliver explained each suspect's condition.

"Who do you think it might be?"

Oliver thought and said: "Definitely not Sebastian. No secrets that he got to the crime scene first but the Sebastian I know, isn't able to hurt a bug."

"So, we've got Pietro and Theodore left. Who do you think?"

Oliver, who could no longer stand starve, politely said: "Arthur, I haven't eaten yet. Can we please talk it through when we arrived?"

Arthur whispered: "Sure."

Oliver closed his eyes, put his head on the window and reviewed Brad's voicemail in his head; over and over again. As he recalled the mattress part, he opened his eyes and said out loud: "He said a name!"

Arthur looked at him angrily and yelled: "Couldn't you say that faster?"

"He said it! He said that I should check his mattress if anything ever happened to him. The mattress, Arthur, *the mattress*!" Oliver yelled excitedly.

Those twenty-two words caused Arthur to drive faster to Brad's house; and passing a red light!

They got to Brad's house in the exact moment as Ezra. Arthur said without his lips moving: "Why is he here?"

"I told him to come," Oliver said, "I thought we might need help."

"With a mattress?" Arthur grumbled.

"Don't grumble! He's Brad's brother!" Oliver said in low voice.

"And I'm a police officer with a damn job that does not allow me to let a victim's family know about everything!" Arthur said angrily even though he was trying to remain calm.

"Take it or leave it. Ezra saw Brad the same day Brad left the message. They went to their aunt's house. Ezra might know things."

Arthur frowned in a scary manner: "Then he'll be so sorry for not telling us." He said and got off the car.

Oliver shook his head: "Oh, Arthur. You damn idiot." And followed Arthur: "Don't do anything inconsiderate!"

Arthur stopped and frowned at him again: "*Inconsiderate*, Oliver? You made a completely thoughtless choice and now you're calling *me inconsiderate?*" he continued: "Just *shut up*. I'm so mad at you right now but I don't have a gun so you'll die painfully."

Oliver didn't dare to say another word. Arthur went further and started the three members conversation: "Hi Ezra."

"Hi. What's going on? Why are we here?" Ezra said and looked at them for answers.

Oliver handed the keys to Arthur. Arthur explained: "We're here because your brother left Oliver a message, almost a month ago. Saying that a man wants to kill him and that he put the killer's name under his mattress. It worth a search."

"*What?*" Ezra asked amazed "When did you find the message?"

"I just found out about it." Oliver answered.

"Jesus." Ezra whispered and covered his eyes with his hand and exhaled.

"Ezra, did you and Brad have supper at your aunt Marina's house a month ago?" Oliver asked Ezra.

Ezra though and explained: "Yes. Yes, we did. She invited us and the rest of our cousins to her house. She made us chocolate chip cookies with earl grey tea."

"How was Brad that day? How did he seem?" Arthur asked while opening the door.

"He wasn't as cheerful as he always was. I remember asking about it and he just said that he had to perform an autopsy on a child that morning. I didn't ask more, I thought it might upset him to remember it." Ezra explained.

Arthur entered the house and went upstairs to Brad's bedroom. Ezra and Oliver followed him. The three of them helped removing the mattress off the bed. They looked all around the empty bed and every side of the mattress but there was no notes or names. Oliver checked the mattress's area but he found nothing: "What the hell? Where's the name?"

"Hold on a moment," Arthur whispered. He touched all around the mattress for a split.

"What are you doing?" Ezra asked Arthur.

Arthur's hand stopped at some point: "Wait."

He put his hand in the mattress and when he felt a paper, he grabbed and took it out. It was a very small paper.

Oliver stole the paper and opened it; once again, he said: "What the hell?"

"What?" Ezra asked. He was tired of receiving no answers.

"Just…four numbers," Oliver said with a blue face and a turned off candle of hope.

"What numbers?" Arthur asked Oliver.

"Fifteen, fifty-three, fifty-two, forty-four." Oliver read the numbers out loud.

"Someone was using different alphabet." Arthur whispered.

They all stood at their places hopeless for a while until Arthur said: "Guys, we must go. I have to report this to detective Henry and verify the information. And Ezra, *don't* tell your parents about this, don't give them hope. And never mention to anyone that you were here with us. You weren't supposed to be here."

Ezra showed his acceptation by shaking his head and said: "I'll be downstairs."

When Ezra left the room, Oliver was so close to weep. He whispered: "But, I was sure. I thought it'll end today."

Arthur sat on the floor next to him and said: "It's just how it works. It's like a matryoshka, you think what you have found ends the job but another layer shows up."

"All I wanted was a name," Oliver whispered with his shivering voice and covered his face with his hands, "why don't criminals just confess? If they're so afraid of paying the price, then why do they even do it?"

"A little madness and rage is enough for committing such crime. That madness and rage aren't among you at the court or the jail. That's what scares them." Arthur continued: "You know what did my first instructor told me when I first joined the police academy?"

Oliver denied with head.

"Hope is venom," Arthur quoted, "That's what he said to me. He believed that too much hope kills you. Takes away a small piece of you every day."

"Hope is not bad," Oliver said with a sad, low voice.

"It is, for my career. It can lead me to a hellish frustration."

Oliver turned his face to Arthur and asked him: "You have—no hope that we'll get justice for Brad?"

"Not that I don't have. I just don't strongly believe it. I wasn't even so hopeful when I was driving here. This case is more complicated than the victim just leaves a voicemail and tell us who the killer is. I hate to remind you of it but this is a real world, Oliver. We're not living a fantasy," Arthur said what he said and left the room.

Oliver looked around him. He was all alone. Although Arthur sounded very rational and there were no signs of anger in his voice, Oliver was mad at him.

How could Arthur be indifference about the murder of a man?

"Does death even bother him?" Oliver thought.

He stood up and read the paper again: *15.53.52.44.*

Oliver angrily crumpled the paper and put in the inner pocket of his sweater. He had all good reasons to cry and break a mirror; but he chose control over crumble.

***

## Flashback, February 9th, Bradly Moore's House, 22:25 P.M.

HE knocked at the door. After the pass of not so many seconds, the door was opened and Bradly Moore appeared with his permanent charming smile: "Hey you! Come in." Bradly invited his cause of death inside the house, not having a clue about what was about to happen in ten minutes.

HE walked in among the Bradly. Bradly asked: "Are you hungry? I still got some tuna pasta left."

"Your favourite, huh?"

"My favourite, yup!" Bradly said and raised his mug "Now that you're not eating, let me invite you to a cup of hot cocoa."

"I'll pass. I'm not here to nutrient. I'm here to talk." HE said with a cold attitude and a clod smile. No signs of hesitate. HE was tired of waiting. HE couldn't wait to achieve a gloomy and sinister goal.

"Hey, what's wrong? Is everything alright? Is everybody okay?" Bradly asked confused. Not that he wasn't familiar with the killer's cold and heartless attitude, he just wanted to make sure. As long as Brad knew, HE wasn't a person of unplanned meetings unless an urgent situation.

"Yes! Everything and everyone are okay. I said I'm here to talk. Let's go to the living room. We should sit."

It's undeniable that Bradly was worried. He could sense that something wasn't right, he just didn't know what.

Putting together any worst-case scenarios including robbery, fighting, hurting and even murdering, Bradly could never guess that he was the worst-case scenario himself; never in a million years thought that HE could even ponder hurting Brad.

Carrying all the anxiety and toxic thoughts like a heavy backpack, Brad walked into the living room with the killer.

They both sat on the two seats couch. Bradly just noticed that HE was wearing gloves, although HE would rarely use them.

HE looked around with a well-covered nervousness and asked: "Where's your dog?"

"Margot's in my room, chasing her tail. She hasn't slept in two days. She's sick and furious," Bradly said it as a threat. HE took it but the only reaction was a little cold smile.

"Okay, well; I should be sleeping in an hour. I have plans for tomorrow." Bradly said and that didn't change the killer's opinion. It didn't melt the killer's frozen heart even a little bit. The killer was too determined that nothing could put him doubt.

"Don't worry. I'll end the talk soon."

"You better do. Go on."

"So, I was thinking…since a very long time ago; I was thinking that the difference between us is so undeniable. It is…full of hatred and anger like we've got a bad blood."

"You're unhappy about that? So cute," Brad said humiliating, "I never had any problems with you. *You* were the one to create problems."

"Think about it, Bradly. Think about the behaviour of those we commonly known, the way they treat you, it is way different than how they treat me! It's filled with discrimination." HE said seriously. No more cold smiles.

"Discri...Oh Jesus! What are you, Seven?!" Bradly said while laughing nervously.

"You, see? This is what I'm talking about!"

"Let me get this straight. You're upset because of the way I treat you? So does the others?" Bradly frowned "Oh, pet! Maybe you're just not mature enough!"

"See? This is what you always do!" HE enraged "You blame everyone else but you for what's done by you!"

Bradly tried so hard not to slap the killer in the face. Brad slowly said: "Do you really think that I wouldn't have treated you better if you were actually matured? I don't care if you're a genius or something, you're still a kid. A kid who doesn't remember that yelling is banned at this house. Besides, does anyone know that you're here, Yelling at me?"

"Yes. I'm out with a friend."

"Excuse me?" Bradly raised an eyebrow, "Are you calling me a 'friend'?"

"I *was* out with a friend. I drove him home. I'm here now." HE continued: "Although, if I hadn't met that friend tonight, I would've meant the great Lord when I said 'friend,' because you and I," HE nodded, "Are not friends. We never were."

"I'm afraid I don't catch your point." Brad still had that frown on top of his light blue eyes.

"Don't be silly, Bradly! You can't say that we were friends when you don't even know fifteen percent of me!" HE said angrily.

"Oh really? And that hurts your feelings? You're an egoist. You can't see anyone but you." Bradly said furious, "I can't have this conversation with you right now. Get out of my house! *Now!*"

He stood up to leave the living room when the killer grabbed his shirt and pulled him over. Grabbing a knife out of their coat and sink it into Bradly Moore's left foreleg, HE whispered, loud enough for Bradly to hear: "This is for the damage you caused me."

Killer brought the knife out and stabbed Bradly again: "This is for my life."

The next strike was so much closer to the heart: "This is for us," HE whispered, "We could've been everything." HE then yelled with tears in their eyes: "*Everything*!"

Bradly's eyes were also tearing rivers. He was unable to talk but the killer saw his lips moving like: "Don't."

"I'm sorry. For everything." HE whispered back, pulled Bradly out to the hallway and stabbed; over and over again...until the poor defenceless man's heart stopped beating and the warmth left the body for the cruel coldness.

HE who saw that scene, who saw HIS prey not struggling anymore, sat next to Bradly and started to weep, holding Bradly's body in HIS arms.

HE *wasn't* sorry because they were sat free.

HE *was* so sorry for the way they had to set himself free.

HE had just took the life of a man that HE could've loved.

Losing someone close to you is hard, believing it is harder and learning to live without them is the hardest.

HE was never capable of living a normal life; ever.

HE whispered next to Bradly's ear: "I would've given you the world...but you made me take it all away from you."

The last thing to do was sending eight of Bradly's friends an emergency message.

It was over...

It was all over...

***

### Oliver Johnson's House, 18:19 P.M.

"You idiot," Olivia said while wrapping bandage around Oliver's hand.

After returning home, Oliver took a cold-water shower, cried in the shower and after wearing dresses, he punched the mirror in his bedroom.

He didn't know that Arthur was taking night shift that night so he drove Olivia to Oliver's house while Oliver was showering.

When Olivia heard a glass breaking, she followed the sound upstairs and she saw Oliver with a red, covered in blood hand.

"Didn't find a better way to evacuate your anger?" Olivia asked.

Oliver looked at him and asked: "Should I answer?"

"No, Oliver, No! You should be ashamed. What are you, eighteen?" Olivia yelled at him.

Oliver didn't answer. He knew that his decision was irrational but so was Olivia's. His hand was in a nagging pain but he didn't say a word, that would've made Olivia angrier. She would've reprehended him for causing himself pain.

Olivia finished wrapping. She said with a blue face: "Done...Ollie, what's the matter? Arthur didn't tell me what happened."

Oliver breathed and looked at the floor: "I checked my answering machine and I found this voicemail that Brad left a month ago. He explained that he was having problems with a friend and that friend might've been thinking of murdering him. Brad said that if anything happened to him, I should check his mattress where he put the guy's name."

Olivia, who seemed extremely amazed, shouted: "Did he? Did Brad say it himself?"

"Uh-huh."

"Oh God." Olivia covered her eyes with hands, "Did you go there? Did you find anything?"

"We went there. We checked the mattress but all we got was a bunch of numbers," Oliver said paralysed.

"What numbers?"

"Fifteen, fifty-three, fifty-two, forty-four."

"What the hell does these mean? What are we supposed to understand?"

"I don't know, Liv. I'm done." Oliver stood up, "I just know that I want to go take a very long nap. Don't disturb me and don't wake me up for dinner. See you, dear," Oliver said with a cold manner went upstairs to sleep...

## March 4th, Pietro Schewater's House, 5:58 A.M.

Pietro woke up frightened. He could barely breathe. He grabbed the glass of water on the drawer next to his bed. After breathing for a while, he succeeded drinking it until there wasn't a drop left.

He laid back on his bed. It wasn't the first time he had a nightmare, clearly. But the sort of nightmares he had been having, yes, they were new.

An idea, turned on the light of his mind. He left the bed to grab a pen and a notebook. He wanted to write all he could remember.

He wrote down:

*Darkness. Blindly touching everywhere. No way out. Collar being pulled back. I fall on the ground. I see Bradly. He is very angry. He doesn't talk. He grabs my throat with his hands. He tends to choke me. I try to stop him. He is unstoppable. I success. He is even angrier. I see a knife in his hand. I don't know where he got it from. He raises his hand. He stabs me. A lot. I wake up.*

Pietro rubbed his face. His heart was still beating fast and hard like a hummingbird and his every breath felt a massive pain in his chest. He had been having the very same nightmare every time he felt asleep for a week now. Even when he slept on the couch, or at the hotel. Not just at nights, no, literally *every* time he felt asleep.

It was getting hard to overcome.

"I'm not a killer," Pietro whispered.

He was standing up when he saw a planning paper was on the table. He looked closer. He had his plans written for March 4th:

- 6:00: wake up.
- 6:15–7:00: do a 45-minute workout.
- 7:30: eat breakfast.
- 8:00: go out for a walk.
- 10:00: buy a cup of caramel latte.
- 10:20: Paula anrufen (call Paula).
- 12:00: visit the GMT.
- 13:00: go shopping and return home.
- 14:00: *mach Kartoffelpüree und Bratwurst zum mittagessen* (make mashed potato and bratwurst for lunch).
- 14:30: watch a random movie and *den Rest des Tages nichts tun* (do nothing for the rest of the day).

Based on the plan, he was supposed to exercise first. It was time to cheer up…

\*\*\*

"Hi Leah."

"Pit! Hi!" Paula said happily to her older brother.

"How are you?" Pietro smiled. He was glad to hear his little sister's voice.

"I'm good. Thank you for asking. Hey, where did you get with that case?"

"It's ummm…in process. I'm taking care of it but I still need talk to the forensic psychologist."

"Why is it not finishing? I miss you."

"I miss you too," Pietro said, "How's…how's Dad? And Mum? How are they?"

"They're fine. Dad was just dealing with flu last week; he couldn't attend any classes. But he is better now."

"Still not asking if I'm alive?" Pietro asked sarcastically and disappointed.

"Stop it. He loves you. You're his first born and only son. He can't stay mad at you."

"I doubt. He has been, for the past four years."

"You are his only son, Pietro. You and I don't know how it is like to have your only son in a foreign country."

"But it must feel really great to have a friend in the same foreign country to spy on your son!" Pietro said sarcastically again.

"Don't blame him, please. I mean, what were you doing at that party anyway?"

"What do people do at parties? I was celebrating a friend's birthday!" Pietro said, "And I know that I was using drugs but that couldn't prove that I was addicted."

"Don't you remember all the drugs you used to be high on? Ecstasy, methamphetamine? Or even alcohol?" Paula said in anger, "Sorry."

Pietro was silent for a while. He then calmly said: "I *do* remember them. I'm not proud of those times. But it doesn't allow you to talk about them like I enjoyed being recalled as an addicted. Do you understand?"

"I do," Paula said innocently. She was sorry about what she said.

"Okay," Pietro said, "Are you and Mum joining me here this summer?"

"Of course!" Paula cheered and innocently continued: "And Pit, what if, just what if you and Dad make up and you see all three of us?"

Pietro closed his eyes and took a deep breath just to prevent throwing his phone on the street. He said with no hard feelings: "Leah, *liebling*, I've said what I should've to defend myself. I have a heavy crap that is disturbing my life right now, I'm too tired to take care of a family issue."

"Daddy issue," Paula whispered but Pietro heard her and asked to end or prevent a very engaging conversation: "*Warum bist du nicht in der schule?*" (Why aren't you in school?)

"Backache. Why aren't you at work?"

"Because I'm doomed!" Pietro yelled.

"Okay, *bruder*! I won't disturb you, *liebling*!" Paula yelled back.

"*Ich hasse dich!*" (I hate you!)

"*Ich hasse dich mehr!*" (I hate you more!)

This was a totally normal conversation between Pietro and Paula. Although Pietro could never do this conversation when Paula spoke English.

She was really good at speaking English but she still had a German accent which Pietro thought it was super cute to fight it back.

Pietro, on the other hand was adopting a British accent, thanks to the citizenship of United Kingdom. British accent was taking over his thoughts but he was still fond of American accent; he knew why.

***

## 14:30 P.M.

Pietro sat on the couch in front of the television and put his plate of bratwurst and mashed potato with the topping of corn on the table in front of him. He turned on his laptop and picked a movie to watch. Meanwhile, when he was surfing the crime genre, he thought of Brad again. About the case and how it was changing his life.

By 'life' I mean his mental health and stability. Having chained nightmares is a disease. Pietro was diseased.

He couldn't stand being killed while sleeping and he just wanted and answer to the questions 'why?' and 'Were they meaningless or meaningful?'

"Should I see a psychologist?" Pietro thought and by the time he thought of the word 'psychologist', Oliver came up to his mind immediately.

Actually, Pietro felt so sorry for him. Burying a cherished person is nothing less than burying memories and feelings.

'Emotional' isn't the right way to describe Pietro but imagining a very long-time friend who happened to be your best friend being buried, that scared him.

He wasn't emotional, but he would've never been happy to see someone upset. NEVER. He found it inhumane.

He heard his phone notification. He looked at his phone. The name 'Oliver Johnson' appeared with a message: *"Good afternoon, Pietro. Our next meeting will be tomorrow at 17. I will send you the address in an hour."*

Pietro breathed out: *"Vom Teufel sprechen."* (Speak of the devil)

***

## March 5th, Greenwich Library, 17:00 P.M.

Everyone was at the library, ready for their seventh meeting; except for Anya whom professor decided to choose 15 to 16:45 as a make-up class with no previous notices.

"We'll wait for five more minutes, Anya said she can make..." Oliver was saying when Anya arrived and interrupted him, saying in low voice: "Hi everyone. Sorry I'm late." And sat on the only empty seat between Marika and Olga.

Everyone greeted her in whispers. Oliver began to talk, in a low volume, obviously: "Thanks to all of you for joining me today. Today's meeting will be a little bit more friendly than our previous meetings. Today, I want all of you to talk about your greatest regret in your life. I want to get familiar with the deepest parts of your emotions and souls."

"Excuse me," Olga whispered, "Are regrets, great?"

Oliver smiled. It feels amazing when a foreigner speaks your language and confuses a word. He bent a quantum and explained: "It means the biggest, as well."

He went back to his seat and continued: "I suggest ladies start the conversation today. Ladies first?"

Marika raised her hand and said: "I'm eldest. I go further...so as you might know, I'm a mother to a two-year-old named 'Nilsa'. My regret goes back to a year and a half ago when my daughter was a newborn...my mother died soon after I was born, she had this infectious disease. I never blamed myself for her death until I gave birth myself. I regret the fact that I was hating Nilsa."

Tears came to her eyes but she didn't want to cry. She continued: "Can you imagine it? A woman hating her own daughter because she never met her own mother! It's horrible! But what I was unaware of, was that I was hating myself, I blamed myself for my mother's death because I was experiencing motherhood and I couldn't find anything unique about it to explain why my mother gave her life over it…but I love my daughter now, extremely and indescribably. When I'm at work, in the hospital, I can barely wait for my shift to be over even though I love my job."

"Thank you so much, Marika," Oliver appreciated, "Sure, you never met your mother but your expectations, I believe they make you the wonderful mother that Nilsa deserves."

Olga raised her hand and said: "What I'm about to say…it might change your whole prospection of me. My oldest sister is 'Melora'. Twelve years ago, we had this argument and it led to physical violence. She slapped me and I was young, I was sixteen or seventeen but I remember that I pushed her. She felt on the floor and before she did, her head hit the corner of a table. Her spinal cord, I think this is the word, her spinal cord got hurt and for the past twelve years, she had been paralysed in both legs. She cannot move her legs and she sits on a wheelchair."

"Did you two talk after that?" Pietro asked her.

Olga confirmed with head: "We did. I apologised to her like a billion times. She said that she forgave me but I can't forgive *myself*, why should I? I stole her life away and I lost it."

Oliver said: "You are valued with your humanity, knowledge and successes not your mistakes and no one has the right to judge you because of them but God, Olga."

Anya bent her head and put it on Olga's shoulder and said: "I'll be next. My grandfather was prone to Alzheimer. I used to visit him a lot so he rarely forgotten me. It didn't happen more than once or twice. At the last days of his life, he was bedridden and at his last day on earth, which was sadly his birthday, me and my brother Luke went to a bakery to buy him a birthday cake. His children and grandchildren were all at his room that day. Long story short, we didn't make it on time and he passed away…my aunt said that he wanted to see 'Annie' before he was gone. I hate to be called Annie but its pronunciation was too difficult for him."

"May he rest in peace, Anya. You were the last thing he was thinking of before the enormous change in his life and that means that he loved you," Oliver said, "Morgan?"

"Oliver," Sebastian called, "I'm not insisting but, will you tell us *your* greatest regret?"

Oliver didn't say anything, just shook his head as 'Yes'.

"My turn," said Morgan, "I was born and raised in a not very wealthy family which was being supported by an alcoholic father. What I regret is my relationship with my sister Karla. So, I was obsessed with how I use my money when I was growing up. I allowed that obsession affect my feelings for people. When my sister and I first moved to Birmingham, we both started to work all the time but at some point, I started to think that she wants to steal all the money I made and get away with it. Lots of arguments happened because of that and our sisterhood was affected and this year's january I could finally make things a little less worse…that's it, that's my regret."

"Thank you for talking about it, Morgan. It's a good sign that you tried to make things right. That means a lot," Oliver said and turned to men's side "Gentlemen?"

Theodore explained: "I can't remember my childhood clearly. I can't say if I regret anything from that time period. But three years ago, I had this Corgi dog. I left her at the house for two days straight without leaving her enough food. What I regret is that I had only one job and I failed. Who would treat an animal like that? Who except psychopaths?"

Oliver didn't say anything about this one. Pietro understood that Oliver will not talk, started to talk about his regret: "I've been addicted for four years, you know that. I've lost connections with my dad; you also know that…you know my father has always been my greatest mentor. He taught me everything. He's an English literature teacher and he taught me that, he taught me how to ride a bike, drive a car and cook and all good things. We used to talk everyday but we haven't talked in four years and that's too much. It seriously is. I texted him for his birthday but I received no answers. I owe the man everything I have and everything I know. He did his best raising a competent son but he got an addicted one. I give him every right to be mad and…and disappointed but he could've reacted better, I think. I regret letting him down."

"Pietro," Anya called, "Didn't you want to talk to him?"

"I did," Pietro smiled sadly, "He didn't text back and answered no calls."

"Pietro, you're a good person. Addiction is so not welcomed but the addicted person isn't guilty of anything. Of course, your father would've never accepted such condition but that's normal for parents to do. None of them want to see their kids' lives being affected by such pernicious matter," Oliver said with sympathy.

"Anyone else?" Sebastian asked with a weird smile, "I don't want to talk about it; it's nothing normal to talk about."

Oliver smiled tiredly: "Say it or you'll never hear mine."

"How can I clarify?" Sebastian whispered.

He sighed and said: "Our stories are so much alike, Oliver. But I lost my friend to suicide."

Oliver raised his eyebrows like he didn't know: "What?"

"Yeah…so I was thirteen and my best friend Matt was suffering from depression…I'll cut it short, one night his parents called me and said that I should've been there immediately. Matt was on the rooftop, ready to throw himself. I rushed there and I arrived on time…I talked to him, tried to discourage him but everything I said sounded like nothing to him and he jumped. He jumped and he didn't make it. He died. I couldn't dissuade him," Sebastian said and smiled innocently, "Don't tell me anything pleasing, Oliver. I want to know your regret."

"Is Sebastian more broken than I am?" Oliver thought once more.

He made Sebastian a so-called promise to tell them his greatest regret. He was a man of his word. He said: "I never told Brad how a perfect friend he was. He was always there for me and he took care of me. But I never told him how lucky I was to have him by my side. And now the only one I can say these things to is a cold grave at the Chingford cemetery."

Oliver paused and closed his eyes to get ready for the rest: "Like I said, our past and its actions and decisions does not define us. What truly matters about a person is how humane they are, is how they try to evolve, is how much they try to grow and how much they care for themselves and others. You can't change the past, you're not Barry Allen…all you can do is to learn what your mistakes were. Once you learn something, you don't say it in the wrong way. We know that water's molecule is $H_2O$, you don't say it's $CO_2$. When you understand where your mistakes were done, you won't make them again. So, keep going forward. Evolve."

## Oliver Johnson's Car, 18:10 P.M.

Oliver was proudly eating potato chips, watching a '90s movie on his phone. He was stuck in the traffic; but he wasn't naïve. He had snacks and fine playlists to get through the traffic.

The movie paused automatically when his phone rang. Arthur's name appeared on the phone. He answered the phone: "Hey Arthur."

"Hi, is the meeting over?"

"Yeah. We finished twenty minutes ago. Why?"

"I increased the investigation and I found criminal records about Pietro."

"Did you?" Oliver put the chips on his legs, "What records?"

"Physical violence in public, he didn't start the fight. Passing red lights and unauthorised speed."

"What was the fight for?"

"Someone confused him with another albinos guy. Pietro only defended himself and had witnesses to testify." Arthur explained, "Although the man who started the fight sued him."

"Sued him? For what? *He* started the fight!" Oliver said surprised.

"Indeed. Apparently, he called Pietro 'Nazi'. Pietro got angry and put his head into a window. The guy's face got twenty stitches!"

"Still think Pietro had every right." Oliver defended Pietro, "What if someone calls you a Kangaroo? Don't you get mad?"

"I mean…I don't get mad but I wouldn't like it either."

"These aren't enough to suspect him as the OG killer. Can you investigate more?"

"I tell Juniper to take care of it."

"Thank you."

"Are you going home?"

"No. I'm going to Brad's house. You know, like a reunion."

"Keep in touch."

"See you."

Oliver hung up the phone and waited for the traffic to lower down.

***

## Bradly Moore's House, 19:00

That was one hell of a traffic. After almost an hour, Oliver had arrived at his dear dead friend's house. He sat on the couch with ice cream's bucket and a spoon. He looked around him. Brad's house was perfectly decorated. John Lewis green chesterfield sofas made perfect matches with brown parquet floor and chocolate tables.

"You had an amazing taste and an artistic soul. Why did you choose to rip people's body?" Oliver thought out loud "Let's do a bit of reverse engineering here, shall we?"

Oliver breathed out and started to complain: "I have only a week to rescue my career, why? Because I failed recognizing a killer. Why I had to recognize one? Because you were murdered. Why were you murdered? Because a friend of you killed you. Why did he? That is what I don't know. Why don't I know? Because you never told me. Why didn't you? Because you were a jerk? I don't know that either!…all I know is that my career and all my life is being affected *because of you*!" Oliver yelled the last sentence, leant back and angrily ate ice cream.

"Don't get me wrong. I love you and I miss you as much as you can't believe. But that doesn't change the fact that your death is ruining my life. I'm trying to deal with that," Oliver said out loud.

He texted Ezra after half an hour: "Can I wrap some of Brad's objects?"

When the text was sent, Oliver stood up and went upstairs to Brad's bedroom. He wasn't really asking Ezra for any permissions; he was just informing.

Oliver started with Brad's closet. He already knew that Brad used to keep a few boxes of useless stuff at the bottom of the closet.

He brought the boxes out and put them on the ground and sat next to them.

He opened the first box. It was filled with comic books. Oliver remembered when he and Brad used to go to libraries after school to buy comics. Brad was fond of Batman and Daredevil. He had a full collection of their comics. Oliver, on the other hand, liked the Green arrow just because they shared a name. He also thought Moon Knight was cool.

Oliver opened the second box. He faced some notebooks, books, stationery and Brad's first handwritten periodic table.

Oliver grabbed the periodic table and studied every block with a beautiful smile.

He remembered when they were seventeen, Brad made his choice of becoming a coroner. He was so into periodic table that he drew the very same table over a night.

Oliver finished reading them all. He smiled and thought: "You really liked chemistry, didn't you? Chemistry, puzzles, animals and superheroes were your interests, huh?"

Oliver laughed at what he said. But his smile faded away when he noticed a point.

He checked his sweater's pocket for the paper he found inside Brad's mattress. He found it inside of an inner pocket.

He opened the crumpled paper and put it next to the periodic table.

Fifteen, fifty-three, fifty-two, forty-four were numbers of elements Phosphorus, Iodine, Tellurium and Ruthenium.

They were shorts for: P-I-Te-Ru.

He whispered: "Pietro killed Brad."

Oliver could not believe what he just found out. It was as unbelievable as keeping him grounded for an hour and a half, overthinking.

An hour and a half of resolving, deducing, putting theories together like a thousand pieces cloth. It did and did not make sense to him. *Why* would Pietro kill Bradly and *how* did he manage to escape the charges?

*How* long it took him to apply his sinister and vile inclination?

A tear dropped off Oliver's left eye. He closed his eyes and tried to imagine what exactly happened on that night. He wanted to, but he couldn't picture the agony and discomfort that Brad went through on the very moment his body started to freeze and his breaths were fast.

Now that he was actually thinking about it, Brad was a billion times braver than Oliver ever was and ever could be.

He slowly moved his hand inside his pocket to grab his phone. Calling Richard was the rightest thing he could think of. He called Richard and unlike ever, Richard answered with peace: "Oliver?"

"Detective...I found out who's guilty." Oliver hardly said to Richard, "Pietro killed him. He is the murderer."

Richard didn't say anything. Not that he was shocked at that moment, no; he was already surprised by Pietro himself: "Oliver...I think you should come here."

"Wha...? Why?"

"Because…Pietro came here ten minutes ago. He's confessing."

"I'll be there in no time," Oliver said and hung up the phone.

He couldn't remember if he ran or jumped off the stairs, locked the door and sat inside his car. He just remembered that he was never that fast.

## Interrogation Room, 22:29

Oliver walked into the room taking slow and silent steps. He found Pietro putting his head on the table and covering it with his hands. The moment wasn't good and neither neutral at all; it was horrible. Absolutely horrible.

It reminded Oliver of one of his favourite cousins wedding, Joe's wedding. Joe's brother, Simon was supposed to prepare a speech for the wedding; but since Simon was living in a different state and couldn't make it to the wedding, Joe asked Oliver take responsibility.

Truth be told, Joe didn't ask. He ordered. Of course, Oliver didn't accept but when Joe's wife, Melissa asked and promised that that he'll certainly be the godfather of their future children, Oliver couldn't say no. That is the story of Oliver's last minute but perfect and romantic speech.

The point of bringing up the very old story is to clarify that Oliver was gifted and talented enough to present a last-minute speech and get an acceptable result but at that moment, nothing seemed like a wedding. No enthusiasm, no decoration, no maids of honour and no best men were there to take care of everything. No one was joking and No one was gossiping. That place was cold, so serious. No feelings could've been sensed.

"P…Pietro," Oliver called but Pietro didn't catch. "Pietro," Oliver called louder. Pietro looked up to Oliver. His eyes were filled with shame, regret and sorrow. He didn't know what to say to make things better or stop them from getting any worse.

Oliver took place on the other side of the table and looked into Pietro's buried-in-tears eyes. Oliver asked gasping: "Do you have anything to say?" Pietro quietly put his hands down "Do you have anything to say?" Pietro didn't react again. Like he couldn't see and hear Oliver.

All of a sudden, Oliver's anxiety turned into rage and he lost his control. He suddenly stood up, hit the table with two hands and yelled: "Say something, damn it! *Say something!*"

Pietro whispered something. His voice was too low that Oliver couldn't hear. He asked: "What? What did you say?"

"I'm sorry," Pietro whispered embarrassed.

"You are...*sorry*? You killed my friend! You should be *dead*!"

Oliver's shouting was getting louder and louder. Arthur and Richard ran into the interrogation room to prevent him from hurting himself or Pietro.

Arthur tugged him out. He pushed Oliver to the wall outside but Oliver didn't resist anymore. He leant to the wall and slightly sat on the floor.

He covered his face with his hands and that was right before he fainted and heard Arthur calling his name and asking for an ambulance...

## March 6th, The Greenwich Hospital, 01:08 A.M.

Oliver opened his eyes and looked around as much as his eyesight assisted. He was at a hospital. The room was cold, or Oliver felt cold, all the lights were off and all the lights that was brightening the room belonged to the streetlights on the other side of the window.

Oliver succeeded seeing a blonde woman walking quiet and slow in front of the bed. "Liv?" Oliver doubtfully called Olivia since he knew only two blonde women.

She turned to Oliver and as Oliver guessed, it was Olivia.

"How do you feel, Ollie?" Olivia asked with kindness.

"Why...Why am I here? I shouldn't be here."

"Believe me, you *should* be here," Olivia said with no certain feelings but Oliver understood that she is angry, just a little bit.

"Why are you angry? What's happened?"

"I'm not angry, Oliver. I'm sick of you. You're the reason why," Olivia said exhausted.

"Do you mind telling me why?"

"No. Actually it's time." Olivia breathed, "Oliver I'm sick of you. It's been a month since you lost Bradly and you're this devastated. You are broken, Oliver. How can you not see that? Just because his parents asked you, doesn't mean you are given a duty. Elizabeth and Robert are selfish; they don't consider anyone else's sorrow but themselves. If they did, they wouldn't have asked you for such a huge thing!"

Oliver kept quiet until she was over. He said: "I appreciate your humanity. But I do not require anyone's assistance. I have everything under control."

"Oh, I'm sorry; *under control*?! Does that mean 'getting bedridden at the hospital because of low blood pressure?' Are you an actual idiot or you're just trying to make me laugh?" Olivia asked, tried so hard to hide his anger. Hospitals aren't good for arguments.

"What is it? Just because I fainted does it mean that I'm doing my job wrong?" Oliver said angry "Bradly was my friend. I would've taken the case even if no one asked me to. He was my friend and it is what he would've wanted!"

"A dead wants *nothing*!" Olivia yelled at Oliver, "A dead does whatever its name is; being dead. Why do you think that they want something from you? They're *too dead* to ask for anything."

Oliver didn't answer her. He didn't have a clue that his little sister thought that way.

Olivia sadly asked: "Why are you like this, Oliver? Why do you love to be sad?" and she went out of the room, waiting for no answers.

She came back later in ten minutes. Accompanying a middle-aged doctor and two plastic cups in her hands.

Doctor smiled at Oliver and said: "How do you feel, Bill?"

"I'm good. When can I leave?"

Doctor laughed and said: "A young man was here earlier. I assume he is you're brother; he asked me if I could keep you here for twenty four hours!"

Oliver asked: "What did you tell him?"

"There's no reason for you to stay. You can leave in the morning."

Olivia smiled at the doctor and said: "Thank you, doctor. Can my brother drink some hot chocolate? I bought him a small cup."

"Yes. Sweets stabilise his blood pressure. I should be going now, good night."

Oliver said: "Doc, I can't stay 'til morning. I have got work to do."

"Nothing is more important than your health, young man. You can't work if you're not healthy," Doctor said in indifference and left the room.

Olivia sat on the chair next to the bed, gave Oliver the smaller cup and said: "Just because you like it."

Oliver grabbed the cup with a big smile on his face. He was so ready to thank Olivia when his smile faded away because he saw that the liquid in the cup wasn't hot chocolate, it was white chocolate.

"Seriously?" Oliver asked, disturbed, "What is wrong with you?"

"They didn't have hot chocolate," Olivia said, "Hey I've got this question about the suspects. May I ask?"

"Would you keep your question if I say no?"

"Absolutely not."

"Then you may."

"Did SCIs find any hair at the crime scene?"

"If you mean SOCO, yes, they did. Dog hair that belonged to Margot. Why?"

"The other day, I went to the department to take Arthur to lunch. I was waiting for him at the hallway. I overheard two officers; a case was solved that day and they were talking about it. They said that the killer was identified by a hair. They left a hair at the crime scene. I thought that this might help you guys."

Oliver smiled and said: "Liv, I appreciate the fact that you're trying to help us, but SOCOs didn't find any hair. They bluntly told us that the murder was a hundred percent planned. It couldn't be a self-defence or some random and sudden misunderstanding."

"Understood," Olivia whispered. She started laughing a few moments later "You know what's funny? When I tell other people that my husband is a sergeant, they wonder if the excitement of watching crime movies is double or not!"

"What do you tell them?"

"The truth, of course. I tell them that in real life, crimes doesn't always get solved by a tall, good looking and handsome detective who always solve a crime in an hour long episode. I tell them that the criminals doesn't leave their wallet at the crime scene, they don't usually come back and they care a lot about the security cameras."

"That sounds pretty generous!" Oliver smiled, "I have this question. I wanted to ask you on your wedding day but I thought it might be sad. How do you know if Arthur comes back home? I mean, he is like Sherlock Holmes. He is great but when he gets a high-risk case or gets in a situation where he has to use guns, how do you know if he ever comes back home?"

Olivia smiled and said calmly: "I don't. I never know when the last time might be. But not being capable of accessing knowledge, doesn't mean that you are not allowed to hope for it."

"What do you mean?"

"I mean that I never know if he's coming back or not. But every morning at seven o'clock when I watch him leave, I hope to see his face again by evening.

Because I trust Arthur Black, the man I love and the man I married. I believe that sergeant Black always finds a way to come back home."

Oliver smiled and drank his hot chocolate. He wanted to ask Liv for a favour. He just wasn't sure if it was the perfect timing. But you know about that saying, 'if you don't take risks, you'll have a wasted soul.'

He kindly asked: "Liv? Can you do me a favour?"

"As long as it's not stupid and I can ask for the reason," Olivia said without looking at Oliver.

"I can leave in the morning, right? Can we go to…" Oliver was saying and Olivia interrupted: "Oliver, there's *no way* I'm letting you see Pietro again."

"Olivia, I have to go and see him. I need a reason." Oliver insisted.

"He's at the interrogation room, confessing. You can watch the tape later."

"Olivia *please!*" Oliver yelled, "I dedicated an enormous part of my life to get here! Don't I deserve to be given a reason?"

Olivia had never seen Oliver insisting so bad on anything before. She looked Oliver in eyes: "Fine. We'll go there. But I will not take any responsibilities for upcoming consequences. You understand?"

## London's Police Department, 7:09 A.M.

He played the video and the first thing that could be heard was Arthur's voice, saying: "Introduce yourself, please. Give us a complete biography."

The man in front of the camera, on the other side of the table was Pietro, clearly. He looked exhausted and his straight hair was messy. He spoke tiredly: "My name is Pietro Adolf Schwarter. My birthday is July seventh, nineteen ninety. I was born in Erfurt to a teacher couple. My mother worked as a kindergarten teacher and my father is an English teacher."

"How old were you when you first came to London?" Detective Henry's voice added.

Pietro gave it a little thinking and answered: "I can't quite remember the exact date but I just remember that my parents and I had three tickets to London and at the airport, my mum was asked to return because she was pregnant with my sister so she went back home so I visited here with my father. I was nine," Pietro said the memory with a sad smile but that smile disappeared shortly after Richard asked the next question: "How did you know Bradly Moore?"

"I'm a musician and I sometimes post videos of myself working. Brad somehow found me on social media and we met after one of my performances."

"And how was your friendship?" Richard asked.

"It was…it was not perfect. We were both stubborn and that was the main problem. Made the whole friendship problematic and complicated."

"Be more specific," Richard requested "what do you mean by complicated?"

"I mean," Pietro said, "from day one, I knew my red lines. I knew which parts of Brad's life relates to me, I knew the ones I had the right to interfere and I never crossed them. But Brad did and he got far from them that he was almost invisible."

"What lines are you talking about, Mr Schwarter?" Arthur asked.

"My family is the most important part of my life and I'm sick of saying it lately but I was addicted for four years until I was all clean on august twentieth last year. I let my family down over a stupid addiction and I was trying to make things right between us taking baby steps but Brad took control of everything and called my father. He made things much worse and my father didn't speak to me and didn't let me reach my mother and sister."

"Since when did you start to think of ending his life?" Arthur asked Pietro.

"I don't know the exact time. After my problems with Bradly got serious, I begun drinking again, but I ended it right after the murder because I knew how it would represent me. I remember that I've been keeping his house under control for three weeks," Pietro said and looked down.

"Tell us about February ninth. What happened that night?" Richard asked.

"I went to Brad's house and he invited me in. We sat in the living room and talked. I was wearing gloves and hoodie and that was when he understood that something was weird," Pietro breathed deeply and resumed: "I remember drinking before I did it to decrease the pressure of the guilty conscience but I seem to be suffering more than I deserve."

"What happened when he realised that something was wrong?" Arthur asked.

"He tried to end the conversation. He said that I should be gone because he had a lot to do the next day…I gave him a chance to change my mind…I explained my concerns to him but he made fun of them and you know…" Pietro said regretful.

"What about coming back to the crime scene?" Richard asked.

"While we were talking, I noticed Brad was sending a message. I bent a bit and I could see that it was an emergency text. He had already told me that I was on his emergency list. My plan was escaping but at that point I thought that his message was my ark of Noah. I could go outside and come back in like I was never there. And I did it. I escaped. My name came among the suspects."

"And what motivated you to confess?" Arthur asked.

Pietro didn't answer the question for a minute. He then was filled with courage to say it. Admit it: "For the past month; since the night it happened, I've dreamed of Brad. Endless nightmares didn't leave me alone. They were all regarding switching places between us. That *Brad killed me*. And each time, I woke up with ache in my chest and weak lungs, too weak to breathe normally. That made me realize how did I made Brad feel when I did it to him and...I would never want anyone to do such thing to me."

"Do you regret it?" Arthur asked after a minute.

Tears came to Pietro's eyes. He sadly smiled: "Gray. I hate that I took a life but I'm happy that he isn't in my life anymore."

The video came to an end. Oliver shut the laptop and looked at Arthur: "Is that it?"

Arthur—who was using his phone—confirmed with head. Oliver angrily breathed out. "Gray," Oliver said, "What a nonsense. Didn't you find a better way to kick someone out of your life?"

"Oliver," Arthur calmly called, "it's over. There is nothing else we can do. Pietro admitted being the killer of Bradly Anton Moore the second. We just have to wait for the justice to decide."

Oliver looked at his hands: "Have you told the Moores yet?"

"No" Arthur answered, "Richard and I were waiting for you. We think that you might be the best to tell them."

"Me?"

"Yeah, you. Don't you think?"

There were no such things as 'other options' for him. He removed his car keys off the desk and said: "I'll go right now. But I won't bring them here, okay?"

***

Oliver knocked at the door and kept waiting. He has been busy with choosing words since he left the station; but he still had problems with putting them together. "I'm the boss, I'm the best, I'm the bear." Oliver thought, "What the hell?"

The door was opened and Elizabeth appeared with a courteous smile: "Oliver! Hi! Come in."

And she put a step back so that Oliver could enter the house. He nervously smiled: "Hi Elizabeth. Are Robert and Ezra home?"

Elizabeth closed the door and walked behind him: "Yes, we were having breakfast."

"Oh," Oliver whispered, "Am I interrupting?"

"Absolutely not! Come on, join us." Elizabeth invited Oliver with a maternal smile.

Oliver smiled back and made his way into the kitchen, where he found Robert and Ezra were having breakfast. They also greeted him nicely and Robert asked: "Have you had breakfast already?"

"No, actually. I spent the night at the hospital and I went to the station next, so…" Oliver smiled and shrugged.

"Hospital, why? Are you alright?" Elizabeth asked Oliver.

"Low blood pressure, no big deal. I'm alright." Oliver answered.

"Ollie" Ezra called Oliver, "Cereal or oatmeal?"

"Cereal, please." Oliver answered with dried mouth.

"So, Oliver, how's the case going? Listen to me, give yourself a break. Low blood pressure is as dangerous as being high." Robert said to Oliver.

"You're probably right. I'll consider that and…there's something about the case that I meant to discuss," said Oliver.

Ezra put a bowl of milk and ring-shaped chocolate cereal in front of Oliver and asked: "What about it?"

"Did you find the killer?" Elizabeth asked excitedly.

Oliver looked at their plates and bowls. They were almost empty. Oliver closed his eyes and slightly shook his head as a 'yes' to Elizabeth's question and said: "Sit down, please. I'll tell you everything."

Elizabeth covered her mouth with hand and sat on the other side of the table next to Oliver. Robert sat straight and Ezra took a seat next to Oliver.

Oliver stirred his cereal and began: "There is no easy way to say it but I have to…I did…find the killer. But he got to the department to confess sooner than I called detective Henry."

"*He*?" Ezra asked Oliver.

Oliver turned to Ezra and said: "Yes, Ezra. He." He turned to Moores and said: "Robert, Elizabeth, the man who got Brad's life was Pietro Schwarter."

Not even a second after Oliver finished his sentence, Elizabeth started to cry out loud. Robert hugged her and turned his crying face and hid it from Oliver and Ezra. Oliver turned to Ezra to see his reaction, he had tears in his eyes. Breathing shortly and fast.

Ezra's voice quavered: "Why?"

Oliver explained: "Pietro has been addicted for nearly half a decade and his father found out and the two of them haven't spoken ever since. Brad tried to make things right but he only made them worse and Mr Schwarter thought that Pietro got addicted knowingly. They got into bigger arguments and his father banned Pietro from reaching his mother and sister. Pietro said that he was secretly in touch with the two of them. Pietro couldn't accept what indirectly was caused by Brad. And then you know…"

Ezra put his elbows on the table and grabbed his head. He started to weep. That was all too much for him to take. He wished he wasn't home that morning to know what happened to his brother.

Meanwhile, Oliver was just as sad as Moores were. It's no lie that Oliver and Brad didn't share any DNAs or RNAs but they shared a lifetime and uncountable memories that recalling any one of them would ache Oliver's heart to death.

Brad's stopped heart was capable of stopping so many more…

***

**10:01 A.M.**

After a gloomy hour and a dreary half, Moores weren't better but they'd cut the tears and were all settled in the living room with Oliver. Elizabeth was holding a glass of water and sugar to stabilise her low blood pressure.

Elizabeth, who was shaking, asked with a shivering enigma: "Can I see him?"

"See who, Elizabeth?" Oliver asked.

249

Elizabeth looked at him like a child, asking for extra candies: "Pietro. I should see him."

"I'm afraid I can't allow it. It's for your own good." Oliver answered peacefully.

She resumed crying: "But I *should*! He killed my son!"

Oliver closed his eyes angrily: "Did I not make my point very clear?" he thought, "For God's sake!" but he said very gently: "Elizabeth, please. I need you to respect my recognition of the circumstances."

"Oliver's right, mum. We're not ready…I mean, what would you do if you go there right now? What can you possibly do? What can any of us possibly do?" Ezra said to Elizabeth.

"Will he be punished, Oliver? Can you assure that?" Robert asked Oliver.

"Due to his own decision to confess, I highly see it coming." Oliver answered Robert.

"For how long?" Ezra asked.

"At least ten years, I assume," said Oliver.

"*Ten years*?" Elizabeth yelled and stood up, "My son aged three decades and all that filthy pathetic monster will get is just *ten years*?"

"I said, *at least* ten years. Ten years is the least verdict for homicide in England and Wales. Richard is still processing the arrestment and confession." Oliver explained in peace, with a flaming fire of enragement inside him that was caused by Elizabeth's irrationalism.

"Why don't he get a life sentence? He took a life!" Robert asked.

Oliver was ready to yell and emphasize '*least*' but Ezra took care of the moment and explained: "Dad, Mum. He is saying *at least*, ten years. Pietro is still not even introduced to the jury. It takes time. They guy confessed ten hours ago!"

"Thank you, Ezra." Oliver thanked him, "Robert, Elizabeth, I'm going to the office now. But I won't take either of you because you'll definitely experience a madding mental breakdown. I'm taking Ezra with me, alright? He knew Pietro and his actions seem to be a bit more under control. I'll be in touch with you, Ezra come on."

***

# The Police Department, Interrogation Room, 11:00 A.M.

Oliver was staring at all three of them through the glass, Pietro, Ezra. And Arthur, who accompanied Ezra to the room in case of any unexpected reactions occurred. None had occurred until then. Ezra had been staring at Pietro for the past five minutes—as Pietro avoided making eye contact—with arms crossed, heavy breaths and eyes that only blinked every forty seconds. Ezra finally spitted four words out and made a question: "What were you thinking?"

Pietro finally dared to make eye contact with Ezra. He looked Ezra in his eyes and slowly asked: "Repeat again?"

"I asked, what were you thinking of when you took my brother's life?" Ezra asked in a scary voice, "Do you understand or should I switch languages?"

Pietro tiredly stared at Ezra with his eyes half open and whispered: "*Ich habe nicht nachgedacht.*" (I wasn't thinking.)

"You were *not?*" Ezra groaned, "You weren't thinking of my mother? Y…you never cared to think what would happen to *my parents*, to *me?*"

Tears occupied a layer on Ezra's eyes and made his voice shivering and even more groaning: "Didn't you even think about *yourself?*"

"I didn't even think about Paula," Pietro yelled, louder than Ezra and allowed his eyes to cry rivers.

Ezra stood up. Even though he was weak in the knees, he couldn't take the room anymore. He bent on the table and said: "You were my friend, Pietro; me and Brad's…This isn't how friendships work. Now, I don't wish your death but I so do beg the God to give you your self-torment," Ezra said all his last words to Pietro with tears dropping on his face that he was trying to not let them leave his eyes.

He left the room.

He decided to say no more.

"Now the court had a lot to say."

# Chapter Seven
# The Monster Inside Us

The overcame silence felt like a swamp. Oliver's eyeballs were starting to switch into two taxidermy balls, he had been staring at the court's door for a long time, waiting for Judge Alasdair Clark. Judge Clark was supposed to represent the jury's sentence, but he was late by two minutes. Two minutes that passed nothing less than two centuries for the Moore's—and Oliver, of course.

Oliver took a quick look at the others. Robert and his permanent frown; Brad would do anything for his father's frown to disappear. Robert was always having an ugly, frightening frown that would scare Genghis Khan. No one ever knew why. Even Brad's might rest in peace soul left his body without knowing why.

There was this one thing that no one talked about, but they all knew it, Oliver recently learnt about it: Robert was not a good father. Not to Brad, not to Ezra; and it was not just about frowning because frown was just level one. Mental pressure and being obstructive were just two leaves of Robert's weeping willow of not being a good parent.

He was even frowning at the trial for his son's gone life's justice.

Oliver's next target was Elizabeth. The supportive mother with an opposite personality comparing to his husband. She was crying with her eyes full of hope, her hands crossed and lips praying to God.

Ezra was next; the mastermind brother with nerve issues such as shaking legs, lack of saliva and feeling cold in his shoulders.

At that moment, he was clearly suffering from lack of saliva because he was constantly licking his lips. And he was also shaking his legs.

He seemed to care the most about the outcome; he was never ever the perfect brother but that didn't make him the villain. In fact, he always had brotherly feelings for Brad although he was literally a piece of ice for everyone else and everything else.

Brad had never treated Ezra like a real brother. He would always follow an indifference algorithm that he had learnt from Robert.

"Raise to the great Judge Clark," A policeman said and everyone raised, sat back on their seats after the judge did.

After a few moments, the Scottish judge started to clarify a man's destiny: "The court had made its decision but before that, I shall speak to the young man." He continued to Pietro: "Mr Schwarter, you own a loving and respectful family who care for you. Who love you and who would shelter you in the hardest times...because you are a good man. I've listened to your work, its indeed audible and worth being heard by the world. Just a simple choice of moving on to resuming your life would've given you a different life...different and greater. You deserved so much better than being called 'the addicted' or 'the killer' or anything similar. You deserved to be called 'the musician better than Beethoven.' But you chose the wrong path to walk and I couldn't be any more sorry about it."

Meanwhile Judge Clark's speech, Pietro only looked at the desk in front of him and bit his cheeks from inside.

The judge sympathetically closed his eyes and opened them to read the sentence: "Under the great law of Britain, you, Mr Pietro Adolf Schwarter, are sentenced to seventeen years in prison for the premeditated murder of Mr Bradly Anton Moore the second with the possibility of parole...dismissed."

Everyone raised again and Oliver was the only one looking for Pietro's family. He found Pietro's mother and sister on a far side of the court, hugging and crying. And Mr Schwarter next to Pietro holding on to his son so tight as if he didn't mean to let go.

Truth be told, Oliver didn't know if he was happy or sad. Like what Pietro said on his confession video earlier 'grey'.

Actually, he was more upset about Pietro's family. His mother, his sister and the father who was holding his son for the first time in years.

On the side that Oliver was sitting, everyone was happy, literally. He felt a touch on his left shoulder. Oliver turned back and faced Arthur, who was ready to congratulate him. But Arthur's smile disappeared when he saw Oliver unwell: "Oliver, what's wrong?"

253

Oliver didn't answer. All he could remember was feeling empty and leaving the court to the yard. He needed to breathe.

As soon as he got to the yard, he kneeled on the grasses and looked around him.

Was everything over?

Was Brad gone for good?

And was his murderer going to prison?

Was Oliver supposed to get used to his new life without his best friend?

Was the case, the last thing that related him to Brad?

All these questions were stairs, brought him a step closer to the destination of cry.

He cried out loud and freely.

Like there was no one out there to hear him.

He didn't want to get used to the new world that its creation was out of Oliver's decision.

He didn't...

*** 

## March 17th, London's Police Department, 16:59 P.M.

Oliver was spinning on the task chair, whistling and waiting for the clock's hands to show numbers '5' and '6'...And another reason regarding making an announcement to his family and friends. After the succession at the court five days ago, Moores announced a memorial for their dearest Brad and to thank Oliver, Richard and Arthur.

Oliver hadn't seen, called or met anyone in five days, started the day after the court. He had left London to Oxford for two peaceful days. Just before he left, he texted Dakota: *"Hey D. I'm heading to Oxford. Alone. Tell everyone. Be back in two days. XOXO."*

That night after the court, Oliver and Ezra spent it on walking in London's streets and talking about Brad and Oliver just came to and understanding that how badly Ezra needed a brother; as they were talking, Ezra said one thing about Brad that melted Oliver's heart right away: *"I can't wait to see his pretty face when I'll tell him everything that happened in these days."*

Brad's connection with Oliver was exceptional but with Ezra, it was just different.

Oliver might've eventually forgot that he ever had a best friend named 'Bradly'; or at least he would've reached a level of recalling their memories? Not sensing them.

But Ezra?

That man lost a biologically connected person, that must've been painful. Brad was gone but still, parts of his existence were alive in Ezra's DNA. Guess we're all truly more than words. Aren't we?

One other thing that Oliver learnt was that *most people don't care.*

Why would they spare their precious time to think about the death of someone they didn't know?

Or why would they want to be sympathetic to a dead's alive family members and friends? People didn't know the dead or if they knew, they would move on and live unaffected.

Not having high expectations was the exact thing that he had learnt recently, unlike his own will.

Because *most of the people don't care.*

Oliver's philosophical thoughts ran away when he heard his phone rang. He looked at the screen and faced the name 'Sebastian Bell'. Oliver answered the phone: "Hello?"

"Hi Oliver. Can you speak?"

"Yes, go on please."

"I'm with Olga now and we thought that we should see you before the memorial. Is it possible?"

Oliver raised an eyebrow: "How do you guys know about the memorial? Are you invited?"

"We are. Mr Moore called us last night. I think Morgan and Anya are coming too but Theodore said that he might not be able to make it on time."

"Okay, that's not bad at all," Oliver said, "Excuse me, what's the occasion?"

"Nothing, just Olga and I want to talk to you. It's nothing shady, I promise."

Oliver looked at the clock, 5:10 o'clock. He said: "Fine, I'm at the police department now. Can you come over?"

"Yes, thank you. We'll catch up," Sebastian said and hung up the phone.

Oliver wasn't exactly satisfied about seeing Sebastian and Olga but that wasn't a bad opportunity to see how do they feel about Pietro's crime. They were all gathered at the court, but Oliver was ill enough to leave the court without sooner than anyone, drive back home and cry in his bed until he falls asleep and wake up by Ezra's call.

After five minutes, the door was knocked and Sebastian and Olga entered and sat on the brown leather chairs.

Oliver gently smiled at them and said: "I must apologize, we don't have any nutrition supplies here, but we do have water. Delicious water!"

The three of them laughed. Olga placed a classy black box on the desk in front of Oliver and said: "Oliver, this is for you."

Oliver opened the box and brought out the bottle inside of it. It was black glass of perfume.

Oliver smiled at it when he remembered that Brad had bought him the very same perfume for his birthday last year. He removed the head and smelled the cool, unique and tangy perfume. It was the exact same perfume.

Oliver thankfully smiled at them and said: "Thank you so much, it's very peculiar."

Sebastian said: "We're glad you like it."

Olga said: "You know, last year's June, Brad asked me to help him purchasing a birthday gift for his best friend. He didn't give me a name. But I remember he chose this perfume and he said that his friend loved it. After we met, I realised it was for you and now is the best time to revive some memories."

Oliver smiled gratefully and said: "Not that I don't like it, I love it, I appreciate it but my birthday is…like four months away?"

"Yeah, about that," Sebastian laughed shamefully "we might've been mad at you and we might've said mean things behind your back and we're extremely sorry about them."

Oliver chuckled and said with dignity: "It's alright. I…wasn't treating anyone properly for the past month. I'm sorry if I hurt you with my words."

"It doesn't matter, Oliver," Olga said, "We didn't get to know Brad half as much as you did and none of us were alright. You were surely not better than us."

"So, how do you think about Pietro?" Sebastian asked Oliver.

Oliver took a deep breath and answered: "You know, I'm in doubt. Pietro was a good person, or at least that's how he seemed; I'm a judgmental person, I know you've noticed it. I judged Pietro and by my perception, he was a good person...it was impossible to think that he was the killer."

"Who did you think the killer was?" Olga asked.

"I never allowed my judgment or emotions decide that," Oliver said hastily. He whispered: "I have a perspective of such people."

"What is that perspective?" Sebastian asked.

"We all seem pretty normal, we're all beautiful. We're all children of God. For this very reason, we always have the chance to ask for redemption. The court judges people only by their actions which contradicted human values but God judges us by look into our hearts, he judges by our souls. And you know what I think? I think that there's a monster inside us, the monster inside us is made of hatred, anger, greed, the feeling of guilt, fear and hate and it grows when someone hurts us, it grows when we hurt somebody. The monster is living at the margin of the darkest side of a soul. The monster is guilty of the sins we commit. The monster is guilty of the worst feelings that we keep recall. It supplies its nutrition from all the words we never allowed to leave our mouths, the ones we never spoke. The monster doesn't always stay in the darkness, it makes a way through the dark to the world outside. It allows itself to make up emotional shortcomings. Whatever life took from it. It imposes all the suffer it has been through to the people who might not be as guilty and broken as the monster."

"How do you see this monster?" Sebastian asked.

Oliver looked at Sebastian in the eyes and said: "Like a yeti. But covered in some asphalt liquid. Or petroleum. That is the thing I used to call a 'monster' as a kid."

"Is this how you see Pietro?" Olga asked.

Oliver didn't answer. Instead, he stood up and said: "We better get going, shall we?"

"Lead the way." Sebastian stood up and said to Oliver.

## Moores' Family House, 17:59 P.M.

The door was half open and Oliver just pushed it through and entered with Olga and Sebastian behind him.

The first picture that gave Oliver a massive but disgusting and upsetting nostalgia was the crowd at the Moores' house, the people.

Brad's friends, family, cousins, aunts and uncles, co-workers and generally, a remarkable percent of the people that Oliver saw at Brad's funeral were there. This time not to mourn but to celebrate.

But among the guests, Oliver noticed this one guest from behind that he didn't think would make it, never in a century. Harry Henry didn't notice Oliver came in since he was talking to Dakota.

"*No way!*" Oliver shouted out cheerful.

Harry turned to Oliver, smiled charmingly, opened his arms and said: "There's a way!"

Oliver put steps forward and gave him a warm, friendly cuddle. Oliver whispered next to Harry's ear: "I missed you, idiot."

Harry whispered back: "I couldn't miss you, jerk. But look! You did it, Ollie!"

The two of them separated. Oliver looked around and asked: "Where's your family?"

"Oh, God knows. But Dad said that they will be here." Harry answered, "Go see the others. I'll be in the back yard."

Oliver shook his head. He saw Olga and Sebastian went to someone. The closer he got; he saw that they were talking to Ezra.

Ezra hugged Olga shortly and smiled at her: "Thank you so much for coming." Then looked at Sebastian and shook hands with him: "You must be Sebastian. I'm Ezra. Bradly's brother."

"Nice to meet you," Sebastian said as he was looking at Ezra so amazed "You…look so much like him…you've got different colours in your hair and eyes."

Ezra laughed and pointed somewhere: "I get that a lot…please, enjoy the ceremony."

After Olga and Sebastian were gone, Ezra went to Oliver and hugged him, tapped him on the back and said: "Hello, stranger."

"Hi," said Oliver, "Could you sleep the other night?"

"Hell yeah, I could! I slept at half past six, Mum woke me up at seven to buy get ready for the ceremony!" Ezra complained in a funny-angry manner "I bought and ordered everything new you see today! You're welcome!"

They separated and stared at the population. "It's over, I think," Ezra said with a paradoxical smile out of satisfaction and melancholy, "Everything about him is over but his memories."

"I wish he was here…to see all the people who loved him," Oliver said and sighed.

"Or to see the one and only person he loved the most," Ezra said to make a point.

Oliver turned to him and asked surprised: "Are you serious? Is she…"

"Yup. She's in the kitchen, trying her head off not to cry. Her eyeballs might fall out any seconds now," Ezra said and nodded to the kitchen.

Oliver rushed to the dark kitchen and he closed the door behind him. He found Elma behind the table, staring at picture frames of Brad with tears in her eyes.

Elma noticed Oliver walked in. Turned her head and hardly smiled: "Hello Oliver."

"Hello Elma," Oliver said sympathetically and went to her slowly and sat on the chair next to her.

Elma said with her voice shivering, with eyes ready to cry a hurricane: "You know what? For the past thirty days, I've been pondering that…eh…wh…what if things worked different between us? L…like, if we were still together, wou…would he die like this? This soon? Would've he even died of a ho…homicide?"

The remembrance of her ex-husband's shocking death, made her lose control. She started to gasp and then weep: "If I had n…never a…abandoned him, would any of this su…suffer happened t…to him?"

"Elma…" Oliver whispered. He wanted to take the chance of calming her. Like *he* was alright! "We can't say that for sure…look, you can't blame yourself for Brad's death and please don't…Because if he was here, he would've crumbled all my bones for letting you think of such thing and for blaming yourself for anything…Elma, Brad adored you, respected you. If he didn't, he would've forced you to give up on your dream instead of letting you go for it. He thought of every consequence, everything about himself, about *you*…about both of you. He loved you so madly that he saw the best remedy in letting you go other than imprisoning you…He was preoccupied with you…It was his reasonable, logical choice. You are not guilty of anything."

"I loved him so much." Elma said noiseless with her had down, looking at the sheet of tissue that she was ripping.

Oliver smiled: "I know."

Oliver as well, looked at the floor and thought about Brad and Elma.

He perfectly kept in mind how excited Brad was when he decided to propose to Elma. He perfectly remembered when Brad said: "She is the rest of my life."

Living with the rest of his life ended in five months.

The two of them dated for six months until Brad proposed on March 15th, 2011, and they got married on June 1st and Oliver also remembered that Brad was excitedly saying: "She wants to design her own wedding dress!"

And she did.

There was no time to recall memories, even good ones.

Oliver stood up and said: "Come on, Elma. Wash your face. I'll be waiting in the living room."

Oliver said and left the kitchen. He meant every single word he said to Elma: everything he knew that Brad never had the chance to say to her. Whether if it was for Elma and her second husband's life's sake, or it was just those group of words which Brad decided not to let them spit out of his mouth.

"Oliver! Dear!" Elizabeth called out loud and cheerful.

Oliver turned to the voice's source and saw Elizabeth, so vivacious and alive. The opposite point of what she hasn't been for the past thirty-seven days.

"Hello Elizabeth, you look lovely. Your dress looks good on you." Oliver charmingly smiled at her and complemented.

"Thank you, son." Elizabeth said enthusiastically as if she heard the best news in life and just a complement "Are you enjoying the ceremony? I know it was a last-minute decision to make but we did our best."

"And it couldn't be better, seriously. This is remarkable. Everyone's having their best," Oliver assured.

"Thanks, dear," Elizabeth said and comfortably exhaled "I asked Harry a speech if you don't mind. Where are your parents?"

"I saw Dakota when I walked in. So, I guess Mum and Dad are somewhere around," Oliver said and searched for them in his surround.

"I didn't see them enter. Just find them, will you?" Elizabeth said and didn't wait for a confirmation.

Oliver was alone among the crowd, looking for a familiar face but instead, he got a familiar voice: "Look at this handsome guy!" And Olivia appeared with Dakota next to her. Olivia dramatically complemented: "You know what I think? I think fashion models should thank God on their knees every day, praising him that you chose to be a forensic psychologist!"

"I have to admit it, if we weren't siblings, I would've probably married you!" Dakota joked with a sad voice.

"That's very optimistic of you to think that *I* would've ever married you!" Oliver joked back and received a not-so-painful punch on the shoulder from her.

Olivia laughed at 'Idiot one and idiot three' and asked: "How are you doing, Ollie? Did you enjoy your time in Oxford?"

He breathed deeply and heavily and lied in a believable, professional way: "I'm fine, actually and yeah Oxford was too good to be true…And seeing that I served my duty, getting justice for Brad and getting answers to so many questions has actually cured my melancholy. I'm not quite fine, obviously. I still need time to recover. But I will be well soon."

"We know you will. We believe in you," Dakota said and hugged Oliver.

Oliver warmly cuddled his sisters like they were all he had. On the same pose, Oliver said: "Ladies, I think I've made a decision. Let's sit."

They sat on a three seats sofa in the middle of the living room.

"What is it?" one of the sisters asked. Oliver couldn't say which, the place was getting louder every second.

"I want to get away from work for a while. I'm going to visit America."

Both sisters bent their heads and listened more carefully.

"Are you sure?" Dakota asked Oliver.

"Why would you do that?" Olivia asked.

Oliver smiled ridiculously: "I mean, why not? I have enough budget and I have had enough of work lately!"

"Who else knows?" Olivia asked.

"Me, you girls and the airline!" Oliver said and laughed shortly.

"You haven't told Mum and Dad?" Dakota asked, "Where are you even staying?"

"Mum and Dad don't know yet. I've been meaning to tell you tonight. And please don't act like we don't own a house in America!"

"So, when are you leaving?" Olivia asked.

"I've got ticket for March thirty first. I'll return a month later." Oliver answered.

"I mean…not that we're unhappy, but we didn't see it coming. You know, if we even knew that you were going to take a break, we never thought you would choose America!" Dakota said and Olivia shook her head.

261

Oliver shrugged and said: "Well, I am. I'll tell Mum and Dad."

Ezra walked pass them and said: "Hey, Harry is about to make a toast so, end this conversation." And went to sit on a couch in a far spot from them.

"Ladies and gentlemen, may I have your attention?" Harry said and tapped his glass of wine with a butter knife. When everyone's eyes were on him, he began his glorious speech: "For those who don't know me, I'm Harry Henry and before you ask, yes, I'm detective Henry's son, his last born. Today, we're all joined here to utter our respects to one of the finest, dearest, most considerate men ever, Bradly Anton Moore. Of course, three words aren't even close enough to describe such man but emotions won't let me say more...Ever since I was a boy, I began to consider every act of nature as a lesson, death particularly. Death always taught me to be careful, it taught me to survive; but this perspective of mine has changed recently by looking through Bradly's life. Remembering how someone lived the life in the way he desired, how he lived, he laughed, he loved and he believed; it just keeps me awestruck every single second. So, by remembering how desirable Brad's life was, I don't get survival lessons from death anymore, I've gained the knowledge of *living life* and by living life I certainly don't mean breathing! I mean, living it in a way that when death comes to me, I say *'you're late!'* And I have no doubts that if Brad was now here among us, he'd be asking us the same. He's out no more in our houses but forever in our hearts. To Bradly."

Oliver was mesmerized by Harry's encouraging speech. Although if he was in a proper condition, those extraordinary words would've had more positive effects on him.

You asking why he wasn't?

Because, Oliver, after he was totally sure that someone's a criminal, he would see them as if they were the asphalt liquid yeti.

But Pietro? He was different.

Nothing Oliver had seen or experienced before.

Pietro hadn't appeared to Oliver as 'the monster'. He was just Pietro.

That would've feared Oliver to death. It doesn't sound quite interesting to manage a more spread investigation at night and receive a call about your investigation's plot's memorial by the morning.

Oliver felt his entire muscles shivering. He heard all voices and sounds around him as if they were enigmas or as if he was hearing them underwater. They were echoes. His forehead was being drenched by cold sweat.

He slightly gazed around. Just to find the nearest exit but his eyes suddenly were locked on Ezra, sitting on the other side of the room.

Oliver wished that to be a delirium.

Wished that his eyes were mistaking.

Wished that monster to leave Ezra's seat.

Wished that wasn't Ezra.

He would've begged the lord for that to be wrong.

Who or what was sitting on that couch, it wasn't Ezra, no. It was a creature, a yeti covered by gross and oily asphalt liquid. Wearing a scary, evil and proud smile. Not because his brother's killer was found, but because he *wasn't* found.

From Ezra's prospect, it felt joyful that nobody understood that he had murdered his own brother, that he put the sin on someone else. It felt awesome that Pietro never realised the extra amount of Diazepam that was purred in his drink and that killing Bradly was just his own delusion and he never had anyone's blood on his hands. Poor Pietro was completely innocent, and Ezra was truly sorry and regretful that he'd put him in jail, but Pietro was going to stay in England for a while, and Ezra was flattered by that. It felt delightful to him that now he was his parents' one and only and of course, dearest child since Brad never gave him time to be. Oh! Brad! Nothing felt better than the fact that the only one who witnessed Ezra taking life, was Brad and he was so dead to say a word!

Ezra's eyes caught Oliver's. For one thing, Ezra knew how kind and caring Oliver was and how devastated he would've been to see his best friend's dead body and getting duty to find his killer.

Oliver was ill, unwell and devastated that he would've never revealed Ezra's secret if he knew. And if he did, no one would've believed him or if anyone did, Ezra had already been through that plan. Just a bunch of fake tears and a false, paid witness had already proved that Ezra was innocent.

He had a perfectly set plan to achieve his wicked intention.

As Oliver was gazing at him as if he was gazing at a wild animal, Ezra raised his glass and said: "Cheers, to Oliver and Bradly!"

Everyone else raised their glasses and cheered: "To Oliver and Bradly!"

**The End?**

I'd like to remove my hat to my English teacher, Narges, whose effort have equalled every single word I've written for my book.

I can never thank my family enough for telling me: "You are meant to be remarkable. You were born to accomplish the greatest."

Last but not least, thanks to Austin Macauley Publishers for the opportunity of working with them and producing this book.

An endless thanks to uncle Milan and Selma for their guide and support.